Fire on the Mississippi

In A Foreign Country – *Journeys of a Southerner*
Book 3 of a series

I0637875

Pat Martin

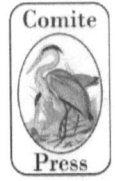

This is a work of historical fiction. With the exception of historical figures, names characters, places, and incidents are the products of the author's imagination, and any resemblance to actual persons, living or dead, events, or locales is entirely coincidental.

Publisher's Cataloging-in-Publication Data

Names: Martin, Patrick H., author.
Title: Fire on the Mississippi : in a foreign country – journeys of a southerner book 3 / Pat Martin.
Description: Clinton, LA : Comite Press, 2024. | Series : In a foreign country – journeys of a southerner ; 3. | Includes 14 illustrations and three diagrams and maps. | Summary: Percy Moorhead works with the Confederate Secret Service in England, dodges Yankee spies, and runs the Union blockade to supply the South. President Davis and Secretary Judah Benjamin secretly send him to New Orleans to deliver orders of surrender. He confronts his past as a Union fleet sweeps up the Mississippi.
Identifiers: LCCN 2024910873 | ISBN 9781964075068 (hardcover) | ISBN 9781964075075 (pbk.) | ISBN 9781964075082 (ebook)
Subjects: LCSH: Spies – United States – History – 19th century – Fiction. | Spies – Confederate States of America – Fiction. | United States – History – Civil War, 1861-1865 – Fiction. | New Orleans (La.) – History – Civil War, 1861-1865 – Fiction. | BISAC: FICTION / Historical / Civil War Era. | FICTION / Action & Adventure. | FICTION / Thrillers / Espionage.
Classification: LCC PS3613.A78 F57 2024 | DDC 813 M--dc23
LC record available at https://lccn.loc.gov/2024910873
ISBN (Hardback): **978-1-964075-06-8**
ISBN (Paperback): **978-1-964075-07-5**
ISBN (ebook): **978-1-964075-08-2**

Copyright © 2025 Pat Martin. All rights reserved.

No part of this book may be reproduced, or stored in a retrieval system, or transmitted in any form or by any means, electronic, mechanical, photocopying, recording, or otherwise, without express written permission of the publisher.

Published by Comite Press, a Louisiana LLC
Clinton, Louisiana

PatMartinauthor.com

This novel is dedicated to

Betty Malone Hingle

Wise, sharp, thoughtful

For we are strangers before thee, and sojourners, as were all
our fathers: our days on the earth are as a shadow . . . .
        1 Chronicles 29:15

Time past and time future
What might have been and what has been
Point to one end, which is always present.
        T. S. Eliot – *Burnt Norton*

The past is a foreign country: they do things differently there.
        L. P. Hartley, *The Go-Between*

Contents

In a Foreign Country
Journeys of a Southerner

About the Series

In a Foreign Country – *Journeys of a Southerner* is a series of six historical novels sprawling over the nineteenth century, focusing on a New Orleans lawyer and two generations of families, one free and one enslaved, on a Louisiana cotton plantation. The stain of slavery tainted Southern Whites who did not want to secede but remained loyal to their state and region when war erupted. The series, set in America and England, is a fresh look into the divisions that led to secession's failure. The reader is drawn into the profound conflicts of the era by vivid characters in a tale of adventure, romance, tragedy, and family conflict.

Books in the Series

1. CANNONS AT THE GATE

   1815-1849: The story of the Moorhead family begins when the father, Howard, flees England to reinvent himself as a successful cotton merchant in Louisiana. It shifts to his son Percy, raised on the family plantation and educated at Princeton, whose ambitions are forged in cannon fire in the American conquest of Mexico.

2. INSURRECTION AT BAYOU SARA

   1850-1859: Percy Moorhead establishes a successful New Orleans law practice but then loses his family and his inheritance to an imposter. He must rise above personal loss to subdue a slave insurrection that threatens the Feliciana parishes.

3. FIRE ON THE MISSISSIPPI

   1861-1862: The Confederacy recruits Lt. Percy Moorhead, now in Virginia. First, he becomes an agent in Liverpool to secure ships for the Navy. Next, he is sent to New Orleans to order its surrender. There he finds that the man who stole his inheritance has been murdered; he must begin anew to restore his fortunes.

4. ESCAPE FROM RICHMOND

   1862-1863: After further missions in England and France, Percy returns to Richmond only to be challenged by false charges. To save himself, he must choose between loyalty and principle.

5. EMPIRE'S FOREIGN AGENT

6. RETURN TO BOLINGBROKE

Mortar-schooners engaged against Fort Jackson.
Distance of leading schooner from the fort, 2850 yards.
Duration of fire, six days. Total number of shells fired, 16,800.

About the Author

Pat Martin taught at the LSU Law Center until retiring. He holds B.A., M.A., and Ph. D. degrees in History from Louisiana State University and a J. D. degree from the Duke University Law School. Among his publications is *Elizabethan Espionage: Plotters and Spies in the Struggle Between Catholicism and the Crown.*

Chapter 1

On Board the *Doubloon*

April 24, 1862

Just before two a.m., the small steamer *Doubloon* passes Quarantine Station and approaches Fort St. Philip, almost silent, engine disengaged, carried now by the current. Nearby, a single fire-raft has just begun to burn, sputtering sparks into the dark.

Percy Moorhead strains but can see little. When the wind shifts, he is hit by the stench of dead fish. Peering starboard, he can see their silver bellies, trapped in the eddies near the riverbank, rotting in moonlight, reflecting fire light from the burning raft. Looming in the blackness off to port, the raft's flames silhouette the massive hulk of the *Louisiana,* the Confederacy's largest ironclad, anchored just above Fort St. Philip, lamps unlit. Inert, she could be a ghost ship, manned by the dead and damned.

Suddenly, flames cascade from forty blazing portals, breathing out fiery contagion. Score on score of shells, their burning fuses trailing, traverse the sky all at once, like shooting stars, as a furious barrage opens. Percy follows their arcing trajectory – up and up, then down, down, down, delay, ka-boom! Ka-Boom! BOOM! When a fuse is too short or burns too hot, the shell explodes overhead, like fireworks on the Fourth of July – bombs bursting in air, raining hot shrapnel on men and two forts below. Captain John Stevenson, commanding the River Defense Fleet, belatedly sets on fire eight more of the fire-rafts held in check beneath Fort Jackson. Futilely, he tries to direct them against the Union fleet now churning upriver. The Mississippi River is quickly engulfed in flame!

Standing next to Lt. Percy Moorhead, General Mansfield Lovell grips tightly the *Doubloon*'s handrails – as if he can hold back the Union's ascending flotilla. Cannons are blasting from the decks and portholes of each of Farragut's seventeen ships as they pass through a breach in the line of chained rafts. The rafts have failed their sole purpose: to prevent this onslaught. The Yankees have cut the chains in darkness. Lovell's worst fears are now in front of him, the burning boats lighting the late April night, the furious cannon and mortar fire from both forts and from the Union ships. The fires on the Mississippi River signal defeat for New Orleans.

Taking it all in, Lovell no longer doubts that disaster is hot upon him. "Goddammit," he exclaims to no one in particular, "the Union fleet will anchor in New Orleans within a day. Goddammit. Goddammit all to Hell!"

The orders brought in secret by Lt. Percy Moorhead from Richmond for Lovell's eyes only will prove as necessary as they are drastic. Percy has come home to the city he abandoned three years earlier, returning as the instrument of its capitulation. The grim message he has brought: "Look on my works and despair." Only surrender will deliver New Orleans from total destruction. Not Carthage, he thought, but New Orleans *delenda est*.

cᴏ⟩ - ⟨ᴏ⟩

The sight of the flaming river was vivid in Percy's memory three decades later, when he told me how he had gone from a college classroom in a sleepy Virginia town to the deck of the *CSS Doubloon*, commanding a Confederate general to surrender the city he was charged with defending, Percy's own paternal city.

"How did this come about, Tom?" he said. "Let me tell you. Let me take you to the classroom where I first found myself suddenly standing in a foreign country, on the day of Virginia's secession. Only twelve months passed between the one and the other. What an enormous year it was."

I knew the story in part. Now it would unfold in full.

Chapter 2

Wren Hall

Open windows of the second-floor classroom of Wren Hall welcomed mid-April breezes and birdsong. New leaves gently unfolded on the trees outside, turning brown trees green. Smiling flowers bloomed anew along the walks below the renovated building - tulips, peonies, azaleas and bluebells.

In a spacious, freshly painted, pleasant room, Percy Moorhead met with his class, the semester nearing its end. Who better to teach rhetoric than a lawyer who has moved beyond his practice? His assignment for today was for each student to compare Pericles' *Funeral Oration* to Mark Antony's speech over the bloody body of Julius Caesar. Class discussion confirmed that they more readily would see Antony's speech as rhetoric than Pericles'.

Percy had served as William and Mary's Professor of Rhetoric and Belles Lettres for nearly a year now, since late August 1860. The new employment had invigorated him, renewing in him a sense of purpose. Relocating to Virginia from his native Louisiana carried risk. He was glad that he had made the move. It was a happy transition from persuading jurors to teaching students.

Wren Hall — 1860-62
Source — https://www.wm.edu/

"Why do you say one is rhetoric and the other not?" Percy asked Mr. Harrison, a Goochland County youth of seventeen. The lad was a great-nephew of the ninth president of the United States. Knowing him to be studious, Percy called on Harrison with the confidence that he would provide a thoughtful answer. Percy was fond of his students, some more than others – but all were his "boys." Their earnest purpose and polite manners, their coltish spirit, made Percy happy to be in the classroom.

The young man stood, as was expected of every student who spoke in class. Without hesitation, Harrison answered, "They have different audiences. Antony is inciting a mob to an uprising. Pericles is appealing to the virtue of his fellow citizens." He was certain of his answer.

"An interesting way to put it. Incite versus appeal." Percy probed, by his tone, by his questioning expression. "Aren't both just another way of saying the speaker wants to persuade his listeners?"

Pacing in the well of the room separating his desk from the

students' elevated seats, Percy preferred questioning the students to lecturing them. Questions held their attention better, even if they took fewer notes. He expected his boys to learn to think, not to parrot. Extemporaneous speech was superior to recitation, as he himself had learned in Professor Hope's class at Princeton.

Harrison was unhesitant. "Yes sir. Antony is manipulating the crowd. He's turning them against his own enemies. He's stirring their passions, not engaging their reason."

"And Pericles?"

"Well, sir, he draws on the better character of his audience. Pericles – he speaks of honor and valor and duty. These are noble qualities. But Antony uses 'honorable' to mock his enemies. You said that is an example of irony. He doesn't want honor from the mob, only vengeance."

"Very well put, Mr. Harrison," Percy said approvingly. "You may be seated." He turned his attention to another student, four seats closer to the window than Harrison. "And what use does Pericles make of honor, Mr. Poindexter?"

"Sir?" responded Poindexter, who hastily stood. Poindexter had been looking outside, distracted by events miles away from this quiet campus. He was one of the eager ones, the impatient ones, among the students. Lads like Poindexter prompted Percy to assign *Caesar* and Pericles. Many of the William and Mary students were keenly aware of the writings and orations issued by would-be Antonys and Pericles in Virginia, and throughout the South, for months.

"I'll put it another way," said the patient Percy. "What does Pericles want his listeners to do?"

"He wants them to live with honor. He says, the love of honor never grows old. Honor rejoices the heart of age and helplessness."

Okay, so Poindexter had read the assignment. Percy pressed Poindexter.

"Those are his words, Mr. Poindexter. But isn't Pericles like Antony? Doesn't he want the people hearing to his words to go out and fight and die? Isn't he inciting them to war?"

"Are you saying, Mr. Moorhead, that a man shouldn't fight for honor?" The edge in Poindexter's voice showed he regarded with suspicion his professor's questions. He and his younger brother were from Richmond, sons of a merchant tailor. Percy knew that they both were signatories to the petition presented to President Ewell, in January, to form a student militia company right after five states had proclaimed their secession from the Union, including Percy's Louisiana.

Poindexter continued, politely challenging the professor. "If we in Virginia are threatened by others, shouldn't we take up arms and defend ourselves? That's what I see Pericles telling us. That's what a man of honor would do."

There was implicit criticism in the young man's response. Poindexter questioned Percy's commitment to Virginia and to the Southern cause. The students all knew he was from Louisiana, not Virginia. Though he had married a Randolph of Richmond, he had attended college in the North, at Princeton, New Jersey. He was an outsider, though his legal studies were here, at William and Mary. Professor Moorhead had not embraced the declarations from South Carolina and the other states that had followed just after the new year. Perhaps that was what started the rumors about Percy – that he was a Jew from New Orleans, that he was a bastard, that he was an abolitionist. The rumors were shadows of truth. He repeatedly turned aside questions in class about states' rights and slavery. This was enough to raise suspicion and prompt whisperings.

If Percy was now belittling *honor*, then it had come to this: Teaching a Greek oration and a Shakespeare play was now a suspect political act.

The assignment was as close as Percy could come to suggesting the South's rush to secession was ill-considered. He wanted the class to see that men should be ruled by reason, not passion. It was a lesson he had learned from hard experience. "He died for honor's sake" makes a poor epitaph, giving little comfort to a grieving parent, wife or child. Percy had stumbled on bodies of dead men who fought beside him at Churubusco thirteen years ago. He had watched other of his countrymen hanged as the American flag was raised in Mexico City, because they had forsaken their oaths of allegiance to that same flag and had raised guns against their former comrades-in-arms. Were the secessioners not equally guilty of treason as they seized federal forts and arms depots in the South? Percy did not share such thoughts with his students nor with his faculty colleagues. But some sensed his meaning. They were unaware that his sleep was still troubled by memories of the deaths he had caused during his year in Mexico.

Young Poindexter guessed Percy's subtle purpose – to use rhetoric to persuade his scholars that appeals to *honor* summon young men to death. Mr. Moorhead didn't want his boys to die in battle. He liked them, despite the possibility that one of them had been a source of rumor. He was once one of them on this campus.

As a lawyer in New Orleans, Percy had avoided political stands that might affect the interests of his clients. Pronouncements by politicians were often no more than posturing and preening. When South Carolina declared that it had seceded from the Union in December, he thought it was a hollow gesture and would soon be abandoned. A weak effort to foster secession a decade ago had quickly faded. He was surprised when other states followed South Carolina's example. Virginia, one of the principal founders of the Union in 1787, was now declaring its separation. For the upshot, Percy was not prepared. Nor had he anticipated the sudden appearance of a man whom he had not seen in more than three years.

◦◦ - ◦◦

Class was nearly over. Percy noticed two men had entered the door in the back of the lecture room. President Ewell was in front and obscured the shorter man behind him. Percy dismissed the class. Ewell and the man now walked in. Percy was surprised to see that the other man was Judah Benjamin.

Percy exclaimed, "I thought you were in Montgomery." When he had last seen his former law partner, Benjamin was returning to his Senate seat in Washington.

Benjamin wore his familiar enigmatic smile on a face that remained unlined. He was six or seven pounds heavier than Percy remembered, more portly on his short frame. In a soft, melodious voice, he said pleasantly, "My dear Percy. You are of course entirely correct. I am in Montgomery but am now in Richmond, with this brief side-trip to where we stand. As the commotion outside shows, the Virginia convention has just this day proclaimed secession and is joining her sisters of the Confederacy."

"But what brings you to Williamsburg?" Percy had followed the news of the state-by-state secessions. Louisiana had seceded at the end of January, and Benjamin had resigned as Senator, along with John Slidell, at the beginning of February. When President Jefferson Davis formed a Cabinet for the newly-established Confederacy in February, Benjamin was named Attorney General. Percy had sent to Benjamin, who had first employed Percy in his New Orleans law office, a congratulatory note. That's how Benjamin knew Percy's whereabouts, though he had not had time to reply.

With a wry expression, Benjamin said, "I've come to see if President Ewell will consent to relieve you of your duties, should I be able to persuade you to accompany me as I return to Montgomery. Happily, he says with Virginia's secession, it is unlikely that classes will continue."

Benjamin looked at Percy as though he expected an answer. He added, appealing as only Benjamin could do, to Percy's ingrained sense of loyalty, "Your country needs you. With Virginia and Louisiana both seceded, you are now a Confederate."

Percy turned to President Ewell, who nodded to affirm that

Percy's departure would be with his blessing. Ewell was about the same age as Benjamin, but his facial hair made him appear older. Percy felt deeply indebted to both men; each had employed him at crucial moments in is life. Before responding Percy paused, as if looking for the right words. Benjamin's presence in Williamsburg was solely for the purpose of recruiting Percy. For the Attorney General of the Confederacy to make this detour, Percy had to be a high priority. With Virginia's secession, encouraged by Judah's trip to Richmond, war with the North was certain. The college would close. Percy would be unemployed.

Percy now replied with an ironic smile, unwilling to refuse outright, knowing it would amount to a betrayal of both men. "I'm not sure an ex-lawyer and teacher of rhetoric is what the Confederacy needs at present."

"You are exactly the sort of man this new country needs immediately, Percy. More than any man in Montgomery, I know the truth of this."

"If President Ewell will excuse us, perhaps we could repair to the lounge below."

Seated in the lounge's comfortable stuffed leather chairs, Percy uncharacteristically spoke first to the mentor under whom he began his practice of law in New Orleans a dozen years earlier. Courteous but firm, he said, "Judah, as much as I respect and admire you, I'm unwilling to follow you down this road. I just cannot."

Benjamin did not show his surprise. Even when his father was ill and Percy was needed to manage their plantation, he had accompanied Judah and his delegation to Mexico City to save their railroad concession for the Isthmus of Tehuantepec. Benjamin responded smoothly, "You know I have always accepted your judgement, even if it might appear hasty in the circumstances. Calling on our long friendship, may I ask for my reasons?"

"It has nothing to do with you, Judah. And I can say that the

Confederacy could have found no man better qualified to be Attorney General than you. I could give you a hundred reasons, but it all comes down to this. Secession from the Union is a horrible mistake. More importantly, I cannot fight to uphold a legal system in which men and women are held in bondage as chattel property."

Judah gently asked, "Is this because of your loss of your family plantation? I did not know of your legal troubles at the time because of my work in the Senate. When I visited New Orleans, you had moved to Virginia. I know it was a terrible blow. I could have helped with a court appeal."

"No. My views were formed before my heritage was lost. Months before my father had a stroke and was incapacitated, I agreed with his plan to free the slaves on Bolingbroke. But we couldn't."

As Percy had found out, the Louisiana legislature had made manumission impossible just as he and his father were making plans for giving freedom to Bolingbroke's slaves. Always uncomfortable with the idea of humans constituting property, Percy had persuaded himself that slavery was a transitional institution that benefitted the African, and that its harshness could be ameliorated. But the *Dred Scott* decision of the Supreme Court and the acts of other slave states led him to the depressing conclusion that the system was hardening, not easing in its severity.

Percy added with uncommon directness, "Now I see slavery is an immoral institution."

Judah was imperturbable even when others disagreed with him. With equanimity, he replied, "Let's say for the moment that you are right. You are a man of integrity, and you are astute. Please tell me how you see events unfolding in the coming months or years."

"I can tell you what should happen. There should be a gradual emancipation of the African, with compensation to their owners and a means provided for the freed men and women to acquire skills and property." Percy's words were not uttered with conviction.

"Will Lincoln and the U. S. Congress furnish us with such a program? Remember, they have said they have no wish to abolish slavery. They say they want only to preserve the union."

"No, you're right that the Northern states would refuse to purchase freedom for some four million slaves. Nor would they allow those millions to migrate into their borders. States like Lincoln's Illinois won't allow their entry now."

"Then how is your gradual emancipation to be effected?"

As always, Percy was forthright. He admitted readily, "I have no answer."

"And if with a stroke of his pen Lincoln were to proclaim the immediate end of slavery throughout the United States, north and south, what would ensue?"

"Horrors unthinkable. We nearly had a slave insurrection at Bayou Sara just before I moved here. The Louisiana militia company that camped there was prepared to kill all who revolted."

Benjamin raised his eyebrows, saying, "Governor Wickliffe assured us that the story of an uprising was unfounded rumor."

Percy shook his head. "No, Judah, it wasn't. I was there. My own brother-in-law brought it upon us. Slavery brought that upon us. But it would be people who don't own slaves that will be the greater threat to freed Africans. They fear the black man and have no use nor tolerance for their continued presence in the South. The poor whites will subjugate or murder most of them."

Benjamin took a different tack in his argument to Percy. "I know you have thought all this through. I won't ask you what you plan to do or where you plan to go to absolve yourself of any responsibility for the continuation of an unjust system. President Ewell tells me the College is closing for the duration of the conflict. It may be short; it may be long. I'm sure that most colleges in the south will close too. You understand, of course, that if you leave the South in its crisis, you'll never be able to return to it. Even if you go north, if the conflict is prolonged, you'll be subject to conscription into the Union army."

Percy acknowledged the truth in Benjamin's statement. "I suppose I'd have to accept that. I just cannot take up arms against the American flag. In Mexico, I fought for that flag. In Mexico, I executed men who had turned against their own country. If I fight for the Confederacy, would I not be as much a traitor as they were?

"No, I would disagree. The difference is, as I'm sure you understand, it is the North that is seeking to overthrow our own state governments. We only want to defend our own homes."

Percy could not refute Judah. He explained it more personally. "You know that I've avoided politics. I distrust most politicians, present company excepted. To be completely honest, I'm resentful of the fire-eaters of secession for disrupting my life once again. I've settled in here and have known happiness that I lost in Louisiana. Now it's being taken away by them and by forces far beyond my control. I don't see how I could work with those people in Montgomery devising new laws to keep slavery in place."

Seeing further discussion would be futile – for now – Judah Benjamin stood to leave. Looking down at Percy, his parting comment was friendly, even conciliatory: "Let's not close the door just yet. Think on what we've talked about. Ask yourself, who will benefit if you isolate yourself from this conflict? I have a few hours before I return to Richmond on my way back to Montgomery. I'm still negotiating the time and manner for moving the Confederacy's capital to Richmond. Let's meet back here after lunch, say in two hours, and I'll tell you what I have in mind for you. It may surprise you."

༺ ‧ ༻

It was at moments like this that Percy wished he had more religious faith. He did not doubt the existence of God. He was only dubious about God's character. Was He Yahweh of the Old Testament, a vengeful God who inflicted punishment on the wicked and showered tribulations on the righteous only to test them and their loyalty, raining on the just and unjust alike? Was He a loving deity who forgave all manner of sin for those who would open their arms to saving grace? Or was He the Great Clockmaker, the Infinite who imposed order on the swirling chaos and set it on with organized motion through invisible gears and springs, but now indifferent to His Creation, whether they be sparrows or innocent children – like Percy's own son, stung to death by wasps of God's creation? No, he would not walk now to the chapel to seek God's guidance. He would have to find it in himself.

Chapter 3

War Comes to Campus

Half of the students at the College of William and Mary had been eager to prepare for war for months. Six weeks ago, a company uniform was hastily imagined by a sallow-faced boy of fifteen from drawings found in a library book – homespun pantaloons, a red flannel shirt and fatigue cap. The would-be militia armed themselves with Bowie knives and shotguns and muskets. Five deep and three abreast, they marched on the college grounds to the beat of a lone drummer, a company at odds with other students who initially were less partisan. Divisions of opinion there had been about appropriate reactions, but few among the student body doubted the grave consequences of a lop-sided election in which Northerners alone put Abraham Lincoln in the White House. His inauguration on March 4 had occurred little more than a month earlier. No abolitionists were among the students enrolled in Williamsburg. No Unionists dared speak aloud.

Percy Moorhead understood the martial spirit of the youths. When he was their age, he had felt the call to war, the excitement of bearing arms for his country. Only, his enlistment had been to engage against a foreign enemy, the Mexicans who had invaded an American state, Texas. A life-time ago. A thousand miles away.

These young men, most Virginians, were ready to fight other

Americans, in their own yards and fields, on the streets of their own towns. If need be, they would march on Washington where President Lincoln now presided over a government they believed was set on destroying their way of life, to their dishonor.

In this corner of southeast Virginia, secessionist fever had now seized collegians and citizens alike. Calmer heads of the small faculty, Percy among them, silently shared with the college president, Benjamin Ewell, the opinion that breaking up the union of states could end badly. Resistance, however, was as futile as a straw hat against a storm. Should Virginia join its Southern neighbors in rebellion? Students in class with Poindexter and their fellow secessionists had bridled at their state's reluctance to join the Confederacy. Southern manhood was at stake. Southern honor was threatened. The Southern way of life was in jeopardy. Now, Virginia had decided. The die was cast. Thought Percy, the Rappahannock, if not the Rubicon or Potomac, had been crossed.

Whatever his students' political views, Percy enjoyed engaging with them in the classroom and sharing in their daily activities. His year studying law with Judge Beverley Tucker on this campus had been a pleasure, both for his intellectual development and his relations with other like-minded law students. And here it was that he had met Philomena Randolph. These young scholars were little different from the friends he had made when he was studying.

But it seemed a lifetime ago. Personal losses had brought him back to William and Mary and a sense of renewal. In despair at the loss of his father, his son, his wife and his inheritance – even his name –he had relocated from New Orleans to Richmond, where he and Philomena had married seven years earlier. His happy memories had led him to a new home and a feeling of belonging, on this campus. He found friends among the faculty.

That last indignity – his father's succession was opened under the name of Boyle! Not Moorhead. Boyle. That name was odious to him. Grady Boyle, the cursed Irishman, claiming to be the legitimate son of Redmond Boyle, aka Howard Moorhead, had opened the succession and had looted everything that should have gone to Percy Moorhead. Boyle! A name as ugly as its homonym.

Grady Boyle's lawsuit surely was the foundation of the campus rumor that Percy Moorhead was a bastard. The whisperings that Percy was a Jew came from the fact that Percy had been in the practice of law in New Orleans with a Jew – Judah P. Benjamin, the most prominent lawyer in the Senate until he resigned when Louisiana seceded from the Union. That Percy was an unenthusiastic Episcopalian only confirmed that he must be a Jew hiding his race and faith. And abolitionist? Someone had heard that the new professor at William and Mary had effectively freed two slaves by conveying them to a free woman of color in New Orleans before moving to Virginia.

As fate had it, Percy Moorhead (he would never accept that his father was a Boyle or that he was a Boyle) had arrived in Richmond only a short time after the disaster at William and Mary that led to his academic appointment. In February 1859 a great fire had consumed the principal building of the college, disrupting the academic program. Several faculty members decided to move on, among them the professor of Rhetoric, leaving an opening that President Ewell needed to fill.

Upon Percy resettling in Richmond, one of his Princeton classmates allowed Percy the use of an office and the law firm library. Five months later, Percy had attracted few clients and was not part of a social network that might lead to a decent income. He was still despondent over his losses, drinking more than was good for his health or his state of mind. He had begun to wonder if a fresh start in Missouri or California would have been better. Then, a chance encounter with the president of William and Mary, outside Corinthian Hall, near the Capitol, led to a dinner invitation. Benjamin Ewell had briefly served as president of the college in 1848-49 when Percy was Judge Tucker's student – the year when only the law school held classes.

At dinner in the Columbian Hotel Ewell had said, "You may have heard of our disaster in February. That was about the time you returned." The college president was about fifty, with ruddy cheeks, a receding hair line and closely trimmed mustache and beard. The sadness in his eyes stemmed from his family relations, the particulars of which Percy only later learned. Ewell's quiet manner and empathy reminded him of his own father.

"Yes. I was sad to learn it had consumed Wren Hall. The papers all covered it a few days after I opened my office."

Ewell said, with obvious pride, "We're rebuilding with the help of generous patrons. But we've lost several faculty. I've filled some positions recently, with men of whom Judge Tucker and you would approve. Judge Tucker said you were the ablest student he had taught."

Percy deflected the compliment. "Perhaps I was one of the few who had read his novels and would discuss them with him."

"Oh, what were those? I have to confess I've never paid much attention to literature. That, and my West Point education, has made some faculty members skeptical of my qualifications to be president of the college."

Percy had little appetite and welcomed a chance to talk about books. After his wife had died of pneumonia in a Mobile hospital, Percy had become withdrawn and little capable of small talk in social settings. Perhaps that was why he was attracting few clients in Richmond despite his Tucker and Randolph connections. He had difficulty mustering enthusiasm for wills and petty property disputes after his work on international cotton transactions and an inter-ocean route across a Mexican isthmus. With books, he came to life and could re-engage with others.

Percy was especially glad to talk of Tucker's books. He admired many of his teacher's qualities, if not his political beliefs. "I thought *George Balcombe* was a well-written story, in the manner of Sir Walter Scott. It's true-to-life in its treatment of human nature, setting, manners, speech, and customs. A younger man named William Napier is on a quest for recovery of an inheritance. Balcombe, the title character, is a man rather like Judge Tucker himself, a Virginian who moved to Missouri and back again. Missouri is where Judge Tucker married his third wife."

Ewell smiled, "Yes. It was over the objections of her parents. They thought he was much too old for Lucie. Her father was a hide-bound former army general, but he finally blessed the union."

"How is the Judge's widow? Is she still in Williamsburg?"

"She is. She is well," Ewell was happy to report. "A couple of the children are at home with her."

With some reluctance, Percy alluded to his own loss. "You may remember my late wife, Philomena." Ewell nodded with a sympathetic expression. Percy continued, "She was Judge Tucker's niece and could discern the family members on whom he modeled his chief characters. The other novel he published under a pseudonym the same year was *The Partisan Leader*. It could have been written yesterday."

Percy's cryptic allusion to the *Partisan Leader* elided over Judge Tucker's strong political beliefs on the subject of states' rights. Though he was careful to respect the opinions of his students, he was known among Southern leaders as a fire-eater of the first rank. Judge Tucker's novel demonstrated his conviction that the federal government had changed from a political union of independent states to a consolidation of Northerners determined out of self-interest to usurp the principles of states' rights. He was convinced that the federal government had assumed the character of a military despotism controlled by commercial interests intent upon destroying the fabric of Southern economic, political, and social life.

"I understand he thought the South should secede from the Union. Did you come to share his concerns?" asked Ewell with a veiled expression.

Percy tried to read Ewell's thoughts but could not. Uncertain of the political inclinations of his host, he was slow to respond. "Judge Tucker was an excellent lawyer and a great teacher – patient, quick to encourage, learned. But I think he was in error in the merits of secession and on his praise of slavery." Percy paused, trying to read his host with the same discernment as he read books, and added, "I hope my candor gives no offense to you."

Ewell and Percy barely knew each other. Percy had briefly made his acquaintance at Judge Tucker's home a decade earlier, and Ewell had attended Percy's wedding to Philomena in 1851 as a friend of the bride's family.

"None at all. May I be equally frank with you?"

"Of course." Percy had been surprised by the invitation to dinner. And he had the impression that Ewell had been measuring him throughout the evening.

The dessert torte was untouched as the two men sipped after-dinner coffee from china cups that rang brightly on return to their saucers. Ewell continued, "I have no doubt that in good time your practice of law here in Richmond would be as successful as in New Orleans. So, when I suggest the possibility of an alternative employment, please do not think it reflects on my assessment of your legal abilities. After I saw you earlier today, I made inquiries among the lawyers in the community who know you and your wife's mother, Mrs. Randolph. They all confirm what I had suspected. I believe that your experience in law and the breadth and depth of your learning in literature make you the ideal person to replace Professor Totten as Professor of Rhetoric and Belles Lettres."

For a man whose occupation depended upon words, Percy Moorhead was at a sudden loss. From his silence, Ewell thought Percy may not have heard him. He said gently, "Perhaps this is a conversation we should have in Williamsburg. I can understand that you would need to see the state of the campus and talk with the remaining faculty before discussing it further."

Percy quickly responded, "No, Mr. President. My silence doesn't reflect any hesitancy. The thought of teaching has never occurred to me. Only now I am struck dumb that it never entered my mind before. Once you've raised it, I cannot imagine anything that could please me more."

Chapter 4

Percy – Friends, Colleagues

Within two weeks of meeting with President Ewell, Percy had closed his law office and had taken rooms at the Steward's House that was serving as temporary housing for faculty. He began an intense several months of reading and note-taking to prepare his lectures. Daily, he walked the grounds and watched as workmen renovated the college building. The rebuilt Wren building had a strikingly different appearance from its old, now relieved by two Italianate towers, one tower containing the college bell and the other serving as an observatory.

Ewell did everything possible to make Percy feel at ease in his new position. The evening after Percy arrived on campus Ewell held a reception in the President's Residence to introduce the newcomer to seven of his colleagues on the faculty, all recruited by Ewell in the past three or four years. Percy found his hostess was the president's delightful mother Elizabeth, who was often assisted on social occasions by his sister Rebecca. Where was Ewell's wife? The lively Mrs. Ewell, much younger than her husband, had returned to her parents' home in Pennsylvania rather than live in Williamsburg as a professor's wife. Sadly, Percy reflected on the joy Philomena would have experienced living with him on the campus where she had spent weeks at a time with her beloved uncle, Judge Beverley Tucker.

The college president led Percy to a group of men and their wives who were gathered near the punch bowl on the dining room table. Percy quickly surmised that he and Ewell, at thirty-four and fifty, were the two oldest men in the room.

Ewell introduced Percy first to Edwin Taliaferro, Professor of Latin and Romance Languages. Almost ten years Percy's junior, Taliaferro had lean cheeks, dark hair and beard, and a high forehead that made him appear older than twenty-five. Taliaferro was to become one of Percy's closest friends, admiring one another's learning and insight while diverging, always amicably, on political inclination. The younger professor shook Percy's hand warmly and, with a mischievous smile, said, "Well, Percy, welcome again to the College. I believe you know my wife."

Percy struggled to recall where he might have met the young woman next to Taliaferro. She was about twenty, slender and of average height, with brown curled hair and penetrating eyes. Suddenly he recognized her. "Frances? It has to be you." Percy was immediately overcome by emotion. He managed to say warmly, "You look more like your mother than your father. I regret I haven't been here long enough to call on her." Percy had first seen Frances as a girl of only seven or eight in the home of her parents – Judge Beverley Tucker and his young wife, Lucie. Frances Tucker was with the other Tucker children and their friends who played with Philomena on the day he first laid eyes on his future wife.

Professor Taliaferro's young wife brightly replied, "She asked to be remembered to you. You were one of her favorites, one of the judge's last class of students before he passed."

As he met his other colleagues, Percy became aware that he was an outsider among them. Like Edwin and Frances Taliaferro, they and their wives were all from the Virginia aristocracy.

Here was Robert Morrison, professor of history and political economy, married to Catherine Harrison, related to President William Henry Harrison. Here was Edward Joynes, Professor of Greek and German, descended from the Virginia Eastern Shore's earliest settlers and whose first two degrees were from the University of Virginia. Joynes's wife was daughter of a wealthy Williamsburg merchant. Percy was finally introduced to Charles Morris, professor of law, a University of Virginia graduate married to the daughter of a Virginia Senator and Governor.

Percy was a foreigner in this tight-knit gathering of Virginians, though his late wife, a Virginia Randolph, would have been one of them. More so than the citizens of any other state, Virginians considered themselves the natural aristocracy of the United States, bred and educated to assume the mantle of authority to rule over more humble persons – whether black or white. Percy was determined that he would make a place for himself among them.

Percy walked over to the corner that the unobtrusive president of the College had taken for his vantage point. The look on Benjamin Ewell's face was one that reflected satisfaction. He had reason to be: The cadre of intelligent and capable young men who now made up the core of the College's full-time faculty were all recruited by him. They were men of learning and character, devoted to the highest ideals and to inculcating those virtues in young men like themselves. Percy himself was aware that they were far more cohesive than the faculty body that was riven by disagreement and controversy when Ewell first became temporary president in 1848, when Percy was a student. Yes, Percy was committed to living up to the trust placed in him.

In a matter of weeks, not more than six, Percy had become fast friends to this group of faculty hired by Ewell over the past three years, a bond growing out of the shared experience of the fire and the rebuilding in its ruins. Percy became the newest and most enthusiastic member of the Augustan Society, a weekly faculty seminar of six of Ewell's scholars, taking their name from the Roman emperor who favored the poets Horace, Virgil and Ovid. In approach and method, it was similar to the recitations that Percy had enjoyed at Princeton. Devoted to close examinations of poetry and excerpts of classics, each week one of the group selected a poem or a short reading from a work they were familiar with. Sometimes they called themselves the Augustans and at other times they joked they were the Seminarians.

The Society met at a lounge in Brafferton Hall, formerly the Indian School but now serving as a residence for some professors and for a few classes. It was conveniently located on the south side of Wren Yard. The presenter would give a reading of the work, chosen not to exceed seven minutes (though not always observed by the more garrulous of the members), followed by a twenty-minute talk on the author and the context of the poem or reading. At that point, the meeting was thrown open for questions and discussion and, yes, to drinks; whiskey for the serious imbibers, wine for those who were more likely to encounter disapproval if they appeared at home at too late an hour. When the latter activity began to exceed the former, the group on occasion was known to burst into spontaneous song or raucous laughter at repetition of some humorous line from the night's chosen reading.

Percy was impressed with the powers of invention and imagination that his friends brought to their assignments. Joynes was the ablest scholar among the group, doubtless due to the rigor of his education in Germany. One of his memorable events was a comparison of Marlowe's most famous lines from Dr. Faustus with his own translation of what he claimed was one of Marlowe's sources, Aeschylus's *Agamemnon*.

On a cool evening near the end of September, Joynes stood at the speaker's dais in the Brafferton lounge. He began by reading aloud from an open book of Marlowe's works but then closed the book. With greater drama, he finished the lines from memory:

> Was this the face that launch'd a thousand ships,
> And burnt the topless towers of Ilium--
> Sweet Helen, make me immortal with a kiss.--
> Her lips suck forth my soul: see, where it flies!--
> Come, Helen, come, give me my soul again.

> Here will I dwell, for heaven is in these lips,
> And all is dross that is not Helena.

To illustrate his point that Marlowe had relied on an ancient Greek source, he then began reading from Aeschylus, first from a leather-bound text in Greek then pausing to pick up notes he had made of his translation to English:

> Nine years have fled on Time's eternal wings
> And now the tenth is well nigh flown,
> Since the Atreidæ, of this two-fold throne,
> By grace of God, the double-sceptred kings-
> Prince Menelaus, Priam's adversary,
> And Agamemnon-from our coast
> Weighed anchor with a thousand ships ,
> Mustering the valour of the Argive host .
>
>   . . .
>
> A phantom court, a phantom king,
> The loveless ghost of Love-longing:
> She beckons him yet, she bids him come
> Over the sea to Ilium.
>
>   . . . . .
>
> Helen ! Ay, Hell was in her kiss
> For ships and men and polities ,
> When, from behind her amorous veil ,
> She sallied forth with proud, full sail,
> And Love's dallying wind blew fair,
> That Iris to earth-born Zephyr bear.

The performance had solidified Joynes's reputation as the most serious and committed of scholars on the College faculty. Yet friendly competition continued among the Society members to outdo one another when occasion served.

In his first turn as session leader in the group on the following Friday, Percy initiated a discussion of the relation between religion and poetry. His principal reading for the occasion was William Blake's *The Tyger*, asking the group the meaning of the poem, especially the lines, "Did He who made the Lamb make thee?" This elicited lively exchanges from three other members who spoke of the nature of evil in Milton's *Paradise Lost* and of Dante and John Donne.

A month later, humor was joined to serious purpose when Charles Morris, a lawyer like Percy, related lines from a Wordsworth poem and told stories of the poet's unique friendship with Coleridge. As a prank upon the group, he had teamed up with Ed Taliaferro. After apologizing that Wordsworth's *Ode: Intimations of Immortality from Recollections of Early Childhood* was too long, Morris read from *The World is too Much with Us*, affecting an exaggerated British accent to perform as Wordsworth.

As Morris began, Taliaferro quietly slipped around the corner. Morris finished the line in a booming voice:

> Great God! I'd rather be
> A Pagan suckled in a creed outworn;
> So might I, standing on this pleasant lea,
> Have glimpses that would make me less forlorn;
> Have sight of Proteus rising from the sea;
> Or hear old Triton blow his wreathèd horn.

Immediately, Ed Taliaferro stepped out and blew loudly on a conch shell horn borrowed from a display in the College library. Then Ed pretended to hobble up to Morris as a bent old man and took his arm, saying in a raspy voice, "There was a ship . . . " Recoiling in mock horror, Morris shouted, "Hold off! unhand me, grey-beard loon!" With this, the room dissolved in laughter as the men recognized Coleridge's *Rime of the Ancient Mariner*, and each man in his turn blew on the conch horn. As the evening drew to an inebriated close, the lines *unhand me, grey-beard loon!* had been repeated dozens of times and the gestures of taking each other by the arm pantomimed.

The first two sessions of November were allotted to Morrison and Percy. Both were more serious in their selections after the fun of the previous gathering.

For his part, Morrison gave an account of Keats' *Ode on a*

Grecian Urn, reflecting the poet's contemplations about relationships between the soul, eternity, nature, and art, and drawing on classical Greek art as metaphor. Impressed at Morrison's unexpected lyricism, Percy hesitated but then asked, "You've wonderfully invoked the beauty of the scenes depicted on the urn, joy, love, sacrifice, immortality. Dare we inquire the purpose of the urn itself?"

Grinning in delight, Morrison exclaimed, "Indeed, Percy! Well done. I think you are suggesting the urn to be a burial urn. Perhaps Keats himself was unaware that in ancient Greece and Rome funeral urns were far more common than coffins. To be without an urn was to be unburied, as I recall from some lines of Lucan, in *Pharsalia* I think it was."

Percy's most personal selection was made after a sleepless night in which he dreamed of his late wife, Philomena. On the second Friday in November taking his turn at the dais, Percy read an extended passage from Book 2 of John Dryden's translation of *The Aeneid,* when an apparition speaks to Aeneas as he calls out for his dead wife Creusa. He did not tell his colleagues it was a parallel to his own loss of a wife but instead used it as an introduction to the topic he wanted to invoke: how ancient was the theme in literature of a hero's journey, the hero who prevails over personal loss and adversity to serve as champion to his people.

> Creusa still I call; at length she hears,
> And sudden thro' the shades of night appears.
> Appears, no more Creusa, nor my wife,
> But a pale spectre, larger than the life.
> Aghast, astonish'd, and struck dumb with fear,
> I stood; like bristles rose my stiffen'd hair.
> Then thus the ghost began to soothe my grief
> 'Nor tears, nor cries, can give the dead relief.
> Desist, my much-lov'd lord, t' indulge your pain;
> You bear no more than what the gods ordain.
> My fates permit me not from hence to fly;
> Nor he, the great controller of the sky.

Long wand'ring ways for you the pow'rs decree;
On land hard labors, and a length of sea.
Then, after many painful years are past,
On Latium's happy shore you shall be cast,
Where gentle Tiber from his bed beholds
The flow'ry meadows, and the feeding folds.
There end your toils; and there your fates provide
A quiet kingdom, and a royal bride:
There fortune shall the Trojan line restore,
And you for lost Creusa weep no more.

Stepping aside from the lectern, Percy opened the discussion of the hero's journey by relating other examples, saying, "Before Virgil gave us Aeneas, Homer gave us Achilles in the *Iliad* and Ulysses in the *Odyssey*. Early English literature gave us King Arthur in Sir Thomas Malory's *Le Morte D'Arthur*." His reading evoked exchanges among the Society members that showed their breadth of learning and shared belief that literature was a guide to living well in a challenging world.

Leaning forward in his stuffed leather lounge chair just in front of Percy, Ed Taliaferro spoke up. He drew on his time at Trinity College, Dublin, to remind the group of Edmund Spenser, the poet who had settled on Irish estates. Spenser's exemplary heroes in the *Fairie Queen,* such as the Redcrosse Knight and Sir Guyon, represented the same sort of heroic knight's journeys.

"Yes," said Joynes, sitting at a sofa next to Robert Morrison, as he recalled his studies in Berlin: "The Germans call this the *Bildungsroman*. The German poet Wolfram builds on the same foundation as Malory and Spenser in his *Parzival*. The hero goes from chaos and self-doubt to become the Grail King after a journey to maturity in his spiritual quest."

Charles Morris, the law professor, responded, "You fellows know Shakespeare better than I. Is there a journey in any Shakespeare play like this?"

Answering was Morrison, the historian, who had been silent until now. He volunteered, "I think the closest or most likely candidate would be *Henry V.* Shakespeare develops his character across several plays, transforming him from a protégé of the dissolute and even cowardly Sir John Falstaff to become the resolute leader of his people who conquers the French. I couldn't call this a spiritual quest." Laughing then, he added, "And all we Americans have to offer are Natty Bumppo and Chingachgook or Ishmael and Queequeg.

Ed Taliaferro said, "Bumppo I know is the woodsman from the pen of Cooper but who the hell is Ishmael?"

Morrison answered, "Ishmael's the narrator of an obscure novel published a few years back by a New Yorker, Herman Melville. It's called *Moby-Dick*. Nominally it's about a whale, but really, it's about an obsessive quest of the ship's captain, Captain Ahab, to get revenge on the great whale for severing him from his leg. No one bought it, but if you have the patience to work through it, it's really pretty good. The native sidekicks to the heroes of Cooper and Melville are feeble attempts to emulate Falstaff or Sancho Panza, but I can't say I find them very entertaining."

With a dismissive snort, Taliaferro concluded the evening by scoffing, "I think it shall remain in well-earned obscurity."

ᛋᏻ - ᦯᠔

Nearly two hours had passed since Judah Benjamin had left Percy alone to reconsider Judah's offer of a role in the Confederate government. Percy emerged from Wren Hall deeply troubled; memories of many happy experiences with his friends weighed on him.

In the bright sunlight he saw students carrying bags as they prepared to leave to enlist in Virginia's army. He saw eagerness and excitement on their faces. They welcomed the arrival of secession and the certainty of armed conflict. They could not envision their own death or maiming. They could not imagine the losses and deprivations their friends and families would suffer as the inevitable consequences of arrogant decisions and enactments in

Southern legislatures and now in Montgomery. They saw only their own heroic journeys capped by accolades for honorable victories over the hated foe. Percy wanted to grab them by the arm and issue his warning of the dark days to come. But he knew it would be futile.

Percy's attention shifted from the students when he encountered the two Eds, Edward Taliaferro and Edwin Joynes. These two colleagues had just come from meeting with President Ewell. They had been told Percy would be going to the capital in Montgomery to work with the Attorney General. They were cheerful, even jaunty, as they happily greeted Percy.

"What an exciting assignment," exclaimed Ed Taliaferro, who was eager for a military appointment himself. He had long been in the shadow of his eldest brother, William, a high-ranking officer who, as a commander of the state militia, was responsible for the execution of John Brown. Without hiding his envy, Taliaferro said, "Congratulations. How did you land such a plum of an assignment?"

Unable to confess his unwillingness to accept the appointment, Percy replied stiffly, "The matter is still under discussion. In my prior life, I was associated with Mr. Benjamin before he was elected to the Senate."

Ed Joynes, obviously impressed at Percy's connection with the new Confederacy's administration, asked, "Is it true that the capital will be relocated from Montgomery to Richmond? If ever I've heard of a capital ideal, that would be it." Percy and Taliaferro groaned in unison at Joynes's pun. At least, it lightened Percy's sense of gloom.

Lacking the deep Virginian roots of Taliaferro and Joynes, Percy could give a neutral assessment of the shifting of the capital. "A change would have advantages. Richmond is much larger and has far more resources. It's closer to the Atlantic and access to trade routes. But it's awful close to the national capital and would be more vulnerable to attacks from the North. An inviting target."

Taliaferro was quick to counter, "Don't be a doubter, Percy. Lincoln's call for volunteers is all talk for public consumption. When our neighbors to the north face the real prospect of facing Southern arms, they'll fold up their tents and trundle back to the safety of their own homes. Richmond will outshine the District of Columbia."

Sensing that Percy was somewhat distant, Joynes showed his concern: "You are going to join with Benjamin, aren't you?"

Percy again was evasive, knowing he risked alienating the best friends he had. He gave a half-hearted chuckle. "Well, I'd be foolish not to follow Judah, wouldn't I? What would be my alternative? The College is closing. I would not expect to find a warm welcome at Princeton or Yale. Maybe the Attorney General's office is the best offer I'm likely to receive."

Ed Taliaferro said, "We've guessed all along you'd go back to Louisiana. You're as much a Louisianan as we are Virginians. Home is home. It's hard for any of us to give it up."

"So true," said Percy, preparing to move along, uncomfortable in dissimulating with his friends. He shook the hand of each man and continued his walk, torn by the encounter. Now he was even less decided than twenty minutes ago. These were his friends. One was married to Judge Tucker's daughter, his first mentor in law. The other thought so much of Percy that he had made him his child's godfather. They would feel betrayed and even deceived after this last encounter if he were to flee the South. If Virginia had not just seceded, he would certainly have remained in Virginia even as it continued slavery. His scruples against slavery had not led him to oppose it when he returned here two years ago. Why would it be so different to accept a position with Judah Benjamin in Montgomery? It was his fear that his legal talents would be used to re-create the laws of slavery, to strengthen and embellish them, forging tighter the iron shackles upon the African. He could not do this.

But Judah was right: if he went north, he was likely to be conscripted into the Union army should there be a prolonged conflict. If he was reluctant to be an instrument to legislate slave law, he could never take up arms against his friends here or his students, some of whom greeted him warmly as he continued to walk on the College grounds. His boys! He had killed a young boy, a stranger, in Mexico and had difficulty living with the memory. Never, never could he fire at one of his boys nor at Taliaferro or Joynes or Morrison or Morris or any one of his other friends here. And President Ewell: surely, as a West Pointer he would become a general now that Virginia was joining the Confederacy. How could he fight against Ewell? North or South: either choice was impossible; neither was acceptable to his conscience or his emotions.

Still unresolved, his time was up. Just ahead on the walk was Judah, returning to campus for his answer. His future was balanced on a fulcrum.

Chapter 5

Judah is Persuasive

Instead of returning to the lounge at Wren Hall, the two men sat on a bench near the President's office. Judah seized the initiative, saying to Percy, "Before you speak, your grim expression tells me you have not reconsidered your position. Your resolve is one of your great strengths. But I know you to be open to persuasion and reason. Indulge me. I think I can assuage your misgivings."

Reluctant to cut off his mentor of a decade of practice, Percy would listen before declining. He said, "I owe you that at the very least, Judah."

"The work I envision for you will not require you to draft laws for the politicians you disdain. Nor will you have any direct involvement in the enforcement of the institution of slavery. If you accompany me to Montgomery, you will remain there for a few days at most."

Percy assumed Judah was speaking of the move to Richmond. He did not readily pick up on the hint that the work might be radically different from heeding the demands of legislators or accommodating a regime of human bondage throughout the newly established government. He saw no reason to rethink his decision. He said, "Surely, the capital cannot be shifted to Richmond in so short a time."

"I wish we could. Montgomery can't supply the most basic facilities of our government. We will move to Richmond with all due speed but not immediately. Our Treasurer, Chris Memminger, has found Montgomery has no engraver to prepare the bonds, certificates and treasury notes we must issue. There's no printing shop to reproduce them. The town's three hotels are overwhelmed. I have three rooms at my disposal, so you will have a place to stay before you are off again." Benjamin had a sly look on his round face as he saw he had found Percy curious, as though solving a puzzle. Now Percy realized that Judah was baiting the hook that might draw his interest.

"Oh? Where are you sending me now?" Interest and uncertainty sounded in Percy's voice. His thoughts turned to his last experience with Benjamin, four years ago. It was a journey to Mexico City for the Louisiana Tehuantepec Railroad. Percy, Benjamin, and two others had met with Ignacio Comonfort, then briefly president of that deeply troubled country. Percy recalled that the result was highly satisfactory to Benjamin and Emile La Sere, the nominal head of Benjamin's long-term project for connecting the Atlantic and Pacific Oceans. Percy had returned to his family's plantation, Bolingbroke Hall in St. Francisville, without collecting a fee for his month-long services, but he had no regrets for accepting Benjamin's invitation. Now .... Was Percy weakening in his resolve?

Judah Benjamin was a man of great talent and far-reaching vision – and outsized ambition. He was also astute in taking the measure of others. Percy had thought that Judah would appoint him as deputy to the Attorney General and that he would work with the Confederate Congress and cabinet. He was unprepared for Judah's surprising response, a project of international reach and intrigue.

Benjamin enticed Percy, "From Montgomery, we would send you to go post-haste to Charleston – to set up arrangements with the Fraser, Trenholm company. Then to Liverpool."

"Trenholm? Liverpool?" Percy could not immediately see the Confederate connection to the English port.

Observing Percy's renewed interest in what he had to say, Benjamin continued, "I've just heard from Bev Tucker's wife, Jane. You remember Bev, Philomena's cousin."

This was a surprise to Percy. Bev had given Phil to Percy at their wedding a decade ago, but Percy was unaware of Judah knowing Bev Tucker. "You know Bev, I gather."

Smiling Judah continued, "I helped Bev get his appointment as American consul in Liverpool four years ago. Jane arrived in Richmond two days ago. When our first states seceded, he resigned as consul in Liverpool. But he's still in England. We must have a network of people working with us in Liverpool. There is no city in the world more vital for all that we must have. Shipping, munitions, small arms, uniforms, soldiers' kits. Liverpool is where we must purchase ships and build a navy. Liverpool is where we must continue to market our cotton."

Percy understood immediately the crucial role of Liverpool. He knew the Union would see it too. "Didn't Lincoln and Seward just announce a blockade of our entire coast?"

"You see their mistake, don't you?"

Percy had some awareness of blockades. "What? That it's not valid because it can't be enforced? It's more than 3000 miles. Paper blockades aren't effective in international law."

Benjamin had long respected Percy's quickness. It was that quality that led him to hire him when Percy first applied to him. "Your point is well taken, Percy. It will take them time to make a blockade effective. But I don't doubt they will – if the conflict lasts more than six months. That country lawyer in the White House and Seward have made a fundamental blunder. They've called it a blockade. A blockade is something one country does to the ports of another country. They should have said they were closing the ports of the South. A country *closes* its own ports, it doesn't *blockade* them.

Words matter. The British and French will have to give us the status of a belligerent, if not recognize our sovereignty outright."

Nodding in agreement, Percy wasn't sure why Judah was bringing this up. "I recall now. We blockaded the Mexican ports in 1847 to prevent supplies from going to Santa Anna. But I'm at a loss how this relates to me going to Liverpool."

Benjamin persisted, "We must act quickly. Our ardent secessioners understand the urgency for raising troops. But they don't see we must look to Britain and Europe for arming them and supplying them. That's where you can help."

"Me? I can write a brief against a blockade but that doesn't arm an artillery company or launch a ship."

Judah's enthusiasm grew as he drew Percy in. "Quite right. You see that we have no foundries and no navy. Virginia is seizing the Navy yards at Norfolk. Federal authorities will destroy as much as they can before we take over. We'll have no facilities to build ships. Our coastal states are impounding U. S. naval vessels and private ships. But we will need more. Many more. Liverpool must be our source. Liverpool must become a Confederate port."

Percy understood Benjamin's urgency. What this meant for Percy and the Attorney General's office still wasn't clear. "Let's go back a little, Judah. It's been a few years since my last cotton transactions in international markets. The Trenholm company I dealt with was in New York and Liverpool."

"Of course. Yes. Their principal is George Trenholm of Charleston. You'll find no man more loyal to our cause than he is. The New York office is closed."

Percy's eyes narrowed as he absorbed the import of Benjamin's points. He and Judah were hardly aware of the increased activity all around them on the college campus. Excited young men were rushing past them, eager to pack their bags. They were heading to their homes as quickly as possible to see family and girlfriends before enlisting in the state militia or the Confederate army. Where would Percy go? He was suddenly aware that he had given no thought to what he might tell Emily Randolph, his mother-in-law. Could he possibly say to her that he was abandoning Virginia and the South?

Percy told Judah, "So, it sounds like you would like me to be a commercial agent of some sort." Percy wondered what his father would have thought of that. Howard Moorhead had established himself as a cotton factor in New Orleans after immigrating from Britain. His work as an agent in cotton and sugar transactions, as well as astute investments, had made possible his purchase of a thousand acres of land in the Felicianas and the building of Bolingbroke Hall. Certainly, Percy could make use of his knowledge of the business from cotton boll to the delivery of bales to the wharves of Liverpool if a role were created for him.

Benjamin nodded and elaborated, "That, certainly, and more, Percy. You will be working with government representatives and businessmen in England and France. You've done business in Liverpool and London for our law firm. You know how the British are fixated on official documents. They must see a man's credentials. Documents must be notarized. You will be an attorney-in-fact and notary for the Confederate States of America. The lifeline of our new country will be its connection to England, especially with Liverpool. We will be entirely dependent on Liverpool and its ability to get to us ships, arms, munitions and many other goods."

"Sounds like a lot will be riding on Trenholm."

"Our financial survival will depend on the Fraser, Trenholm office in Liverpool. The question for you . . ."

Before Benjamin could finish, both men were startled by the repeated loud peals of the bell atop Wren Hall. Ordinarily, the bell was rung once each hour to mark the end of one class and beginning of the next. Now it was almost half past.

Percy said, "The repeated rings can only signal the last day of classes. President Ewell must have announced an early end to the semester."

Benjamin used his keen wit and his understanding of Percy to turn the moment to his advantage. "Is this not also a sign to you, Percy?"

"A sign?"

"Surely you recall the bell in *Hamlet*. And Hamlet declares 'The time is out of joint'. And surely, this is just such a moment for us." Percy could not help but smile at Judah's inventiveness in seizing the moment for its persuasive appeal.

Judah continued, "But I digress. We were discussing George Trenholm, with whom you would first work. Without the Fraser, Trenholm company – we have no means to buy arms and ships and gunpowder. We cannot engage in commerce with England and France and Russia without a dependable intermediary. When we sell our cotton and tobacco and sugar abroad, we will depend on Fraser, Trenholm to make the transactions possible. I need you in Liverpool for that and more."

Percy knew that Benjamin was not a man given to exaggeration. He was the best commercial lawyer in New Orleans, and he had only enhanced his reputation as an effective attorney after entering the United States Senate in 1853. Nothing had prevented his continuing a lucrative law practice while representing Louisiana in Washington. In fact, it made it easier; for a Supreme Court argument he needn't even leave the capitol to appear before the justices whose court was housed there. He had been offered a seat on the court but declined. He could not have lived on a justice's salary. He had a wife and child living extravagantly in Paris. He had sisters, a brother, and a brother-in-law who were entirely dependent on him. But had he accepted an appointment to the Court, would he have resigned on secession, just as he had given up his Senate seat when Louisiana seceded? Benjamin thoroughly understood business and finance and could just as well have served as Secretary of the Treasury in place of

Memminger in President Davis's cabinet as he could Attorney General. Davis's cabinet was chosen as much for geographic balance as for competence. Each state had to have a seat at Davis's table.

"Financial transactions require financing. What does the Confederacy have in gold and specie?" Percy asked.

Benjamin frowned. "Not much. We seized the mint and customs office in New Orleans. We have United States dollars but they're rapidly depleting on goods we need in the North before everything shuts down and all borders are closed. We don't even have paper to print our own currency." With wry understatement, he added, "What credibility has a bank note printed on wrapping paper?"

Percy's attitude was visibly shifting as his interest grew in the role Benjamin outlined for him. The Attorney General added another weight to the beam to shift the balance decisively.

"Percy, I know you to love your Aristotle as you love your Shakespeare. Recall in the *Politics* where the Philosopher says, 'And he who by nature and not by mere accident is without a state, is either a bad man or above humanity; he is like the tribeless, lawless, heartless one, whom Homer denounces. The natural outcast is an isolated piece at draughts.' Will you become that man with no home and no friends?"

Rueful, Percy could only respond, "I was making a new home here. And new friends."

"You can stand with your friends and work to make the Confederacy a functioning country that will not descend into the chaos you already have admitted will come if the North succeeds in destroying us. I'm not asking you to fight to maintain slavery. Nothing you do can end it. But you can prevent the destruction of the only life and society you and your family have known."

Percy now knew he could not abandon his friends, nor Philomena's mother, to satisfy his own conscience. Judah was not asking him to shore up the legal institution of slavery but forestall an invasion. The North might yet abolish slavery, but Judah was right in saying it would destroy all order in the South and institute only chaos. And will Percy have done nothing?

Standing up, Percy said slowly to Judah, "Do I have two hours to get ready? It seems like I must prepare for a long voyage."

Chapter 6

Two Men on a Train

B enjamin and Percy shared a hotel room at Richmond's
American Hotel, at Twelfth and Main. The Attorney-General
slept soundly, but Percy was kept awake much of the night
by the excited crowds on the capitol grounds celebrating secession.
Early the next morning, the two men boarded the first of several
trains that would take them circuitously to the Confederate capital
in the small Alabama town serving uncomfortably as seat of a new
government.

Hotel staff had presented the Attorney General with two dozen
telegrams delivered in the night. From a station vendor, Benjamin
picked up the *Daily Dispatch* and the *Enquirer* to gather the latest
news. Both papers published Governor Letcher's secession
proclamation, adding Virginia to the seven states of the
Confederacy. Letcher's brief but forceful statement cited President
Lincoln's own Proclamation calling for "a force of seventy-five
thousand men, to cause the laws of the United States to be duly
executed over a people who are no longer a part of the Union." As
Percy expected, Letcher asserted that Virginia's honor was violated,
requiring an armed response: "and it is due to the honor of Virginia
that an improper exercise of force against her people should be
repelled."

Busying himself with the telegrams, Benjamin scribbled notes in dark pencil for sending when the train stopped at a later station. Percy glanced at the newspapers, smiling in surprise to read that the first shot of the war was a cannon fired on Charleston's Fort Sumter by General Beauregard, the same Beauregard, then a lieutenant, who had saved Private Percy Moorhead's arm from amputation when he was wounded at Cerro Gordo. Percy had last seen Beauregard as a captain in New Orleans when the Army had put Beauregard in charge of Mississippi River navigation and the construction of the Federal Custom House.

In the same paper, he read that the Union's army was under General Winfield Scott. His surprise there was that Scott was still in service – and a Unionist despite his deep Virginia roots. When Scott commanded the invasion force in Mexico, he had made Percy a scout for a brief period. And Scott had recommended Percy for the study of law with Judge Beverley Tucker at Scott's alma mater, William and Mary.

Looking out the window, Percy wondered how many others from his past would be in this war, and on which side. He regretted killing Mexicans. He couldn't imagine shooting fellow Americans from the north.

Everywhere along the railroad route could be seen the eruptions of war fever. Men harangued on street corners against the Black Republicans who were raising armies in every Northern state to attack the South and free the slaves, invaders who would arm slaves to kill their masters – the men, the women, the children. Signs on office windows told where men could volunteer to serve, in defense of the homeland. Men and women and wagons filled the streets of every town they passed through, stocking up goods that soon would be in short supply.

Over the clatter of the rail car wheels, Benjamin finally put aside his bundle of telegrams and papers. "Let's talk further of the part to be played by Percy Moorhead. I'm sure you have questions. But first, a bite." Standing to stretch himself, Benjamin took from the overhead compartment a bag of rolls, cheese, and fruit he had picked up in the train station in Richmond and offered some to Percy.

Having eaten a roll earlier, Percy declined an apple. "You've indicated I'm to be a sort of commercial agent and will work with George Trenholm. I guess my first question is what will the Confederacy do for money. I suppose the newly independent states and their banks could each issue their own currency, if they are sovereign. But to protect their sovereign states' rights don't we have to first consolidate military and economic authority in a strong central government? Or am I missing something?"

Putting aside his bag of food, Judah replied, "Ah, dear Percy, you're quick to see the contradictions. Not one of the seceded states, not even mighty Virginia, could oppose the collective strength of the Union by itself. Would Georgia make bank notes of Virginia legal tender in Georgia? Such are the anomalies of sovereignty. We have no choice but to fashion a central government rather like the government from which we are severing ourselves. But our constitution makes clear that we are a confederacy of states, not a new Leviathan. We will establish a currency and issue bonds redeemable in Confederate dollars."

"That's reassuring." Percy's words did not conceal his doubt.

Judah acknowledged that the Confederacy faced an enormous challenge: "For now, we have sufficient gold and American dollars to begin our work in England and Europe. Through trade we will generate funds to sustain us as we gain acceptance by other countries. At present, President Davis and the Cabinet are dispatching a few key agents to Charleston and then Liverpool and London to establish working relationships for finance and commerce. You will take part in these meetings and assist in preparation of contracts for letters of credit and other instruments for payment of the debts we incur abroad. It's little different from what you were doing with our law firm in New Orleans. It will require imagination and improvisation. We can't do it without men like you."

Percy was warming to a return to the law. "You know I love a challenge. With no position at William and Mary, I'm at your disposal."

Benjamin pared a slice of hard white cheese. "That shouldn't be too long. England and France will recognize our independent status within the year. The northern states won't have the fortitude to wage a long war." As was his manner, Benjamin displayed no doubts about a position he advocated. Always confident in appearance, even when the inner man knew better.

"I'm not so sure about that." Percy was the more cautious, younger man.

Shrugging, Benjamin said, "You may be right. Even so, with the steps we've taken already, there's no turning back. What were the lines in Julius Caesar? There is a tide in the affairs of men, which taken at the flood, leads on to fortune. Omitted, all the voyage of their life is bound in shallows and in miseries."

Percy smiled, "You've always bested me on Shakespeare. But, as I recall, it didn't turn out so well for the man who spoke the lines. Should we wade no more, returning would be as tedious as going over."

Chuckling, Benjamin conceded, "You are right. Once again you improve upon my recollection of the swan of Stratford. We have crossed a line. There's no room for compromises or half-way measures. We know that. Lincoln and Seward know that. Doubt can defeat earnest efforts."

"Does the cabinet know of my role? I'm not nearly as qualified or experienced as a many other people serving the Confederacy already."

"Don't underestimate yourself. Two of the cabinet know something of our plans. Only President Davis and I know of your more important functions abroad. And you are uniquely qualified."

False modesty did not contribute to Percy's candid response. "That sounds ominous. What do you have in mind? Something more than commercial transactions?"

Benjamin leaned forward again in his seat, his forearms resting on his knees, drawing closer to Percy who was opposite him. "They involve Bev Tucker and the Tehuantepec Railroad Company."

This did not register with Percy. "I don't see how they fit together." Tucker's newspaper had published stories supporting the Garay-Hargous grant when Tucker was editor, but Percy had never associated Tucker with the Mexican railroad project.

Benjamin teased the conversation forward, making associations for Percy and waiting for his reaction. "Not directly. As we've discussed, Bev Tucker was American consul in Liverpool for the past four years."

Still in the dark, Percy said, "Yes, I know. He spoke at my wife's funeral while on a visit home."

"I was so sorry about Philomena." Benjamin had been unwilling to speak of Percy's losses until Percy himself brought them up. For two years Benjamin had known Percy's wife as a charming hostess, helping Benjamin's campaign on his path to Senator. "I loved her like my own daughter. I didn't hear of your loss until months afterward. And your subsequent difficulties. It must have been awful. Your plantation. Your brother-in-law."

Judah paused before resuming. "But to the point. Bev Tucker, you know passing well. He will trust you completely. He, with your backing, must set up a network of confidential friends in Liverpool."

Benjamin's plan rapidly became clearer to Percy. "Agents? Spies?"

Benjamin leaned back in his seat. "I wouldn't use those terms. Friends of liberty would be better," he said, smiling slyly at his euphemism.

"And Tehuantepec?"

"Someday, Percy, you must share with me what you said to President Comonfort to persuade him to give our company a new grant of the route across Mexico. Whatever it was, it was timely and effective. However, he lost his government only a few months later. After he was succeeded by our friend Benito Juarez, we were able to improve the terms. As I recall, you built a good relationship with him, didn't you?"

"I admire the man. He seems to embody the spirit of Mexico, like the stone jaguars the Aztecs carved from lava to guard their temples." Percy didn't add that he couldn't think of Juarez without remembering the young Mexican goatherd whose life he ended one night to save the American assault at Cerro Gordo from discovery.

Benjamin resumed, "Going forward, we obtained a Federal postal contract and satisfied its requirements with a coach road and boat transport across the isthmus. I made a trip to Britain but failed to secure financial backing to undertake the rail construction. We're burdened by debt and saddled by the Mexican government with repaying a million dollars owed to Francis Falconnet, but we are holding the funds in his name."

Percy hoped that Benjamin would not use his new cabinet position to advance his private wealth in the same manner as he did with his Senate seat. Instead, he asked, "Are you going forward with that project despite the war upon us?" He knew that many men would see a war as a means to enrich themselves. Where most see only chaos and disorder, others see opportunity of the rarest sort. Focused by the imperatives of survival, guardians of the public good will pay little attention to a minor vice of greed – self-benefit in service of the greater good.

"Out of the question entirely," said Benjamin, shaking his head slowly. "But it's an opportunity of a different sort. When the North makes its blockade effective, it will prevent any foreign vessels entering ports of the Confederacy. If the British remain neutral, all ships leaving England will be closely examined by the authorities for violations of their neutrality laws. The most important for us is their Foreign Enlistment Act. The Union will use it to demand that the British government interdict ships bound for the Confederacy."

"But you have a way to work around this?"

"Yes, through you, Percy. You are the unique man for this. What I want you to do is transfer the interests of the Louisiana Tehuantepec Company to a new undertaking. We'll call it the Anglo-Mexican Tehuantepec Company. It will be nominally held by Mr. Falconnet or his assignees. The ownership of the company will remain the same, and the concession will still be held by the Louisiana Tehuantepec Company, but the new Anglo-Mexican Tehuantepec Company will act as its agent. All transactions will be conducted in its name."

Nodding in comprehension, Percy advanced Benjamin's proposition. "Yes, I see where you're going with this. Ships in Liverpool will be loaded with cargoes of equipment, gunpowder, arms etc. with a manifest showing their destination in Mexico. Then what?"

"Whether going by steamship or sail, the ships will need to stop in one of the ports we will use for shipment into the Confederacy. To pass any blockade that the North tries to impose, we'll have to transfer cargos to fast steamers. The ports we will use will be Havana, Bermuda or Nassau. Once there, the cargo will be taken off and put on a blockade runner."

"Do we have ships that can run through a blockade?" Percy was little familiar with such shipping.

Observing that Percy was already speaking of the Confederacy as "we," Benjamin knew he was right to make the side trip to Williamsburg to recruit Percy. Only three years ago, the younger man had lost all that was dear to him, and Benjamin had not known how it might have affected him. In quick succession, Percy's son, his father, and his wife had died. An Irish half-brother had dispossessed Percy of his inheritance of a plantation as well as his

New Orleans townhouse. Somehow, the details of which escaped Benjamin, his brother-in-law was killed in a slave insurrection. Benjamin had pieced together a story that Percy's mother estranged herself from him when she would not support his claim to the plantation against an Irishman, who was Percy's half-brother. In despondence from the several blows, Percy had started a new life in Virginia.

Had his traumas diminished Percy? To Benjamin, he seemed as sharp as ever. Would he be able to serve Benjamin's larger purposes? Time would tell.

Benjamin's position as the Confederacy's Attorney General was more impressive as a title than as a position of power. As he had indicated to Percy, the future of the South as a new country was dependent on England and Europe. They were essential for Confederate arms, ships and commerce. The Confederate Army and Navy were already sending their own agents who would work abroad, and President Davis and the Secretary of State, Robert Toombs, would have their own commissioners to England and European capitals reporting to them. If Benjamin were to gain influence in the Confederate government, he needed his own man overseas to serve as his eyes and ears, to be attentive to his interests, to gain intelligence that would be useful in countering those who might undermine Benjamin. Already, there were nattering voices whispering against Davis's "fat little Jew." The assignments that Benjamin would lay out for Percy would certainly serve the Confederacy's needs, but his long relationship with Benjamin was assurance enough that Percy would, in good time, advance Benjamin's interests as well.

Benjamin now laid out the Confederate plan to counter the blockade. "Some blockade runners will be available. We are acquiring more. They will have to be fast steamships, with shallow draft to go where the Union war ships can't follow. We'll have to buy or build these in England, Scotland, Ireland or France."

Noting Benjamin's inconsistency on the duration of the war,

Percy commented, "If you're talking about building ocean-worthy ships, we're looking at a timeline of six months or more. And large expenses. Do you expect the war to go that long?"

Benjamin's response was without pause. "If we don't act now, we guarantee that we will lose a long conflict." From his expression, Percy could see that Benjamin did not really expect a quick end to the war.

"And will the British allow their shipyards to supply the Confederacy?"

Putting his index finger on Percy's knee, Benjamin insisted, "Oh, Percy, you don't miss a thing, do you? That's part of your lawyer role. You'll need to become intimately familiar with England's neutrality laws."

"The Foreign Enlistment Act you mentioned?"

"Yes. It forbids either of two belligerents to equip, furnish, fit out, or arm any vessel within Britain, for the purpose of making war upon the other. Every detail in the fitting of a ship must be carefully reviewed so as to avoid its application. You and Bev Tucker must see to our strict compliance in working with the shipbuilders. Lincoln's Secretary of State, William Seward, was my greatest foe in the Senate. He'll bring as much pressure to bear as he can on the English to prevent us from acquiring ships. He's forceful and wily, even if a son of a bitch. But have them we must. You can be sure Seward will see to it that Liverpool and London are swarming with their agents. He's as devious as they come. My fellows in the Cabinet underestimate him."

Percy sensed Benjamin's antagonism towards Seward. Such a display of feeling was uncharacteristic of Benjamin. This was personal, two old foes becoming locked in mortal combat, the fate of a continent turning on their old feud and grievances. Percy wondered if their mutual animosities would impair their critical judgment. "I don't know much about Seward. From New York?"

"Yes. You were never very interested in politics, were you?

Seward was their governor. Then Senator. He poses as a radical, but he's a man of low cunning and few principles. Do you know what he said to me after a heated exchange on the Senate floor on the Kansas question? I had scarcely finished my speech when he said to me, 'Come Benjamin, give me a cigar and I won't be mad with you'. I could never trust the man, but I'll grant his ability."

Percy reflected that Benjamin's grudging respect for Seward stemmed from the fact that the two former Senators, both now in opposing presidential cabinets, were more alike than different; both were facing similar challenges. "Let's say Seward's men don't stop our vessels. What happens to the ships we've built or hired that deposit their cargoes in ports friendly to us?"

"Outbound steamships from Southern ports will slip the blockade and bring cotton bales to warehouses in Caribbean ports. The bales will be relabeled, as originating in Mexico, and put on board the ships returning to England. The Union can't stop them if they're British property and carried on British ships."

Percy was puzzled. "All of this will be done out of your Attorney General's office?" A growing hunger made him seem distracted. He hoped they would stop at another station before Tennessee where a meal might be available, while the engine took on fuel and more water. It would be good to get out and stretch and walk on stable ground. Train travel was better than horseback, but he preferred a well-appointed steamboat, where he could walk around or read more comfortably, where a meal was always available. "Maybe I'll have that apple now."

"Sure," laughed Benjamin. "I brought extra for you. When you travel as much as I do, you know that the next meal may be a long time coming. Just a few months ago I was in California on a mining title case. I expect it'll end up in the Supreme Court. I would have liked to have argued it. No looking back now."

Benjamin sounded regretful. The twenty-five years he had devoted to making himself one of the most eminent attorneys in the United States were now behind him. It was not a path he had chosen – nor would have chosen. What had he gained in trade? He wasn't given to second-guessing his own actions. Nor could he present himself to Percy Moorhead as regretting the dissolution of the Union. He could not ask Percy to make sacrifices for a man not fully committed to the success of the Confederacy. The moment passed.

Judah continued, "To answer your question. I'm Attorney General, but President Davis looks to me for guidance on many fronts. Working with me, you will wear two hats. The first is as legal counsel to the Attorney General. That is your public title and role. But you will be named as a special agent to the President. You'll be appointed as an officer of the Confederate Army's Secret Service."

"Will I know any of the people I'll work with, besides Bev Tucker?"

Judah pulled aside the opaque window blind, squinted at the light, then released it. They had rounded a curve and were going downhill at a slight grade, gaining a little speed. "No doubt you will. We've already sent a delegation of diplomats to the capitals of Europe to plead our cause. They are William Yancey, Pierre Rost, and Dudley Mann. Rost you know from the Louisiana Supreme Court. You've probably not made the acquaintance of the other two, but you'll remember the secretary to their mission. He's Walker Fearn."

"Of course," replied Percy, reaching the core of the apple. "Chief of mission for Ambassador Forsyth in Mexico City. Able fellow."

"Precisely. Fearn was formed in the same mold that produced a Percy Moorhead. His uncle is LeRoy Walker, our Secretary of War. You'll meet him soon. Perhaps, too, you'll recall Thomas Pickett."

"Pickett, the consul at Vera Cruz?" Percy did not have favorable recollections of Pickett. "He did some work for the

Tehuantepec Railroad, didn't he?"

"Yes. He'll be our envoy to Mexico. He knows all the right people there, as well as the business interests of Britain, France and Spain. They're threatening to intervene in Mexico's civil war to collect debts owed them."

From his experiences in Mexico, Percy knew the country could be important to the South's independence, but he doubted that Pickett was the man for a mission requiring tact and diplomacy. He turned to ask about another old acquaintance. "Since you seem to know everything happening in the South maybe you can tell me what's happened to my old regiment commander, Colonel De Russy."

"Which one?" asked Benjamin, raising his eyebrows.

"I know of only one. Last I saw him two years ago he was head of the Louisiana militia."

"That would be Lewis. He's now Colonel of the 2nd Louisiana Infantry. President Davis plans to send his unit to Virginia soon. I thought you might have meant René, his brother. René is also a West Point graduate. He worked for us on the Tehuantepec Railroad up until a year ago. We hired him right after we obtained our new charter from Mexico in September of '57. Unfortunately, he's staying with the Union in the conflict. Brother against brother, I'm afraid."

The iron wheels of the train screeched in complaint as it slowed and stopped. The engine wheezed loudly and then heaved a great sigh as the engineer released pressure from the boiler. Percy looked through the window and saw a metal drop-spout lower from a water tank to the train's engine. Without a regular supply of water, there will be no steam. Percy smiled at the timeliness and aptness of the analogy. No replenishment of supplies from Liverpool, no Confederacy. They had arrived at the depot in Abingdon, Virginia.

Chapter 7

The Ineffable and the Inevitable

Now seated at a table inside the Abingdon depot as their locomotive took on wood and water, Percy again reflected on his prospects as he ate. He couldn't go back to Williamsburg – the college was down for the duration of conflict. He couldn't return to Louisiana – Grady Boyle had his townhouse and his plantation. And he had no more clients in Louisiana. He'd had no communication from his mother and sister since he had left them in February two years ago. He couldn't go north – he knew no one there. Even though he distrusted secession, he had no sense of identity with Northerners who hated the South for its benighted state. How could he embrace their cause? They wanted freedom for the slaves but would bear none of the costs of their emancipation themselves. If chaos throughout the South followed universal manumission, the Northerners would regard it as the wages of sin, the just punishment of Southerners for preserving an unjust institution.

No doubt the North would first strike at Virginia. The boys he had been teaching for the past year were now in arms, or soon would be. His boys. How could he support the Union if they were to try to kill his boys? Percy's future was bound to the Confederacy and to Judah P. Benjamin, whatever may come. There was nowhere for him to sit it out, even if he wanted to.

Benjamin was outside, sitting on a chair leaning with its back against the depot wall, smoking slowly on a cigar. Percy could see part of him through the window. If Philomena were alive, she would tell him the same thing she had said when Benjamin had telegrammed him in St. Francisville, asking him to go with him to Mexico. "Trust Judah," she would say. Oh, how he missed her voice, her gentle encouragement. Her intuited judgment was better on most matters than Percy's analytical conclusions. He could hear her now, "Judah wouldn't do wrong by you. He's wandered since birth. He knows impermanence. When's he's found a friend, it's a friend for life. He sees the best of himself in you. If he were to make ill use of you, he would betray himself."

Still hearing Philomena, he would heed Judah. The doubts? They would intrude later.

Many years later, I asked Percy about that moment in April 1861 when he was in that train depot. "And if you had known then what you know now, would you have done what you did?" He was slow to respond. Was he reluctant? I asked again. "Let me be a little more direct: If you were again seated at that depot in Abingdon, Virginia, would you have not reboarded the train? Would you have remained there, leaving Judah Benjamin to continue on his own?"

Percy looked at me with mild amusement, as though my question was naive. From his perspective, it was naive. That explained his pause. He called Florio, his brown retriever, over to his side, by the fire. Scratching Florio's head, he fed the old dog a dried sow's ear from a bowl on the mantel. And he responded, though with patience, even indulgence.

"Tom, you mean to ask, if I had understood then as I understand now. For the gulf between knowing and understanding, while not unbridgeable, is often wide. Just as often, it is ineffable."

Percy would do that, deflect to throw me off. *Ineffable*. How like

Percy to linger and savor a word that conveys just the sort of uncertainty and mystery he wants. It distracts his auditor. I persisted, affably. "As amended, that remains my question."

"Well, now. Knowledge comes quickly. An announcement in the public square. One of your newspaper articles. A report of a sergeant from headquarters. One's own eyes and ears and hands. Understanding creeps at a petty pace, forming itself from multitudinous bits of disparate knowledge. Knowledge and experience must come together for understanding. On that April day in 1861, on a chuffing train to the Confederate capital, I knew Judah Benjamin as well as I knew any man. Perhaps even better than I knew my father. But I understood neither man. Not as I do now."

"Please explain. Even if ineffable." Was that a wink I saw?

Here, I'll condense his response so as not to take you down the sidetracks, at the risk of a tedious monologue.

"Yes. Similarity is more readily perceived than difference. Both Judah and my father were ambitious. Both were competent and successful in their professional lives. Both were married to a younger woman who depended on her husband for financial well-being but not for emotional fulfillment. For Judah Benjamin and Howard Moorhead, a marriage was a fingerpost on life's road. One arrow pointed in the direction from whence the traveler had come and another in the direction of a future that lay ahead for a fully formed life. The Benjamins and the Moorheads were similar couples, each joined legally though not in spirit. Judah and Howard were also similar in being immigrants to Louisiana with English-speaking roots. Both sought and achieved professional success in selling their services to others, my father as a cotton factor and Judah as a lawyer. Each had crowned his financial and marital status by establishing a plantation, Howard's cotton plantation – Bolingbroke – and Judah's sugar plantation – Belle Chasse. What I knew, others knew. The two men were accomplished, and I wished to emulate them, enjoy success as they had. Knowing all that, there was no reason not to return to the train. Nor would knowledge that a great civil war would follow and would end as it did have compelled me to stay off the train."

"So, you've explained *knowing*. But you spoke also of *understanding*. What of understanding?"

"The understanding could only come later, when I could appreciate the differences between these two men who were my pole stars. They sought different ends. My father was ambitious. He sought and achieved wealth, as I have said. But Howard Moorhead avoided public recognition, preferring self-effacing obscurity. And he possessed a special quality that he seldom allowed to be seen: his sentimentality. His quiet demeanor was the manifestation of an inner settlement, a self-awareness, a sweet-sadness at the sum of his experiences. I never saw him treat another person with the slightest degree of disrespect, even those who were identified as his property. Nearing the end of his life, he wanted only to free them."

Percy stood. He stirred the fire. He put his hands in his sweater pockets and resumed. "Now Judah? When we were on that train, transiting from Richmond to Montgomery as the great war began, he was one of the founders of a new country. His acumen in law was shaping the legal system of that country. What lawyer would not want to be present in that act of creation? Yet, not having had contact with the man for several years, I had forgotten the contrasts with my father. At that time, they seemed negligible. And I was uncritical. I attributed desirable attributes to a man I already admired. We do that, don't we? We see only that which confirms our own desires and inclinations. The contrasts became more pronounced as I continued to work with Judah. Of course, even then I knew that Judah flourished in being the brightest, cleverest, most successful man in any setting. I came to observe that he seldom ventured into an arena where he could not show off his talents. His imperturbability arose from immense self-control, from the suppression of anger or anxiousness or frustration or any other emotion that might impede achieving his immediate purpose – not from their absence. As much as I admired the man for his talent, as much as I was drawn to him for his mastery of the profession and the strength of his intellect, I slowly became uneasy that every word, every act, of Judah Benjamin was an expression of calculation. Even now, after all that has occurred since, I remain flattered that in his cold, dispassionate calculation I was a worthy instrument to further his purposes. Where my father was sentimental, Judah was cunning. Where my father sought the care of others, Judah sought the use of others."

"Where does this take us, Percy?"

Again, the slight smile, indulgent that I wanted more from him but weary of the memories; his response, "It takes us to the decanter that awaits us on yon shelf. From it we will imbibe of the best offering of a Western Cape vineyard, the Vin de Constance, newly arrived in Bristol aboard one of my vessels. I think you will admire its bouquet and the forgetfulness it brings."

Chapter 8
Montgomery

Two days after re-boarding the train in Virginia, Benjamin and Percy arrived in Montgomery. Early the next morning, Benjamin took Percy to a large brick building, at the corner of Market Street and Commerce Street, down from the state capitol. The offices had been hurriedly transformed into the new Executive Building of the Confederate States of America. A Confederate flag floated lazily above it, incapable of comprehending the passions aroused by its threads, fabric, and colors and by its status as the symbol of a new sovereignty among the countries of the world, though still unrecognized. The Commerce Street door stood open, and gave on to a large, unpretentious whitewashed hall. Names of government departments were handwritten on sheets of paper tacked to doors off the bottom floor hall.

Benjamin and Percy walked upstairs to the second floor, which was surrounded by doors opening off the open court. On one of these off to the right was another handwritten paper saying, "The President," so modest a plaque for the august chambers of the chief executive of a proud and defiant new nation.

A half-dozen men, some in uniform, were at work in the outer office, the office of the private secretary to the President. Three other men could be seen through the open door into the President's office. Standing next to another, shorter man at the desk in the center of the room was Jefferson Davis. Percy had seen his likeness in newspapers but was unprepared for the imposing figure of the man himself. Davis appeared taller than others, a consequence of his erect, military bearing. Austere in appearance because of his lean figure, he was dressed in a rustic suit of slate-colored material, with a black silk handkerchief around his neck. A fine full forehead, square and high, set off a face covered with fine lines and wrinkles. His features were regular, with high cheek-bones, and recessed jaw – lips, thin and flexible; chin, square and well defined; nose with wide nostrils, and eyes deep-set and large. One eye seemed at odds with the other, the result of spells of neuralgia and fever. His face ended with chin tufted by a small goatee.

Benjamin went in alone. After a moment, he returned and declared to Percy, "The President will be glad to see us." Percy followed.

Interrupting his conversation with an aide, Davis walked around his desk and stiffly took Percy's hand into his own. "You must be the agent Judah wants to send abroad – Moorhead, is it?"

Percy returned Davis's firm grasp. "Yes, Mr. President. Percy Moorhead."

"A cotton planter like myself," Davis declared. Benjamin had prepared Davis to receive Percy on favorable terms, not mentioning that Percy no longer owned a plantation.

"Yes sir. Down river on the Mississippi from your plantation. I was raised at Bayou Sara and St. Francisville."

"Splendid. Judah tells me you were a scout in the Mexican War. What was your rank?"

Without hesitation or apology, Percy answered, "A private in the Louisiana volunteers. Later I was assigned to General Twiggs's division." Percy could tell from Davis's expression that he was asking himself how a planter's son would have been no more than a private. No matter – if the man had Benjamin's confidence, he had Davis's too.

Davis inquired, "Are you now in a company from Louisiana? Our General Beauregard resigned as superintendent of cadets at West Point to volunteer in a Louisiana regiment."

"No Mr. President. I was teaching at William and Mary College when the Attorney General recruited me. I served with General Beauregard in Mexico, at Cerro Gordo." He might also have mentioned his night-time reconnoitering with General Lee before the battle, but it would have presented a false appearance to his modest services.

With a small chuckle, Davis said, "Well, *Private* Moorhead, you're promoted. I'm appointing you a Lieutenant in the army of the Confederate States of America." The Confederate President added, "If I hadn't made Beauregard a general in our army, he might still be a private in the New Orleans Guard. The army must love privates because it makes so many of them."

Again, the presidential smile and chuckle. They were intended to set others at ease. But they were not natural gestures for Davis. From his political experience, he understood that his military demeanor was off-putting for most civilians. He was stiff and uncomfortable with common pleasantries. But, with his wife Varina's encouragement, he made the effort.

Benjamin later explained to Percy that Louisiana's Governor, Tom Moore, had offered Beauregard only a colonelcy in the state's army, an army Beauregard had expected to command, while the generalship was given to Braxton Bragg. Beauregard had deeply resented the affront to his honor when Moore promoted Bragg over himself. Beauregard expressed his dissatisfaction by volunteering as a private in the New Orleans unit: he'd prefer being a private to serving as an officer reporting to Bragg. Beauregard, however, did so because he was confident that the new government in Montgomery would seek his service. Davis's elevation of Beauregard to general in the national army of the Confederacy did not prevent Beauregard from regarding his own military judgments as superior to Davis's, a conviction that would grow with each battle and campaign.

Benjamin believed, not without cause, that Percy's appointment as an officer would serve more than one end. It would give Percy a sense of commitment more than employment as an attorney for the new government. Percy's occasional references while working for Benjamin in New Orleans to his service as a private had suggested an embarrassment at his inferior military status. Percy's effectiveness in dealing with officials and others abroad would be enhanced by a rank as an officer. Perhaps, too, should Percy be captured by Union forces, he would be accorded treatment as a prisoner of war rather than sentenced to a spy's execution.

Benjamin and Percy left the President's temporary office to go to the Attorney General's office nearby. They were passing a room housing the Secretary of War, Leroy Pope Walker, when a loud voice called out, "Judah!"

The voice belonged to Secretary Walker. A tall, lean, straight-haired man, with fiery, impulsive eyes and manner, he had been closeted with two officers in a room full of maps and plans. Now he stepped out to speak to Benjamin. With some urgency, he began asking about the blockade President Lincoln had declared a few days earlier. Benjamin interrupted him to introduce Percy.

"Leroy, this is Lieutenant Percy Moorhead. He's working with me on a presidential assignment from the Army. Like you, he studied law in Virginia."

"Charlottesville?" Walker responded, suddenly more attentive. He had attended the University of Virginia.

"No, Mr. Secretary. Williamsburg, with Judge Tucker."

Suitably impressed, Secretary Walker said, "Yes, Judge Tucker. A fine man, an early advocate of secession. We should have heeded him earlier."

Benjamin returned the conversation to the blockade. "A declaration means nothing in law. Without at least five hundred ships, Lincoln and Seward cannot maintain an effective blockade. And they are caught in a contradiction."

"A contradiction?" Walker was curious.

As an attorney summarizing the law to a client, Judah explained, "I am certain that the English law authorities must advise their government that the blockade of the Southern ports is illegal so long as the President claims them to be ports of the United States. Lincoln's paper blockade can do little harm. The season for shipping cotton is over. By next October, when the Mississippi is floating cotton by the thousands of bales, and all our wharves are full, it is inevitable that the Union must come to trouble with this attempt to coerce the British by excluding their commerce with the Confederacy."

"That's reassuring," said Walker. "Can we count on the British government to do the right thing?"

Putting his hand on Percy's right shoulder, Benjamin said confidently, "We're sending Lieutenant Moorhead to England, where he will urge the finer points of the law of blockade to the merchants in Liverpool and to the government in London. He will persuade them that they may safely and in good conscience ignore the Union's usurpation of international laws of commerce."

Slapping Percy's left shoulder, Walker warmly urged Percy, "Give 'em Hell, Moorhead. They need our cotton more than we need anything from them."

Percy agreed, adding, "I have found men are more open to reason when their pocketbooks are in peril, Mr. Secretary."

Confederate Cabinet at Montgomery
Source - Library of Congress

Attorney General Benjamin - *Secretary* Mallory - *Secretary* Memminger - *Vice President* Stephens - *Secretary* Walker - *President* Davis - *Postmaster* Reagan - *Secretary* Toombs

Chapter 9

On to Benjamin's Office

From the Secretary of War's office, the Attorney General's office was two doors down, just opposite the President's across the open court. Arriving there, Benjamin took a few minutes to sort through the mail and telegrams handed him by an assistant, while Percy looked around the office. There were no more than fifty volumes on the sparse shelves of the spartan office, but Percy glimpsed enough of them to see that even as Attorney General of the Confederacy Benjamin had given space to a half dozen recent novels, an edition of Shakespeare and two anthologies of poetry. Seeing Percy's interest, Benjamin inquired, "What books did you carry with you from Louisiana?"

"Virgil. A collection of the Stoics. Florio's Montaigne."

Benjamin approved of Percy's interests. He said, "What a man reads tells you much about the man."

Laughing, Percy asked, "And what do our books say about us? That we'd rather live in another place and another time? Books are an escape."

Taking off his spectacles, Judah drawled, "I know you better than that Percy. They're your maps. You look to them as a guide to your own actions."

Changing the subject, Percy replied, "You and the president

surprised me. I had not expected to be appointed an officer in the army."

Benjamin saw that Percy was pleased and smiled broadly, "As much for the President's benefit as yours, Percy. President Davis enjoys making appointments. You have to give the man credit. He foresaw clearly one of the defects we face as a new union of independent states. From his experience in the Mexican War and as Secretary of War for Pierce, he knows the dangers of irregular levies. If our Confederacy had to depend solely on volunteers from the states, our new nation would be at the mercy of volunteers whose service might expire in the middle of campaigns that require months to plan and execute."

Percy agreed. "I recall well when we spent three months in the summer of 1847 at Puebla. Many volunteers had to be replaced. Their enlistments were up, and they returned home."

"Whatever his shortcomings might be, Davis understands the complexities of getting conflicting military temperaments to work together to a common end. Much of the correspondence that cross his desk are complaints over rank and status of our officers."

On reflection, Percy realized that may have been another subtle reason for his lieutenancy in the Confederate army. While he might be an attorney in Benjamin's department, he was also in the chain of command directly subject to the orders of the commander-in-chief. It left no doubt about who Percy answered to. He asked Benjamin about the other man they had just met.

"Does Secretary Walker have any military experience? I don't recall his name in connection with the Mexican War."

Benjamin was frank. "The President wants administrators in his Cabinet. That, and a balance of states must be represented in the Cabinet. A lack of time in uniform is no hindrance for Leroy Walker. President Davis was Secretary of War for the four years of the Pierce presidency, and he expects to do much the same job now as President of the CSA – if the war continues for any length of time."

Percy inquired, "Would I be wrong in assuming the President and Secretary Walker are your principal clients?" This was also another way Percy was asking as to whom he reported.

Benjamin took his time answering, showing apparent discomfort at the difficulties he faced. He was reluctant to be fully candid with Percy: "I wish it were a simple matter of attorney and client. Everything we do has such enormous consequences. It's not like an argument to persuade a judge or tribunal. Consider the blockade question. What response do we make? We might authorize privateers and issue letters of marque and reprisal."

"Are privateers still lawful?"

Benjamin smiled. "Perhaps, if they are authorized by our government." Holding up the pen with which he had been writing, he continued, "Is this the pen that launches a thousand ships? But what happens then if we launch even a hundred privateers? England, France and other great powers decreed the abolition of privateering at the end of the Crimean War. They might declare our privateers are no more than pirates and hang every one of them. It would be nothing more or less than a declaration of war against us, and we would have to meet it as best we can. Of course, we cannot possibly have war with the North and with England, so we must tread very carefully, even if we are not bound by the Paris Declaration on Maritime Law."

"Wouldn't that be something in the jurisdiction of the Secretary of State?" Percy sensed that the lines of authority in this new government were murky, if not chaotic.

Benjamin sighed and shrugged. "Not if we can help it. Robert Toombs wanted to be the first President of the Confederacy and had to settle for an office for which he is singularly unsuited. He has a volatile personality and pettiness resides in every limb of his body. And that's what he's like when he's perfectly sober, which is not very often."

Wryly, Percy responded, "So, his name alone is not sufficiently ominous. His character, too. I've not met the man. Is his appearance similarly grave?"

Benjamin chuckled, relieved that he could count on Percy to share his outlook and also amuse him. Percy's dry wordplay, subtly acerbic when not cynical, had impressed Benjamin from his first meeting more than a decade earlier, when Percy asked to be taken on as a lawyer by Benjamin. "You haven't lost your taste for puns. It's difficult to imagine a man less suited for the office than Toombs. At a time when we have no paper, Toombs meets with his staff to discuss paper dimensions and margins within which writing must appear so that all correspondence may be uniformly bound. Each letter to his attention must have headings and marginal notes to highlight key points he should address. Instead, he should be devising ciphers and establishing communication routes and confidential couriers. Of the Cabinet, he alone opposed our engaging the enemy at Fort Sumter. He said we were striking a hornet's nest which extends from mountain to ocean, and legions now quiet will swarm out and sting us to death."

Percy suppressed a shiver at Benjamin's choice of metaphor – whether it was by Toombs or Benjamin. Surely Benjamin, who was always empathetic and gentle, would never have repeated it had he been aware of the circumstances of Percy's son's death, by the stings of a thousand swarming yellow jackets.

Percy merely said, "I take it then that Mr. Toombs is unaware of the activities I am to undertake with Bev Tucker and others?"

"Precisely. You are an attorney with the Attorney General of the Confederate States of America who, for the time being, is acting abroad. Toombs would not want you or me acting in matters he claims are within his jurisdiction." Benjamin's attention was interrupted by a figure coming into the outer office. He informed Percy, "Ah, one more with whom you must meet. An old friend of yours, I believe."

Percy turned in his chair as a lean man of middle height and years stepped in. "An old friend?" Percy had no memory of the man who took his hand and gave him a sly smile, amused at Percy's confused expression.

"Rufus Jordan," said the man with a voice that bore no accent that could be identified with a region. "Good to see you again, Percy." His hair was dark and long, parted on the left side of his angular head.

Percy struggled; there was something vaguely familiar about the man. He could only shake his head slowly in apology. "I'm sorry, Mr. Jordan. Please forgive me. I can't recall that we've met."

Chuckling, the man said "The fault is mine, Percy. You knew me in a different life." He took a comb from his pocket, and swept his hair so that it streamed from his forehead back and to his neck. He put a monocle over his right eye and subtly shifted his shoulders forward. "Ve knew one another ven I was the Count, Luigi Ottavio."

The Count was one of the three men who in 1852 had employed Percy as an attorney for a casino they set up in New Orleans – Toulouse Gardens. Percy had taken an ownership interest in the enterprise but sold it as his finances collapsed due to Grady Boyle's intervention in his life.

Percy could not withhold a burst of laughter. "My God, so you are. I would never have guessed. Was it an act all along?"

"No," Rufus replied with a broad grin. "There was never an intent to deceive you. When we launched our syndicate of gaming emporiums, we thought it would add to the allure to have a European association. Unquestionably, it did."

"You were very convincing."

Rufus Jordan settled comfortably in his chair. "It was not so much an act as an alternate identity, no less genuine than Rufus Jordan of Baltimore, Maryland. My parents sent me to seminary in Rome when I was eleven. After seven years with the priests, it was mutually agreed that I was ill-suited to wear the cleric's cassock. I lacked piety and had no capacity for celibacy. For the next eight years I served as gentleman companion to an Italian nobleman who traveled among the capitals of Europe, gambling. When my master was killed by a jealous husband, I returned to the United States speaking five languages and in possession of both Italian and French identity papers that allow me to travel freely abroad."

"Fascinating!" Percy again laughed. "And a fluid identity. A shape-shifter."

Benjamin now spoke again. "And that brings us to why he is here to meet you today, Percy. Rufus will return to New York shortly where he will employ his considerable talents as an undercover agent of the Confederacy. You will not know his name or his location or the business that will disguise his activities. When you arrive in New York in a couple of weeks, he will know how to contact you at the Astor House Hotel. And now you must gather the materials one of my staff has prepared for you. Return to your hotel for rest before you set out for South Carolina early tomorrow."

After Percy left, Rufus Jordan said to Benjamin, "Moorhead's a good choice for your man in England, Judah. Able. Experienced. You won't have to worry about him feathering his own nest at your expense."

From behind his desk, feet propped on a stool, Benjamin said, "Your words are reassuring, Rufus. But your expression shows misgivings."

"I like Percy. I always have. He earned the trust of me and my associates. But this is now war. Will he prove to be the dove when circumstance requires the serpent? He may prove squeamish."

Turning to look out his window, Judah said, "The Jesuits trained you well. Don't they have a motto, *exitus acta probat*? If the end doesn't justify the means, then what does?" The Attorney

General paused as he reflected on his protégé. "Rufus, I'll grant you that Percy Moorhead is not so calculating as you and I. This war may make beasts of us all. His peculiar notions of integrity can be become tedious, and he doesn't yet fully understand what we are throwing him into. But I know him to be resourceful when he encounters obstacles. If he proves too scrupulous for an undertaking, we find a substitute."

Rufus Jordan stood to take his leave. "You know him best. We do make a pair, Judah, don't we? A non-observant Jew and a failed priest, in the service of slave-holding Bible-thumpers who detest Hebrews and papists in equal measure. Will their God punish us for our sins? For the record, however, Ovid was long before Ignatius."

Judah Benjamin smiled as Rufus Jordan left. The day had been productive. He would have a Percy Moorhead serving his purpose in England and a Rufus Jordan at work for him in the North.

Chapter 10

Grady's Townhouse

Grady Boyle had had his eye for several weeks on the woman now in charge of the Dennett Pharmacy on Carondelet. Today, he commented on the absence of the proprietor who usually sold him medicinals.

"I've not seen Mr. Dennett in a fortnight. I hope he's not taken ill," he said to the woman, using his best Irish brogue and imagining a twinkle in his eye. She looked to be in her late-thirties. From her hands and complexion, she was a woman who had spent little time in physical labor.

Her voice was not unpleasant, carrying none of the annoyance that some New Orleans shopkeepers gave out to customers. "He's been called up to the regiment. They're gone to Pensacola as I hear tell."

The smiling Irishman said, "So, you must be the young lady employed in his absence?" Describing the woman as "young" was generous. And "lady" conveyed, in the Southern parlance this Irishman was acquiring, a sense of elegance that the woman behind the counter visibly lacked.

"If you mean me, I'm his wife," she replied pleasantly. If he would entertain the fiction that she was a Southern lady, she was willing to share it. "I'm not registered by the pharmacy board, but

I can sell the potions and sundries that are on hand. Does Mr. Dennett run an account for you, sir?"

"Boyle. Grady Boyle, Mrs. Dennett. No, I'm a cash customer." When she spoke, Grady took note of the small gap in her front teeth, always a promising sign back in Dublin, where he had spent most of his life.

"What can I get for you today, Mr. Boyle?" She pressed her apron, placed her smooth, uncalloused hands on the counter, and smiled at her cash customer. The store's stock was running low now that the military was competing for supplies. Cash would be welcome.

He looked at the shelves just behind the woman, a few feet above her head. "A friend has recommended those Holloway's Pills. If it's not too much trouble, I'd like a small bottle."

"No trouble at all, Mr. Boyle." She maneuvered a small sliding ladder and ascended three steps to reach for the Holloway's Pills. Boyle admired her slender ankle and the fluidity of her movement as she returned to the floor. It was near five in the afternoon, but she showed no sign of weariness. Her expression as she handed the pills to him suggested that his attentions would not go unreturned.

"These just came down from Vicksburg," she said. "Perhaps you would let me know if you find them to your liking."

"But of course. And may I say how much I admire a lady, who is obviously more accustomed to leisure, who would assume her husband's business activities while he is away to defend us from the radical forces that threaten. It can't be easy for you."

Coyly, she shrugged, "It could be worse. I will admit to a certain loneliness at times."

Receptive to her acknowledgement of a lonely state, Grady said, "Oh? Would you be offended at my boldness if I offered you dinner sometime – as a gesture of respect for the sacrifices made by you and your husband?"

"You are too kind, sir. Ordinarily I would have to decline."

Though she tried not to sound eager, Grady knew better. "But you have the appearance of a gentleman of manners. I'm sure Mr. Dennett would not object if I were to accept the kind hospitality of one of his customers."

At 7:00 Grady returned to the store, which had the pharmacist's living quarters on the second floor. She made him wait a few minutes before descending the stairs, the better he would note how she had dressed for him. She had let down and brushed her brown hair, then re-layered it, clasping it in back. He smiled at her appearance, as if he actually approved her efforts to please.

Dressed in his tailored suit with a bright red vest and his best beaver hat, Mr. Boyle took Mrs. Dennett to Toulouse Gardens. They ate and gambled until 10:00. She was impressed that all of the dealers and croupiers addressed him formally and showed him the deference expected of a part owner of the establishment. Fewer people were attending the casino since Louisiana seceded from the Union, four months ago, the sixth state to do so. Grady had paid little attention to the clamor over states rights. He assumed that each state had the right to withdraw from a voluntary compact. With the firing on Fort Sumter and President Lincoln's call to arms, it seemed serious but likely no worse than a case of the flu that would spend itself quickly. It was no concern of his. Even he noted that fewer New Orleanians were willing to spend their money on the gaming tables. Plenty of gambling and drinking were still going on, but not among the finer sort of people who were conserving their money as prices were rising.

Everywhere that Grady and Marnie walked, they encountered soldiers. Few boats could be seen as they approached the levee: As news of the war's outbreak spread throughout the country, foreign vessels had departed the docks and wharves. Their berths were not occupied by new river traffic from abroad. The few steamboats that were tied up were river craft intended for the anticipated conflict.

The air on this May night was pleasant. The couple strolled for a few blocks under the watchful eyes of sentries in uniform and of civilian vigilantes on the lookout for disloyalists, spies, and secret abolitionists. Boyle's Irish accent raised no alarms – there were at least thirty thousand Irishmen who had settled in New Orleans in recent years.

Boyle took Marnie to his town house, the same that had been in the Moorhead family for four decades. It had been the marriage gift of Howard to Percy and Philomena and was the birthplace of Randolph Moorhead. It was now Grady's because, as his lawyer told him, Percy had thought it would be disrespectful to record the deed; it might mean that he distrusted his own father.

Marnie Dennett admired the large interior and refined furnishings, exclaiming, "I've walked by this place a hundred times in the four years since Mr. Dennett acquired the pharmacy, but I never knew whose it was. It's . . ., it's *grand*, Mr. Boyle." Mr. Boyle was a gentleman of taste to have chosen such appointments. Was there a Mrs. Boyle? She dared not ask.

"Grady, my dear Marie, just call me Grady," he said grandly, as though gifting her with his attention.

"Well, Grady," she said putting her arms around him from behind his back and saying with emphasis in his ear, "it's actually *Marnie*. Mar-Nee. The *n* is not silent. I'm not either."

Grady chuckled and turned to face her. She was about six or seven years younger than he. On the shorter side of life's calendar, she regretted that she had settled too easily for a man with no panache about him. Enoch Dennett, registered pharmacist, had no charm, no mystery. A woman needs a little mystery from a man, even if he seems to carry danger. It quickens the pulse, awakens the senses. She felt it now, behind her eyes which darted rapidly from side to side.

"Oh, you can be feisty, can you?" Grady said. "A good Irish lass is a saucy gal. And I've known a few. Now my grandfather, there was a lady's man. Charming into his old old age. Any of the colleen in you?"

"French, Swiss, maybe a Dane on my mother's side. Have you lived here long, Grady Boyle?"

"Let's just say I inherited it, a few years ago. And the family plantation."

"And you are a planter, too, are you?" Marnie was growing more interested with everything she learned about this charming, tasteful, vaguely menacing man. There was nothing interesting about her Enoch, who was content to close shop at 6:30, then read a paper each evening after dinner and retire after a small glass of beer. He snored. He coughed. Her eyes never danced with Enoch, her pulse never quickened. Surely a fine gentleman like Grady Boyle neither coughed nor snored nor slept in his underwear.

"After a fashion. Cotton." His obscure reply and averted eyes warned her to make no further inquiries about the plantation. Did he say he owns a plantation, or only that he had inherited one?

Grady Boyle had been highly pleased with himself when he brought his plan to fruition a little over two years ago. Lawyers in London had contacted him in Dublin to learn the whereabouts of a Howard Moorhead and his son Percy. They had sought them for some time before identifying Grady Boyle as a close relative.

The lawyers approached Grady Boyle who was happy to accept a generous advance from a dead man's estate to seek out his relatives who might be in Louisiana. The family name of *Boyle*, he was informed by the estate solicitor, had been supplanted by *Moorhead*. He expected to stay no more than six weeks after contacting his long-lost relations.

Grady's revised plan took form when he learned of Howard Moorhead's incapacity – and wealth – and of Percy Moorhead's ignorance of his own father's background. Oh, what a jumped-up Paddy Grady Boyle was to make this townhouse, Bolingbroke Hall plantation, and a 10% interest in a gaming establishment called

Toulouse Gardens all his own!

"Mind you, I planned on keeping the plantation in the family," he told Marnie. "That's what family are for, taking care of one another, we Irish. But I'm no lawyer. And when my Louisiana lawyer told me it would be best for everyone if I sold the plantation and invested the proceeds, well, I couldn't ignore his advice. Turned a right pretty penny, too, I did."

It was true that there were difficulties, but not quite the sort that he would tell Marnie. Grady had at first thought it was to his advantage that Howard Moorhead's widow, Lucinda, had turned over management of her property affairs to her feckless son-in-law by name of Bunch. After settling with Grady a division of the plantation's human properties, whose ownership had been in question, Bunch had promptly and stupidly gotten himself killed by one of his own slaves.

It was true that Grady initially relished the idea of owning a thriving cotton plantation, imagining himself on horseback inhaling the odor the dank, dark earth at sunrise as he led his darkies into his fields, *his* fields, *his* darkies. The real possibility of one of those enslaved hands striking him dead, as happened to Calvin Bunch, changed his mind. He then planned to sell all of the ninety or so slaves of Bolingbroke at auction and to find a buyer for the plantation. The killing of Bunch and the reports of an insurrection immediately depressed the market for slaves from the troubled plantation, as if haunted by the ghosts of the black slayer and the white victim. His lawyer had indeed persuaded Grady that he would fetch a better price if he sold the plantation and the slaves together, as a working enterprise, even in a depressed market.

Grady's "pretty penny" he received for the sale neither glittered nor rang. The money was no more than numbers on a piece of paper. On the strength of his court judgment of inheritance to property worth in excess of a quarter-to-a-half million dollars, Grady had borrowed more than $15,000 in New Orleans and pledged the property as security. It had taken nearly that much to pay off other loans incurred since he arrived in the United States, his attorney fees to Mr. Sumner Clausen, and to hire an overseer for Bolingbroke Hall pending a successful sale of the property.

The overseer had proved unsatisfactory. He stayed at a hotel in Bayou Sara rather than on-site, was a poor bookkeeper, and was unable to create fear in the slave labor of the plantation. Widow Moorhead had moved in with Widow Bunch, her daughter, on the adjacent plantation, Jericho Hill, which they jointly owned. With no occupant, Bolingbroke Hall soon deteriorated, its furniture, tableware, lamps and all gradually disappearing at the hands of persons unknown. Broken machinery was neither fixed nor replaced. Soil cultivation was slip-shod and cotton gathering lackadaisical. With such mismanagement, the cotton crop of 1859 was poor indeed, depressing further the potential price for the plantation's sale. Wide advertising in major newspapers throughout the South finally produced a buyer from Tennessee. Grady signed away the title in exchange for a note – a formal IOU with a notary's seal, its power to bind unequal to its bold flourishes and formidable legal phrases, with *parties of the first part* and *the second part* and a plenitude of *therefores* and *hereinafters*.

Marnie observed that Grady's glass was nearly empty. "Well, my handsome Irishman, you look like you could use another drink. Let me refresh that for you." She caressed his shoulder as she reached for his glass.

"Sure, Sweetie, get one for yourself while you're at it. One of the perks of owning an interest in a gaming casino – I can borrow from the bar. Only the best."

She stepped out of her shoes and walked barefoot to the cabinet where he had several bottles of whiskey. He admired her ample figure. Pausing before pouring the liquor, she took the clasp and ribbon from her hair to let it fall freely to her shoulders. She handed him a glass and stroked the side of his face with the back of her hand. "You've got a nice beard. I like a man with a trim beard.

And so black. Your grandfather, the ladies' man, I bet he had a fine black beard, too."

Grady grunted a reply. "Solid white when I knew him. But he was old then. Very old." Grady Boyle disapproved of old age. It was weakness. "When he took my grandmother to wife, he was thought old by her family. In London it was. He was twenty-two years older than her. An English girl of good family, the gentry. Old enough to be her father. And a divorced Irishman. As old as I am now."

His grandfather may have achieved a certain fame on the stage, but he had not prepared for his future. Grady Boyle was prepared. He was set. He had his townhouse, He had his florid IOU secured by a grand cotton plantation. Had he not proved he was more clever than his grandfather?

"Come now, you're not so old as all that," Marnie murmured. "And a man of leisure besides. With a grand inheritance."

Grady hardly heard her. After an evening of drinking at the casino and now here, he was again a sentimental Irishman, harkening to his family. Family produced sweet memories, even if he had just taken everything from the other grandson of Cormac Boyle. Marie or Marnie or Mrs. Dennett was a warm body, a woman, to listen to him, an occasion for him to reminisce and weave a poignant tale of family background that had at least a few threads of truth in the fabric. He could as well have been talking to a bartender or a terrier.

Remembering, in his drunkenness, that there was a music box tucked at the bottom of a cabinet, he clumsily swayed over to it. He opened the bottom door of the cabinet and took out the walnut box. He put it next to a whiskey bottle and wound the key. The tines of the comb began to play the sweetly sad song *The Last Rose of Summer*.

"Pretty," said Marnie.

"Belonged to me grandmother, given her by me grandfather.

They say he could sing like an angel. He was famous on the stage, a handsome devil, he was. Cormac Boyle, actor and singer. A cavalry man, an Irish regiment, when they discovered he could sing. When he went on stage in Dublin after he mustered out, they discovered he had a gift for acting too. Before long he was appearing regularly in Covent Garden – that's in London, you know – a singing soldier in the operas popular back then, them that was by William Shield, I think it was."

"Is that where he met your grandmother?" She traced her right index finger gently across his cheek and down his neck. He took her hand and led her to the sofa where they sat together.

"That it was. That it was. A handsome devil he was, and she an English lass from the English gentry, her father in the shipping business. Did I say that already? But her father didn't approve of the match, not to an Irishman, not to a man of the stage. He wouldn't give his only daughter so much as a fare-thee-well when she married and ran off with the actor. He wouldn't even let her little brother see her one last time. She was the dearest person in all the world to that little brother. The only real friend he ever had. He never saw her again."

"What was wrong with him, this brother? Problems, you said."

"One problem, really. His speech. He had a brilliant mind, but he couldn't get his words to come out right. His brain was just too fast for the words to keep up. In a word, he stuttered."

"That can't be so bad, can it?"

"Oh, indeed it was. Grandfather took me to see him one time. Grandmother Winifred was long dead and Cormac had married a third time, a well-to-do woman with children of her own and they gave little attention to his. Maybe he felt some guilt, I don't know, but for some reason when he made a return to London, where he had once been famous, he took me along. And so it happened that he took me to see my mother's brother who had inherited everything from their father. He had a big fine manor in a village, and I remember the attached cottage for servants. Yes it was, a fine old English home. And what I remember of the man is all the books he had in the house. And the paintings. Books and paintings everywhere. Grandfather said the books had all the words in them that the man could not speak. He was my great-uncle, and he carried a stout walking stick with him every day when he walked down the country road to the point where it reached the river. His servant said it was to shake at the village boys who would taunt him. You know how mean English boys can be."

The great-uncle was wealthy, but he was weak – unable or unwilling to speak like a normal human being. Grady Boyle resented him for leaving him nothing in his will. But Grady was bold enough and clever enough to seize the opportunity to turn it to his advantage.

As Grady paused his self-absorbed monologue, Marnie said quietly, "I have no sons, only a daughter." She was willing to continue to listen to the Irishman, though she hoped he would not turn maudlin. She would do nothing to discourage his attention.

Ignoring Marnie's mention of her child, Grady resumed his ramble. "There was a verse. Even the London lawyers handling the dead man's estate had heard it and filed it in his effects. I made a copy to show to Howard Moorhead to remind him of his uncle. But I never got the chance."

Grady picked his glass up from the table in front of him and walked unsteadily to the cabinet where he kept the whisky close at hand. He opened the drawer beneath the bottles. Now he read aloud from a piece of paper in his left hand while he poured more whiskey with his right. With a self-satisfied grin, he recited –

There was an old hermit of Halford
Whose tongue stumbled on every word
All day he stuttered and stammered
All night he muttered and yammered
That wealthy old hoarder of Halford.

Grady's sneer revealed his contempt for his great-uncle's

weakness.

Contrary to Grady's expectation, Marnie was not amused: "I don't think it's very nice to make fun of someone's infirmity." Her feistiness had gotten the better of her desire to retain Grady's affection, a man who would not hear her as she spoke of her family while he prattled on about his.

Grady scowled, "Maybe he deserved it. *He* wasn't nice, and *he* wasn't generous. He knew me. He could have done something for me in his will. He was my great-uncle after all. I should not be held responsible for the failings of my father. Maybe if he had been kinder, I would have been generous to Percy Moorhead."

"Who's that?" Marnie's interest was pricked by this new name. "I thought you said Howard Moorhead."

"Never you mind. A former resident. I hear he's in Virginia now." Percy's name was a slip of the tongue. Moorhead was on Grady's brain because of the whiskey. Percy Moorhead was a naïve fool. For a smart lawyer, he could do precious little to protect himself. Despite all that Grady had done to him, Percy had come to him at St. Francisville with that slave woman, Odessa, and told Grady he wanted to buy her and the boy who was in her care, her grandson. Grady Boyle didn't know them and wasn't sure he even owned her or the boy, but he named a price that was in considerable excess of their worth. The two men then appeared before a public notary in the courthouse where Grady Boyle had won his judgment against Percy, and Grady deeded over the woman and boy, with a deprecatory flourish of his pen.

God damn Percy Moorhead! He should have acted like a beaten dog. But he showed no emotion at all. Why he was attached to them was of no concern to Grady Boyle. But he did think it curious when someone told him that Odessa was the mother of the slave who killed Percy's brother-in-law and that the boy was the killer's son.

"Your plantation, Grady. Was it near New Orleans?" Marnie

remembered the Moorhead name. Maybe from an old news story.

"No. Upriver. Up from Baton Rouge." Grady didn't want to talk about the plantation. It was beginning to pain him. This war might make the IOU he held from the Tennessee buyer worthless.

Marnie recalled a slave uprising somewhere north of Baton Rouge. St. Francisville or Bayou Sara, she thought, and it was connected with the Moorhead name. She wouldn't mention the revolt, but she could raise it indirectly. "You must have had a passel of slaves."

"Oh, you know how it is. What's a plantation without negras? So, they went with the plantation when I sold it." Grady himself didn't know 'how it is' to own other human beings. He had never come face-to-face with an African before disembarking in New Orleans. When he had first come to Bolingbroke after the court awarded him possession, Calvin Bunch had showed him around and presented Pompey and Julius to him; they seemed to be in charge of the others. Grady had no idea how to speak to an enslaved person or to give them orders. And within a short time all three were dead, Calvin, Pompey and Julius.

Grady Boyle hadn't had time to think it through when Percy Moorhead reappeared offering to buy two slaves. Why would Percy buy them? What use could they be to Percy if he no longer had his plantation? When Grady had taken possession of the townhouse, a week after Percy had left for Richmond, he discovered that Percy had left behind a folder of papers in a drawer of the living room cabinet. Among them was the bill of sale by which Grady had sold him Odessa and the boy known as Little Jay, dated February 2, 1859. Underneath it was another bill of sale, dated one week later and notarized in New Orleans. Percy Moorhead had sold the two to a Maisie Dastugues of 219 Old Levee Street, New Orleans: a female, age 50 years known as Odessa Moorhead and a male age 7 years known as Julius Moorhead. The price listed was "For $10 and other valuable consideration." So, Percy must have decided to sell the two slaves right after having bought them. Perhaps they had some attachment to the buyer. Who could say? Who cared?

God damn it all! Percy Moorhead wouldn't get out of his head. He was still leaning on the cabinet; he poured a little more whiskey though his glass was half-full. Opening the drawer under the whiskey bottle, he looked at the papers again. Yes, it named the boy as Julius Moorhead. He wondered if maybe the seven-year-old boy was Percy Moorhead's bastard half-breed child. He chuckled at the thought. Percy Moorhead, so educated, so clever, but unable to penetrate Grady's ruse. If Grady couldn't have their great-uncle's legacy, he had something equally valuable, thanks to Percy's ignorance of the labyrinthine family history. But Grady knew it and rearranged it to suit his needs. Percy Moorhead, he was sure, would never have reason to travel to Dublin and would never discover the truth of his heritage. Nor was it likely the London lawyers would persist in their efforts to locate the Louisiana Moorheads, now that civil was raging. Grady was secure in his new holdings. And he had a court judgment adjudicating with finality his claim based on his version of the facts.

Marnie Dennett was still seated on the sofa. She thought she might have offended Grady Boyle. He seemed less distant, but sour now, perhaps angry – whether at her or at the stuttering man who hadn't named Grady in his will she could not tell. Angry or not, he came behind her and reached around to grasp her breast in his right hand. She made no resistance. He moved to sit next to her and put his arm around her shoulder as he kissed her. He was rather rough and demanding, not so much the gentleman after all. Grady was more accustomed to relations with prostitutes. Money, however, was more a concern than it had been, which is why he looked to satisfaction of his needs from a lonely, married woman. War produces many of them. Even a man with so little natural charm as Grady Boyle need do little to draw them to his bed. Unlike a whore, however, such a woman would think she had a claim on Grady Boyle. She would want attention and small affections. No woman had a claim on him.

Grady's financial worries would return with daybreak and sobriety. When the Tennessee buyer had paid Grady $5000 in cash a year ago, he insisted on taking title to Bolingbroke Hall and all of the slaves on the strength of his note for $200,000 of solemn indebtedness, payable over a ten-year period, with interest. This was less than half what Bolingbroke Hall had been worth under an appraisal only a year earlier. Grady's lawyer had approved the sale, and a mortgage on the property in favor of Grady Boyle secured the payment. However, the prior mortgage that he had signed to secure his own debt still bound the property. Thus, Grady's own rights were now junior to a more senior mortgage of his creditors.

The Tennessee buyer was two months delinquent on the annual payment. One ineffective white overseer was replaced by another with no greater success bringing in a cotton crop. Grady Boyle's wealth, which had seemed immense two years ago, was now a matter of paper pledges that could vanish entirely even if the land remained intact. None of the paper could be borrowed against, not in the midst of a war of uncertain scope and duration. For now, he had a warm woman and enough whiskey to numb him to his worries. She was an inexpensive distraction from the unraveling of his plans. He might even see her again.

Chapter 11

Charleston, after Fort Sumter

After three days at the Confederacy's capital, Lieutenant Percy Moorhead boarded a train in mid-morning at the Montgomery and West Point Railroad station. Now on his first assignment for the Confederacy, the special agent of President Davis and Attorney General Benjamin, he was eager to get on with his work.

Crossing into Georgia hours later, the train stopped at the West Point station where it connected to the Atlanta & West Point Railroad, near the bridge crossing the Chattahoochee River. Percy was seated quietly in the station when other passengers were accosted one-by-one by a rowdy group of five men. One man, mid-forties and shaggy-bearded, had announced:

"Listen up, y'all. We're the Georgia Vigilance Committee. Get your papers ready."

Their only badge of office was a small white cloth affixed to their hats. Almost as drunk as they were inquisitive, they were haunting the precincts of the post-office and the railway station, to detect Lincolnites and Abolitionists, demanding identification papers of people entering the sovereign state of Georgia.

In Montgomery, Percy had met educated leaders of the Confederacy, men like himself. Now he encountered the riff-raff of secession — the low-born, quasi-literates who would assume officious roles, encouraged by local militia officers who had been tasked by the governor and state legislature to organize for the defense of the state. When the rowdies demanded some proof he wasn't a Northern, Percy scowled and put his right index finger on the chest of the bearded fellow who had had first spoken. "And you, are you in charge of this sorry outfit?"

The startled vigilancer was suddenly without words. A small group of passengers gathered around. Looking at the others of the band, Percy at his most intimidating said, "I am Lieutenant Percy Moorhead, of the Confederate States Army. I am carrying papers of President Davis to Charleston. Impeding an officer of the CSA on a mission is punishable by the most severe penalties of the law. Do I make myself clear?"

No one could doubt the authority his voice carried, least wise the vigilancers. Percy knew their type well – whether found in Louisiana, Georgia, or any point in-between: rednecks, white trash, hillbillies, clodhoppers, hayseeds. Men who knew they were the bottom-rails of white society, proud of their ignorance because they had so little else in which to take pride. Secession made them bold, but when they met resistance they withered, returning to their condition of inferiority, only slightly higher that the Africans around them.

The vigilance men were to a man cowed. The irresolute pack grumbled at one another and retreated to a saloon. How, Percy wondered, would these Georgians stand against well-armed Union soldiers? Boarding the train again, Percy thought these rag-tag vigilancers were not representative of the soldiers who would defend the Confederacy. After training, they would be more disciplined and orderly, responsive to superior officers. Surely.

In the night, the train experienced a long delay in Atlanta. Percy dozed uncomfortably in his seat. By the time his journey resumed it was late morning. Through the open window of his rail car, he watched the movements of a company of volunteers – one hundred and twenty artillerymen, and three fieldpieces – on their way to the station in Atlanta, bound then for Virginia. The guns had no caissons. They were followed by a crowd, male and female of both races, cheering loudly, a band playing "Dixie." The Georgia soldiers were dressed in coarse gray tunics with yellow facings, and French caps. Their smooth-bore muskets were inaccurate even at close range and impotent at longer distance. Their knapsacks were unfit for marching – simple water-proof bags slung from a shoulder. Their footwear was not standard issue, some wearing boots, others shoes. Children were sent out with flags and tin swords to impede the roads before the marching throng.

A mile farther up the line, just at the outskirts of the city, a plume of gray-black smoke sought the sky over tall hickory and elm trees. As the slow-moving train drew closer, through the trees Percy could see a warehouse and an open field. The smoke came from a huge fire. Cotton bales! A half dozen wagons were bringing more bales to feed the fire. Who could be burning thousands of dollars worth of cotton? The last time he had seen such a senseless loss of cotton was the fire at the New Orleans wharves six years earlier, when his mother's cotton had been lost because of Calvin Bunch's failure to insure the bales in storage. Burning of cotton that was ready for export was the sort of thing Lincoln and Seward would want carried out by Union troops. Yet, here the Georgians were doing it to themselves.

Percy shook his head at the senseless destruction of the South's principal commodity of foreign trade. These fools thought they were showing England their power to bring John Bull to his knees if the Queen wouldn't recognize the South's independence. Percy began to appreciate the enormity of the challenges to himself and to the new government.

In Charleston, Percy took a room at the Mills House, on the corner of Meeting and Queen Streets. Built since Percy had last passed through the city, the 180-room hotel was five stories high.

An iron balcony across the façade reminded him of New Orleans, along with the ornate terra-cotta cornices above the windows and an arcaded entry. From an upper floor room, Percy had a wide view of the city and a portion of the harbor. It was three blocks from the wharves and within a short walk to Central Wharf, near the Custom House, where George Trenholm had one of his several offices.

As he did in any visit to a city, when he had the time, Percy strolled the streets to get a sense of place. He was always curious, eager to learn of new surroundings and customs. The houses he passed were detached, surrounded by small gardens, well provided with verandas to protect the windows from the sun's glare, and were sheltered with creepers and shrubs and flowering plants as April merged into May. Humming-birds and fly-catchers flitted near him as he walked. In some places the streets and roadways were covered with planking, and the wood was pleasant to walk upon. A rich melody of mocking birds filled a grove of trees at the edge of town.

That evening, as the sun was setting and birds returned to their nests, in the hotel reading room and in the dining room every man was reading his paper with close attention or discussing the news with his neighbors. Many were talking about the Northern states' responses to Lincoln's proclamation calling out 75,000 men. Most treated the news with contempt or unsparing ridicule. More than once he had heard the boast that Johnny Reb could outfight any three of the Yankees. Or five. Or ten. The effete Northerners would be whupped without mercy if they dared to attempt an invasion of the South's homeland.

༺ ⁃ ༻

The first thing one noted of George Trenholm was his wavy, well-groomed hair. On the first and fifteenth of each month, Sundays excepted, it was trimmed and groomed by a free man of color named Inglis who worked as a barber in the Mills House hotel. From generous tips of Mr. Trenholm, and others of his social standing who followed Trenholm's lead, Inglis had earned enough that he purchased his own freedom and that of his wife, Elizabeth.

Tall and handsome, Trenholm was in his early-fifties, the second or third wealthiest man of Charleston. He had the confidence of the senior man in a banking, shipping and mercantile house with offices at each vertex of a cotton triangle, Charleston, New York and Liverpool. If all fifty ships of the fleet he controlled sailed together, they would overwhelm the docks and resources of any port they visited. He bore himself with the manners of a gracious prince, warmly welcoming visitors such as Percy Moorhead even when engaged in sensitive matters of utmost importance to the infant Confederate States.

"So, you are to be the right hand of Judah in England," Trenholm greeted Percy with a firm grip and a smile. "His telegram said we should expect you sometime today. Have you had a chance to visit Charleston? You know this is where Judah spent his youth."

Percy was charmed by Trenholm's warm welcome. "I had a chance to walk around late yesterday. Very lovely."

"Good. Good. You'll be busy for the next couple of days before your ship leaves for Nassau."

"Judah wasn't very specific on my activities," Percy was certain that Trenholm would provide ample guidance on financial arrangements between Charleston and Liverpool. He understood he would have to rely on his own experience and instincts for his larger role.

Gesturing Percy to a sofa near his desk, Trenholm spoke, with only a slight Carolina drawl, "We're adapting to a new setting for our business. We've closed our New York office. The New York investors and insurers are now cut off from future cotton transactions. We need you to work out new arrangements with the company managers here in Charleston and then coordinate those with Liverpool and the investors and banks in Liverpool and London. New risks and contingencies from the point of ginning to the wharves of Liverpool must be provided for. Do you follow me?"

Trenholm was politely asking whether Percy Moorhead was up to the assignment he was handed. Percy was familiar with the sort of inquiry Trenholm was making – he was a client taking the measure of the attorney who was proposing to represent him, as had many New Orleans businessmen who had him for his services. He smoothly replied, "I'm sure that together we can establish new working relationships. My father was one of the earliest cotton factors in New Orleans. He pioneered the business methods used when the American South was just beginning to dominate the world in cotton production. I grew up on a flourishing plantation. When I was practicing law in New Orleans, I worked on cotton and other foreign transactions. I'm conversant in business practices in New York and Liverpool."

Trenholm was encouraged. "Excellent. My sons, too, are following me in this business. Judah assured me that you were the man for the task."

What Judah had told Percy about Trenholm's ambitions was that secession meant Charleston could become the New York of a new country. His firm and family would rival the merchant and industrial houses of New York, Boston and Philadelphia. The new South would rapidly expand her railroads, build new factories and increase her foreign trade – all led and financed by Fraser, Trenholm and other Southerners of vision and belief in their future greatness. As usual, Percy saw that Judah's assessment of Trenholm was astute.

"And our procurement agents? The Attorney General said the Confederacy has named several already."

"Right." Trenholm saw that Lieutenant Moorhead was a man to get right to the heart of a project. "Two have preceded you. Caleb Huse and James Bulloch. You'll be coordinating contracts and financial instruments for them. Another man, an officer named Anderson, is going over for our army shortly. Secretary Memminger and Judah Benjamin understand that they will turn money and financial instruments over to us, and we will effect transfers of funds to Liverpool and London for the Confederacy. Y'all will draw upon our resources to purchase guns, artillery, uniforms, supplies and other materiel. Bulloch will be looking at contracts for building ships for us. We'll continue our own commercial transactions. Without them, we would be unable to advance funds across the Atlantic for the Confederacy. A hundred thousand Confederate soldiers will depend on the four of you and this firm to provide them arms and powder and supplies to defend our homeland and keep them alive."

Accepting a cup of strong, hot coffee brought by a company clerk, Percy asked, "Liverpool will be crucial to all our efforts. Who is your man in Liverpool?"

Pointing to a portrait (not entirely flattering to the subject) on his wall, Trenholm identified the man. "That's Charles Prioleau, our office manager in Liverpool. Has been for seven years, since I became head of the Fraser company. There's no older South Carolina family than the Prioleaus. They go back to the 17th Century. Colonel Sam Prioleau was the founder. Charles's father was a lawyer, a judge and mayor of Charleston. There's no one we can trust more than Charles."

Trenholm's slightly impatient manner indicated that if Percy knew anything about South Carolina, he'd already know who the Prioleaus were. Until he saw the written name, Percy did not realize that "Pru-li," as Trenholm pronounced it, was "Prioleau."

Ready to return to other meetings, Trenholm asked Percy, "Any questions before I direct you on your rounds?"

"Just one. Outside Atlanta, I saw bales of cotton burning, maybe two-three hundred bales. Hundred-fifty-thousand pounds of cotton. Can you explain that?" Percy knew the answer but wanted to see if Trenholm shared his judgment that it was folly.

"Captain Ludd, of course," Trenholm chuckled.

"Captain Ludd? These folks have a leader?"

"Captain Ludd was an Englishman, supposedly a real person, maybe just folklore, like Robin Hood. He destroyed the textile machinery that would take away work from home-spinning. Hence the name Luddites for ignorant people. Probably a Georgia vigilance committee composed of our own Luddites. We have citizen committees here. They believe the answer to a Northern blockade is a cotton embargo. There's been a movement for months now to get the Confederate states to prohibit the sales of cotton overseas until Britain and France break the blockade and recognize our independence."

Trenholm picked up a newspaper from his desk and handed it to Percy, telling him, "The paper here says the cards are all in our hands, and we can play them out to the bankruptcy of every textile mill in England and France. The vigilante committees have taken the embargo into their own hands and are destroying the cotton that is still in warehouses. No compensation to their owners."

Percy wasn't surprised. "I encountered a vigilance committee when my train entered Georgia. Mischief makers."

"Fortunately, this year's crop is still in the ground. But there are mobs who are going from planter to planter demanding that they not plant or pick this year until Britain and France feel the pain for not recognizing us." Trenholm's disdain for the vigilancers was not disguised.

"I doubt that many planters would think this is sound policy," nodded Percy in agreement. "No cotton, no income. No export, no revenue to the states of the Confederacy. Idle slaves may get restless when whirl is king."

Trenholm's warm handshake as he was departing showed that he was glad that Percy shared his views. Percy Moorhead was the right man to make arrangements in Liverpool – and to influence Judah Benjamin. He told Percy, "The stupidity should be obvious. A better solution would be for the Confederate government to buy up cotton and warehouse it for sale as needed to finance the war effort. We'll do our part to keep commerce alive and well with our friends overseas."

Trenholm's casual suggestion stuck in Percy's head. "A better solution . . . ." He would reflect on it for the better part of the next eighteen months. Without cotton commerce, the Confederacy could not survive.

◆ - ◆

Everywhere Percy went through the streets of Charleston he encountered drumming and marching as he made his visits to acquire documents, affidavits of authenticity, a notary seal, and letters of introduction. Percy was surprised at the number of Irishmen who were among Charleston's populace. Several Roman Catholic churches were elegant evidence of the Hibernian presence. Familiar with the Irish in New Orleans, he had not expected a substantial Irish presence in South Carolina.

At the Mills House that evening, Percy dined with a group that included an English journalist. Echoing what Trenholm had told him hours earlier, one of the South Carolinians, truculent and dismissive of the talk of an extended conflict, lectured the journalist: "Why, sir, we have only to shut off your supply of cotton for a few weeks, and we can create a revolution in Great Britain. There are four millions of your people depending on us for their bread, not to speak of the many millions of dollars. No, sir, we know that England must recognize us. Tell your readers that."

"Well, sir," replied the foreign correspondent, with a wink in Percy's direction, "shall I tell my readers that the North will annex Canada if the Confederacy is recognized? Mr. Seward is on record favoring the plucking of that ripest fruit of Manifest Destiny. Will Johnny Reb march northward to Canada to help Britain maintain her Empire?"

"That will never happen," sputtered the belligerent Charlestonian. "The North would never fight a war on two fronts." The South Carolina gent leaned over and spit into the cuspidor next to the dining table, his thick lips now moist.

"No?" the journalist continued calmly, a twinkle in his eye. "If Britain and the Union go to war, how would your cotton get to England? Have you a Confederate navy? The Northern fleet blockading your coast would be justified in turning their guns on British merchant ships. Then, we would have no cotton as well as losing Canada."

Aside, after the South Carolinian had huffed away, his bluster spent, the journalist told Percy, "Slavery has aggravated the tendency of Southerners to look at all the world through parapets of cotton bales and rice bags. A merchant I visited near the wharves today said much the same as this belligerent. Look out there, he said, pointing to the wharf, on which were piled some cotton bales, there's the key will open all our ports, and put us into John Bull's strong box as well."

Percy invited the correspondent for brandy and cigars in the hotel salon. He enjoyed the company of the convivial and blunt Irishman, the sort of reporter to gather information in odd corners, even out of youngsters. He said his name was Russell. He was no stranger to combat, having covered the war in the Crimea and then India.

"Sir," he said to Percy, drawing on his cigar, "they are all bombast at the first. Boisterous. Brave and brazen. Until all the spit turns to shite. The most bellicose are also the most cowardly. Aye, sir, then there's the reckoning. The bill must be paid, and the reaper collects what is due in the lives of sons and nephews and sweethearts. And still will they spit and sputter at the wrongs done them."

"Hmmmmm," was all Percy would reply, neither agreeing nor disagreeing. Only an Irishman would have such insight. Percy would not risk a remark that would find its way into an English paper or the journalist's next book.

Chapter 12

General Beauregard

On his way the next morning to the Fraser, Trenholm office, Percy encountered G. T. Beauregard, now wearing the uniform and insignia of a Confederate general. Both were headed towards the harbor.

"Mind if I walk with you again, General?" Percy asked familiarly.

Beauregard turned to see who addressed him. "Moorhead? New Orleans."

Crisply, the newly appointed officer answered, "Lieutenant Moorhead, CSA. On assignment from staff in Montgomery."

"No uniform? What brings you to Charleston?" Beauregard's bearing reflected his pride in his personal strength, which for his slight frame was extraordinary. Beauregard insisted that Southern men had more physical strength, owing to their mode of life and their education, than Northerners.

"There's been no time for me to get a uniform yet. The day after you fired on Sumter, I was shuffled off to Montgomery. President Davis gave me an appointment just a few days ago. The attorney general is sending me abroad to assist with procurement contracts."

General P.G.T. Beauregard

Beauregard paused. His memory was acute. "So, you're still with Judah Benjamin. Maybe your trip overseas will be for naught. If Winnfield Scott is the best they can do for a general, the war won't last long. You remember how he dithered and dallied in Puebla. We had that conversation while I was working on the Custom House in New Orleans, if I recall. When the Union sees we mean business, they'll back down. Still, I'm surprised by the spirit displayed by the Yankees. A good deal of it is got up and belongs to that washy sort of enthusiasm that is promoted by their lecturing and spouting."

Beauregard was lively and in good spirits. He enjoyed the adulation of the Charlestonians. His name was on the lips of everyone in the city. The man who fired on Sumter to ignite the war was a celebrity. Darkly handsome, charming with his south Louisiana accent, he was a favored guest of the ladies of Charleston who hosted soirees and dinners as their contribution to morale among the leaders responsible for the city's defense. He was again in his element, a lover of war.

Such men as Beauregard are needed, thought Percy, but must they take pride in death and destruction? The Beauregards and Braxton Braggs of the world are never so alive as they are in battle.

Percy had volunteered to fight in Mexico, but his experiences left him with no appetite for war. Armed conflict he saw as a failure of tribal interaction, not as a desirable end in itself. More to his liking was the conflict of wits in a courtroom or the challenging repartee with resistant students.

Not wishing to come across as disagreeing with Beauregard's optimism, Percy said, "I hope you're right. If it goes on for a year, I'm afraid they have the advantage in men and materiel."

"You'd be right if that was all that it took to fight a war," Beauregard responded to Percy as he would have to a West Point cadet, tone-deaf to his patronizing manner. "What counts for victory is leadership. We have the superior generals. It will be a complete rout if they try to invade us. After that, they'll slink back across the Potomac and leave us alone."

Coming to a corner at the wharf, Beauregard said, "This is where I'll leave you. Tomorrow I'm going to Montgomery and we'll go over every possibility. We have to be sure Jeff Davis picks the right generals to fight this war." Beauregard's confidence indicated that he expected Davis to let the Confederate generals conduct the war. Percy surmised that Beauregard's understanding of Davis was superficial, based on little interaction with Davis as soldier, Secretary of War, or Senator.

Percy's meeting with the Fraser, Trenholm people finished in early afternoon. He took a long route back to his hotel. Near the market stalls where meat was sold, turkey-buzzards could be seen in combat with dogs for the spoiled flesh discarded when it was ripe beyond selling. The ugly birds were contending with wing and beak against the scarred, grizzled dogs who disputed the cast-off meat and bones. Others of the vulture wake were on-lookers. Percy found it curious to watch the expression of the buzzards' eyes as they peered down, necks out-stretched, from the ledge of the market roof on the stalls as they scrutinized the operations of the butchers below. They did not prevent a disagreeable odor in the vicinity of the markets, nor were they deadly to an active breed of rats. Ancient Greeks may have seen the red-faced harpies as harbingers. Were they? Would the same fowl soon feast on flesh of Southern soldiers?

Chapter 13

A Dancing Bear

Percy again dined with Russell, the Anglo-Irish journalist. In the ballroom next to the dining room they could see a large gathering of uniforms and business suits and ladies in fine attire. In the center of all basked General Beauregard.

"I served with him in Mexico," Percy commented. "And ran into him today. He is supremely confident of victory."

"Is that so?" smiled the correspondent, showing a journalist's skepticism. "Reassuring to you, maybe. Charming, surely, to his fawning throng. But in my interview with him only days ago he expressed concerns. The general is apprehensive of an attack by the Northern fanatics before the South is prepared. And he considers they will carry out coercive measures most rigorously. Most rigorously, if they prove ruthless. He's apprehensive that they will cut the levees up and down the Mississippi, for miles above New Orleans. The Federals may resort to their destruction in order to drown the plantations and ruin the planters. He avers that the spirit of John Brown lives in Northern fanatics who see bloodletting as necessary for remission of Southern sin. The most bitter will take no rest until your plantation system is utterly destroyed. Better that the South be pure than prosperous. "

Percy did not disagree. "If anyone should know about flooding, it would be Beauregard. Those levees were under his supervision for near a decade. I hope that Lincoln and Seward would be more civilized than to wage war on civilians. I grew up on that river. It shouldn't be turned into a instrument of war. The muddy Mississippi shouldn't run red as revenge for slavery."

Sniffing a cigar he pulled from his jacket, Russell inquired, "And you sir. What is your place in the grand scheme of things? You have the manner of an educated man, and I infer you have some association with the Confederacy, though I dare say not sharing entirely in the excesses of fervor of its radical proponents."

With pursed lips, Percy replied, "I confess that I have served as a professional skeptic, that is to say, as an attorney."

"Interesting. And are you for the prosecution or for the defense? And why Charleston?"

Percy laughed and said, "I will give counsel. Soon I am off to England to assure that we comply with English law. That's something you can put in your reports."

"Your assignment will take you to London. I will give you the same advice that I received from an old editor in Dublin. Taking me by the arm, he said, 'Beware the dancing bear.' I readily agreed with the old boy that I would take all cautions against dancing bears."

The reporter was eager to tell a story. Grinning slyly, Percy encouraged him, "I can see there's a tale to be told."

Relishing the opportunity, the journalist paused to re-light his cigar and began.

"There was a time, he told me, my wizened editor that is, when he was a young man beginning as a correspondent, that dancing bears were a common sight in the streets of London. They were discreet, well-tutored, well-mannered bears, and their leaders were of a gentlemanly kind. They made their bears dance to pleasant and pastoral music, to the pipe and tabor."

"Tabor?" said Percy.

"Ah, an instrument seldom heard in America. You favor the screech of a fiddle, the plunk of a banjo or the twang of a jew's-harp.

A tabor is a small sheep-skin drum thumped with a hand or stick. Or by a monkey's paw. You see, the dancing bear was accompanied by a monkey or two and a flute player. The monkey would be garbed in a colorful vest, his little head topped by a vivid cap. The man, usually Italian or Savoyard and costumed accordingly – like your zouaves on both sides in this war – would lead his bear by a rope or chain attached to a leather muzzle strapped around the bear's head. The hairy brute would frisk and gambol in the most grotesque manner, the keeper occasionally touching him in his midriff or fleshy parts with a little goad. At times the monkey would dance a pas-seul on the shoulders of the bear; at other times he would, with many antics and grimaces, hunt the bear's head for nits or lice, to the delight of an audience seeing a human aspect. Hopping to the ground, the monkey would toddle among the spectators presenting a tin cup, bowing from time to time when half-pennies or pennies rattled into the cup. Terrible was the dancing bear; terrible was he and funny, and the more terrible from being so droll with an attendant monkey and musical accompaniment.

"But one fateful day, continued my ancient editor, it happened that one of the dancing bears suddenly was no longer tethered to his master and broke loose. He roared and slashed his fearsome paws and gnashed his jagged teeth at everyone within reach. Within minutes, three were dead, the leader, a woman and a child – four if you count the monkey – and a dozen more injured. The bear calmly loped away. At a nearby construction site, he was killed by workers wielding shovels and picks like clubs and axes. The little vest and cap were found nearby, just off the lane, but no monkey. The pipes and tabor were heard no more. There was no more bear dancing in London after that dismal day."

"Well, that is a sad story," said Percy with a quizzical expression. "But if there are no dancing bears in London, why the warning?"

"Patience, my dear auditor. My editor told me he was assigned to write the story. He spent two days working on it He interviewed dozens. What had happened? Some said it was the bear himself, that he was tired of being led by a chain in the day and caged at night. He used his great strength to break the muzzle and to strike out at the leader and everyone he could reach. Those who rejected this explanation said the bear was too well treated to rebel: it was much better off in the city than in the forest; it was well fed and housed from the elements. There must have been another cause."

"Another cause?" asked Percy.

Was that a smile at the edges of the journalist's mouth? He continued, "But of course. Events have causes, do they not? Some claimed it was the monkey. She was jealous of the attention that the bear got while it was she who gathered the money from the awed onlookers. She was embarrassed to pick lice; it was beneath her station. So she unbuckled the bear and set him loose on the crowd before disappearing into parts unknown."

"Do monkeys get jealous?"

The journalist shrugged insouciantly. "I haven't interviewed many monkeys, but I don't see they shouldn't be susceptible to envy, jealousy, malice or pride. Nasty little creatures in my experience. A simpler explanation laid the blame on the bear keeper. He was lax. He was complacent. The bear had obeyed him for so long, it was unthinkable that the bruin would turn against his master. He thought it was his power that kept the beast in check. He neglected the care of the leather of the mask, so it had rotted, and it broke when the keeper gave it a jerk. Unprepared for freedom, the bear lashed out in desperation."

"What was the truth?"

"That, my friend, is a question of Biblical proportions. As a mere reporter, I can't answer it," he said. "The editor couldn't either."

"Then what's the point of the story?"

"You'll have to come to that yourself. I take it that the editor was telling me that every story I would investigate might be a dancing bear story, with an angry bear, a jealous monkey or an incompetent keeper. Or all three were to blame. The story was mine to write."

"I'm not sure how the tale relates to my voyage to England."

"It's an amusing parable, I suppose. And you are a discerning fellow, Mr. Moorhead. If it doesn't help you navigate through London, I'm sure you'll find it useful in other ways. Perhaps this war you find yourself in is a dancing bear story. With that thought, I'll leave you for the evening. It's been a pleasure."

Chapter 14

New Passage

The next day, Percy boarded a steamship belonging to Fraser, Trenholm bound for the Bahamas. It left Charleston harbor mid-morning and encountered no Union ships. Many of the passengers were foreigners leaving to escape a war that was still in its earliest stage. A few were residents of Northern states who now had no reason to remain in what had become a foreign country. The interim destination was Nassau, New Providence Island, where they would transfer to ships under the flag of Great Britain.

Unlike other voyages Percy had taken, the passengers now did not mingle, distrusting one another's political sensibilities. Percy knew that two of the men aboard were scouts for the South. One was an employee of Fraser, Trenholm who had made Percy familiar with financial instruments to be used in England. Another was a Confederate officer whom General Beauregard had assigned to work with George Trenholm's firm for logistical support. Their assignment was to explore the potential of Nassau as a Confederate depot. If favorable, they would secure, by rental or purchase, office and warehouse space. They would investigate to see if Nassau had the capacity to serve as a coaling station for Confederate ships and as a port of opportunity for transshipment of goods and military supplies. Percy avoided them and they him. Among the passengers might be someone who would report to Union authorities when disembarking later in New York.

Percy's six-hundred-mile voyage was over calm waters and took less than three days. After two nights in a poor hotel in Nassau, he took passage on a British steamship to New York City, arriving in the city on a Thursday afternoon. On disembarking, each passenger was interviewed by Federal officials. Percy passed his first test traveling under a false identity. Although the first state's secession was now six months old, the new administration of Abraham Lincoln was barely six weeks old. Percy relied on the fact that the Union had had little time to establish an internal intelligence network to be vigilant about the comings and goings of Confederate agents. In time that void would be filled, and all passengers bound to and from abroad would be much more closely examined.

When he arrived at the desk of the Astor House, the clerk handed Percy a message in an envelope addressed to P. Moorhead of Vera Cruz, Mexico. It instructed him to take breakfast in the hotel at 7:00 a.m. the morning after his arrival.

The next day, while seated at the table at the appointed time, his waiter handed him another envelope, which a gentleman had just asked him to deliver. Percy found it contained a reservation for a first-class stateroom on the Inman Steamship Company's *City of Manchester* leaving at noon the next day, Saturday, from Pier 44 North River.

After walking around the city for a couple of hours, Percy spent the remainder of the day in his hotel room expecting to receive further information and instructions from Rufus Jordan, or whatever name the "Count" might now be using. He grew apprehensive when he had heard nothing from his contact by 9:00 the next morning. He took his one suitcase and a document case to a hansom that carried him to the pier, where he boarded the iron-hulled, single screw steamship without incident. He had no papers on him that would identify him as coming from the breakaway Confederacy. The documents he had gathered in Charleston from the Fraser, Trenholm people were concealed within folders that appeared to relate to the Anglo-Mexican Tehuantepec Company.

The cabin of his ship was not as well-furnished as he had experienced on the *Baltic* nearly a decade earlier, but it was comfortable enough. When he opened the cabinet door to stow his bags, he found another small suitcase already nestled there, under a blanket. A wax seal showed that it had not been opened since it had been smuggled aboard. Cutting through the seal with his pocket knife, Percy found that it contained the papers that identified him as a lieutenant in the army of the CSA, further instructions from Judah Benjamin, and a number of financial instruments from the now shuttered New York office of Fraser, Trenholm that he was to use to establish three million dollars in credits for the Confederacy upon arrival in Liverpool. Rufus Jordan had been thorough, whatever his cover might be.

After three blasts from its horn, the steamship pulled away from the pier and headed out to sea. Only as he relaxed did Percy become aware how apprehensive he had been since arriving in New York. He was unaccustomed to living by deception. For some, such as "Luigi Ottavio," *alias* Rufus Jordan, it seemed to come naturally, even as an actor assumes a role in a performance. Perhaps it would grow upon him. He locked the cabinet in his stateroom and made his way to the bar in the ship's salon, where he ordered himself a strong drink.

༺ ⁘ ༻

For the rest of the voyage, Percy avoided other passengers, keeping to himself in his room during the day and walking the deck at night if it were not raining. Any of the men or women aboard could be Union agents sent abroad to aid their cause – just as he was doing for the Confederacy. He had reading material with him, always at least three books – history, poetry, Shakespeare. Robert Browning was his favorite for this voyage; he would commit three of the poetic monologues to memory. For Shakespeare, he balanced *The Tempest* against *Othello*, always *Othello*.

Chapter 15

10 Rumford Place

Nine years had passed since Percy was last in Liverpool. The city appeared bigger, busier and more prosperous, with a population now approaching a half-million. For four miles, the quays and docks snaked – a long line of masonry flanking the Liverpool side of the Mersey River. Dock after dock, a chain of immense fortresses: Prince's, George's, Salt-House, Clarence, Brunswick, Trafalgar, King's, Queen's, and more, all filled with carpenters, metalsmiths, sawyers, producing a cacophony of noise – hammers, saws, bellows. He passed wharves that were crowded with bales, crates, boxes, and cases, tumbled about by thousands of laborers moving to and from blocks upon blocks of warehouses. He dodged hand-pulled carts and horse-drawn wagons as they jockeyed for position. Teamsters yelled at their animals and at each other. Dock-masters were shouting; sailors of all nations were singing out at their ropes. The sounds receded as Percy walked past the Custom House up to Hanover Street and connected to Ranelagh. It was less than a two-mile hike to his hotel. It felt good to be on solid ground after two weeks aboard ships. He would soon become more familiar with the Custom House.

As he had in 1852, Percy took a suite at the Adelphi Hotel, signing himself now as P. Moorhead of Vera Cruz, Mexico, agent of the Anglo-Mexican Tehuantepec Railroad Company. He affected the clothing and cool manner of a successful man of international commerce. Viewing himself in the lobby mirror, just such a man smiled back at him. He would walk among other Liverpool business agents, unnoticed for his true purposes as an officer of the Confederate States of America.

Rising early, Percy enjoyed a long walk to the offices of Fraser, Trenholm & Co., admiring St. Peter's Church and St. George's Church, arriving shortly at 10 Rumford Place. In response to the clerk's question at the reception desk, he said no, he did not have an appointment with Mr. Prioleau ("Pru-li"). But he had a letter of introduction from Mr. George Trenholm of Charleston. The clerk's head snapped up; Percy had his full attention and complete deference.

A few minutes later, an ebullient man with a broad smile stepped smartly out. He spoke with the Southern accent distinct to South Carolinians, a quasi-dialect afflicted by a deficiency in the consonant "r," elbowed out by random vowels or consonants – such that "Charleston" became *Chaahs-tun* and "here" was barely discernable to the ear in "*hee-yah.*" More than a few in "Livahpool" found Mr. Prioleau most "chaahmin," including Miss Mary Elizabeth Wright, the socialite whom he had taken as his bride in one of the city's biggest weddings only a year before.

Beaming, the portly Prioleau said, "Lieutenant Mo'head. You must be the professah Judah Benjamin was gonna' recruit. I see that he was successful."

"Mr. Benjamin is very persuasive," Percy replied. Percy was about four inches taller than the nattily dressed, Charlestonian/Liverpudlian, but the latter outweighed Percy by a good thirty pounds – or two stone as the locals would have it. For many Englishmen, girth was a correlative of prosperity.

"Come, suh. Let's go to my office."

Percy followed the managing partner of Fraser, Trenholm –

Liverpool, into a large office, expansively furnished. At his host's direction, Percy sat himself casually on a dark brown leather couch, quilted back, embellished with brass nailhead trim. Prioleau sat opposite, in a matching leather chair.

Percy began, "But how could word of my assignment get here so quickly?"

Prioleau was about the same age as Percy but already his hair was thinning at his forehead and shaggy about the ears, with full whiskers and protruding goatee. His appearance would have struck an observer as eccentric were his manner not so confident and reassuring. The Confederacy needed just such an imperturbable man at the heart of its European finances.

"You were preceded by Captain Huse. He arrived on the tenth by way of Maine. He was privy to the plans to draw on yo' services."

"Is he here?" As Huse had been briefed on Percy, Judah had briefed Percy on Huse.

"The captain is in London. He'll be back in a day or two. It's only a half-day train ride now."

"And Major Bulloch?" asked Percy as he looked around Prioleau's comfortable office. A coat of arms with the family name was hung on a wall next to a Belgian tapestry. An ink-well and gavel, both belonging to Prioleau's father, decorated his desk. A South Carolina flag hung limply on a pole in a sand-filled umbrella stand.

"Huse mentioned the major. But he must have taken a slowah rout. What's your hotel? We can provide y'all both an office here. And anything else you may need."

"Perhaps. The Adelphi. I am instructed to get in touch with Bev Tucker. Can you direct me?"

Prioleau looked at his pocket watch and grinned. "It's nearly 9:00 now. He should be in by 10:30. His office is two dohs down from yours."

A few minutes before 11:00, Bev Tucker arrived. He smiled broadly when he walked into Percy's new office. Percy had not seen him since Phil's funeral. He looked older than Percy remembered and appeared weary. His weight was at least two-fifty now and his round cheeks had become jowls. Percy was glad to see an old friend in this new place, his wife's cousin who had been important in their wedding. Bev's skills were noted more for political astuteness than his business efficiency. The gregarious Virginian could be cast as Falstaff or Don Quixote, reflected Percy. Would he prove more competent than they? At least, he could be an amusing companion and would have connections in the city that would prove advantageous to Percy's assignments.

"Huse said you were coming. Wonderful!" Bev Tucker sat in a well-padded wooden chair opposite Percy. He first wanted news of his family and of Virginia and how secession was brought about. Percy described the excitement of Virginia's secession and the feverish activity he had observed in Montgomery, Atlanta and Charleston and along the railroads connecting them.

"What I would have given to be there! It must have been thrilling." Percy saw that Bev was envious and homesick. The Tuckers had lived well while he served as American consul in Liverpool. Now he was adrift, the family spread over two continents, their future uncertain because of secession.

"For now, the Confederacy needs you here," replied Percy, appealing to his friend's patriotism and seeking to console him. "I have a letter from President Davis and the Attorney General requesting your help before you are to return home."

Bev read the two documents slowly, nodding and looking up to Percy after each sentence. "I'm honored," he said. He continued, "We need to introduce you to the key people you need to know. The first of these is Price Edwards. Did Charles tell you about him?"

Percy shook his head. "No. Who's Edwards?"

Bev enjoyed showing that he was well-connected. "Her

Majesty's Collector of Customs for Liverpool. He's an ambitious man with refined tastes. He is sympathetic to our cause. And you must get to know Liverpool. The neighborhoods, the bankers and brokers and agents. And the pubs. We will need to bring shipyard workers into our confidence. The pubs will give us intelligence as we need."

Encouraging Bev to continue, Percy asked, "Are there are English or Americans working in the American consulate that you trust?" The writer Nathaniel Hawthorne, no friend to slavery, had preceded Bev Tucker as American consul in Liverpool.

Frowning, the ex-diplomat said, "Nobody we can count on. Henry Wilding is vice-consul, acting consul until Lincoln replaces him. He is British of the sort who is loyal to his employer. And to England. He had been a secretary during Hawthorne's consulship. I saw Wilding at the docks to greet Charles Adams, when the new ambassador arrived aboard the *Niagara*. Enthusiastic."

Percy raised a ticklish question. "Not to put too fine a point on it, how shall we do this? I always avoided bribes in New Orleans. The people who may help us will run significant risks if they are exposed. Not like if they were spies in our own country. But embarrassment. Perhaps loss of job."

"They should be compensated," responded Tucker, without hesitation. In business and politics he had long been accustomed to the necessity of incentives to obtain results. He was not offended at Percy's scrupulosity, though he regarded it as unrealistic and hence unproductive. "Call it advance payments on expenses. With Customs Officer Price Edwards, you need a different tack. A payment would insult him."

"Gifts?" suggested Percy. His sense of integrity deemed gifts less offensive than cash transactions. Gifts bespoke friendship, not exchange.

"Yes. Be alert for what might please him. Something personal, something that reinforces his sense of himself. You're good at that sort of thing, as I recall."

Percy took the comment as a compliment. He turned the conversation, "You mentioned Huse. I'm to be working with him. Tell me what to expect."

Seizing the opportunity to share his assessment of a new associate, Bev expounded, "Good man. Competent. Northern by birth but now a Southerner. He's maybe five years younger than you. West Pointer, bright, high in his class. After a year in artillery, he was called back to the academy to serve as a professor of chemistry or some such. His Southern ties stem from his taking a leave from the army to set up a program for the university in Alabama. And his wife loves Alabama."

The background struck Percy as odd when there were so many combat veterans who were Confederate officers. "A college teacher? How does that qualify him to be the chief purchasing agent of arms to the Confederacy? I would have thought we could have drawn a more experienced soldier. Someone who had been under fire in Mexico or in our Indian wars." Percy needed convincing that Huse could get the job done.

Bev was reassuring. "Relax, Percy. You've had a long voyage. Don't worry. Huse can handle this. He brings unique experiences and connections to the job. The army gave him leave to spend time in England and Europe to look into business opportunities for an American relative. His family has a company for arms manufacturing and purchasing. He knows the arms import and export business and the British and European dealers like few others, North or South."

"Sounds like an ideal background."

"Yes, but he's sensitive about his Northern roots and family. In the weeks before secession, many of the Alabama students were ready to mutiny against him. Called him a damned Yankee. But he's as much a Southerner as you."

Percy could not help but note that Bev had not said "you and me." The reason, Percy suspected, was that Bev Tucker felt that he was more southern than Percy or Huse. Bev was a Tucker of Virginia, and Virginia was the premier state of the southern states.

Percy told Bev that he shared something of Huse's experience. "Passions were running high on my campus, too. My Louisiana background helped quell suspicions about my loyalties when I was insufficiently enthusiastic in embracing secession. So you think he'll be effective?"

"Yep. Our government in Montgomery will want your evaluation, of course."

"Montgomery's temporary. I'm sure they'll be moving to Richmond. Jane will probably tell you all about that when you get letters from her. Where are you living now?"

Bev sounded wistful. "I moved from Windermere House to a hotel. Our girls made it to Virginia with Jane. Our boys are at school in Switzerland. I'll need to collect them soon."

Chapter 16

A New Friend

An early morning Liverpool train took Bev Tucker and Percy to London, arriving at noon. Caleb Huse's telegram told them to meet him for lunch at his hotel, Morley's, on Trafalgar Square. Bev saw Huse seated at a table near an open window. Spotting the two, Huse stood. Of average height, Huse had a ready smile framed by a trim beard. The intelligence Percy saw in his dark eyes would be confirmed in the months Percy would spend working with him.

Bev said, "Captain Huse, this is Lieutenant Percy Moorhead, Confederate Army. Like yourself, he was a college professor at the outbreak of our conflict."

Showing keen interest in a fellow teacher, Huse asked, "Really? What field?" He had only been told that the man sent by Judah Benjamin was a lawyer. Huse's experiences with lawyers had not been productive. He had found them dilatory and pickers of nits.

With his ready grin that set Huse at ease, Percy replied, "Letters and Rhetoric, at William and Mary. Before that, I will confess that I was a lawyer in New Orleans, practicing with Judah Benjamin."

"No military experience?" Huse's career was defined by military associations.

"Mexican War. Private. Scott's campaign from Vera Cruz to Mexico City."

Percy's ready reply reassured Huse; this Moorhead might not prove to be a typical, obstacle-imposing lawyer. "Good. Then you've seen more combat than I have. And you know how important it is that we get weapons for our men."

Huse gestured for the newcomers to be seated. He was relieved that the Army was not saddling him with a political appointee. Working with Yancey, Rost and Mann was proving difficult enough. Yancey and Rost were patronizing while Mann was indifferent. Huse was weary of them, especially since their mandate from President Davis was vague at best, their status undefined in law.

A waiter came and they ordered. While they ate, Huse recounted his efforts to enter into contracts for guns. "A short time before the beginning of the war, the London Armoury Company purchased a plant of gun-stocking machinery from the Ames Manufacturing Company of Massachusetts. The Ames company was founded by my uncle. I had visited the London Armoury two years ago, so I went to the office of the company in Bermondsey the day after my arrival in London. I was prepared to enter a contract to secure their entire output of Enfield rifles."

Percy's interest was immediately evident: "I don't know the Enfields. How do they compare with the Springfields the Union manufactures?"

"Better, much better than anything else we can obtain over here. They are simply the best rifles made, with fully interchangeable parts. We must have interchangeable parts. When one rifle is damaged, our soldiers can scavenge parts from it. Unfortunately, the Armoury were already under contract for most of their product, and their capacity for manufacture is limited. Their price is above the cost I was authorized for – they want £3 plus each."

"And the good news?" asked Bev. He knew little about arms, but thought himself a skilled maker of deals.

After a pause, Huse was candid. "In spite of my instructions, I've contracted for 10,000 of their Enfields. They won't be ready for shipping in the immediate future. But I have been able to get help from Archibald Hamilton, one of the directors of London Armoury. He's also the managing partner of Sinclair, Hamilton & Company, commission merchants. They will be our agents dealing with a number of small manufacturers who make Enfields under license in Birmingham and elsewhere. Mr. Hamilton is acquainted with every gunmaker in England."

"Are you concerned about our government backing you?" asked Percy, who sensed Huse's uneasiness.

"Yes, of course." Percy's open manner and perceptive questions reassured Huse that Percy's role was not to serve as a check on Huse. "You two can help me." Huse would trust Tucker and Percy. He needed allies. He expected continuing difficulty with the three commissioners.

"How?" Percy readily saw Huse's plight – and the Confederacy's – if the commissioners balked at prudent purchases.

"By working with our commissioners. They need convincing."

"Convincing of what?" asked Percy. He had no prior experience with two of the commissioners.

"You'll judge for yourselves," said Huse looking at his pocket watch. "We meet with them next"

From Morley's Hotel, the three men took a cab to 15 Half Moon Street, where William Yancey had taken furnished rooms at a home in Piccadilly. The London streets were much more crowded than Percy remembered from his visit years earlier. Large omnibuses, pulled by teams of three or four horses, seemed everywhere, burdened by the weight of twelve to twenty closely-packed passengers. "Hi-yah, hee-yah," called the drivers to their teams. Two and four-wheeled carriages of all types competed for street space, pedestrians dashing among them. The clangings of hooves striking stone. Whips cracking, wheels clattering, people clamoring. "Hi-yah, hee-yah, whuh-up!"

Despite the din and hubbub outside the coach, Percy recalled what he could from newspapers about the three Confederate commissioners. William Lowndes Yancey was a fire-eating orator. Though born in South Carolina, his widowed mother had married a northern minister. They had taken him to New York where he spent his youth. His early career as a journalist in South Carolina and Alabama contributed to his pompous verbosity, his preference for three words where one would suffice. Percy remembered Judah Benjamin's wry assessment of Yancey: "If Yancy enjoyed the sound of his own voice, why should others be denied the same pleasure?"

Upon marrying an heiress with a plantation and slaves Yancey had taken up residence in Alabama. Now a slaveowner, he became an ardent champion of both the institution and of states' rights to maintain and extend slavery. A volatile temper led to a prison sentence after he killed a doctor in a street brawl on a point of honor. Failing as journalist and as planter, Yancey had turned to the practice of law; tiring of its tedium, he finally found his niche as an Alabama politician.

Percy knew Rost from New Orleans where Rost had served as a Supreme Court justice with Thomas Slidell, John Slidell's brother. Mann proved more a mystery to Percy.

In the cab, Huse shared what he knew about the commissioners' efforts with the British government. None received a warm reception. Lord John Russell, the foreign secretary, had met privately with Yancey a month earlier and was noncommittal. The Prime Minister, Lord Palmerston, was understood to prefer a divided, and thereby weakened, America, but he cautiously adopted a neutral policy. The commissioners' advocacy of slavery fell on unreceptive ears and undercut their practical arguments for recognition of the Confederacy as a new sovereignty. Their aggressive stance added to fears that the Confederacy would expand in the Caribbean and reopen the international slave trade if they achieved independence. Percy was not reassured when he met them.

Chapter 17

A Confederate Troika

Huse introduced Bev Tucker and Percy to Yancey when the commissioner greeted them at his door. The Carolina native turned Alabaman was dressed casually, indicating he had remained in his residence since breakfast.

"Beverley Tucker? You must be related to the Judge who was at William and Mary," exclaimed Yancey.

Bev was glad to have his family recognized, though he was surprised that a Confederate envoy to England would not know of his own prominence as consul in Liverpool. He acknowledged, "That could be my father or my uncle. Both taught at William and Mary. You probably mean my uncle, for whom I am named. Percy Moorhead here was one of his favorite students."

"I'll be damned," exclaimed Yancey. "The Judge was a prophet. Yes, a prophet if ever the South had one. A seer. A man in advance of his times. We were at the Nashville Convention together ten years ago, supporting each other on the necessity of secession. If more men had listened to him, we'd have been a free country long since. By damn, we should have listened. Y'all come on in." A small bit of dark, wet tobacco was at the corner of his lip. Percy noted that Yancey seemed to have more interest in slavery's cause than the South's commercial relations.

Three other men in the drawing room overlooking the street stood as the new arrivals walked in. Percy recognized two of them. The younger was Walker Fearn. Shaking his hand first, Percy said, "Judah Benjamin told me you were the delegation's secretary. I hadn't expected to see you so soon."

"Welcome to London," said Fearn with unfeigned warmth. He remembered Percy as a kindred spirit from their acquaintance in Mexico, four years earlier, when Percy was one of the delegation to secure the concession of the Tehuantepec Railroad Company.

Yancey said, "You two know each other?"

Fearn turned to Yancey and the other two men. "Percy and I met in Mexico City three years ago. He cast a spell on President Comonfort and walked away with a two-hundred-mile right-of-way across Mexico." He asked Percy, "Did you get your railroad built yet?"

"Still working at it," Percy replied with a wink. "I hope we can turn it to our advantage. In the meantime, Judah Benjamin has recruited me to look after some of the legal work for our agents, here and in France. He introduced me to your uncle when I received my lieutenant's appointment." Percy was gratified to see Fearn as the delegation's secretary. At least he was knowledgeable about the need for Confederate trade with England and Europe.

Smiling, Walker Fearn said, "I hope Uncle LeRoy didn't disown me. It's how I got my name. My mother's his sister."

The other two men were the Confederate commissioners Dudley Mann and Pierre Rost. Mann, a sixty-year-old Virginian, was the only commissioner with any prior diplomatic experience. Percy was aware that he was designated as Confederate envoy to Belgium, as Rost was to Spain; both appeared to prefer London.

"Moorhead?" asked Rost as Percy shook his hand. "I'm sure I know you." Rost, in his mid-sixties, was French by birth. Before emigrating to Louisiana as a young man, he had been a soldier in Napoleon's army.

"Yes, Judge," replied Percy. "New Orleans. When you were on the Supreme Court. I appeared before you in an insurance case."

Dudley Mann   Pierre Rost   William L. Yancey

"Weren't you with Benjamin back then?" asked Rost, making a dim connection.

"Yes," said Percy. He recalled that Benjamin did not much care for Rost, but as a prudent attorney he always concealed his feelings about any judge before whom he might appear. Rost thought his French birth gave him unique insight into French law, though his introduction to the subject came some years after his arrival in Louisiana. He referred to the Napoleonic Code as his "patrimony." When Percy was first to appear before Rost on the court, Benjamin had raised his eyebrow and said, "You'll find him Polonius – full of words and wind, with greater self-regard than depth." Percy's experience would confirm Benjamin's shrewd assessment.

"Of course," Rost replied. "Now I remember. You were Judah Benjamin's protégé. And wasn't your father a factor in New Orleans? Represented the Destrehan family when I bought their plantation, I believe. How is he?"

Percy appreciated Rost's effort to be friendly. "I'm afraid I never knew much about his business affairs. He passed two years ago."

"Pity," said Rost, his tone suggesting he was thinking more of his own mortality than sympathy for Percy's loss. He had none of the vigor of Yancey and was pale next to Mann. His selection as a commissioner was based on an erroneous assumption that his respect as a state Supreme Court justice would bring esteem overseas; what the post required, however, was vitality, not complacency.

When everyone was seated and enjoying afternoon tea and coffee, Yancey, as leader of the delegation, asked "What can we do for you today?" He made it clear that he was in charge and that the three visitors were supplicants.

Huse laid out the details of his negotiations with London Armoury and with Archibald Hamilton. Before proceeding further in concluding agreements, he wanted to secure the commissioners' endorsement. He hoped that they would communicate their support of his plans to President Davis and the Confederate cabinet.

Yancey's eyebrows furrowed as Huse proposed his purchase approval. "Ten thousand you say? Twenty? Should we commit for so many?" Yancey was skeptical of Huse's extravagance. And mildly annoyed he had not been consulted in advance, though Huse was under no obligation to do so. Yancey continued, "What if the war ends next week or next month? You may have committed our new government to purchasing ten or twenty thousand weapons we'll never need." Yancey spoke from the experience of a man who had lost ownership of newspapers and plantations to his debts. His failures were from his inability to grasp the necessary consequences of his actions. Zealotry for slavery was no credential for a diplomatic mission to a country that had abolished the institution throughout their empire thirty years earlier.

Huse was deferential but firm on his proposal. "With all respect, Mr. Yancey, the Union is planning for a long war. I've encountered their buyer, a man named MacFarland, as I've made my rounds with gun manufacturers and dealers. He's buying up everything he can but lacks available funds – just as we do. If we don't act quickly, the Union will drive up the prices. Don't forget the Yankees have factories to make guns. We don't. Without these Enfields, our men will go up against their Springfields armed only with hatchets and hoes as weapons. How will we explain to their widows that we didn't supply them with arms when they were available?"

Huse's words had their intended effect. Reluctantly, after more dithering, the three commissioners pledged their support and made credit available to the extent that they could.

"Gents, you must understand the difficulties we face in spending our funds wisely," said Rost. "I had a meeting about loans to the Confederacy with Joshua Bates, the senior partner at Baring Brothers, but he turned a cold shoulder. He's a Union supporter. Mann here had the same result with an American banker, George Peabody, who resides here."

Percy spoke up, hoping that he could shape the conversation. "A few early victories in the battlefield may change that. When the English raise the issue of slavery, instead of defending slavery, we need to focus on the British dependence on cotton. They must see that British finance is necessary for our people to supply their mills with cotton." One of Percy's principal functions as a Confederate agent was to reconfigure the arrangements for the South's cotton commerce. He wanted the commissioners to see this as among their goals.

But his words missed their mark. It was immediately evident that Yancey was sensitive on the slavery question. Feeling that he had already lost face in his exchange with Huse, Yancey turned to this other impudent Confederate agent, who, like Huse, had no political experience to his credit. Yancey took Percy's statement as an implied criticism of the representation the commissioners had made so far in their mission: "Son, we'll leave the contracts and acquisitions to y'all. You leave the diplomacy to us. We must impress upon the governments of Britain and Europe the justness of our cause. When they understand we are right about the African, they'll see why we must fight Northern aggression."

A good judge of character – and of a man's shortcomings – Percy quickly saw the futility of trying to counter Yancey. Any questioning of slavery was an affront to Yancey's honor – and the South's. Yancey thought the English had to be made to understand that honor must not only be defended but vindicated. How could they not see this?

In the cab taking Percy and Bev Tucker to the rail station for their journey back to Liverpool, Huse said, "I'm glad you two were along. You see what we face with our commissioners. They've accomplished little here, nor much more in Paris or Madrid. Emperor Louis Napoleon favors us, but he won't do anything without the British acting first. Spain still has slavery in Cuba but thinks we're the more likely to try to take over the island than is the North. Of course they distrust us. The most we can hope for from the commissioners is that they'll send reports to the government giving us support."

Sympathetic to the challenges Huse faced (and in which he might share) Percy asked, "Tell me what Bev and I can do to help your effort." He had little hope of changing the course of the three commissioners.

Huse replied with gratitude. "They were more receptive to me with you there. I can't make headway with them on what sort of arms our soldiers need. Guns are all the same thing to them. They think the war will be over quickly and none will be needed. And they won't shut up about slavery. You were right to take it up, Percy. The English just don't want to talk about it. If the Confederacy tries to resume the international slave trade, it puts them in a terrible position."

Percy passed a restless night in a small hotel near the London train station. The experience with the commissioners was not encouraging. Fortunately, the Confederacy had younger and more able agents, like Walker Fearn and Caleb Huse. And he had yet to meet the forceful and effective James Bulloch.

Chapter 18

The Customer of Liverpool

It was a straight walk from Rumford Place down Fenwick, around St. Georges Church, then a couple of blocks to the Liverpool Custom House. Percy made his way up a flight of stairs to the large office of the Collector of Customs, uncertain how best to make a favorable impression on the man who could be essential to his mission. Bev Tucker had tried to prepare him, but Bev's assessments were not always trustworthy. He would have to rely on his own judgment.

Arriving at the outer office, a dull clerk of indeterminate age took Percy to meet Samuel Price Edwards, a man of distinguished appearance, aged about sixty. Price Edwards was at the peak of his career, having begun his employment with the Board of Customs at age twenty-four. The Customer of Liverpool stood and shook Percy's hand, firmly, in the American manner. Southerners, to whom Edwards was partial (according to Bev), were frequent vistors to this office.

"Thank you for seeing me, Mr. Edwards," began Percy, showing deference to the man and to his office. "Mr. Beverley Tucker, whom you know well, is related to me by marriage. He advised I should make your acquaintance so that should questions arise relating to the Board of Customs for the interests I represent you will know who I am."

"Very good counsel from Mr. Tucker." Price Edwards gestured to Percy to sit in the comfortable chair near his desk. "I hope my friend is well. And what interests might you represent?"

"Bev is well. This unfortunate conflict, however, has disrupted his family." Leaning forward, Percy continued as he watched for the official's reactions, "As to my interests, I suppose I should start with the Anglo-Mexican Tehuantepec Company. It has succeeded to the interests of several predecessors in the grant by Mexico of a railroad right-of-way for sixty years across Mexico. The route has been fully surveyed. A ship is in operation. And a mail contract with the United States government was successfully initiated. Rail was being laid when civil conflicts in Mexico and in America necessitated a cessation of operations. We are directing all of our activities from England now, with English investors."

Edwards nodded but smiled in indulgent skepticism. "You are from the South, Mr. Moorhead. How is it that you represent an English-based company?"

Clearing his throat, Percy explained cautiously, "My association with the Tehuantepec railroad project began ten years ago through Senator Judah Benjamin, who was among the first to lead the undertaking."

The name and man were familiar to Price Edwards. "I met Benjamin twice. And he's now a cabinet officer in President Davis's government. Yes?" The positive expression on Price Edwards's face assured Percy that his invocation of Benjamin's name was well-received.

"Yes. He's our Attorney General." Percy sat back, more relaxed now that he and Price Edwards need not ignore his greater concern. "Which brings me to my second reason for being here. Mr. Benjamin has asked me to assist the Confederacy in conducting its business in England. He and President Davis, of course, would like to see the Queen recognize the Confederacy. Until she does, they wish to fully respect Britain's neutrality in the unfortunate conflict which President Lincoln has brought about."

The English official continued to peel away the layers of relations prompting Percy's visit. "Am I amiss in assuming you are a lawyer in the employ of the Confederacy?"

"Your inference is correct." Percy was unapologetic. "It is my role to see that the agents of the Confederacy comply with the strict letter of the Foreign Enlistment Act and all other English laws. My practice of law in New Orleans with Mr. Benjamin often involved the mutual interests of England and the Southern cotton export. Liverpool for many years has been the principal port for all Southern commerce with England."

Price Edwards nodded agreeably. "Please continue."

Percy asked, "Would Liverpool be the city it has become in this century without our cotton? Without our cotton, what will become of Liverpool? I hope to see to it that the trade between England and the Confederate States will only increase in coming years. If there is ever a question concerning the Foreign Enlistment Act or other laws, I will take all measures to assure you and the Crown that all issues are immediately addressed."

Price Edwards replied without the indirection of other government functionaries whom Percy had encountered. "I understand your concern. A terrible calamity has befallen your country. While I am in sympathy with the new government in the South, you understand I am bound to carry out my duties to Her Majesty."

Percy assured Price Edwards firmly. "We expect no less, Sir. We can ask for no more than a fair reading of the English law. But let me not slight my duties to the Anglo-Mexican Tehuantepec Company. They are separate from my efforts on behalf of the Confederate government. There's no reason to cease work on the railroad across the Mexican isthmus while the Confederacy awaits the Union's acquiescence in our independence."

The Customs officer acknowledged Percy's point. "Our merchants here believe trade with the East would benefit greatly if our ships could avoid the Drake Passage or Strait of Magellan."

Percy embraced the opening. "Our Tehuantepec isthmus route is far superior to the competing Panamanian or Nicaraguan passages. If our company fails to fulfill our development obligations, we will forfeit our rights from the Mexican government. I hope we can count on your cooperation without regard to the South's struggle for independence."

The administrator reassured his guest, "Of course, Mr. Moorhead. The Mexican rail project presents no conflict for Her Majesty's government. This office will extend to you every courtesy."

From Price Edwards's expression, Percy understood that he would be able to avoid a heavy-handed interference of the Customs office by disguising suspect transactions through the use of the Anglo-Mexican Tehuantepec Company. "Very good. Now, that covers our formal discussion. Before I take your leave, I must ask you about the paintings you have displayed on your walls. You have exquisite taste."

"Thank you," said Edwards, pleased at Percy's discerning interest. "I began collecting art two decades ago. What do you like?"

"The one behind you. What is it?"

Turning his head, Price Edwards smiled and said, "Oh yes, that one is very special. It's called *Corfu, from Ascension*. It was painted for me by my friend Edward Lear. Mr. Lear describes himself as a painter of poetical topography. He's not only a painter, but a poet and a traveler. A most interesting fellow. They say he gave art lessons to our Queen some years ago. *Corfu* he painted for me under commission three years ago."

Percy continued, "Ethereal, I must say. I love his treatment of light, the detail of the native costumes." Percy's admiration was unfeigned. "They must be the Greek goatherds. It looks as though you could count the leaves on the trees. Simply magnificent."

Price Edwards was flattered by Percy's praise of the painting. Very few Americans visiting his office paid the slightest attention to the fine collection of art in his office. What captured a man's interest said more about his character than his words or his public associations. In a friendly manner, Edwards inquired, "What is your background? Moorhead is almost a familiar name. Is your family English?"

"Anglo-Irish. I hope time will allow me to explore my family roots while I am here."

"Irish, too, you say. Well, if I can help, please do call on me. I know the importance of family. I was Collector in Dublin for six years before posting here. Please give my regards to Mr. Benjamin when you see him again. Did I mention he paid a visit to me a few years ago, just as you do now? Yes, I did."

Chapter 19

Arma virumque cano

On Wednesday, June 5, Percy Moorhead was in the Fraser, Trenholm conference room at Rumford Place when James Bulloch opened the door and stepped in. Bulloch was three years older than Percy, of medium height, with dark brown receding hair over a broad forehead. His black eyes, beneath dark eyebrows, punctuated Dundreary whiskers and mustache; at his chin he was clean shaven. The stoutly-built Georgian's eyes fixed first on Charles Prioleau then took in Percy and Caleb Huse, as though connecting them with what he had learned about his future associates before leaving Montgomery a month earlier.

"Good morning, gents," he said cheerily. "Unless the *North American* took a wrong turn in the Azores, I surmise I'm in the right place." He extended his hand across the conference table and shook the hand of Charles Prioleau first, saying "I'm Jim Bulloch. From the portrait in George Trenholm's office, you must be Mr. Prioleau."

"Indeed, I am, sir." Prioleau was standing now to welcome the newcomer.

"Then to you I present these papers from President Davis and from George Trenholm which will establish my bona fides. May I sit?"

"Of course, Major," insisted Prioleau. "And it's Charles, please. Do you know either of these two? Lieutenant Percy Moorhead and Captain Caleb Huse."

James D. Bulloch

"My pleasure," said Bulloch, shaking their hands in turn. "Captain Huse and I just missed each other in Montgomery. Lieutenant Moorhead's reputation precedes him, a good one I should add, if I'm to believe our Attorney General."

Smiling Percy responded, "We shall see whether his confidence has been misplaced. How was your journey?"

Bulloch reported that he had been in transit for nearly a month, beginning by rail from Montgomery through Kentucky, a border state that remained neutral as he passed through. From there he had traveled to Detroit, crossing into Canada via Lake Erie, then making his way to Montreal where he boarded the Allan Line steamer, *North American*.

Prioleau excused himself to allow the three men to get to know one another and to plan their next moves. Benjamin had told Percy in Montgomery that in fifteen years with the navy and another six with a private shipping company, Bulloch had traveled much of the North and South Atlantic, the Pacific coast, and the Mediterranean.

He knew ships as Huse knew ordnance and Percy law. The combined competence would prove to be in stark contrast to the ineffectiveness of the trio of commissioners sent by the Confederacy — Yancey, Mann and Rost.

Percy's initial impression of Bulloch, based on his confident manner and knowledgeable background, was favorable. Percy began, "Captain Huse and I have an understanding of the needs of the Confederacy that we can fulfill here. Buying arms, munitions, uniforms and other supplies that can't be produced at home and finding a means of transporting them before the Union navy can interdict our efforts. What are your assignments? Let's see what we can do together to help achieve them."

Bulloch was no-nonsense; small talk was a waste of time and words. "It's a challenge. We have to build a navy to take on one of the strongest navies in the world. Maybe second only to the British and itching to surpass them. We have to work quickly. And we have limited resources. What's more, we are 4,000 miles from our country's government. Nine million of our countrymen are counting on us."

"Is that all you need?" Percy asked with a smile. "A few miles from where I grew up, the Louisiana legislature established the State Insane Asylum. Then they emptied all the asylums in New Orleans into it. If I didn't know better, I'd think you got your marching orders from patients who had escaped."

For Percy, small talk was exploration, an interval for scrutiny, to explore another's personality and character, an opportunity to build a relationship – if one were possible. He would listen and absorb before passing judgment.

Bulloch perked up, taking new interest in Percy Moorhead. "Are you from Louisiana? So's my wife," said Bulloch with surprise. "I was told you're from Virginia."

"Only a couple of years in Richmond and Williamsburg. I grew up in St. Francisville. For a time, I practiced law in New Orleans.

Where's your bride from?"

"Baton Rouge. Just downriver from you."

Percy said, "Small world. You'll have to tell me more after we build your navy."

Loosening, Bulloch commented wryly, "The only people whose sanity I would question are the ones who think this war will be over in three months." Bulloch, Percy saw, was blunt.

Taking Huse's nod as agreement among the three that the war would be long, Percy said, "Since we concur on that, where does that take us in building and arming a navy?"

Bulloch was eager to move forward. He had had two months of anticipation. "There's no one, Union or Confederate, who knows more about the needs of a modern navy than our Secretary of the Navy, Stephen Mallory. He was on the Senate Committee on Naval Affairs for years before this war started. He knows what the Union navy has and what it will likely do. President Davis and the rest of his cabinet know nothing about naval affairs and will leave it all to him. Mallory told me the Union will mobilize rapidly and use its navy to the fullest. They will concentrate on gaining control of the Mississippi and on making the blockade effective along the entire length of our coasts. We don't have the raw materials, the shipyards or the machine works to match the Union's capacity for rapid expansion."

"All too true, I fear," conceded Percy. "As I was leaving Virginia, the governor was seizing the U. S. Navy's shipyards at Norfolk. But the Yankees were already scuttling most of the ships and machinery that were there. I doubt we were able to save much. Where does that leave us?"

Bulloch stood and walked over to the window, looking at the street below. He spoke with resolve. "Gents, the success or failure of the Confederate navy is just outside these curtains. We're here in Liverpool because it has the best shipyards in the world. It has all the experience of building vessels for the Royal Navy. The city also happens to be our chief trading partner for cotton. That means it's the best hope we have for financing and construction."

"That's true," said Huse. He was impressed by Bulloch's directness and ready to follow his leadership, though Percy saw a small frown on Huse's lips as he watched Bulloch spit tobacco juice into a cuspidor near Huse's feet. After a pause, he continued, "And London is of near equal importance. It is where the agents of the armament manufacturers are to be found. I've established contact with several who are ready to work with us. So, where do we start here?"

Bulloch picked up notes from the table where he had left them. "Mallory's first priority is to weaken or destroy the blockade before it can prevent our commerce with Britain and France. We lack the force to confront the Union warships directly. So the strategy will be to draw off the blockade's ships. We will both purchase and build commerce raiders to attack, capture or destroy Northern shipping. The Union will be forced to reassign the majority of its blockading fleet to defending their sea routes. In short, we will make them chase us. The fox is swift and wily. He leads away the baying hounds."

Huse was enthusiastic about Mallory's strategy. "Do you have ship plans?" he inquired. He took notes of his thoughts and questions stimulated by Bulloch.

Sitting down again, Bulloch replied with confidence. "The plans will almost draw themselves when we tell the shipwrights what we require. A cruiser must have steam and sails so it can continue under sail when coal is unavailable. It must be a screw ship, not a paddle-wheeler. Sail and paddlewheel are a poor match. It must be made entirely of wood, except for her copper bottom. In remote locations, repairs can be made to a wooden ship, but not to a ship with a damaged metal frame or hull. Wood is going out of use in the British merchant service. Their iron ships, though fast and well built, are too thin in the plates and light in the deck frames and stanchions to carry heavy guns."

"What ordnance will we need for your cruisers?" Huse understood that was his department for both land and sea.

"A raider preying on merchant ships need carry relatively few guns, enough to intimidate and sink a merchantman. Guns enough to defend itself if engaged by a ship-of-the-line while speeding to its escape. The shallower the draft, the more ports she can put in to. The Union navy will have to chase our raiders. Every one we put to sea will draw off ten Union ships. They'll have to patrol the whole world while we dart in and out of commercial shipping routes. Fox and hounds. We will drive up the insurance costs for their merchant shipping, make them pay heavily for warring on us."

Huse continued, "All right. What's Secretary Mallory's second priority?"

Percy closely observed the interaction between Huse and Bulloch. He concluded that they would make a good team. War throws all sorts of men together without regard to their compatibility. Even with a common purpose and the best of motives, they often clash as to methods or even the pettiness of personality.

Bulloch had anticipated such questions. "If we're successful in drawing off the Union's ships, this will give us time to consolidate a formidable, home-based river and coastal fleet of ironclads. Mallory knows that ironclads are the future of a navy. Powerful, steam-driven ironclads don't need speed to deny the inland waterways to any attacking Federal vessels. They simply must be heavily armed and impregnable. But they won't be suitable for ocean crossing. So, that's outside our responsibilities for now."

Percy tried to be candid without sounding flippant. "Frankly, I don't know a topsail from a mizzenmast. Tell me what I can do."

Turning to Percy, Bulloch, who appreciated candor, especially in a lawyer, answered, "An old salt like me has never had much need for the law. I'm at home afloat, where the captain's command is the law. Neptune's jurisdiction, we sometimes say. On land, I've been given my marching orders, which is to give you the helm. Mallory and your friend the Attorney General warned me to be prudent so as not to involve the agents of the Confederate States in embarrassing complaints over neutrality laws. They directed me to acquaint myself, as soon as possible after my arrival, with the reach of the Foreign Enlistment Act and the Queen's Proclamation of Neutrality. I was told to count on you for counsel on complying with English law in all my undertakings to get cruisers afloat with the quickest possible dispatch."

"I've studied their laws," Percy told his two associates. "The directives are clear enough, but they are untested in court."

Huse sounded disappointed. "That's too bad. Then we don't know what the British will do?"

With a smile, Percy responded emphatically: "No. It's good for us. Where there is no precedent, there is opportunity. And unlike our own fire-eaters, the English ruling class are cautious by nature. Their hereditary inclination is to wait-and-see. It's in their blood. They will be reluctant to intervene. Why would they stop us while we are doing business here and in London and Birmingham? We need to let them know that the ships we get here will make it possible to keep the cotton trade going despite a Union blockade. Their ships, our cotton."

Bulloch enthused, "I'm convinced."

"Let's hope we can convince the British. Our people depend on us. We must do our utmost to justify the confidence they have given us. Where competence is not alone enough to win the day, we must use wile and stratagem."

"Lawyer's tricks?" Bulloch winked.

With a warm grin, Percy responded, "We prefer to think of it as lawyer's craft."

Chapter 20

Hull, of Fletcher & Hull

The ride in a hansom cab from the Fraser, Trenholm offices, was uncomfortable. Bev Tucker, Percy and Bulloch were shoehorned into a fly that was designed for two passengers, with the driver on the elevated seat behind the cab. Bev Tucker's bulk required a tight squeeze for his two companions, Percy lean but tall, the Georgian Bulloch shorter but broad in chest. The horse pulling the small carriage struggled as it reached Upper Duke Street and turned left, swaying awkwardly, at St. James Cemetery. A light rain had fallen. As the sky cleared, they were spared from arriving for their 10:30 morning appointment at the law offices of Fletcher & Hull on Rodney Street wet.

Bev Tucker had recommended the firm to Percy based on his dealings with Frederick Hull while he was the American consul. He introduced Percy and Bulloch to Hull and left it for Percy to explain their needs. The English solicitor was lean, with an angular face and long graying hair.

Percy began with indirection, as he had with Price Edwards, uncertain of how the lawyer's views on the Confederacy. "Mr. Hull, we have a common acquaintance, Mr. Judah P. Benjamin. I am here as attorney and agent of the Anglo-Mexican Tehuantepec Company, which is presently organized under English law. We hold a concession for a railroad right-of-way across Mexico at the

Isthmus of Tehuantepec. We are looking into the feasibility of purchasing or building steamships in Liverpool. The purpose we envision is transportation of material for construction of the railroad and for use on the Coatzacoalcos River, which is part of the transit route. We may also desire the building of steamships to engage in merchant shipping on both the Atlantic and Pacific coasts, for transportation from California and the China trade to England and France. As I am sure you are aware, there is a civil struggle in Mexico to determine its constitutional government. To ensure that we do not violate British law, we would like a legal opinion that we can take to the shipbuilders so that we can assure them of strict compliance with the Foreign Enlistment Act of 1819."

"I see," Hull acknowledged, adding, "And our mutual friend Mr. Benjamin has become Attorney General of the Confederacy, has he not?"

"Yes."

Hull was no stranger to indirection and circumlocution. "Though you have couched your inquiry in respect of the Mexican political context, shall I assume you are interested in an authoritative opinion that would equally apply to Mr. Benjamin's present office and circumstances?"

Percy replied cautiously, "Only if you think the two cases are equally similar." He did not appear disingenuous; his meaning was transparent.

"Have you made your own review of the Foreign Enlistment Act?"

"I have."

"So, you must have your own interpretation." The English solicitor raised one eyebrow.

Percy continued in his more formal manner. It was a formal occasion, and he would follow form. "Though I am not an English lawyer, I can read a statute as well as another lawyer. But I read as an advocate, not as a jurist. And no British shipbuilder is likely to defer to an American's reading of a statute when there is no English precedent. We need a written opinion that we can share with a shipbuilder should any question be raised over the lawfulness of their activity. It is as essential to us as a letter of credit upon a banking house."

Hull replied cordially and formally. "Mr. Moorhead, you are right that there is no precedent. But it would help me to have a context on which I might opine. What would you seek of a shipbuilder here or in Glasgow?"

Percy did not need notes to provide the essential context. His discussions with Bulloch had been an informal education on contemporary ship characteristics for naval warfare. He explained that the ideal steamship for their purposes would be a fast screw ship made entirely of wood that could proceed under sail when coal was unavailable. In a remote location such as the Yucatan or Tehuantepec, repairs to a wooden ship would be possible. Such a vessel might need openings in the hull for a few guns, as would be necessary for defense against pirates or privateers or to pacify a hostile tribe at a coastal inlet. But a builder should be informed that no arms would be supplied to the vessel in British waters. Percy concluded: "The purchase with the shipbuilder will be in my name, as agent of the Anglo-Mexican Tehuantepec Company, or in the name of Mr. Francis Falconnet, a British citizen."

Turning to the third member of the group seeking legal services, Hull inquired, "And Mr. Bulloch, is he also with the Anglo-Mexican Tehuantepec Company?"

Bulloch took this as his time to speak. His words, spoken slowly, indicated that his interests, though aligned, were not necessarily identical to those of Percy Moorhead. He would cut through the polite indirection, a dance at which he was awkward. "No, Mr. Hull. As you have correctly surmised, the questions of Mr. Moorhead would pertain equally and more forcefully to the Confederate States." Bulloch was impatient with the periphrasing of lawyers. "I'll come right to the point. If you find that Mr. Moorhead's client would be able to undertake construction of vessels in Liverpool without the British government interdicting them, then the interests I represent would have you review other proposed contracts. These would be between myself or the Fraser, Trenholm Company and local ship builders. We would expect that you would be in a position to defend such contracts should they be called into question."

Hull replied with equal frankness. "Thank you for your clarity, Mr. Bulloch. Having my office consider the matter for the Anglo-Mexican Tehuantepec Company would spare us of awkwardness if you thought our law firm might be reluctant to represent the newly formed Confederate States of America."

Showing deference to the English lawyer's possible scruples, Percy again spoke. "Your Queen has issued a proclamation of neutrality. Her government is under continuing efforts from the Union to prevent the Confederacy from obtaining ships and arms and supplies from any British sources. Minister Adams, as you know, is the son and grandson of American presidents and has long ties to English interests. Several of the leading banking companies in London already have been disinclined to associate themselves with our new country. Before we formally engage your services, it would be helpful to have an insight into your initial thoughts."

Hull appreciated the gesture of a face-saving way of declining representation. His manner was receptive but noncommittal. "Yes, a most prudent course. For the time being I will look to the Anglo-Mexican Tehuantepec Company as my client. Let me assure you, we in this firm would have no reluctance in representing the interests of the Confederacy. The great importance of the South to this city and this region has led to numerous of our dealings with businesses in the South. And we know some of your leading men well, including Mr. Benjamin. I believe this is sufficient information for me to begin. Please come to see me this time next week, and we will see where we stand."

Outside, Percy asked Bulloch and Bev Tucker their reactions. Bulloch said "I see no reason to be discouraged."

Smiling broadly, Bev said, "Hull's a fine man. He'll come through for us. Like I always say, hitch your wagon to a moonbeam and you'll rise with the tide."

Percy chuckled. "Bev, I almost forgot you used to make your living slapping words together for a newspaper to make a distinct impression on your audience."

Chapter 21

From Hull to Keel

A week later, Percy and Bulloch returned to the offices of Fletcher and Hull, without Bev Tucker. They were hopeful of a positive response. A clerk showed them into Hull's office again. The English lawyer stood and walked around his desk. He greeted his guests warmly and begged them to sit. He assured them, "With the proper precautions, I believe that the Anglo-Mexican Tehuantepec Company can proceed on its proposed course of having ships constructed within Britain. Building a ship is no crime under the Foreign Enlistment Act. Based on a strict reading of the statute, in my opinion, three things are necessary to make the building illegal."

Putting on his glasses, lawyer Hull picked up a piece of paper on which he had written, and continued, now looking at the paper, now looking at his two clients. "These are 1) that the vessel be within the United Kingdom. The person to be charged with a violation must 2) equip, furnish, fit-out or arm, or procure to be equipped, furnished, fitted-out, or armed, or shall knowingly aid, assist, or be concerned in the equipping, furnishing, fitting-out, or arming of any Ship or Vessel. If these are present, then the government must clearly establish 3) intent that such . . ."

Hull paused. "Please forgive me for reading, but any court decision will turn on the exact language of the Act. I must be precise

. . . Ship or Vessel shall be employed in the service of any Foreign Prince, State, or Potentate, or of any Foreign Colony, Province, or part of any Province or People, . . . as a Transport or Store-ship, or with intent to cruise or commit hostilities against any Prince, State, or Potentate, ... with whom His Majesty shall not then be at war.'"

Bulloch did not pretend to follow Hull's discussion, allowing simply, "I'll have to trust you two lawyers on this. Is there a layman's version?"

Setting aside paper and glasses, Hull answered, "In short, the Anglo-Mexican Tehuantepec Company or, for that matter, a business firm such as Fraser, Trenholm and Company with associations with the Confederate States of America can lawfully have ships built in England."

Percy added his own explanation. "Jim, it is the fitting out or arming for hostilities *within* England that is prohibited. If the ship is built in England without being armed, it is okay. Once it leaves English waters and then becomes armed, it is beyond the jurisdiction of British law to punish." Having said this much, Percy was reluctant to add more on English law; it was important that he let Bulloch and Hull establish a relationship that did not depend on an intermediary.

Nodding in agreement with Percy's explanation, the solicitor added, "A necessary precaution would be to avoid the Confederate states having a direct hand in contracting for ships. You should take steps to negate an intent that the ships would be used in hostilities. And no crew can be enlisted *within* England for service with a belligerent."

Bulloch leaned forward, saying, "Yes, we are closely watched. Almost simultaneously with my arrival in England there came in a New York paper, the *Times,* with a half column of telegrams, purporting to have been sent from Montgomery via Petersburg, Virginia on the 19th of May. My departure for Europe, with the precise service assigned me, the total amount of money furnished, and even the banks and bankers through whom the credits were to be arranged, was as minutely detailed as if the particulars had been furnished direct from our Treasury Department or from the pages of my instructions. This was before either the money or the orders had reached me!"

Percy interjected, "All of us who are supposed to be in the service of the Confederate States are closely watched. The Union's consuls here and in London employ detectives for the purpose." Pointing at the window, he added, "Without doubt, there's an agent or two across the street as we speak."

Hull nodded in sympathy. "I've been told that Mr. Wilding and the ambassador in London have engaged many agents. This has discouraged British shipping companies from business dealings with the Confederate States. From my own inquiries I've learned that the Queen's neutrality proclamation is almost an exclusive barrier against shipments to the South. Have you any alternatives?"

Bulloch sat back. His years of dealing with government agents in numerous foreign ports had prepared him to anticipate contingencies. "We do. Or hope to. In addition to having vessels built, we will hire ships outright. Maybe we'll buy them to transport what we need. Are you willing to guide us in the steps that allow us to stay within the strict letter of the Foreign Enlistment Act?"

Firmly, Hull replied, "We can make no guarantees of government non-interference. But I can promise you vigorous representation." Exchanging glances, Percy saw that Hull had impressed Bulloch as a man equal to his assurances.

Opening the worn leather valise he carried with him, Bulloch took out papers for Hull. "Then, sir, in my own name I will engage your services. I have brought with me rough drafts of contracts. The first is with the engineering firm Fawcett, Preston & Co. who will build our vessel's boilers. Through a subcontract with William Miller & Sons, we will have the ship's hull built." Bulloch's weathered leather bag had accompanied him on countless voyages, its surface showing the assaults of the briny elements.

Hull nodded with approval. "We know both firms well. They are less than a mile apart. It is advisable that ship and engines should be as near together as possible. Have you a design and name?"

With pride showing, Bulloch pulled from his valise a folded paper which, when opened, revealed a sleek design. "Mr. W. C. Miller had a scale drawing of one of her Majesty's newest ships, which we will adopt as a base to start from. We'll draw her out in the mid-ship section, and flatten the floor so as to get greater carrying capacity. Her name: The *Oreto*."

"Interesting," said Hull, raising querulous eyebrows. "Does the name have meaning?"

"It's from the Italian, *ore'zzo*, suggesting a gentle breeze. The papers will show it is intended for an Italian buyer."

"And financing?"

"The contract price is £45,600. Fraser, Trenholm & Co. has agreed to advance the sums in five installments."

Hull was not accustomed to clients as well prepared as Bulloch and Percy. He said, "Excellent. I will give these my immediate attention. Can I assume, Mr. Moorhead, that your hand was at work in these drafts?"

Modest in the face of Hull's implied flattery, Percy replied, "Yes. I make no representations as to their adequacy under English law."

"Understood. Every lawyer has his own phrasing and flourishes. I'll respect those flowing from your pen. In a few days, I will send word through Mr. Prioleau that they are ready."

The *Oreto's* keel was laid in early June, less than a month after

Bulloch's arrival in Liverpool. Percy's preliminary work had made the speed possible, and he had carried out the details with Fawcett, Preston and Miller & Sons while Bulloch made extensive design changes from the British gunship plans with Thomas Miller, who was managing the yard.

Within a few more weeks, Bulloch had Hull reviewing contracts for a second ship that was a larger version of the *Oreto*; with a length of two hundred feet, it would be nine feet longer and at 1,000 tons would weigh in at 300 tons greater. Her price was £2,000 more than the *Oreto*, £47,500. She was to be built across the Mersey, at Birkenhead, by the firm of Laird Brothers. The company founder, John Laird, had recently retired in favor of his sons. He was now a member of Parliament, which could be a help or a hindrance with the government. The ship's name was only a number: No. 290, for the vessel was the 290th to be built by the shipyard.

Leaving lawyer Hull's office after completing the documents for the 290, Percy said to Bulloch, "For someone as unflappable as you, you are rather more enthusiastic than I've seen you. Is it this ship? You seem to have invested more effort in her than to the *Oreto*."

Bulloch cocked his head to one side. "Yep. I guess I'm not good at hiding my feelings. Percy, I've been on or captained ships most of my life. They've always been some other man's vessels. What captain has not wanted a ship of his own making? Now, I've designed a ship of my dreams. Secretary Mallory promised me her command. She will be my very own ship. Damn me if anything comes between us."

"Even the war's end?" Percy's meaning was clear.

Without hesitation, Bulloch responded, "We both know she'll see service long before this war ends."

Percy was unsure whether Bulloch was expressing reality or desire. An army man like Beauregard can only flourish in armed command facing an enemy; a naval captain needs only a ship at sea, seeking mastery of time, tide and tempest.

Chapter 22

Enter Major Anderson

Near the end of June, the Confederate agents operating in Liverpool and London were joined by two more men sent by Navy Secretary Mallory – Major Edward C. Anderson and Lieutenant James North. Although Anderson was outwardly affable on first acquaintance, Percy noticed that he was reticent in his dealings with Caleb Huse. This struck him as peculiar until some months later Benjamin explained that certain members of the Confederate cabinet distrusted Huse because of his Northern origins and his family connections. Anderson had been instructed by President Davis to observe Huse and to remove him if he were failing in his duties. Anderson and North were expected to work with Bulloch in acquiring more ships, including iron-clads. The Confederate Congress had appropriated $2,000,000 in May 1861 for their purchase.

Lieutenant North impressed Percy as too taken with his own abilities. Early on, North had made clear that he planned to command one of the raiders that Bulloch was building. Could he expect to captain the *290*? That would be a blow to Bulloch. Percy thought it odd that Anderson and North had sailed in a racing yacht, bringing North's wife and daughter with them. The yacht was formerly the *America*, which the Confederacy purchased from her Irish owner, Henry Decie. Apparently, someone in the

Confederate government was persuaded that a fast sailing ship could be useful for special missions, despite the disadvantage of lacking steam power. As the ship's name would likely cause confusion as to her loyalties, she was re-christened the *Camilla*. Decie remained her captain as he sailed her to England with Anderson and North. Sleek and fleet she was, but the *Camilla*'s talents were not coupled to her purpose.

Percy observed that the first meetings between Huse and Anderson had been awkward. Anderson, having gone to sea at seventeen, lacked Huse's West Point education and army training. His was the jealousy not only of inferior credentials but of limited capacity. However, Anderson was Huse's superior officer and sixteen years his senior. He was reluctant to acknowledge that Huse had a far better understanding of small arms needed for a large army facing a long engagement.

Though Huse did not intend to, Percy observed that Huse talked to Anderson as though he were instructing one of his students at Alabama or West Point. Huse had expected ignorance of the three Confederate emissaries, none of whom had significant military experience. Nearly a half-century had passed since Rost's French service. Dudley Mann was a West Point dropout, who, despite his suavity, resented the fact that Huse had taught at the Academy. Huse was surprised that Anderson and Bulloch knew so little of the advancements in design and manufacture of small arms in the last six or seven years. Because both men had left the U. S. Navy for civilian life years earlier, both needed guidance on heavy ordnance, as well as an understanding of recent innovations in small arms. Bulloch was ready to learn, but Anderson remained obtuse, unwilling to acknowledge Huse's superior knowledge.

Huse, with patience that was visibly strained, told Anderson in Percy's presence, "Sir, like Major Bulloch, you spent your service in the navy. The small arms used on a ship and by marines are vastly different from the needs of an army who will be in the field for months at a stretch. Ideally, all the soldiers in a unit should have rifles that are capable of effective firing to the same range. Now, your best Enfield rifle will reach out a thousand yards with 90 grains of powder and take a man down with a 520 grain .58 caliber bullet. An older musket may only carry to 150 or 200 yards. How can a major order his unit to open fire at an approaching army 900 yards away if a half or more of his soldiers are wasting their powder and bullets?"

Percy cringed as he listened to Huse lecture Anderson.

"If all your infantry in a regiment have the same caliber weapons, then bullets and cartridges can be mass produced and used by all the soldiers. No infantryman will have to spend his time casting balls from a hand mold. We should make every effort to obtain rifles and pistols with interchangeable parts, so repairs can be made quickly in the field without requiring a gunsmith's shop at hand. A naval engagement may last a few hours. An army battle, four days or a week. The siege of a city or stronghold may be a month or two or more."

Anderson's resentment showed. He in turn patronized the junior officer with sarcasm. "You will agree, *Captain* Huse, that a working musket is better than fighting with a sword or a woodsman's axe, will you not?"

Annoyed, Huse replied, "None would argue otherwise."

Having bested his opponent's arguments, Anderson declared, "Then we should buy and send what we can now, not wait for the *ideal* rifles to present themselves to us in an *ideal* world. Let's give Johnny Reb a weapon he can use, not a receipt for an order."

Anderson insisted on winning an argument. However, he knew that Huse was right and would not interfere as Huse went about his work securing the best weapons for the Confederacy. For Anderson, it was a simple matter of reminding an inferior officer of his position, lest he become accustomed to having his own way to the detriment of good order. With his own superiors Anderson would accept the credit for the prudent purchases made by Huse.

Anderson's less-than-subtle rebuke of Huse was designed to convey a message to Percy as well. But Anderson was more wary of Percy Moorhead. Percy, he surmised, would be a dangerous foe if crossed. Give Anderson credit for sensing that Percy could be a threat to "good order" as Anderson saw it. His instincts would prove correct. But Anderson would have ample opportunity to inflict damage to Percy.

British purveyors of weaponry proved to be staunch supporters of the Confederacy, even if silent on the institution upon which its economy and political ideology were based. When in London, Anderson and Huse together called upon British gun and supplies dealers. Percy sometimes went with them, other times with Bulloch and North, dividing his services between the Confederate army and the Confederate navy. With Anderson and Huse, Percy made repeated calls at the offices of Isaac, Campbell & Company of No. 78 Jermyn St., St. James, run since 1852 by Samuel Isaac, an army contractor.

Over a period of three weeks, the agents of the Confederacy made purchases of more than a dozen rifled field pieces, several heavy coastal guns, more than thirty thousand Enfield rifles and Genoese muskets, and many thousands of bayonets, cartridges, sabers, knapsacks and uniforms. In addition to the London Armoury and Isaac, Campbell, they entered into contracts with John E. Barnett & Sons, Sinclair Hamilton & Co., Benjamin Beasley, Robert Adams, Ross & Co., Thomas Bissell and Charles W. Lancaster. Samuel Isaac was their agent in dealing with some of the suppliers of guns, accoutrements, and uniforms, earning a commission on each transaction. He showed his appreciation by providing dinners and tickets for them to entertainments in London and Liverpool.

One play would prove especially important to Percy.

Chapter 23

An Evening at the Theatre

W hat a splendid view of the stage! Percy, Bulloch, Walker
Fearn and Anderson were amazed at the luxury as they
took their seats in cushioned chairs in an upper-level
stall of London's Adelphi Theatre. The lavish theater had been
entirely rebuilt three years earlier. Now it was filled to capacity
with a seated audience of 1,500, with standing room for another
500. The interior was lighted by an array of gas mantles passed
through a chandelier of cut-glass. In early July, after a week of
successful transactions, Samuel Isaac had provided the box seats
for the Confederate officers. Huse and North had already returned
to Liverpool.

This evening's performance was Dion Boucicault's play *The
Colleen Bawn*, a success in New York where it had first opened,
before the American war, and now highly popular in London. The
set was extravagant. When, in the second act, Percy viewed a lake
on the stage in which the body of a young girl was seen, he
whispered to Walker Fearn that it must have been inspired by a
painting portraying the drowning Ophelia that he had seen a week
before at the Royal Academy of Arts. The action was no less
spectacular than the sets. The act was brought to a triumphant close
when the author/actor Boucicault dove into the water to rescue the
girl. Bulloch only yawned; Anderson shifted uncomfortably in his

seat.

In scene five, a young woman was identified as Kathleen Creagh. It was a small part, but there was something familiar to Percy about the actress. He borrowed a copy of the playbill from Fearn and strained to read it under the dimmed gas light. He was surprised to find that Kathleen Creagh was played by Miss Grace Tarkenton; she was also identified as the understudy for the principal role of Eily O'Connor. The young lady who had annoyed him as a precocious teen ten years earlier aboard the *Baltic* and at the Tarkenton home in Godstow, outside Oxford, had finally made it to the stage as she had dreamed of doing, following her girlhood heroine, Fanny Kemble. The performance ended with thunderous applause for the actors and author.

At the back of the Adelphi was a tavern for after-play entertainment, named the Cider Cellars. While the four Confederates were enjoying a drink after the performance, it occurred to Percy that he had been in England for the span of five weeks, and he had made no inquiries about Grace's father, Sir James Tarkenton. Since he had passed a pleasant three days at their home in 1852, he had given no thought to the family. When last he had visited with Sir James, the English lawyer and diplomat was planning to go into the government of Lord Derby with the Board of Trade. He would be a good man to call upon if he were still active. He must be in his early sixties now.

Anderson and Percy took a cab back to Hatchetts Hotel, Piccadilly, Dover Street, where Major Anderson had taken several rooms. In the swaying coach Anderson bluntly asked, "What's your assessment of Huse? You've been with him longer than me or Bulloch."

Aware of Anderson's critical views, Percy with no hesitancy replied, "I find him honest and very diligent in the discharge of his duties. He's untiring in his efforts to acquire weapons and supplies for the Confederacy. He understands our needs completely. For a

West Point man, he's more kind-hearted than most I've known."

Anderson wasn't satisfied. "I don't doubt his knowledge of weapons and the Confederacy's needs. Kindness, however, is often a fault in an army man. And is he prudent in undertaking commitments obligating the Confederate government to pay for goods?"

Percy continued to defend Huse. Concealing his annoyance at Anderson's patent effort to turn him against Huse, Percy said evenly, "Do you mean, does he drive a hard-enough bargain? I think Huse, better than most men, knows that time is of the essence for us in the present conflict – as you yourself have called to his attention. We are in competition with the Union government, which has more men and money than we have or will be able to get. To haggle over prices today and lose a deal will require us to pay half again as much tomorrow, if the guns are even available. He has developed good-will among the merchants who supply us by not using hard tactics in his dealings."

Reminding Percy of his junior rank, Anderson intoned, "When a few more years wrinkle your brow, Lieutenant, you'll see better that following regulations is essential in all tasks, great and small. They are indispensable to good order, even if we do not immediately see how."

"Even in a crisis, Major?" Percy's voice was more polite than he actually felt as he pushed back.

Anderson became more emphatic. "*Especially* in a crisis. Men who can't comply with procedures fall into disorder. I have the impression that the good-will you speak of is reciprocated by the commission agents who share a commission with the purchasing agent. Is that your understanding?

"I believe it is a universal custom among English merchants and agents."

"But we are not English, are we. Do you know if Huse is receiving such payments?" Anderson demanded sharply.

"I can't speak to what he does or does not receive," Percy said cautiously. He liked Huse and thought him extraordinarily knowledgeable and efficient. He did not wish to convey to Anderson anything that might be used against Huse. And he knew that Anderson was probing Percy himself about his own dealings with the English merchants. "For myself, I credit any amount that may be set aside for me to the monies the Confederacy owes to reimburse the account of the Anglo-Mexican Tehuantepec Company that I have drawn upon for the Confederacy. The net to me is zero. This shows in the figures I submit to Charles Prioleau who disburses the funds he receives from our government. The accounting is scrupulous, I can assure you."

Anderson replied with a hint of smugness, "Of that, I'm confident, Moorhead. I've adopted a similar procedure. The commission agents insist on setting aside money for me as it would be improper to their way of thinking to retain such customary payments for themselves. I learned this when I made a series of purchases from Ross & Company. When I drew a sight draft for £10,000 on Fraser, Trenholm & Co., Mr. Ross returned to me a voucher in full for the same as my receipt. After a few more minutes of what I took to be idle conversation, he quietly passed over to me a check for two hundred and fifty odd pounds, payable to myself individually, as a return commission for my transaction with him. I told him I understood this was the English way of doing business and that his government permitted its officers to receive these commissions. But it is not our lawful custom. I declined to receive the check, and I asked him to make out the bill I had run up with him, less my commission and to let me change my order on Fraser, Trenholm & Co. for that amount."

Percy asked, "And did he?"

Scowling, Anderson said, "The man positively refused to comply, telling me it was an established rule with them to render their accounts as they had done with me and that they could not and would not deviate from their rule. So, I have adopted the practice to subtract such amounts from the prices reported to the government."

"I'm sure that will be appreciated in our capital." Percy doubted that Anderson detected his irony. Could Anderson be unaware that war profiteering was common, even rampant, in the Confederate legislature and among many other government officials?

Finding Percy reluctant to criticize Huse for any breach of ethical duties, Anderson shifted his ground. "In your opinion on the zeal of Captain Huse, I perhaps concur. However, I have concerns that he lacks discretion and judgment in his intercourse with men. In his peculiar position as chief purchasing agent for the Confederacy he is too ready to mix in with men from the North whom he chances to meet with here. They are now the enemy, and he must put aside his friendly instincts even if they were friends before. They are no longer his countrymen."

Percy would not relent in his unqualified support of Huse. He asserted, "Captain Huse is a man given to common decency and unfailing courtesy. More cogently, I've observed that Captain Huse's manner has disarmed his Northern counterparts, resulting in them inadvertently yielding valuable intelligence to him about their methods and purposes. If these are faults in the circumstances, I shall call them to his attention."

Anderson continued, obtuse that Percy patronized him, "Yes. And if you should find that Huse is accepting commissions and retaining them, you would do him a favor to caution him against it."

With exaggerated courtesy, Percy responded, "Of course. I will relay to him word of your commendable practice."

Anderson would not let it go. He was now lecturing Percy as a warning. "It's not just a matter of good order for Huse. It's the English who must be made to understand we receive no commissions. We pay no bribes. They must learn that if they want our business, they must conduct business as we insist."

Percy snapped back, "Without us, they lose a sale. Without them, we lose our country. Where else can we acquire arms and ships?"

Undeterred by Percy's gibe, Anderson continued doggedly, "We can't be weak, Moorhead. As to the Anglo-Mexican Tehuantepec Company, if you are in fact using the company's funds for the Confederacy, shouldn't you turn over all of its assets to the government for its disposition?"

"I beg to differ, Major Anderson. That would amount to expropriation of private property owned by more than a few investors. Should the owners of slaves, such as yourself, turn over their own property to the cause of the Confederacy? In reality, the funds are in the nature of a debt still owed to a Mr. Falconnet, a British subject, not a Confederate. I am merely in a position to borrow against them in these exigent circumstances."

"You and Attorney General Benjamin?"

Smoothly, and suppressing his growing irritation, Percy replied, "My role as agent of the company is entirely separate from my duties to the Attorney General and President Davis."

Percy had the uncomfortable sense that Anderson was looking for improprieties on his part and on the part of Judah Benjamin. He was a politician storing away intelligence that he could use against rivals should the need arise. One never knew who might prove to be a rival.

Chapter 24

A Paris Excursion

Meeting at the Fraser, Trenholm offices the following Tuesday, Percy, Anderson, Bulloch and Huse reviewed the status of their arms and supplies that were to be sent to the Confederacy. Anderson began by stressing the urgency of the circumstances. "We can't consolidate what we have procured until we know from what port we will ship to the Confederacy. We must begin sending everything soon before shortages become critical. But we have no ships." He relished the role, acting as a senior officer to subordinates, generously seeking their input, but reserving decision to himself. Their purchases were stored in a dozen locations under innocuous descriptions or were held by their suppliers in London, Manchester and Liverpool awaiting instructions for delivery.

Percy knew that Bulloch had already made the necessary arrangements without consulting Anderson. Bulloch would not make an enemy of Anderson. But he would not let him interfere with his carrying out his mission. Percy had observed the antagonism growing between Anderson and Bulloch: Anderson had tried to interfere with Bulloch's ship building by his criticism of the plans Bulloch and the two shipyards had drawn up. Bulloch pushed back strongly against Anderson's calls for changes and his proposals for cost savings in construction.

Bulloch said to the group, rather than to Anderson, "This morning Charles Prioleau and I talked about a ship that his firm is acquiring to send a load of commodities. She is the *Bermuda*. Edwin Haigh, of Liverpool, is the registered owner of the ship. He'll remain on the books as owner of record. She's an iron-hulled merchantman. Screw-driven, large capacity."

"For our use alone?" Anderson was surprised that he hadn't been consulted. Bulloch's force of character prevented Anderson from saying more.

"No," explained Bulloch. "His firm is sending goods on their own account. Some military supplies they intend to sell to our government and to some of the states. From other private goods they expect substantial profits. They're selling space to other people, probably speculators, as best I can tell. They'll give us space on the same terms as the others." Bulloch quoted the price per square foot.

"Damn, that's piracy!" Anderson exclaimed angrily, resentful of both the charges and that all this was news to him. "Aren't they making enough money with the commissions they charge for every financial transaction that passes through their hands? Hell, this amounts to extortion."

Prioleau was a civilian, thus outside the military chain of command. And Prioleau controlled all funds, even those for Anderson's activities.

Bulloch understood the realities and risks better than Anderson. Matter-of-factly, he said, "Prioleau says it's a huge challenge. If the ship is sunk or intercepted, they lose the vessel and all their own goods. Insurance is out of the question in this war. If this were an ordinary commercial voyage last year, I'd say the price was too high. But the *Bermuda* must first make it out of England and then face the Union Navy across the entire Atlantic. They will be eager to seize contraband of war. Without the private goods aboard, we couldn't pay for the voyage at any price."

Sullen, Anderson continued to complain. "We have no choice? At these rates, we need to think about buying our own ships." He was as much upset by his own limited authority (about which he would not speak) as about the charges.

More concerned about security than costs, Percy redirected Anderson's concerns, shifting the discussion. He was determined that Anderson's pettiness should not disrupt cohesion of the agents. "Will the *Bermuda* be loaded in Liverpool? When we start consolidating our supplies, we're bound to draw attention."

"No word from Prioleau on that yet," replied Bulloch, not keen to suffer another harangue from Anderson. "Liverpool has advantages. But we're being watched closely here."

Percy nodded. "True. In the meantime, I suggest we label most of the crates, wherever they are, as destined for the Tehuantepec Rail Company, Vera Cruz, Mexico. This should draw away the attention of Union agents."

Anderson regained his composure, perhaps aware he seemed endlessly disagreeable. He outranked the other three but needed their goodwill to carry out his assignments, ill-defined as they were. He, too, changed the subject, saying, "I've gotten letters from France that we might secure a large lot of good French muskets. Judge Rost has been in Paris for a couple of weeks. He's been approached by an ex-New Orleans resident he knows, a Paul Pecquet du Bellet. He claims he has influence enough with the French Emperor to get all the muskets we want. Is he someone you know, Moorhead?"

Percy was noncommittal and vague. "A nodding acquaintance. He practiced law in New Orleans when I started out, but we never engaged in litigation. He moved to Paris six or seven years ago. I can't vouch for his character. Rost was on the Louisiana Supreme Court at the time. He may know him from there. Or socially. It's worth looking into." Percy was skeptical of Rost and Pecquet, but Anderson's temper and ego needed soothing.

Anderson brightened, relieved that he could recover at least the appearance of leadership. "Then I say, let's see what Paris has to offer. Who will join me? It's a surprisingly short trip." The other men readily agreed.

The next morning, the four Confederate agents took an early train from Liverpool to London. By two that afternoon, they had transferred stations and were on a pleasant seventy-mile run by the South Eastern Railway to Folkstone. They said little to one another lest they call attention to themselves. When they arrived at the harbor, the tide was out. The little steamer that was to ferry them across the English Channel was almost hidden by the dock alongside of which she was moored.

After a calm passage across the Channel, they reached Boulogne where another rail connection awaited them. The route from Boulogne to Paris was well developed and smooth; they reached the French capital before midnight. At the depot their baggage was sorted and examined by the Custom House officials who immediately refused to clear their arrival on learning they had no passports.

With hauteur equal to that of the French bureaucrats, Percy took the lead, in French he had learned from Odessa, denying vehemently that they needed passports. "Nous sommes Anglais!" The skeptical French officials were in no mood for a confrontation at so late an hour and had no means of denying that the four were Englishmen who were not required to present passports. Before three a.m., the four were safely registered as guests at the Hôtel du Helder, north of the Boulevard des Italiens.

Following breakfast, the party called on Judge Rost and his friend from New Orleans, Paul Pecquet du Bellet. The man with them was introduced as Thomas Butler King, a former Georgia Congressman who now represented his state's interests in Europe. Pecquet had impressed Rost and King as a person of consequence.

Anderson and Bulloch took an immediate dislike to Pecquet du Bellet. Percy and Huse assessed him as merely an eccentric who was to be ignored unless he had something exceptional to offer. The ex-Louisianan was comfortably established in luxurious apartments, near the Théâtre Séraphin, Boulevard Montmartre. Though noon was only an hour away, he was still dressed in a fancy parti-colored morning gown.

Misjudging his audience, Pecquet talked in an excited lisp about arms and ships as though he was thoroughly familiar with the nation's war matériel. He strove to impress them with his knowledge and importance. Anderson quickly surmised he was a *poseur* and took the conceit out of him within the hour by a succession of withering questions. Pecquet became conscious of his own inferiority in the discussion and wilted. He sat down, meekly defiant in his facial expressions. Anderson determined the group should have nothing to do with him, a self-promoting humbug, too greedy to meet the exigencies of the Confederacy. But the group still had to deal with Georgia's agent and with Rost. They could not be dismissed so easily.

Anderson had known Thomas Butler King, though not well, when both were Georgia politicians. King had represented Savannah in Congress, the city for which Anderson had served as mayor before the outbreak of the war. Despite Anderson's disdain for Pecquet, King prevailed on Anderson to pursue the purchase of muskets from the French government's arsenal at Vincennes and to give Pecquet another chance to establish his ability to assist. Anderson and Percy agreed to meet again with Pecquet, though Bulloch and Huse would have to return to England for business before visiting the Vincennes arsenal. Exaggerating his own influence, King told Anderson that he had been invited to spend three days with the Count de Morny and that the Emperor wished to see him sometimes towards the close of the month.

King confided to Anderson that he was awaiting money from the Georgia government; if he were to make a suitable presentation as a representative of the Confederacy, it would be desirable for Anderson or Percy to lend him a thousand or fifteen hundred dollars from their Confederate funds. King had a card to play that he had withheld until this moment. He informed them that the French police had visited him to inquire about the four "Englishmen" quartered in the Hôtel du Helder. The police prefect was now aware that they were Confederate agents and were in need of passports, which King would be happy to assist in obtaining.

Anderson took Percy aside. "Do you have the impression that we are being taken advantage of?"

Percy nodded ruefully, commenting, "Paris is like New Orleans. It's a city that serves as the refuge of impecunious exiles. They trade on the only currency they brought with them – their patriotic ties to visiting countrymen. At most, we owe them a respectful hearing and vague assurances that we will do what we can on their behalf."

Anderson couldn't disagree. "Suggestions?"

Percy proposed, "I think we can give Mr. King fifty francs to pass on to the police for proper passports. I know that you are an old friend of his, but I think we must impress upon President Davis and the Cabinet that each state of the Confederacy cannot conduct its own foreign policy. The Confederate States of America must speak with one voice in the courts of Britain and Europe. We cannot let the French or British think we are fractious. Even if we are."

Anderson nodded, agreeing reluctantly with Percy's acute assessment. He was undecided whether to treat Lt. Moorhead as an ally or as an impediment. It was, for now, best not to make an enemy of Judah Benjamin's protégé.

Before Bulloch and Huse departed, Commissioner Pierre Rost invited them all to dinner at the restaurant of the Hôtel du Tiber, just down from their own quarters. He said he would recount his recent interview with Edouard Thouvenel, the French minister of foreign affairs who had welcomed him as a native son, a true *fils de France*.

That evening, the group dined on *canard aux navets*, roasted duck with turnips, and *petits pois au beurre*, green peas in butter. The fare was a bit rich for Percy's taste, but he ate politely with the others. Rost was in good humor, telling the Confederate agents that he was encouraged by Minister Thouvenel's positive outlook and willingness to share the Emperor's favorable impressions on the South's fortunes. Thouvenel had told Rost they should be patient on the matter of recognition: either a decisive Confederate victory or the great demand for cotton in England and France would likely accomplish their objective.

"Time is on our side," regaled Rost. "As our French brothers would say, *tout va bien* – all goes well. Two questions occupy the attention of both the English and French governments. First, how to obtain cotton from the Confederacy next fall, and, second, how to pay for it without depleting their gold supply."

"And what do you recommend?" asked Anderson.

Rost was as expansive in his pronouncements as he was unrealistic on their prospects for success. "We need to make sure that 4,500,000 bales of cotton are available for export in Southern ports by early fall. The iron law of necessity will justify European ships in coming for it, blockade or no blockade. As to the difficulty over gold, I've suggested to Parisian bankers that the Confederate Congress might be willing to make, for a limited time and at a determined value, the notes of the Bank of France real tender in payment of debts, so as to give them currency in our states. We would dispense with the importation of gold." Rost took another bite of *canard* and looked pleased with himself. Life as a diplomat he took to be the fulfillment of a career, concluding now as a statesman of a new nation, the Confederate States of America, returning to his hereditary home, *la belle France*.

Anderson looked to Percy. "Lieutenant Moorhead, you know the cotton business better than any of us. Your thoughts?" For now, he was outwardly treating Percy as an ally.

"A sound idea, Judge Rost." For his part, Percy would say nothing to dampen Rost's enthusiasm, no matter how unsound his ideas. He knew the group of four would not benefit from negative reports that Rost might send to Richmond. He explained, "Cotton is the key to our success. May I urge you to write our government and impress upon them that under no circumstances should they embargo the shipment of cotton. Moreover, they should prevent the states of the Confederacy from suppressing the cultivation or export of cotton."

Percy had not fully appreciated the sensitivity of the issue. Rost responded quickly, "But this war is being fought over the sovereignty of each state." He was immediately concerned that a bedrock principle of secession had been questioned. King, the envoy of the sovereign state of Georgia, made his agreement with Rost known by the sharp expression he directed at Percy and the vigorous shaking of his head.

"True, sir." Percy's reply was polite but no less firm: "But a strong centralized government in the North will defeat a fractious collection of states with inconsistent policies. This is true of cotton as our major diplomatic tool. It's also true that your wise suggestion of currency policy can only be implemented if Treasury Secretary Memminger has centralized authority over state monetary matters."

Rost was untroubled by his own inconsistencies or that Percy might be patronizing him. Was it not self-evident that the Confederate Congress had to have the final say on currency, despite the individual preferences of the states of the Confederacy? Percy had seen clearly that when Rost was on the Louisiana Supreme Court, he was often inconsistent, but seldom in doubt, the sort of judge for whom legal principles needed to conform to his opinions.

Rost, wishing to remain the genial host, replied without

addressing Percy's cotton concerns. "I'm sure President Davis will be able to navigate through the problems. *Tout va bien.* I've spoken with the two other commissioners. Here is what we need from you. When you return to the South and meet with the government in Richmond you must stress the great importance of secure communication between us and the Department of State. We must have the power to employ messengers. Secretary Toombs has deemed it too expensive a mode of communication, unless we are to announce the fact of recognition or of a treaty we might make."

Ready to find common ground with Judge Rost, Percy informed him, "I plan to return to the South soon. What message shall I deliver?"

The envoy had considered the matter: "If we might be allowed to suggest a plan, it would be this: that our government employ a resident agent upon the Confederacy's frontier, and another at some proper point in Canada, and that every week, or every fortnight, or as often as occasion requires, a messenger should carry dispatches over the intermediate country, both to and from the commission. This will be attended with some risk and expense, but it must be conceded that communication across a hostile country can only be carried on by incurring both."

Anderson expressed agreement with Commissioner Rost. "You can count on us to do exactly that, Judge Rost. We have the same frustration of being unable to communicate freely with our government."

Percy remained silent. He could have said that Davis and Judah Benjamin had already begun a Secret Service and that the South had a very effective agent in New York City, Rufus Jordan. But the others need not know.

Two days later, the follow-up meeting with Pecquet at King's request produced even less satisfactory results than the first. The visit to the arsenal at Vincennes was deemed unnecessary by Pecquet: He had obtained samples of the muskets for inspection by Anderson and Percy. At his apartments, Pecquet proudly displayed three of the guns, which he said could be purchased in unlimited number. Although the normal French commission was higher, as a patriotic gesture he said he would expect the Confederacy to pay him only three francs on each weapon that they should contract for. Major Anderson and Lt. Moorhead made a show of handling the muskets and dry-firing the mechanisms while aiming at a wall. Then they went down the stairs and exited to the boulevard as quickly as they could.

"Those samples were the worst trash imaginable," Anderson declared in exasperation.

Responded Percy, "More dangerous, I would suppose, to the soldier firing one than the intended target," happy to agree with Anderson on something. "And no doubt these are the best he could come up with. The French must be trying to sell arms that remained after Waterloo. Or were already retired before the battle."

Despite himself, Anderson laughed at Percy's wit. The two agreed that Huse would be tasked with future negotiations for French arms, but not through Monsieur du Bellet.

ᕧ — ᕦ

Percy and Edward Anderson left at five p.m. for London by the night train. In the railway carriage with them was a traveler who was evidently a Yankee. He regarded them with special attention. Not concealing his disdain, Anderson said aloud to Percy that the man must be part of the Union's espionage system.

They reached Boulogne at midnight. The weather was more stormy than the journey over to France. The same little channel steamer awaited them, nearly hidden away under the lee of the pier which loomed high above her bulwarks. She revealed only her stout smokestack.

Although the channel waters were choppy, they arrived at Folkstone three hours later. The London train left at four in the morning, arriving in London at half past six o'clock.

The man who had boarded the train in Paris right after them never let them out of his sight.

Would there be others?

Chapter 25

Manassas

The first accounts of the great Confederate victory at the battle of Manassas reached Percy, Anderson and Huse while they were conferring at the Fraser, Trenholm offices in Liverpool. The news was carried aboard a steamer from New York that called at Queenstown, Ireland on August 4, 1861. These first reports were relayed by Reuter's telegraph to newspapers in Liverpool and London.

The Fraser, Trenholm clerk at the front desk rushed into the conference room with the morning's first paper. Excited by the headline "Rebels Rout Yanks at Manassas Junction!" the three agents spread the paper on table. The article described the first large-scale engagement of Union and Confederate soldiers that had taken place twenty-some miles from the District of Columbia two weeks earlier, on July 21. Aloud, Caleb Huse gleefully read: "The Union army under General McDowell initially drove back Confederate forces under General Beauregard, but the arrival of troops under General Joseph E. Johnston by rail from the Shenandoah Valley started a series of reversals for the Northerners."

Eager to celebrate and to share the exciting news with their host, the three men summoned a cab to go to Charles Prioleau's country estate outside Liverpool. Cheering the welcome victory, the four Southerners ran a Confederate flag up on Prioleau's housetop and shot fireworks into the air.

ᴄᴏ⥾ - ⥾ᴏᴄ

Three days later, Percy found himself among the guests at a grand London soirée that began at six in the evening. The event took place at the home of Sir Alexander Beresford-Hope, Arklow House, near Hyde Park. Sir Alexander was not only very wealthy but also highly sympathetic to the Confederate cause. Such was the excitement in Liverpool and London that he immediately planned a celebration to bring together many of his like-minded and influential friends to applaud the news and to introduce them to representatives of the Confederacy.

The hostess greeting the hundred and twenty guests was Sir Alexander's wife, Lady Mildred, a fixture of London social life. More importantly, she was sister of Lord Robert Cecil, a member of Parliament who was close by his brother-in-law visiting with the attendees. Lord Robert bore the name of his ancestor who was principal minister to Queen Elizabeth and King James I. He would himself become Prime Minister under Queen Victoria when opportunity arose, virtually by hereditary right.

Yancey, Mann and Rost, the Confederate commissioners, were the featured guests of the reception. They had brought with them their secretary, Walker Fearn, and the four agents who were working together – Edward Anderson, Percy Moorhead, James Bulloch, and Caleb Huse. Lieutenant North and his family were on board the *Camilla* off the Isle of Mann, participating in yacht races. Again, North had passed up an opportunity for good public relations with the English supporters of the South.

Beresford-Hope delighted in describing the details of the fighting that he had pulled together from the American papers. He flourished his monocle in his right hand as he recounted to his guests the dramatic role played by a brigade of Virginians under General Thomas J. Jackson, who stood his ground like a stonewall against the Yanks and rallied his troops. The Confederates had then launched a strong counterattack that sent McDowell's army in a panic, retreating back to the defenses of Washington. An aide of Beresford-Hope had prepared a board posted on a wall in the ball room with clippings from the American papers. Under headlines from the *New York Tribune* that said of the Battle of Bull's Run (as the Unionists called it): *Desperate Conflict and Repulse of the Union Troops by an Overwhelming Force: Retreat of the Union Forces.*

Percy stood with a group as they examined another article describing the rout. A guest, a businessman of about forty, read aloud with jaunty approval and dramatic emphasis on the North's chaotic defeat :

> At the beginning of the retirement, a few ambulances and baggage wagons were driven hurriedly away, the noise of which seem to spread terror among the troops within hearing, who instantly broke ranks and ran pell-mell toward Centreville. This contagion caught the rest, and in less than ten minutes our army was flying in the utmost disorder. Everything was abandoned. The wounded were deserted in the hospitals, and the only thought was of individual safety. Guns were thrown aside, and blankets and knapsacks were lost and trampled upon.

> The artillery shared the panic; the guns were cut loose, and the gunners used the horses to escape the more swiftly. Those on foot begged piteously to be allowed to share the horses of those who rode. Many strove to clamber into wagons, and were pushed back by the bayonets of those who occupied them. The ground was strewed with food, weapons, and clothing of every kind. Many of our guns were left to fall into the enemies hands, including the large 32-pounders which had done so much service during the fight. All courage, all manliness seem to have forsaken our terror-stricken men.

Amused by the report, Beresford-Hope was charming in his own way, a distinctive character with full beard. He parted his hair on the right, where it was most receding from his forehead, and combed it severely over to the left, so that he perpetually looked as if he were standing in a gale.

"Don't you find," Beresford-Hope asked Commissioner Yancey, "that Lincoln's background as a rail-splitter, bargeman and self-taught attorney proves him the social inferior to President Davis? He's an atavist of the uncouth Andrew Jackson."

"Indeed," chuckled Yancey, pleased that his efforts as a diplomat were now met with success. "And no general. Lincoln immediately replaced McDowell with McClellan. But who the Union general might be is of no moment. The Union soldier will not fight for a man with no more substance than Lincoln. McClellan will do no better against Johnny Reb than General McDawdle."

Biting into a Cornish prawn held in his left hand and gesturing again with his monocle, Sir Alexander laughed at Yancey's wit and expounded to the group gathered around them, "Talleyrand said that a blunder was worse than a crime. But in President Lincoln we seem to have a man, all whose blunders are crimes, and all whose crimes are blunders."

"Hear! Hear!" enthused several of the speaker's ardent guests.

Raising a glass to his guests, Sir Alexander winked and continued, as though taking them into his confidence on a little-known secret, "I have it on good authority that Mr. Lincoln was foisted into his exalted place by a sort of joint stock company that had been set up as a speculation in politics, on the Republican side in New York. Lincoln was set up by it to oppose Douglas in Illinois, on account of Douglas's then local popularity. Mr. Lincoln gained fame in the East as an orator, but in fact he had not delivered any of the speeches that were attributed to him. It was all a ruse. The New York newspapers sent round a staff of writers and reporters, who accompanied Mr. Lincoln on his canvas. Douglas would make his speech, and whenever Lincoln stuttered, muttered, and mouthed something in reply, the writers and reporters set to work and fabricated a telling speech in Lincoln's name. So much for the political wisdom of the United States."

Hearty laughter resonated throughout the throng of listeners, the most enthusiastic being the three commissioners of the

Confederate government. Sir Alexander rolled on, "And now that the rail-splitter has taken up residence in the White House, Lincoln is reduced to being the hand puppet of the beak-nosed master of the country, Mr. William Henry Seward."

Upon learning that Judge Rost and Percy Moorhead were from Louisiana, numerous guests asked them if they knew General Beauregard – the man who was regarded as the hero of the battle. Percy acknowledged that he had served with him in the Mexican War and knew him from his law practice in New Orleans.

"Is he as handsome as they say?" gushed a baron's wife.

Percy indulged the buxom lady with a smile. "Pierre Toutant has Gallic charm, and his name translates from the native French of his region as good looks, perhaps because of his deep black eyes."

The English lady's ardor only increased. Percy excused himself lest any of her infatuation with the Confederate Napoleon carry over to him.

An hour into the evening, Percy felt a hand upon his shoulder. Turning, he immediately recognized Sir James Tarkenton, older, grayer, but still vigorous.

"I was told a Lt. Moorhead was among the Confederates here. I wondered if it might be my old friend, Percy Moorhead," he said with a warm smile.

"How marvelous to see you here," exclaimed Percy. "I've been meaning for weeks to look you up. But I wasn't sure where. As I recall from my visit in Oxford, you were prescient in seeing the coming of our civil strife."

Sir James replied ruefully, "And tis a pity that it has arrived. You must tell me what has happened with you in the nearly ten years since we were together. You were practicing law in New Orleans. You and your wife were expecting a child, weren't you?"

Percy regretted conveying sad news on this happy occasion. "That's too long and too sad a story for a celebration such as this.

When the war began, I was professor of Rhetoric and Letters in Virginia and a widower. I'm still a lawyer and work for the Attorney General of the Confederacy."

"Interesting," the English lawyer commented. "And how does the Attorney General need a presence in England? I assume you have a State Department for envoys like the commissioners here this evening. Are you an attaché with them?"

"Your observation is acute, as I would have expected. My role is curious. Somewhat like yours when we met. You had just been a commercial consul in New York City. My portfolio includes the facilitation of cotton transactions in the conditions of war." Without providing more detail, Percy redirected the conversation to Sir James. "When last we spoke, you were perhaps going to work with the Board of Trade. Or return to the practice of law."

The Englishman chuckled modestly. "Life might be simpler if I had. Unfortunately, friends prevailed upon me to stand for Parliament. Despite my lack-lustre performance as a candidate and the inadequacy of my qualifications, I won my seat."

"And Clare? How does she take to being married to an MP?"

"Indeed, it was Clare who set me on this misadventure. She is in her natural element. My seat was held by her father twenty years ago. She and her friends persuaded me that I had a duty to seek a seat and restrain the more radical elements who would take over the government. It would have been churlish of me to disappoint her."

"And Grace? Was it not she whom I saw recently in *Colleen Bawn*?"

With a wry smile, Sir James said, "She is as head strong as always. Like her mother. If the two of them do not think the theatre life is beneath her station, who am I to disagree? Grace's friends of the stage take a similarly dim view of those of us who participate in political office. My daughter and I have entered into a mutual compact not to embarrass one another with our activities that might catch the public eye. We are both performers after a fashion. We have our audiences, differ as they may."

Turning to a more serious matter, Percy asked, "Does your presence here indicate that you embrace the Confederacy as does Sir Alexander?"

Sir James was reluctant to appear critical of Percy and his role representing the Confederacy in England. He chose his words carefully. "Percy, I must confess to ambivalence. I found much to admire in your country when I was there for three years as consul, both North and South. It troubles me to see you divided. That said, I would hate to see your Confederacy defeated. President Davis has shown he can win a battle. Can he win a war? I've met with Minister Adams, and he seems as determined to fight this out as you rebels are. Your cause would be easier to defend were it not linked in the English mind with the institution of African slavery."

Percy appreciated his friend's candor. He would be equally open. "Sadly, neither North nor South offered a middle ground. Slavery cannot continue and must be replaced. Many thoughtful Confederates understand this. But what will replace it? An orderly transition is needed even if the Confederacy prevails. Did I say 'if?' That makes me appear doubtful. A good advocate should never display uncertainty."

Sir James paused to sip from the drink he held in his left hand. He looked Percy in the eye. "When advocacy and honesty come in conflict, I dare say I know which side Percy Moorhead will come down on. Clare will be disappointed to have missed you. We would love to have you be our guest in Godstow again. Do your responsibilities allow you time?"

"I look forward to the opportunity. But it will have to wait. I plan to leave shortly to report to my superiors in Richmond."

"Oh? But isn't the Union blocking all ships from entering the South?"

"We shall see," said Percy with a wink. "Words alone do not a blockade make. Proclamations are easily issued. Creating a 3000 mile wall of ships is quite another undertaking. What was it that Glendower says? Something like, *I can call spirits from the vasty deep. And Hotspur replies, So can I, so can any man, but will they come?"*

"Ah, Percy. You must identify with Hotspur. But you will need to excuse me. My colleague, Sir Robert Cecil motions to me, and I must come to his call and attend to ceremony. Do come see us if you return to our island."

Chapter 26
Pub Talk

Percy and Bulloch arrived from Liverpool in late morning to Anderson's commodious London quarters, which were on the second floor at No. 58 Jermyn Street. Anderson admitted them into a large sitting room, verging on the yard below. It was covered overhead with glass to admit light and air. Because it reminded him of an armored enclosure for cannon, Anderson called it the *casemate*. Caleb Huse was already there, seated on a sofa. The four agents would muster at the *casemate* almost daily in the next few weeks to review plans for loading the *Bermuda*.

As they began, Anderson seemed upset. He attributed it to frustration with commissioner Yancey. A few days after the reception at the Beresford-Hope house, Anderson complained to Percy and Bulloch, he had begun receiving visits from Englishmen who were eager to share in the military glory surrounding the unexpected rout of the Yankees at Manassas. The would-be soldiers told him that Mr. Commissioner Yancey had assured them that they could join the army of the Confederate States and that passage by ship to the South would be arranged for them.

Anderson groused, "I called last night on Mr. Yancey to protest. One young man has been hanging around my quarters seeking an army appointment. I put him off. From all I could gather he's an unprincipled, trifling fellow. He went from me back to

Yancey, who gave him letters to the Secretary of War that would procure him employment as an officer. I then learned he was a Yankee spy. When I called on Yancey to express my disapproval of his recommending unknown men to be put in service, I myself being the representative of the War Department in England, I was met by only rudeness from him."

"Why?" asked Huse. "What did he say?"

Anderson's quick change of expression toward Huse showed Percy that the real purpose for criticizing Yancey was to register his dissatisfaction with Huse. Anderson's voice took on a sharp edge. "We had some very plain talk together, in the course of which Yancey became very much excited and as if to back up his venom, he said that you had told him that 20,000 muskets had been lost to us in France in consequence of a delay of one day on my part to authorize their purchase. I told the commissioner that you had nothing whatever to do with my purchases and that all guns submitted to our inspection were worthless."

At this accusation, Huse was visibly disturbed. He disliked confrontation, responding emotionally in defense, "I never said it was your fault or responsibility. The commissioner has entirely misinterpreted me. I distinctly told him that your delay *saved* us from buying guns of an inferior quality. More likely, Judge Rost was upset that his friend from New Orleans wasn't able to get a sale, and he carried this to Yancey. It is a canard of the most disreputable sort, a calumny against me."

Seeing Anderson was spoiling for a quarrel, Percy interjected to try to calm the meeting, "Let's reflect for a minute on the problems of the commissioners. They came over here just as the Confederacy was being formed. They were sent by an unelected president for an undefined assignment of an indefinite duration. They were given very little money and no authority to conclude treaties or enter into contracts on behalf of the new country they represent. If they feel that they are making no progress, they may suggest it is us and not they who are responsible when their mission produces little to help our cause." Percy paused, then continued, appealing to the fact that his three colleagues were military men, "Neither Yancey nor Rost knows anything about muskets and rifles, and they will not have to carry a weapon we buy into battle. Come what may, we four sink or swim together. Together, we have to get arms and powder for the next battles our men will face. Quibbling, we fail."

Bulloch approved the sentiment, adding, "In his absence, I'll have to say I think several of you share my wariness at the contributions of James North. We need to be on the lookout that he not sow discord, either among us or with the commissioners."

"Right," said Anderson moving on, sensitive to the implied rebuke from Percy and Bulloch. *Quibbling* had stung. "Let's get the *Bermuda* loaded and purchase our own vessel so we don't put off getting guns and supplies to our people back home."

Bulloch appeared grateful that the subject was no longer Huse. "Prioleau has the *Bermuda* across England from us. She's tied up at West Hartlepool. The rail connections from Liverpool, Manchester, and Birmingham are very good. The distance from London is not much farther. I've long had experience with customs and cargo manifest protocols, so I'll spend the next few weeks organizing the loading myself. Prioleau will have his own man superintending the goods that they're sending."

Anderson, conciliatory. "Agreed. Let's pool our resources and coordinate with our contractors. Do we have a date for sailing?"

Bulloch, shrugging. "About August 20, says Prioleau."

"That soon? Do you still plan to go with her, Percy?"

Percy laid aside the pen with which he had been taking notes. "I feel I should. If the Confederacy is going to look to cotton to finance this war, I need to see how we can make it happen. This year's harvest will soon be baled. We've got to find ways to get it here. The Confederacy isn't a cotton grower, so we're going to have to tax private sales or have a tariff on exports. Or we're going to have to buy and sell cotton like a broker. If someone in Richmond has thought this through, we need to have that information over here. Our people in the capital need to know the problems we're having with the spies working for Adams and the Union's consuls and the difficulties they cause for us with the English government."

Anderson, agreeably. "You're right, of course. We have to have our own counterintelligence. Percy, you must impress upon President Davis and his cabinet how difficult are our conditions – to cope with spies, the lack of cash, competition from Union purchasing agents, poor communications."

Percy smiled amiably, as though he was accepting direction from Anderson. What he would impress upon Judah Benjamin was the need to counter negative reports and unproductive recommendations Anderson was surely sending to Richmond. Judah had the cunning to undercut Anderson's influence with Davis and the others of the cabinet. Percy was all the more certain he needed to sail aboard the *Bermuda* in advance of Anderson to shore up support for the work of Bulloch and Huse.

The four spent the next two hours cataloging the goods they had purchased or were on order that could be shipped on the *Bermuda*. Anderson continued to lead the planning. "Okay, it's clear we've got to arrange a second shipment and then more. How shall we go about it?"

Bulloch spoke up, "We can't look to commercial shipping to carry anything into the South. They're afraid of the blockade and the obstacle of a war. We can see if Fraser, Trenholm will offer another ship. It's costly, and it wouldn't be under our control. Or we can consider buying one. There's no shortage of ships to purchase in Britain."

Anderson supported the suggestion. "As much as we owe to Fraser, Trenholm, it comes at a heavy price. I favor buying our own. What do y'all say?"

All three agreed readily.

Satisfied that the others followed his lead, Anderson in good nature volunteered, "Let's adjourn to the public house across the street for a few drinks. On me this time."

Five minutes later the quartet of Confederate agents, the South's operatives controlling the acquisition of more arms than commanded by any Confederate general and more ships than sailed under any Confederate naval commander, strolled casually into the pub under the sign of the Turks Head. No heads turned at their entrance. Few in London had an inkling that the success or failure of the Confederacy depended on their exertions. They would not be mistaken for Englishmen, but whether they were Americans from the North or from the South was not apparent.

Shortly after being seated in leather-upholstered chairs, Bulloch observed, "I suppose our consensus shows we share the assumption the war will not end soon."

"No, I think not," admitted Anderson reluctantly. "Lincoln is in office for three more years. He has shown determination, and the northern states have answered the call for troops. They have more men, money, munitions and resources than we can muster. We must prevail by our determination and the justness of our cause."

"Well, that's a cheerful thought." Bulloch was trying to sound jocular.

"I don't intend to remain here longer than necessary," Anderson continued. "I believe I will be more useful returning to command."

Percy was not surprised. Anderson would prefer to be in charge of a regiment rather than here. From the start, Percy had seen that Anderson was uncomfortable: all three of the other men were more competent at their work than he. He was out of his element, trying to be a leader by virtue of rank among men who needed no leader.

Percy changed the course of the conversation, as he often did to maintain cohesion of the group. "And after our war, where will your inclinations take you?"

Anderson was taken back by the question. Perhaps Percy was attempting to get him to confess doubts about victory. He realized, however, that Percy may have given him an opening. "I plan to become the first post-war senator from Georgia to the Confederate Congress."

Percy looked to Bulloch. "And you, James? You are a Georgian. Will you enter politics?"

Bulloch scoffed, good-naturedly. "I'd rather beg alms than votes. These business transactions are not disagreeable. I rather fancy the idea of working for my own account and not be subject to the direction of others. Business it is for me. Care to join with me, Caleb? We make a pretty good team."

"Don't we all just want to go home?" mused Huse. "Aren't we doing this to protect our families and friends? I've been happiest in a college setting, at West Point and Alabama. I'm more scientist than soldier. I feel more at ease with students than with men of affairs and professional soldiers."

Percy objected to Huse's self-deprecation: "But Caleb, look how much you've accomplished in so short a time. You have a knack not found in books."

Huse deflected the compliment. "I've done no more than what had to be done. And we've a long way to go. Others may do better. A man must know himself. Negotiations and confrontation are not my pleasures."

Anderson let Huse's statement stand, turning instead to Percy. "Moorhead, we haven't heard much from you. Didn't you inherit a cotton plantation in Mississippi, as I've been told?"

"Bulloch's heard my story, but you other two haven't. I'm afraid I lost my family and my home in Louisiana before this war. I can't blame it on Lincoln or Republicans. It was fate and an Irish scoundrel who claims he's my brother."

Huse was affected. He put his hand on Percy's arm. "That must be hard to bear. You've never let on."

Shrugging, as though indifferent, Percy said, "It was long ago. Or it was yesterday. My father . . . . ." He was silent for a moment and looked at each of his three companions. He saw no reason to share his sad tale with these three. "I guess I'll teach after this. Or practice law. And I'll write about how we founded a new country." After a pause, he added, "Or why we failed."

Huse again spoke. "Don't you believe in destiny?"

Shaking his head, Percy said flatly, "Destiny is what's left when our plans fall apart. I had one life, and most of it was taken from me. I began another in Virginia, and this war interceded. Destiny has swept aside all my plans. She is likely to do so again. I've learned the wisdom of the philosopher who wrote 'Do not want what you cannot have.' It is pleasant here. I am among friends and doing work that is worthwhile and important for others. So, *carpe diem*. Cheers, my friends. Let us raise our glasses in a toast to the Confederate States of America. May she and we live long and prosper."

Percy made his way to Hatchetts Hotel by himself. He was tiring of his self-imposed role as the unofficial mediator among the Confederate agents. It required that he dissemble to them and to the three commissioners, but dissimulation was necessary if the parties were to maintain cohesion to fulfill the responsibilities given them.

The hour was late. As he passed beneath a gaslight, he heard a woman's voice. Turning to his left he said, "Did you speak to me?"

"I said you look lonely."

In the dim light she appeared about Percy's age, maybe a little older. She showed a bare ankle and calf from the opening in a light coat. Her hair was reddish-brown beneath a grey cap.

"Very perceptive of you, Miss." Wryly, he asked, "Is that your professional opinion?"

"It's what is. I can be good company." She stepped closer, so she could be seen in the light.

"For a price, madam, and I'm sure it is money well-spent. But I would prefer not to." With a light bow, he returned to his walk, his spirits curiously lifted by the encounter. The hotel was only two blocks more. Percy realized he was lonely, yes, but not desperate. His self-respect would not allow him to engage in a transaction he regarded as demeaning to both parties. This, he still retained.

Percy wished he had someone in whom he could confide, to express his frustration, especially at being unable to see whether his efforts in England would bear fruit at home. But where was home? Louisiana? Virginia? The Confederate States of America? He missed Philomena. Could another ever take her place? Could he find another place he could call home?

Chapter 27

Memories of Maguire

C oncealing his nearly instant distaste for Edwin de Leon was
difficult for Percy. He had heard enough from the former
American envoy to Egypt in the first fifteen minutes of his
meandering discourse to form a firm opinion of the man. Although
this occasion was a mid-August dinner for de Leon at London's
Westminster Hotel arranged by Commissioner Yancey, weeks
earlier Bev Tucker had told Percy to expect de Leon sooner or later.
Like Bev, de Leon was American diplomat stranded in Europe with
no portfolio as his position had been dissolved by the solvent of
secession.

Percy had asked, "And when I expect him, what should I
expect?"

"Take him in small doses," was all Bev would allow, with a
knowing wink.

"Meaning?" Percy didn't like intelligence withheld. He
insisted on a reason.

"Let me put it like this. He and I were both publishing
newspapers in Washington ten years ago. He was already so ardent
in pushing for secession, President Pierce found the only way to
calm the waters was by sending de Leon to Egypt where he'd be a
thorn in the bonnet to Arabs and mummies." Bev Tucker had also

told Percy that De Leon's father was a Sephardic Jew whose family had emigrated from Spain and had prospered in Columbia, South Carolina. Now, he considered himself a natural aristocrat.

Looking around the Westminster Hotel dinner table and seeing new faces, Percy thought London had become a crossroads for Confederates coming and going. This to be his last dinner in London before himself returning to the South. In addition to Percy, the dinner was attended by Mann, Rost, Anderson, Bulloch and Walker Fern, as well as two others: A Dr. Smithers of Texas, a round faced, round headed, round bellied man, with gold spectacles across his nose who remained as silent as a Cheshire cat; and a Mr. Tarleton of Alabama, who was in England with, he said, £300,000 from the state, for the purchase of arms. The guest of honor was de Leon, who was both coming and going. He had come to London to ingratiate himself with the three Confederate commissioners and to arrange a voyage to Richmond to join the government at a level commensurate with his high regard for himself.

When Yancey introduced Percy to de Leon as a Confederate lawyer from Louisiana working with the procurement agents, de Leon must have thought he was being clever when he quipped, "I was a lawyer once myself. But I found it more rewarding to excite thousands of readers through the newspapers than grinding out pro forma documents with hackneyed legalese. You must have found it tedious too, did you not?" Percy found de Leon was condescending, if not outright arrogant.

"Oh, indeed, Sir. Indeed, I did, which is why I became a professor of Rhetoric," said Percy, speaking as though he agreed fully with de Leon but adding slyly, "Yet, I find that it is the hackneyed legalese, as you put it, of contracts that allow us to get ships built and arms purchased. Tedious? Yes. But crucial."

De Leon appeared uncertain whether Percy might be mocking him. He turned as Yancey began the dinner.

"Edwin," announced Yancey to the assembly of Southerners, "has shared with me some of his observations as someone who has been away from his home for an extended period."

Percy could see how pleased de Leon was to be able to present himself to his fellow citizens of the Confederacy. It gave him an opportunity to rehearse the presentations he would need to make in Richmond, when he would advise President Davis and the Cabinet of their need for a presence in the newspapers and other publications of Britain and Europe.

Standing to address the other guests, de Leon began, in a manner that struck Percy as officious and arrogant, "Let me say first I mean no criticism of present company, especially of you commissioners of the Confederacy, or of you gentlemen who have been laboring so hard to supply our army and navy. The procurement of weapons and vessels is of the utmost importance. What is lacking, however, is attention to public opinion in Britain and France. The Union controls the sources of news going to them. All they learn of the Confederacy is one-sided and most negative. All they know of slavery is what they have read in Mrs. Stowe's *Uncle Tom's Cabin*. We have a story to tell. Recognition of the Confederate States will come from the British and French leaders when their people are persuaded it is the right thing to do."

"I beg to differ, Mr. de Leon," interposed Dudley Mann in his customarily diplomatic, understated manner. "While I agree that we suffer in Europe from the false statements which are furnished by the Union for dissemination on this side of the Atlantic weekly, we have not been quiescent. Mr. Paul Reuter, owner of the Reuter Telegraph & News Agency, has a monopoly of the telegraph here in London for the newspapers of all Europe. A short time ago I had two interviews with him. He is not only willing but anxious to furnish his correspondents everywhere with the latest reliable news and intelligence from both sides."

"Oh?" responded de Leon, with obvious interest. "How can we capitalize on this?"

Mann, with some satisfaction, added, "I have proposed to our

Secretary of State that his office prepare a short statement of the most important occurrences, and transmit it per Cunard steamer to us, under cover to M'Iver, agent of Cunard Packets, Queenstown, Ireland. Reuter has agreed to give him directions to telegraph the contents to us the moment the steamer touches at that place. If it were deemed important to communicate twice a week, then a dispatch should be sent to Joseph Sharpe, Southampton, England. The steamers which touch there carry the United States mails and leave New York every Saturday. Both M'Iver and Sharpe are the paid confidential agents of Reuter, and he will have them cooperate with us."

De Leon sought more about the owner of Reuter's. "Is this Reuter such a supporter of the Confederacy?"

Mann admitted that Reuter was motivated more by gain than allegiance. "It seems Minister Adams was approached first by Mr. Reuter but was unwilling to compensate Mr. Reuter for the services he could provide."

"So, we can buy him?" asked de Leon, flashing a lupine grin.

Mann winced at de Leon's crude way of putting it. "We have a commercial arrangement in which we will pay for services. He gains access to exclusive news from Southern sources that he can transmit to his English newspaper clients and those in Europe."

Anderson laughed, "I don't think Adams has any money left to spread around after spending so much on detectives and spies in London, Liverpool and other ports in England."

De Leon, recovering from his excess of candor, said, "I've just arrived here after being away in Egypt. You must tell me more."

Anderson was eager to relate their experiences, "As we sit here, there is somewhere nearby at least one, perhaps two, paid agents of the Union noting our every move. One is writing in his notebook a description of you and will follow you back to your hotel. Another is surely writing down the name of each man at this table. Our waiter will be questioned as to what he may have overheard us say to one another."

De Leon was surprised. "Should I worry about my well-being? I would if I were being followed in Cairo."

Bulloch reassured him. "No. There is no danger. We have all learned to be cautious, to disguise our transactions. My steps as well as those of Anderson and Huse have been dogged by a set of the cleverest London detectives employed by Minister Adams. These men are indefatigable in their attentions, following me wherever I go. My attention was brought to these people by Mr. Isaacs who came over to my quarters one morning and asked me if I knew I was watched. I replied that I had no idea of any such thing. 'Come with me to your window then' said he, 'and I will point out to you a shadow that never loses sight of you,' at the same time directing my notice to a rough looking fellow standing across the street on the corner."

De Leon was reluctant to believe that the English would tolerate such ungentlemanly practices. "Really!"

Bulloch discreetly rolled his eyes and continued. "Determined to make the acquaintance of the gentleman, I passed into the street. Walking up to him, I scanned him carefully from head to foot and asked for direction to some street nearby, which he very civilly complied with. He was a plain, countrified looking man, roughly clad and by no means bearing about him the appearance of a detective. When I came to know him better I was impressed with the effect produced by dress, for when I met my man on the following day, he was accoutered in a neat suit of black clothing, like a gentleman, and on subsequent occasions in different costumes. Sometimes as an English lackey in brown shorts, and again in a semi-military coat. Sometimes with mustache and whiskers, sometimes clean-shaved. I never failed, however, to recognize my shadow. Assisting him were one or two others, employed in like manner in the pay of the American minister. They certainly manifested both zeal and fidelity in their devotion to Mr.

Lincoln and Mr. Seward."

Yancey, still seeking to regain the confidence of Anderson, said, "Major Anderson has had similar experiences. Tell Edwin de Leon about your confrontation with Detectives Brett and Maguire."

Anderson was ready to relate his own surveillance tale. "Last week, I was leaving London for Liverpool from my Jermyn Street quarter. Just as I had put my foot on the cab's step, I saw a detective on the opposite side run rapidly to the corner and jump into another hansom which was evidently awaiting his orders. He was equipped in a neat suit of black clothes, dark hat, stand up collar frock coat and heavy walking shoes, and when I passed out of Jermyn Street into St. James, my shadow was seated in his cab, waiting for me to take the lead. He followed me at a short distance behind to the Eustis Square Station, and as I got out of my vehicle, passed on unconcernedly, leading me to suppose that he had satisfied himself in the information thus far gained that I was leaving London for Liverpool."

De Leon again interjected, "So, another replaced him?"

"No," resumed Anderson. "I had passed into the station house and was counting the change for my ticket when I chanced to turn and look at the person just behind me. Behold, there stood my friend of Jermyn Street. He had completely metamorphosed himself since I saw him pass the depot gate. Now he had on a shiny white beaver. His shirt collar was turned down, a jaunty little black mustache and goatee adorned his face, while his feet were neatly cased in a pair of light walking shoes. I recognized my man in a moment and facing him within three feet of his person deliberately scrutinized him from head to foot, walking around him the while with an amused expression which I did not attempt to conceal. The boldness of my scrutiny absolutely abashed him. That one who he had been hired to watch, and most probably to regard as a suspicious character who would shrink from his presence, should stand up and sneer at him, was something utterly beyond his composure, and to relieve his embarrassment he fidgeted about in evident distress."

Yancey shared his disdain for ungentlemanly London detectives. "The chap is probably more accustomed to tailing a cheating husband than a military officer of rank."

Anderson nodded. "Even so. Just at this time a newsboy came up and asked me to buy a copy of his paper. I declined as I had already bought one, while keeping up my amused scrutiny on my friend. The fellow actually winced, and in desperation sought to relieve himself by remarking very awkwardly, 'There is a change Sir in the price of the Times, the stamp duty has been taken off today.' With a grin I thanked him for his gratuitous information and replied that I was aware of the fact, but that I noticed before me some other changes beside: that I had seen him only a few moments before in Jermyn Street with a clean shaved face, a black hat, stand up collar, frock coat and heavy walking shoes, and now he stood before me with a six weeks beard at least on his face and all his garments correspondingly changed."

"That must have taken the wind from his sails," said de Leon.

Anderson was pleased to explain. He enjoyed holding forth to a captive audience. "It was piteous to see the mortification of his embarrassment. To help him along I enquired if he was travelling that morning, inviting him if he was to take a seat with me in my railway carriage. He said he was travelling but that he was going to Bristol. 'Well' said I, 'my friend, I thought the London detectives all knew that people going to Bristol generally started from the Paddington Station by the Great Western Railway instead of from the Euston Square Station.' He made no reply and I continued to torture him until the departure was sounded, when I got into the train and my detective sneaked out of the station house. I never saw this man afterwards, but on reaching Rugby another specimen of the genus made his appearance and accompanied me on the train to Liverpool. He was not sure I was his man, however, and it took him some days to be assured, as I used to see him hanging about the curbstone in front of the Queens Hotel narrowly scrutinizing everybody."

Yancey interjected, "You must mean Maguire."

"Yes," said Anderson. "My new friend was Matthew Maguire. He's an ugly, red-headed villain whose faculties are by no means so acute as those of his metropolitan brother, and whose propensities for gazing innocently into the sky are remarkable. Look for Maguire in Liverpool. Tip your hat and bid him 'Good morning, Maguire' then observe how his cheeks will flush, and he will turn from you muttering to himself."

Percy and Huse had heard other of Anderson's and Bulloch's spy stories. Anderson presented himself as outwitting the best that Minister Adams could throw at him from London's private detective agencies, known for their thoroughness and expense. Bulloch related his tales with less embellishment but likewise enjoyed the sport that the mutual intrigues had become.

Yancey said, "I'm afraid the agents of Adams and Wilding have met with more success than we would like. I received a telegram message a few hours ago from Charles Prioleau that they have learned the names of the captain and pilot who are to take the *Bermuda* to the Confederacy."

Huse showed his worry aloud. "That's awful. Shouldn't we stop all shipments from our contractors?"

"Relax, Huse," said Anderson calmly. Anderson was much more adept at managing such problems than Huse. While Huse was superb on technical matters regarding guns of all types, his inexperience in crises made him timid when confronted by exigent circumstance. Anderson directed the conversation to Percy. "Even if the embassy of the United States can identify a ship captain and pilot by name, what do they have? Let's ask our lawyer. Do you have an opinion, Lieutenant?"

Percy was unable to discern whether Anderson was giving him an opportunity to demonstrate his own *sang-froid* in managing adversity or expecting him to share in Huse's embarrassment.

Percy, without hesitation. "I've spoken with both gentlemen, Captains Tessier and Peck. If questioned by the British authorities, they will honestly state that it is their understanding that the steamship *Bermuda* is owned by an Englishman, Mr. Haigh, who has arranged for a shipment of goods to Havana on behalf of the Anglo-Mexican Tehuantepec Company for further shipment to Mexico. They have no reason to know the contents of any goods to be shipped aboard the *Bermuda*. There is nothing about the equipment of the *Bermuda* that makes her subject to the Foreign Enlistment Act. Our only concern for secrecy at this time is guarding against revealing the dates and ultimate destination the ship might take. The Union has no grounds to stop the *Bermuda* from sailing with any cargo whatsoever, but armed with that information Mr. Adams could alert the Union Navy to be on the lookout for a ship of the same description attempting to run the blockade. I will be on the *Bermuda* myself."

Bulloch and Huse were satisfied with Percy's guidance. Anderson said nothing, and his expression showed no disapproval. But there was cold calculation in his eyes, behind which lay the resentment of the military man, who thrived on action, against the lawyer, who prevailed by guile and craft.

Departing the dinner, Percy came away less impressed with de Leon than the latter was with himself. De Leon, he could tell, prided himself on his friendship with President Davis and expected to see him as soon as he could make his way to the Confederacy, where he would volunteer his services. De Leon seemed confident that he could accomplish what the three commissioners had so far failed at, namely, to gain the recognition of the Confederate States of America by Britain and Europe.

Bev had been right about de Leon. Percy believed that the former envoy would prove a "thorn in the bonnet" to the work of other Confederates in Europe. His return to the South before de

Leon would allow Percy to warn Judah about the danger he could pose. The subtle Judah would know how to undermine him.

Chapter 28

Liverpool to Hartlepool

Percy yelled to the coachman, "Hurry up, please. It's time." He was afraid that he would be late for the train that was to take him from Liverpool to Hartlepool where he was to arrange for the loading and departure of the *Bermuda*. His two bags were on the hansom packed for the voyage back to the South.

"Can't," came the coachman's surly reply.

"Why not?" Percy had hopped quickly into the waiting cab on Rumford. He could see nothing of what was in front of the vehicle, which has just turned the corner.

"Blocked."

"Blocked?"

"Blocked. No room to turn around."

Percy swung open the cab door and put one foot in the street as he looked to see what was the holdup.

"Damn," he muttered. He saw an overturned dray wagon, a brewer's wagon. Barrels and casks, large and small, were on the street, some broken, some rolling. An overworked horse had collapsed and was now lying on his side, struggling to raise his head, gasping for breath. The dray's driver was slowly getting to his feet. He had lost his hat. His forehead was bleeding. He was dazed. A crowd was gathering around him, around the overturned wagon. A few who had watched from a window or open door now grabbed mugs or bowls to fill with beer. Others were scooping brew with cupped hands, supping brown liquid. A yeasty odor permeated the air. Other horses, wagons and walkers arrived at the intersection. Movement in any direction for Percy's coach was impossible. Percy grabbed his two bags, tossed his coachman a coin, and began to jog in the direction of the station, awkwardly with the burden of the cumbersome bags.

Percy did not see the barrel-chested, red-headed man who began jogging behind him. The man thought Percy was jogging to get away from him. This was the notorious Matthew Maguire. He had followed Percy from his hotel to the Fraser, Trenholm offices. Something was afoot, he knew, and Percy was a participant in plans for the *Bermuda*. His instructions were to stay close to Lt. Moorhead wherever he may go.

The street commotion added to Percy's sense he was forgetting something. There was unfinished business, besides the business he must finish in Hartlepool. Getting the *Bermuda* out of Hartlepool would be a challenge. The Confederate agents would have to employ trickery. Minister Adams's own agents would be expecting them.

Sweating, Percy presented his ticket to the ticket agent as he boarded the train coach, just in time. He placed his bags overhead and sat next to a middle-aged man smoking an acrid pipe. The man ignored him. Percy had a book in a pocket but did not feel like reading as he caught his breath and settled in. He looked out the window. He did not see the forlorn figure standing at the landing back at the train station. Matthew Maguire was not so fleet of foot as Percy. The detective was breathing heavily; his forehead was wet, and he had lost his hat. He will have to report to Consul Wilding that Lt. Moorhead had eluded him. The smell of beer from sploshes on his trouser cuffs would have to be explained: "Sir, beer was running in the streets as I ran behind the subject." The acting consul will not be impressed.

The weeks had passed quickly, Percy mused as the train swayed rhythmically at each joint in the tracks. Clickety. . . . Clickety. . . Clickety. He yawned. August had ended her second week. Her third was not beginning well. What had he accomplished? Two ships were being built, others purchased. It remained to be seen if the Union could persuade the British government to prevent their completion using the Foreign Enlistment Act. If words can shape the construction of the ships and serve to shield them from interdiction, then Percy will have accomplished something of value. He had facilitated the purchase of arms and ordnance and supplies for the Confederacy. The next few days would be crucial to seeing them safely at sea. He had plans – snares and stratagems – to work his will. Only at the ship's sailing could he feel it had been worth it, after all.

Could he have accomplished more? Had he enjoyed himself too much – the plays, the bookstores, the museums, the walks in the parks? There had been time for these, without skimping on his work for the Confederacy. Wasn't the Confederacy just another client? Work for a client had never prevented him from enjoying leisure time. Yet. Yet. . . Men were dying in a war in which he was active. He still thought of the Mexican boy he killed with a knife at Cerro Gordo. He remembered his friend Jed Barclay, who died as they rushed the convent at Churubusco. And there came then to his mind the image of his fellow Americans who were hanged as traitors by Col. Harney at Mixcoac. Percy had not hanged them. He only drove the wagon that left three of them suspended. They were traitors because they had left the United States Army to fight with Mexicans who were defending their country from invasion by a northern aggressor. Were those traitors so different from the Confederate soldiers shooting and killing soldiers of the Union army? Was the South like the Mexicans? If the South's cause was just, then wasn't the Mexican War an unjust war in which Percy himself had taken an active part? What constitutes a just war? What justifies rebellion against a lawful sovereign?

One of the bags on the rack overhead held books he intended to read on his upcoming voyage. There would be time to study and consider. If study and reflection matter. You find yourself in one place or another when others bring about a war or rebellion. Doesn't that determine which side you must support? The ties of place, family and friends bind you, don't they, not your philosophical reflection? Not so, he told himself. He chose to enlist in the Louisiana regiment in 1847 that took him into Mexico. But he was a boy then, full of patriotism and the romance of Harfleur and Agincourt, wanting whole-heartedly to be in solidarity with a band of brothers. Now he was more mature, capable of reflection and informed decision.

Yet he had allowed Judah Benjamin to persuade him to come with him to join the Confederacy, when Judah showed up in his lecture room and invited him to come to Montgomery. Shouldn't he have resisted? But . . . how could he have told Judah no, I will not go with you? It would have been a betrayal of trust. Unthinkable. And having accepted the invitation, he now had a duty. He had been given responsibilities which he must fulfill. To do less would lessen who he was.

The train slowed as it went around a curve and began to ascend a grade. The man next to him coughed and re-ignited his pipe. Percy decided to nap. A nap would be more productive than reflection. Clickety. . . . Clickety. . . Clickety.

Chapter 29

The *Bermuda* at Last

After taking a room in Hartlepool, Percy immediately went to the Jackson Dock to get his first look at the *Bermuda*. Although it was near dusk, he quickly located the two-masted, brig-rigged, iron-hulled steamship, launched only weeks earlier in Stockton-on-Tees. Charles Prioleau had informed him that he had arranged her purchase when the firm that contracted for her construction defaulted on its obligations. Percy appreciated Prioleau's nose for deals and eye for detail. As he walked her length, he saw the lower part of the ship's funnel was painted black and the upper part red. Her black hull was set off by a narrow red stripe around the molding, level with the deck. The wheelhouse was white; six auxiliary boats painted with the same white were slung in iron davits. At her bow, she had neither figure-head nor bow-sprit, a strong lady whose features needed no adornment or embellishment. A little over 200 feet in length, she was two-thirds the size of the *Baltic* on which Percy, a decade earlier, had made his first trans-Atlantic crossing and was half her width. Her four guns were suitable for defensive purposes but inadequate to fend off a warship. Satisfied the Bermuda was a worthy vessel, Percy retired to his room.

The next two days in West Hartlepool Percy took up an observation post on the second floor of a building seventy yards from the *Bermuda's* dock. With binoculars he was able to identify two men and a woman who were likely agents of Minister Adams, up from London. They were milling about, taking turns trying to determine the contents of the crates, cases, and barrels on the dock that might contain arms and ammunition. Bulloch joined Percy in mid-day on the second day. Together they identified the British customs inspectors on duty and took note of how they conducted their business.

Handing the binoculars back to Percy, Bulloch groused, "We can expect an examination of the ship some time tomorrow."

Percy wryly asked, "Magic binoculars? You can tell just by looking from here?"

Bulloch grunted, "That, and a little help from a friend."

"Must be a well-placed friend."

Bulloch, more somber now. "There are things it is best to keep as little known as possible. Know this much, that complaints were filed on Thursday by Minister Adams to Lord Russell alleging that the *Bermuda* has been taking in crates and containers believed to contain arms and ammunition of all kinds ordinarily used in war. He claims she is an armed steamer about to be dispatched with the purpose of making war against the people of the United States. Adams asked for the Foreign Minister to stop her so as not to violate the act prohibiting the fitting out of vessels for warlike purposes. Lord Russell promised an inspection by tomorrow."

Percy, with ironic earnestness. "Then we shall make her ready for inspection." He was impressed with the specificity of Bulloch's information, inferring he must have a source inside the British Foreign Ministry. It was unlikely that Adams would have someone disloyal inside the American embassy. He wondered what other sources of information Bulloch had developed without his knowledge. Were Anderson and Huse privy to the source or sources? Eventually, he would have to ask Bulloch to take him into his confidence. Secrecy was all well and good, but something might happen to Bulloch, and then what would happen to a valuable source of intelligence within the British government? The risk to secrecy had to be weighed against the possibility of loss of the source if his sole contact were suddenly taken away. Perhaps there was an intermediary between Bulloch and the source.

That evening, Percy and Bulloch and a trust-worthy man named Alston "Al" Gamage, sent by Charles Prioleau from Liverpool, repacked some of the crates. The trio descended into the hold of the vessel and set to work by oil lamps. What the Union's detectives had suspected to be crates of rifles on the dock became boxes of rail spikes when the top layers of the Enfield rifles were replaced by a layer of spikes. The crates were labeled as bound to Vera Cruz via Havana for the Anglo-Mexican Tehuantepec Railroad Company. In the same manner, a layer of construction nails covered over barrels of cartridges prepared to fire in those rifles.

"These uniforms. Where do you want them?" Al Gamage called out softly. He had personally accompanied them from a warehouse in Manchester where they had been stored.

"No need to move them," returned Percy. "It'll be easy to toss a few dozen bundles of blankets over them."

"And these medical supplies?" said Bulloch.

"Easily explained. This ship is taking a large quantity for a crew of hundreds of workers building a railroad in a semi-tropical region of Mexico. They will have needs for treatment of disease and numerous injuries or even wounds from attacks by the local tribes. But Jim, you've not showed me where you have hidden our heavy ordnance."

Bulloch laughed quietly. "You walked right past it and over it coming to this part of the ship."

"Oh? Is there a false deck?"

Bulloch led the two others from the forward hold. "Let's walk aft." After passing the engine room, he pointed, "There."

"All I see is coal."

"That's all the inspectors will see. Hidden within these tons of coal of our fuel bunkers are eighteen rifled field pieces and four heavy coastal guns. From Germany. We loaded them at night a week ago. No inspector will dig through a ship's coal in search of contraband. They'll require a little cleaning when you get them to a Southern port, but that's all. They're indestructible."

"Well, gents, I think the *Bermuda* is ready for inspection," Percy grinned. "To celebrate I suggest we find the captain's quarters. I have it on good authority from the captain himself that there's a bottle of French brandy that we can help ourselves to."

Bulloch's unnamed informer proved accurate. The British customs inspectors on Tuesday, August 20, examined the *Bermuda*'s cargo manifest filed by her owner of record, Mr. Edwin Haigh of Liverpool. They spoke with the ship's captain, Eugene Tessier – a Frenchman sailing under English colors who had signed a declaration that her cargo was destined to Havana, Cuba. Standing by was Percy. The inspectors then interviewed him. He related to them that he was an agent of the Anglo-Mexican Tehuantepec Company, an English company engaged in building a railroad across the Isthmus of Tehuantepec, and that he was one of the persons who had purchased space for shipping goods aboard the vessel. Finally, the inspectors were shown some of the crates and barrels of the railroad company, a few still on the dock, others in the holds below, which they asked to be opened. Prying open the wooden containers, they found only spikes and nails and medical supplies such as would be needed by railroad workers. Percy told them that he would be accompanying his shipment to Havana to see to the safe trans-shipment of his cargo to Mexico. Satisfied, the head of customs for the port signed the papers that would allow the *Bermuda* to sail on Thursday.

At dinner that evening Percy assured Bulloch that he would get the shipment into the hands of President Davis and the War

Department.

"I have no doubt that if anyone can give such assurance, it is you," Bulloch said. He had grown to trust the Louisiana lawyer.

Percy accepted the compliment in silence. Would he see Bulloch again? He had come to enjoy his gruff company, his wry, understated observations about the Confederate commissioners, the British and French officials and business agents with whom they dealt, the Southerners who visited them. He would not want to lose Bulloch's trust. And when he did, he felt acutely the loss.

The *Bermuda* sailed from its dock on August 22, 1861 in mid-afternoon bright sunlight. Percy Moorhead stood on the forward deck, exchanging glances with the three London detectives who looked on unhappily as the inspection they had sought turned up nothing matching the suspicions they had related to the American minister. How could Adams's operatives have gotten such misinformation about the *Bermuda's* cargo? False reports to the British authorities would call into question all of the claims made by the Union.

Percy felt no smugness. He had won this engagement, but he knew that there surely would be more.

ᦔ — ᦔ

Captain Tessier charted a route that avoided the shipping lanes which the Union's war ships were likely to haunt, though it added four days to the voyage. At this time of year the weather was favorable. They made good speed. Percy bunked with the first mate. Although he visited with Gene Tessier, the captain, and Fenn Peck, the ship's pilot, during meals and played cards with the crew on some evenings, he spent most of the crossing in his cabin with the canvas bag of books he had collected in London and Liverpool. He welcomed the time to consume his selection of books on civil wars.

On the English Civil War of the time of Charles I and Oliver Cromwell, he had purchased cheap editions of Cattermole and

Hume; there were too many volumes to carry any of the classic work by Edward Hyde, Lord Clarendon. Of Shakespeare's plays he had chosen slender reprints of *Richard II, Henry IV* parts 1 & 2, *Coriolanus, Macbeth,* and *Julius Caesar.* From Roman times, he had chosen Lucan's *De Bello Civili,* the *Pharsalia.* Of more recent events he had brought Lord Mahon's *War of the Spanish Succession.* Recalling its importance for justifying the American Revolution and the founding of the Constitution, for political theory he had Locke's *Second Treatise of Government.* He also had Hobbes's *Leviathan.*

Occupied with his heavy reading, the days of Percy's voyage passed quickly and pleasantly. He was struck that the books he most admired, though for very different reasons, were written in exile. Locke had expatriated himself to Holland and lost his Oxford teaching position at the time of Charles II. Hobbes had gone into exile in France to escape the English civil war at the time of Charles I. The greatest works of Locke and Hobbes were nurtured in a foreign country. Did history or literature offer any lessons to a man who found himself a participant in a war between citizens over their proper governance? His books gave him no grounds for optimism. No civil war ended happily. Would America's be any different? Would it produce its own Locke or Hobbes?

ᜄᜄ - ᜄᜄ

Alerted at breakfast by Captain Tessier that they were approaching their destination, Percy was on deck when he first saw the brownish water of the Savannah River. It was about a half mile wide where the *Bermuda* entered it coming in through Tybee Roads. As they passed a sand fort that the Confederates had erected near the lighthouse on northeast Tybee Island, the Savannah appeared to Percy to be muddy, with a strong current. From the ship's chart, he knew her two channels were separated by Cockspur Island, which was mostly marsh, about a mile long and half a mile wide. Soon, stout Fort Pulaski loomed into his view. It had been built there by the Federal government over a two-decade period of intermittent construction and occupied it in 1847. Because it was little used and in bad disrepair, Governor Brown of Georgia had easily seized it in January 1861, even before his state seceded. The fort, bristling with cannons, commanded both channels of the river. According to the chart, the fort was distant from the town of Savannah by some fourteen miles.

As the *Bermuda* approached Fort Pulaski, Percy heard the captain direct the crew to fire a gun and run up the Confederate flag. In return, they received three welcoming cannon blasts. Men stood at the parapets of the fort and cheered the arrival of the South's first commercial ship defying the embargo. At a signal from the fort, the *Bermuda* dropped anchor to receive a rowboat bringing officers from the fort.

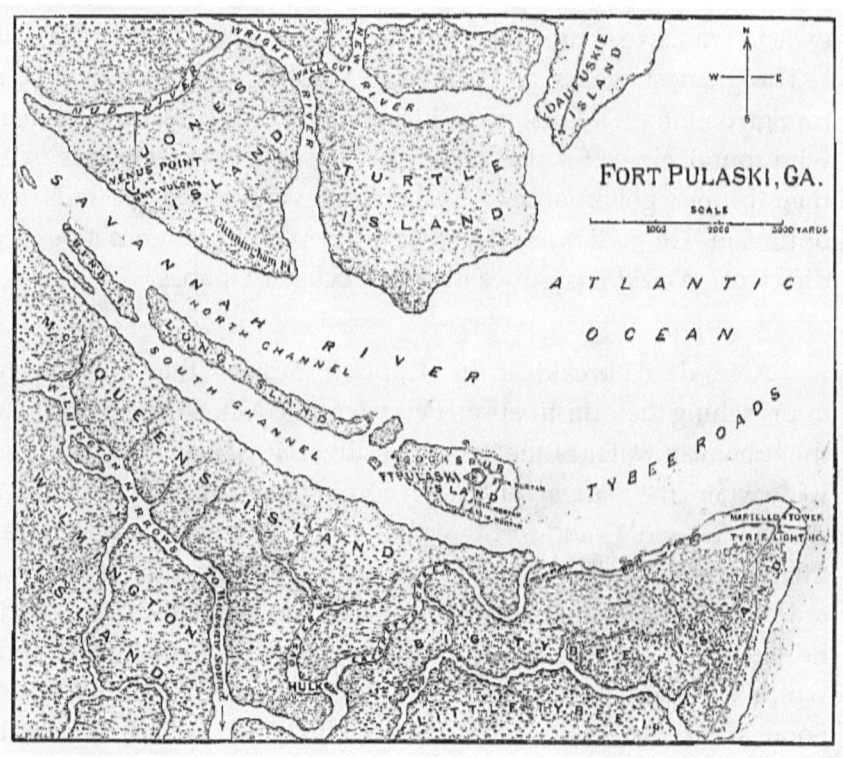

In his baggage Percy had packed a Confederate uniform with lieutenant's insignia. There was no occasion for wearing it in Liverpool or London but it was entirely appropriate dress for his return to the CSA. It fit as though measured for him, which in fact it was. When he and Caleb Huse had ordered 10,000 uniforms of cadet gray wool jackets with two rows of yellow-metal buttons and blue, gray, or brown pairs of trousers made in various sizes to the specifications of the Confederate War Department, the clothing manufacturers had volunteered to tailor a complete outfit for each of them at no additional cost, to be certain of their satisfaction at the design and quality. He had put his uniform on as the *Bermuda* awaited the boat from the fort.

Coming aboard the *Bermuda* was Fort Pulaski's recently named commandant, Major Charles H. Olmstead of the Georgia militia. A decade younger than Percy, Olmstead was confident of his post. He had the highest forehead of any young man Percy had ever seen. It was given emphasis by his heavy beard. Olmstead eagerly greeted Captain Tessier and Percy in a preternaturally deep voice. "Welcome to Georgia. Our state has spent months preparing the fort to guard the entrance to our only major port. We now have near four hundred men and fifty cannons to protect the fort."

Impressed by the young commander of a major installation, Percy asked, "What's the fort's construction?"

With the pride of a parent for his offspring, Olmstead gushed, "You can't get a full view from here. It's a brick work, with five faces, including the gorge. It's casemated on all sides and has walls seven and a half feet thick, and twenty-five feet above high water. We have one tier of guns mounted in embrasures and one in barbette. The Yanks will get a hot greeting if they try coming up the river from either side." Olmstead had prepared well and was proud to show it to a fellow officer. "I'll ride the fifteen miles to the city with you, if you don't mind. I've got a man telegraphing your arrival. A lot of people will be happy to see us."

∽ - ∾

Percy's first impression of Savannah was that its location was both charming and ideal. Now he understood why Jim Bulloch and Edward Anderson were so taken with the city. It was built atop a bluff of low elevation, maybe twelve feet above the mean high-water mark. The houses stood on a little eminence over the river, affording convenient wharfage and slips for merchant vessels. Opposite it, on the other side of the river, were rice-swamps where the land was low and stretched away as far as the sea in one level green – smooth as a billiard-cloth.

The pilot, Fenn Peck, maneuvered the *Bermuda* smoothly up the river til she was safely docked at the wharf. A large crowd had gathered and were singing Dixie and waving flags and banners. Percy assumed that the soldiers in uniform with horses and wagons were there to help. Percy also assumed that representatives of Fraser, Trenholm and Company would be dockside to take possession of the goods that Charles Prioleau had sent. Both of his assumptions were flat wrong.

Instead, the troubles began.

Chapter 30

Standoff at Savannah Harbor

On the voyage across the Atlantic, especially as they neared the Georgia coast, Percy had anticipated the possibility of an attack by Union ships, sweeping in with guns blazing and grappling hooks ready to board the *Bermuda*, to seize all her cargo and to imprison her crew. He had not expected a dog-fight-over-bones among his fellow Confederates – Georgia, South Carolina and Florida militia and political figures and cash-wielding speculators from all over the South, all in a frenzy to claim and acquire the cargo of the *Bermuda*, by purchase, persuasion, or brute force.

Pushing through the throng of civilians lined up next to the *Bermuda* was an officer in a black and grey uniform, a colonel, followed by six other soldiers bearing carbines. Theirs was no friendly greeting but a campaign aimed at a hostile takeover.

Ignoring Percy, the colonel addressed Captain Tessier, courteously enough but demanding, "Captain, before this vessel is unloaded, I am to serve you these papers from Governor Joseph Brown and General A. R. Lawton. I have been authorized by them to examine your cargo and to take possession of such arms and artillery as I deem necessary for the defense of the sovereign state of Georgia."

The diminutive Frenchman was not cowed by the larger

Georgian. He refused to accept the papers thrust at him by the officious colonel. "You must take that up with Lieutenant Moorhead," pointing to Percy. "He's in charge of the cargo."

Percy strode the seven steps across the wharf to bring him nose-to-nose with the scowling colonel. Politeness dripping from his voice, Percy introduced himself: "Percy Moorhead, Lieutenant, Confederate States Army, at your service, Colonel ....?"

"Colonel *Goodbie*, Georgia State Troops, Volunteers, First Regiment. In the name of the state of Georgia and by the authority of its Governor, I will take possession of all arms and artillery on board this vessel."

Percy, still smiling, "Would you be so kind as to allow me to review your papers, Colonel Goodbie?"

It was not the response the colonel usually received from his demands. "I see no need for that, Lieutenant. Are you in the habit of challenging a senior officer?" His was the snarl of a dog's warning. The soldiers standing behind their colonel tensed, gripping their carbines.

"Indulge me, Sir." Percy's voice bordered on condescension. "You may have a superior rank, but we serve separate sovereigns. I am not in your chain of command. You are answerable to the state of Georgia and to your governor. The appointment I hold is in service to the Confederate States. My superiors are President Davis and the Attorney General, Judah Benjamin."

"Two sovereigns, my ass," exclaimed the colonel. "We are here in Georgia, and you are under its full authority. Besides, you must have been away. Mr. Benjamin is no longer Attorney General."

Percy was momentarily taken back. What had happened to Benjamin? No news had reached England or France that he had fallen from office.

Major Olmstead had been listening closely to the confrontation and demands of Colonel Goodbie. He quietly interjected, speaking to Percy – but for the hearing of the colonel, "The colonel is partially correct. As of a couple of days ago, President Davis appointed Mr. Benjamin acting Secretary of War. However, he continues as Attorney General until a replacement is named."

Percy smiled slightly. His status was in fact raised; he now served both the Attorney General and the Secretary of War, as well as President Davis.

Goodbie frowned at Major Olmstead and persisted despite the new information. "Governor Brown sent a representative of our state to Europe to acquire arms. The guns you have aboard are surely a portion of the supply he has sent."

No longer smiling or cordial, Percy insisted bluntly, "Most assuredly, Sir, they are not. The representative you speak of is Mr. Thomas Butler King. I met with him in Paris a few weeks before the *Bermuda* set sail. As of that time, Mr. King had received none of the funds necessary for him to purchase arms. I personally supervised the loading of this vessel in England. We received no consignment from Mr. King."

A small crowd was now gathered at the wharf, curious as to the commotion taking place before the *Bermuda*. Those who had been elated and cheering were now piqued. Some sort of confrontation was taking place.

"That is of no consequence," demanded the colonel with greater heat. "Pursuant to Governor Brown's authorization and General Lawton's orders, we can requisition any property necessary for the defense of the state." His face was reddening in frustration. He wanted to tell his men to seize Percy, but something in Percy's cool demeanor dissuaded him.

Percy refuted the Georgian. "Again, I assure you, Sir, that you do not possess such authority. It may be true that you have the power to appropriate *private* property within the jurisdiction of the state of Georgia. However, as I have said already, we serve different sovereigns. You, your governor, and General Lawton have no power to requisition the property of the Confederacy."

Getting nowhere with Lieutenant Moorhead, Goodbie turned his back to Percy and sought to intimidate Captain Tessier. "You, sir, are the ship's captain and are in charge of the cargo. I demand to see your manifest."

The captain shrugged with Gallic indifference. "I'm no longer at sea. In port, Lieutenant Moorhead is in full charge of his cargo."

Percy stepped between the colonel and the *Bermuda's* captain: "Colonel, I have inventories and receipts for each and every rifle, cartridge, uniform and all such items from three agents of the Confederate government, each an officer of the Confederate army or navy – as am I." Percy had no more fear of the Georgia soldiers then he had of the Georgia Vigilancers whom he had confronted five months earlier as he had passed through Georgia on his way to Charleston.

Percy looked on as Goodbie assessed his own situation. The looks on the men's faces, new militia recruits without military experience, showed their uncertainty at which officer had the better claim to authority. Nor did the crowd seem to be with him. They looked back and forth between the state's officer and the representative of the Confederacy who had brought the first ship all the way from England with supplies and had successfully run the blockade. Muttering to themselves, they knew he was being tested. If he tried to make a move against Percy and his own men hesitated, he would appear the fool. If Percy resisted, the scene could turn violent.

From the corner of his eye, Percy saw that Captain Tessier had begun assembling the crew of the *Bermuda* on deck, standing in front of access to the ship and the cargo. Some had taken up unused belaying pins from the ship's rails. A few held machine wrenches from the engine room. Goodbie's expression showed that he knew all too well that while his men were armed they were outnumbered five to one.

Percy acted as though he was in full control of the situation.

"Please examine the receipts if you care to. While you are about that, I shall go to the nearest telegraph office and send a message to Secretary of War Benjamin. I am confident that he will immediately send an order to a company of the Confederate army to accept my delivery of the arms and supplies they have been waiting some months for. Rather than meet their superior numbers, it might be prudent for you to report to your governor that there has arisen a question of jurisdiction."

Goodbie remembered that Major Olmstead was standing near him. He looked to see his reaction. Olmstead subtly gave a slight motion to his head in disapproval.

"Jurisdiction?" was all that Goodbie could manage as he tried to find a way that allowed him to defuse the confrontation without backing down.

"Yes. You may tell your governor that you were advised by the Confederate Attorney General's representative that whatever authority you possess in your jurisdiction, it cannot supersede the authority of the Confederate States of America to which your powers are subordinate. You may refer him to Article 6 Section 3 of the Confederate Constitution, to which Georgia has subscribed. It provides that the laws of the Confederate States are the supreme law of the land. The judges in every state are bound thereby, notwithstanding anything in the constitution or laws of any state to the contrary."

Percy's threat of telegraphing Richmond and recitation of chapter and verse of the Confederate Constitution, which the colonel had never read, had the desired effect. Goodbie took his small unit from the dock, with a parting shot, "This will not go unanswered, Lieutenant. It is Governor Brown you challenge, not me. It is his wrath you will feel." The threat was not idle, as Percy would learn.

After Goodbie was safely gone, Major Olmstead shook Percy's hand and with a smile said, "When the Yankees begin their siege of our fort, as they surely will, I'd be proud for you to stand by me at the ramparts."

Percy laughed. "I'll take that as a compliment. But if a lawyer's bluster could do anything to win this war, I'd volunteer for the negotiating table."

The unloading of the cargo resumed. Percy supervised the storage of his goods and supplies in the nearest warehouse. He found two Confederate soldiers and assigned them to guard his shipment. Then he reported his arrival by telegram to Benjamin, leaving the newly appointed Secretary of War to sort out the conflict with Governor Brown.

It was neither the first nor the last time that the Georgia governor would cause difficulties for the Confederacy – and for Lieutenant Percy Moorhead.

Chapter 31
Reporting to Judah

A rriving in Richmond two days after his tense encounter in Savannah, Percy took a room at the Ballard House, on Franklin Street. It was connected to the Exchange Hotel by a footbridge constructed over the street. The Exchange held memories for Percy. He had stayed there twice before. Philomena had surprised him in its lobby when he came to Richmond ten years ago, several lifetimes ago. He couldn't bring himself to enter the Exchange, not yet. He knew he would look for her in the lounge chair where she had called to him in her husky voice. What he would give to hear that enchanting voice again! The Ballard was built after their marriage but was owned by the same man who had purchased the Exchange.

The last time Percy had seen Judah Benjamin, Montgomery was the capital, when Judah was Attorney General. Now the seat of government was Richmond, Virginia; Benjamin's portfolio was now Secretary of War. The hastily furnished offices of Montgomery were replaced with the finely appointed chambers of Richmond's Custom House, newly constructed of granite only three years earlier by the Federal government. It was immediately opposite the south face of the Virginia Capitol and a short three blocks from the Ballard House. Percy's appointment was not until 10:00, so he enjoyed a leisurely breakfast.

Entering the executive office building for the first time, Percy found the offices of the first floor were occupied by Treasury. The President and Secretary of State were in the story above. Although the War and Navy Departments were housed in a building on Ninth street, Judah Benjamin's office was here, close to the President's. Davis insisted that Benjamin have an office near his own. Davis so depended on Benjamin, he wanted to be able to summon him on short notice.

Now seated in a comfortable leather chair opposite Benjamin, Percy recounted some of his activities that had not been in Percy's reports from England. Those reports, along with communications from Huse, Bulloch and Anderson, had reached Benjamin aboard ships successfully running the blockade, so Benjamin was aware of Percy's principal accomplishments in Liverpool and London.

Benjamin, brow quizzical. "Your thoughts on Huse and Bulloch? Anderson was sent over to check up on them – supersede them if necessary."

Percy, unhesitant. "Both men are doing superbly, especially in light of the difficulties of resources. They're arming an army and floating a navy on scraps of foolscap. I rate Huse as near genius on science. He approaches ordnance as applied metallurgy and chemistry and is a master. Same for Bulloch on our naval requirements, though I'm sure he'd love to be at sea."

"And did Anderson share your assessment?" Judah Benjamin sought to draw out Percy. Not knowing the relation between Judah and the selection of Anderson to check on the Confederate agents in Europe, Percy was reluctant to volunteer the information until asked. Now Judah had asked. And he was frank.

"Anderson's not the best choice to assess their work. His lack of knowledge on new arms developments has caused some tensions with Huse, and more so with Bulloch. Anderson went so far as to try to improve on the plans for the two cruisers Bulloch is building and to impose cost savings. Bulloch would have none of it. Anderson's a nuisance. He'd rather comply with regulations than accomplish a goal. He's the sort who will always count on following the rules to deflect criticism of his performance. Effective procurement is secondary to procedure."

Percy was relieved to see that Benjamin agreed. The Secretary of War relaxed and said, "Your observations confirm what seems the import of his reports. I'll see to it that he doesn't return to Europe. He can still be useful."

Percy brought up a subject where he knew Benjamin would differ. "I concur with at least one of Anderson's recommendations. The Confederacy can acquire its own ships."

Benjamin was not so much annoyed as he was frustrated by any proposal that would increase the demands on the resources of his department. "Why not continue to use Fraser, Trenholm's ships and other private shippers?" He preferred private solutions. "Our need is for war ships. Raiders and ironclads. Civilians, Confederate or British, can furnish merchant ships at their own expense."

Percy knew Benjamin would listen to disagreement. "I found Anderson's arguments for purchasing a ship persuasive. The shipping rates of private vessels are exorbitant. Much of their cargoes we have no control over and don't even know what's coming in on them. A blockade runner will make more money bringing in ladies' dresses and French wine than Confederate uniforms, so we have to share space as best as they will let us. Perhaps we could have the Anglo-Mexican Tehuantepec Company be the guise to purchase several steamships in England or Ireland for the Confederacy."

Benjamin ruminated for a minute before answering. "Mallory got dispatches this morning from Anderson and Bulloch that arrived with the *Bermuda* about purchasing a ship for cargo. He's endorsed the plan. Do they have a vessel in mind?"

"Yes. They're buying the *Fingal*. She's a new screw steamship built on the Clyde for the Highland trade. Bulloch says her log gave her speed as thirteen knots in good weather. She'll be coming over shortly with a huge cargo. Prioleau in Liverpool has assured me he's arranged for the Fraser, Trenholm agent in Nassau to service goods marked for our Mexican railroad. We will have him receive our matériel for the Confederacy and give us access to warehouse space. Each crate showing a final destination for Vera Cruz has a code that will tell what the supplies are and where they are to go by blockade runner."

"Does your code specify what port?" Now that he was War Secretary, Benjamin had to consider details of logistics that were of little concern to the Attorney General.

Percy had devoted a lot of time to the logical steps for implementing his plan. "Our people in England will not know which of our ports will be open to our ships. The agent in Nassau has instructions to break up shipments into smaller groups and parcel out the crates to different blockade runners. If he gets 8,000 Enfields, he might try to send 3,000 through Wilmington, 4,000 to Charleston and a 1,000 to Savannah. Not all will be lost if one steamship is caught or sunk by the Union."

Benjamin stood and walked around to the back of his chair and looked out the window, speaking as he went. "Very good. That also helps with another of our problems." As September was nearing its end, the Richmond weather was at its most pleasant. A light breeze came up from the harbor below.

Benjamin, after a pause. "It's not the Yankees that keep me up at night, Percy. It's our own damn people. You already know about Governor Brown in Georgia. Some of our other governors are also trying to confiscate the goods coming in. They have their own purchasing agents running around Europe, and they claim the guns are theirs. When they don't get their way, they threaten secession from the Confederacy."

Benjamin's voice carried more resignation than anger. He

added, "Secession fever is hard to contain once it takes hold." He almost sounded regretful.

Percy stood and walked to the window by Benjamin. As they shared the breeze of the open window, he told his employer, "I don't envy you. And how are we doing with Mexico? The news in England makes it sound like England, France and Spain may use military force to insist that the Juarez government make good on Mexico's debts. Before I left in May, you told me we were sending Pickett to Mexico City to represent our interests." It was as much a question as a statement.

Benjamin did not conceal his displeasure at Pickett. "Ah, Pickett. Yes. Pickett, he's a problem. A brash man of no tact and little discretion. When he's not in jail for drunken brawling, he's insulting the Mexicans. He's made it clear to them he favors the large landowners and clergy and has only distaste for President Juarez. He calls Juarez an ineffective little Indian in his letters to us. Which, of course, the Mexicans have intercepted and have given to Juarez. Pickett is a diplomat devoid of diplomacy."

Benjamin sat down and pulled a file from a drawer. Holding up a copy of a letter from Pickett, he read: "'Courtesy is natural to all Mexicans; but I fear corruption and moral depravity is not less so'. This is a copy sent by Pickett's clerk in Mexico by an alternate route. The original must have been filched by the Mexicans."

Judah tossed the offensive file on his desk. "I'm afraid Pickett's views on Mexico were shared by Secretary Toombs who appointed him. Among the papers taken from Pickett when the Mexicans locked him up were his instructions from Toombs which said a million or so of money judiciously applied would purchase our recognition by the Mexicans and that it is not our mission to mend their morals. No doubt we must recall Pickett, but he has supporters here in Richmond. Toombs has been replaced by Robert Hunter as Secretary of State, but some others are still in the Cabinet who share Pickett's belief that we should break up Mexico and annex parts of northern Mexico. They say we should finish what

Polk started."

Percy took the news gravely. "Mexico's too important to the Confederacy to have Pickett destroy our relationship. Juarez is their best hope for an orderly future. He's impressed me since you introduced us in New Orleans when he was in exile from Santa Anna."

Benjamin picked up another paper. "To repair some of Pickett's damage, we're sending a new man to northern Mexico. He's also lived in New Orleans, where we're more respectful of racial and cultural differences than Kentuckians like Pickett."

"What is it about Kentucky that it produces wild men?" reflected Percy. "My mother was afraid to come to New Orleans half of the year, when the flatboats floated down from Kentucky. She would say they howled all night and fouled the streets all day. Who's your new man?"

"His name is José Quintero. Cuban by birth, Texan by choice. Want to meet him? He's about to leave in a few days for a return to Mexico."

"Sure."

"He's probably in the building somewhere." Benjamin called an orderly into his office and asked him to see if he could locate Mr. Quintero, probably somewhere near Secretary Hunter's offices.

Percy anticipated a swarthy creole of Spanish heritage. But he had not expected a poet in exile.

Chapter 32

A Cuban Confederate

The Cuban who appeared fifteen minutes did indeed bear the Mediterranean complexion of a Cuban of Spanish descent, a dark mustache and goatee. He was about thirty, slim and shorter than Percy. His confident manner arose from his legal experience. Like Percy, he was accustomed to meeting new people and creating trust. Like Percy, he greeted a new acquaintance with a firm handshake, a meeting of the eyes and careful attention to the exchange of names.

"Percy Moorhead," said Quintero with no hint of accent. "I'm pleased to meet you. Mr. Benjamin tells me you are familiar with Mexico." Only now did Quintero look to Benjamin.

"*Mucho gusto,*" Percy responded warmly. "We have an interest in Mexico in common. Judah tells me you are finding success where others have failed. What is your secret?"

"Good fortune, my friend, no skill of mine. A chance encounter with a man who holds great promise for Mexico's future, And our own." Quintero may have hailed from Cuba, but Percy concluded he must have spent time in his youth in the United States. Quintero was now seated in a chair next to Percy.

"Oh. And who is that?"

"Santiago Vidaurri. Have you heard of him?"

"I recall his name. When a new government assumed power six years ago, he was one of the leaders who had opposed Santa Anna. At that time, Vidaurri was on the same side of reform as Juarez."

Quintero confirmed Percy's recollection. "Yes. And he has continued to support President Juarez. He was a friend to President Comonfort when he went into exile. Governor Vidaurri is the strongest leader in the region closest to Texas. That's how I met him. I was in Austin when Vidaurri himself had to leave Mexico."

Percy observed wryly, "It seems a qualification for political advancement in Mexico is a period in exile. New Orleans and Havana have been second homes to many of Mexico's presidents. Why did he leave?"

Gesturing energetically in his seat, Quintero said, "That young upstart, Miramon, who now claims to be *el presidente*. He was part of the reactionary *coup d'état* that overthrew Comonfort. For a time, Miramon held Monterrey. But Vidaurri is back now. He is *el jefé*."

Benjamin had been silent as Percy and Quintero sized one another up, establishing that the two men could work together comfortably. He now spoke. "Our man Pickett has publicly expressed his support for Miramon and his faction. This is causing us problems in northeast Mexico where Vidaurri has his power. There's no place in Mexico more important to the Confederate future than Matamoros and its port of Bagdad. We hold Fort Brown and Brownsville on the Texas side of the Rio Grande. The Union's blockade of Texas extends to it. But they can't blockade a Mexican port. By treaty the Yankees are bound to treat the Rio Grande as an international river. Our cotton crosses the river at Brownsville and becomes Mexican cotton. It then goes out on British ships protected by international law. Our supplies come from the other direction. It's a long trip across Texas, but it adds to what we can get through by blockade runners."

Percy flashed a smile. "A Bagdad, in Mexico. Someone must

have been imaginative."

Benjamin laughed. "Perhaps it was the name that inspired President Davis a few years ago, when he was Secretary of War. He recommended that camels be introduced to Texas. A herd was imported, along with men to train them."

Quintero interjected, "Brilliant, it turned out. A camel can carry twice the load a mule can. And they're faster. Two cotton bales each. It's a sight to see, a caravan of fifty or sixty camels coming from Camp Verde into Brownsville with cotton for Matamoros. Their smell and braying frighten horses and mules, but they're effective. Going back the other way they carry powder, lead, supplies that the Confederacy badly needs."

Benjamin added, "President Davis says they can go thirty-six hours without water, subsist on greasewood shrubs and are impossible to stampede."

Percy brought the conversation back to politics. "Camels aside, where does Vidaurri stand in relation to Juarez?"

Quintero leaned forward, "They are two bears caged together. They must be friends, or both will lose. Vidaurri cannot oppose Juarez, and Juarez cannot counter Vidaurri. When they have a difference, they ignore each other. Each leader has his own supporters, but their supporters often overlap. Vidaurri governs both Nuevo Leon and Coahuila. And no one in the state of Tamaulipas would go against anything Vidaurri might want."

Percy raised his eyebrows. Quintero obviously could judge character astutely. He asked, "What sort of man is this Santiago Vidaurri? Another *caudillo*?"

Smiling brightly, Quintero said, "Why, he's very much like us, Lieutenant Moorhead. If he were on this side of the Rio Grande, he would be a Confederate. He believes in states' rights in Mexico. He wants the people of the state where he is governor to govern themselves and not be ruled from a distant capital, whether it's in Vera Cruz or Mexico City. When I met with him in Monterrey at the end of June he expressed the utmost friendship to the CSA. He wants nothing but peace and commerce along the border. As proof of his sincerity, he handed me a copy of a decree he had issued in April that called for the arrest of Mexicans raiding in Texas. He promised he would never agree to allowing Union troops to cross northern Mexico."

Percy was impressed with Quintero's quick assessment. He asked, "That's very encouraging. Can he deliver on his promises?"

Quintero seemed uncertain whether to share his further negotiations with Vidaurri with Percy Moorhead. Benjamin nodded to Quintero, "We have no secrets from Percy. He's our most trusted agent."

The Cuban Confederate resumed, "In a private interview, Vidaurri told me that he has wanted for years to form a Republic of Sierra Madre comprised of northern Mexican states. He authorized me to report to President Davis that if he would appoint an agent, negotiations could begin immediately for annexation of the Mexican border states into the Confederacy. Vidaurri believes that only one thousand Texans and some artillery would be required. He's sure the northern Mexican states will be Americanized. The Confederacy would respect states' rights, but Washington would not. The border states contain great mineral wealth, but the Mexicans can't develop their own resources. After Coahuila and Nuevo Leon are annexed, the majority of Mexico's northern states would soon go along. Governor Vidaurri promises that he can furnish us with unlimited supplies of lead, copper, and gunpowder."

Percy nodded. "I know he didn't promise any guns. They have no more ability to manufacture guns than we do."

"No, they cannot," Quintero acknowledged. "All of the weapons he commands belong to the Mexican government. He'll see to it that Matamoros is as good as a Confederate port. Any cotton we can bring there can be loaded on to ships going anywhere in the world."

Percy turned to Benjamin. "What do President Davis and the Cabinet say to Governor Vidaurri's project?"

Benjamin made a vague gesture with his right hand. "It's under consideration." Percy could read the subtle shifts in manner when Benjamin had misgivings on a matter. The meeting was over.

☙ - ❧

Coming out of the Treasury Building, Percy enjoyed the warmth of the early afternoon sun. It was too soon after his late breakfast to be hungry. He walked along Bank Street in the direction of his hotel when he found himself at the corner of 12th Street, standing in front of the office of the *Southern Literary Messenger*. He had forgotten that it was published in Richmond. The South's only viable literary magazine, the *Messenger* was a favorite of his since his days as a student at the College of William and Mary. When Percy was in England, he was frustrated that he had been unable to get access to copies of the publication.

Now he opened the door. The interior was very large with partitions rather than walls. A counter a dozen feet wide separated the front part from the rear where a printing press was located. Percy could make out a figure sitting near the silent press at a desk, apparently unaware of the arrival of a visitor. Rather than call out, Percy picked up a brass bell with a handle that was on the counter and shook it a couple of times. The man looked up and growled loudly, "Who goes there, friend or foe, contributor or critic?"

Percy was taken back for a moment but then saw the man's gritty grin that was barely distinguishable from a scowl. Beneath a high, receding forehead were fierce eyes, a sharp nose, and a dark beard. Percy replaced the bell on the counter and placed one hand next to it. "Neither of the latter, sir, nor your foe. I hope to be a consumer of your offerings."

"Did you say consumer? That we can manage, short-handed though we are. Thank God you didn't say you're a patient. I gave up medicine some time ago for belletristic endeavors. But instead of composing couplets, I find myself mending machines while my printer has gone to war. At my back I always hear, Time's winged chariot hurrying near."

Percy, laughing heartily. "As I thought I was giving up law for literature. I was expecting to deal with a clerk, but unless I have mistaken your reference to being a physician, you can only be Dr. George Bagby, editor of this illustrious magazine. Come now, don't be coy."

"Guilty as charged, sir. Illustrious? It is our aspiration, even while we remain firmly unillustrated unlike our competitors in the North who continue to rob me of my subscribers. What business might you have with this diadem of Southern literary delight?"

"I hope I have not interrupted you."

"Interrupted? Indeed, you have and for that I thank you. It is a moment of blessed relief. However right and proper it may be for an editor to make himself a beast of burden, it does not follow by rigorous logical sequence that he should be compelled to stagger under a load of ungrammatical, improperly punctuated fiddle-faddle, or to wade through the mire and filth of a villainous, higgedly-piggledy, tattered, patched, interpolated and dirty manuscript. That is what you interrupted as I must wade through a hundred submissions of the purest drivel." Bagby sighed as if relieved.

"How can that be? Your contributors have included the likes of my professor, Beverley Tucker, not to mention John Esten Cooke, William Gilmore Simms, and Joseph Glover Baldwin."

"Ah, yes. In glorious days of old when prose was vigorous and poetry sinewy. What we receive now are articles on topics selected with great care for their uninterestingness and written by irreproachable gentlemen at odd hours and without the least pains. It should seem that respectable gentlemen of a literary turn are subject, at times, to fits of almost unimaginable stupidity. In the extreme critical moment of these convulsions of dullness they catch at a pen, and the result is a series of what the French would call *idiotisms*, which are sent without exception to the *Messenger*. As for poetry, I receive whole reams of mere rhyme -- sometimes not even that -- absolute, unadulterated, preeminent, sentimentalist twaddle. Such would-be contributors dabble in meaningless sonnets, odes, and the like, and we would wish that they would retain their vapid oozings."

Bagby paused and examined Percy closely. "But we digress. You have an honest face, sir. What may I do for you?"

Percy marveled at the gale-force stream of words coming from the over-worked editor of the *Messenger*. Now he recognized Bagby as the unnamed author of "letters of Mozis Addums to Billy Ivvins" that had first appeared in the *Messenger* while Percy was still living in Louisiana. So, this was the sharp intelligence behind the semi-literate Mozis. Grinning at Bagby, Percy explained, "I've recently returned from a half-year overseas where I was deprived of access to the *Messenger* since last March. If you have them available, I should wish to purchase the issues I've missed."

Bagby's manner turned more serious. "Purchase, you say? By all means, I can find for you instantly what you seek. Most of our subscribers are now relying on credit." The *Messenger*'s editor took four steps over to a set of shelves on the wall and gathered seven copies for the months April to September. He placed them on the counter as Percy counted out Confederate dollars.

Picking up the money, the editor offered, "For another three, you will have a pre-paid subscription, Mr. . . . . . ."

"Moorhead. Lt. Moorhead. A subscription is impractical. For now, my residence is where I have most recently left my bag."

"Then consider submitting an essay on your journeys, Lieutenant. Travel letters by distinguished Southern gentlemen such as yourself have long been a staple of the *Messenger*."

As he left the voluble editor, Percy recalled the last editor of the *Messenger* whom he had encountered in Richmond twelve years earlier, shortly before the man's death: Edgar Alan Poe. He had no reason to suspect that he would soon meet two more former *Messenger* editors.

Chapter 33

And a Poet

Seated alone at a dinner table at the Ballard House that evening, Percy heard voices from nearby tables. A group of Georgia men and women were up from Atlanta were discussing how best to take care of the sick and wounded soldiers from their state who were on service in Virginia, those who had fought at Manassas Junction. They sounded concerned that a Virginia military facility would not give Georgia soldiers the care they deserved. Percy had not yet ordered when someone said his name.

"Lieutenant Moorhead, may I join you?"

Turning, Percy saw it was Jose Quintero, also rooming at the Ballard. He stood and extended his hand. "Of course. And it's Percy. The officer's rank is useful but unearned. Are you still in the Texas militia? And is it José?"

Sitting down opposite Percy, the Cuban Confederate laughed lightly. "Now, I'm officially attached to the Confederacy's Department of State. Joseph will do – José in Mexico, Joseph on this side of the border."

"Judah tells me you studied law in Cuba."

Quintero, smiling impishly. "Yes. But I got over it. Just as he told me you practiced law in New Orleans before teaching philology in college. I was a journalist in Texas at secession."

Chuckling at Quintero's choice of words, Percy said, "Philology would be a grand name for my classes. Language skills would be closer to the truth. Argument and persuasion. When Judah asked me to serve, I could not refuse him. But your English is without accent."

José Quintero was used to that reaction. "The heritage of a Cuban father and an English mother, a Woodville. And when I was twelve my parents sent me to Harvard."

"Harvard?" Percy concluded that that would explain the Cuban's flawless English. "What did you study?"

Quintero laughed again. "I prepared myself to be a poet, not a lawyer or diplomat. I studied with Mr. Longfellow."

"You do have the capacity to surprise, don't you? A poet who studied with Longfellow. The same Longfellow of *The Village Blacksmith*? *The Wreck of the Hesperus*?"

"The very man, yes. I've translated some of his poems into Spanish. Longfellow has encouraged me to write in Spanish. He is very fond of Spanish poetry. His first book was a translation of a Spaniard, *Coplas de Don Jorge Manrique*."

Percy shared a memory. "Then you're the second poet I've met in Richmond. Another of our American poets spoke in the hotel next to this one. Edgar Poe. I was here, shortly before he died."

Quintero raised a toast. "Quoth the Raven, 'Nevermore.' Mr. Longfellow was not kind to his memory."

Percy raised his own glass. "And what sort of poems bear the name José Quintero?"

"The kind that can send a poet to prison. Poetry on revolution. I have one called *Esperanza* that I wrote in the Castle Morro prison in Havana. Another is *En la Muerte de Narciso Lopez*."

"Lopez, the filibuster? Were you with him?"

"To my good fortune, not when he was executed. But, yes, I too sought to expel Spain from Cuba. When I was pardoned, I decided to seek my fortune in another country."

"That was fortunate, that you did not share the fate of Cinna the poet."

Quintero smiled with delight. "Ah, Percy, you know your Shakespeare. Longfellow told us in class about the poet in *Julius Caesar* who shared the name of a conspirator. When Cinna protested that the mob was mistaken as to his identity, one of the murderous pack yells out 'Tear him for his bad verses, tear him for his bad verses.' As I sat in Castle Morro fearing execution, I thought on that class but without the humor that Longfellow attached to the story."

"From Cuba you came to Louisiana?"

"Yes. I was in New Orleans for a short time and found my dear wife there. I liked your city. Soon after, I attached myself to a successful lawyer and politician in Texas, much as you have done with Judah Benjamin. My mentor was Mirabeau Lamar. Do you know of him?"

Percy was warming to his new friend. They had common backgrounds and interests. A waiter appeared and took their orders. "Yes. A president of Texas? I think he is dead."

Quintero confirmed with a nod of his head. "Yes. Did you know he was a poet? I practiced law with him for a short time. He got me employment for the Texas legislature and helped me to be a journalist."

"Forgive me, but I have to ask. Why did you join the Confederacy?"

"I'm a Texan now. The North treats us as a colony, like Cuba. Don't you hate the Northerners for what they're doing?"

Percy, pointedly. "Did Mirabeau Lamar hate the Mexicans?"

"Of course not," insisted Quintero quickly, perhaps offended. "I don't understand your insinuation."

Percy smiled, reassuringly. "I didn't think he did. That's precisely my point. Same for me. I don't hate the Mexicans. But I joined the army and fought against them fifteen years ago. So did Mirabeau Lamar as I recall. The Mexicans fought for principle and sovereignty. The United States fought for principle and sovereignty. A lot of men died on both sides. For principle and sovereignty. I get along just fine with Mexicans now. Same thing in this war. Principle and sovereignty on both sides. Many good men are dying, and more are going to die on both sides. Right now, the Union can't take much from me because I lost most of what was dear to me before this war began. When you're swept by a current you can't control or escape, you strive just to survive. Do the best you can to be a man among men. Live with integrity, fulfill your natural duties to friends and family. Fate will bring you to your destiny. Do you hate Henry Longfellow? He's a Northerner and an abolitionist. I suspect you don't."

Laughing, Quintero said, "*Touché*. I think you must be a better lawyer than I am a poet."

"I enjoy poetry but have no talent. Do have a favorite of yours I can read?"

"When I see you again, I shall bring you *El Banquete del Destierro*."

"The Banquet of the Exiled?"

"Yes. You speak Spanish then."

"Enough to appreciate its romantic potential. I look forward to your poetry."

Leaning towards Percy, the Cuban poet asked, "Do you think President Davis will send me back with instructions for Vidaurri to go forward?"

"I can't speak for him. But I wouldn't expect the president to attempt an annexation just now."

"Why not?"

Percy paused before replying. A waiter served their dinners. Resuming the exchange, he said, "If Governor Vidaurri needs Texas soldiers, it won't be a few. And then we're fighting both the Union and Mexico. One war at a time. I think we can help Mexico and ourselves without annexation."

Quintero poured wine into Percy's glass from a bottle that the waiter had brought. "I see why Mr. Benjamin values your opinion. But tell me, you seem to know Benito Juarez. How is that?"

Percy put down his fork which held a slice of pork. "Judah introduced me to him, when Juarez was in exile, rolling cigars in the shop of Fernando Borrego, Cigar Maker, on Bourbon Street in New Orleans and planning *la Revolucion*. At his request, I took him to our Supreme Court and introduced him to our Chief Justice. Later he helped me on our Mexican railroad project. I would not like to see anything happen to him, even if it were to benefit us."

The two men ate, contented with their food and their company. If Percy thought the evening was at its end, he was badly mistaken. He would be unable to keep his thoughts of his new companion to himself for long.

Chapter 34

A Ship in the Night

Percy thought he had settled in for the night in his Ballard House room. In the comfort of a chair next to his bed, a tumbler of whisky on a night table, he had begun the latest issue of the *Southern Literary Messenger* by gas light from the back issues he had acquired that afternoon from their editor, George Bagby. His interest was aroused by an essay comparing the Battle of Manassas with the victory of Caesar over Pompey at Pharsalia.

Under editor Bagby, the pages of the *Messenger* presented the war as a Manichaean struggle between good and evil. Anything Unionist was bad; things Southern were good. So, at Manassas, General Winfield Scott occupied the figure of Pompey for the writer, and Beauregard was Caesar. The anonymous author was erudite, but Percy could not share his disparagement of Winfield Scott. He retained his warm regard for Scott from the time the general made Percy a scout at Vera Cruz in 1847. More important was Scott's favoring him with a letter of recommendation that assured his admission to Judge Tucker's law school at William and Mary. The *Messenger* essay treated Scott as a tyrant and a has-been. Beauregard had earned his accolades at Manassas, but he was no Wellington at Waterloo, as the article's author claimed. Percy chalked it up to wartime excess of enthusiasm.

Percy recalled his conversations with Beauregard in New

Orleans after the Mexican War, when Beauregard was engineering the Federal Custom House and the navigability of the Mississippi River. Beauregard had expressed disdain of Scott's generalship and repeated it in Charleston only months ago. What had he said? Percy recall, "If Winnfield Scott is the best they can do for a general, the war won't last long." The Louisiana general was a good leader but a poor follower. But was he a prophet? Percy was certain Beauregard would clash with President Davis, who would not leave the conduct of the war to his generals.

A knock at the door shortly after nine interrupted his reading. He put the magazine down. On opening the door Percy was handed a note by a messenger in uniform: "Please come to the Davenport residence, 9 West Main Street. Judah."

Against the night's chill, Percy donned a light jacket. After twenty minutes of brisk walking, he arrived at the residence Benjamin had rented for himself and his brother-in-law, the elegant young *bon vivant*, Jules St. Martin. Jules was not in evidence when a servant showed Percy into Benjamin's study.

Looking up from the paperwork on his desk, Benjamin wasted no time on small talk. "What do you think of Quintero?"

Percy's opinion was favorable. "The man and the moment are met. A poet to boot."

Benjamin gestured to Percy to sit.

Percy settled into the leather chair. "His self-reflection will help him to weather challenges that Mexico poses for anyone. A man of Spanish heritage will serve better than someone like Pickett. He seems to have a good relationship with Governor Vidaurri. I gather he has a friend who is close to Juarez, a fellow poet from Cuba."

"What did you tell him?" asked Benjamin.

Now leaning forward in his chair, Percy responded candidly, "That speaking only for myself, I can't imagine we should do anything to put the Confederacy in the middle of a Mexican civil war. If Vidaurri would secede to form a Republic of Sierra Madre, we would be fighting Benito Juarez, the large landowners to the south of Coahuila and Tamaulipas – as well as the clergy who see us as a Protestant threat to a Catholic Mexico. Then the British, French and Spanish might intercede to protect their interests."

Benjamin offered Percy a Cuban cigar, then lit another for himself. "If only all the Cabinet members saw things as clearly as you, Percy. Without naming anyone, I'll say that some are so confident of our independence, they want to see us expand. Now. Not later."

Examining his cigar as he exhaled, Percy said, "Isn't one war enough for them? But we digress. You would not invite me here at this hour to discuss Quintero."

"Percy, Percy. You know me too well. Let's talk ships. You raised the subject yourself. How would you feel about purchasing a fast, shallow-draft steamship in the name of the Anglo-Mexican Tehuantepec Company?"

Percy thought for a moment. "I could do that. But why not Bulloch?"

"President Davis and I agree that it would be desirable to have the executive branch control a ship that is not subject to the politics of the Confederate Congress. Or the divisions between the army and navy and the competing demands of the states of our Confederacy."

"Hmmmm," Percy reflected again. "I see. This would be for operations off the books entirely. Subject to you, not Mallory."

Benjamin slowly nodded. "It may have advantages." He was silent on the advantages and who would enjoy them.

"Do you have specifics?" Benjamin had never separated his own business and financial interests from the offices he held. Benjamin, with Percy's cooperation, had used his position as a United States Senator to advance the Louisiana-Tehuantepec Railroad project. When secession approached in 1860, Benjamin had been in the far West, in California, engaged in his law practice.

As a secessher, Judah was a Johnny-Reb-come-lately.

"Not at present. At least not after its first voyage."

"Where would you want it located?"

"Somewhere in the Bahamas. Not at Nassau. Too conspicuous. But not too far away. Under a British flag. Maybe George Town. It has a good harbor and is near Nassau."

"And the purchase money? From Fraser, Trenholm and Co.?"

"No. We still have a credit arrangement for the Tehuantepec Railroad Company through Baring Brothers in London with Russell Sturgis. I've heard from him through our mutual friend in New York City. Rufus Jordan has been remarkable in developing a network and lines of communication for us. Sturgis wants to send things to some clients in Georgia and Alabama. There's less risk if we do it with a ship that is unknown to the Union. Or to our own officials, outside, of course, President Davis. He's rather taken with the idea."

Percy's interest showed. "And Barings will facilitate because they have interests in the South? Judge Rost got the cold shoulder when he tried to arrange transactions and credit with Bates at Barings."

Benjamin had read Rost's report. "Yes, he did. But there are divisions within the Barings firm. Sturgis will act discreetly."

"Do you have a name for our ship? I believe new owners traditionally get to rechristen a ship."

"Interesting word," replied Benjamin. "I'll leave christening to you. Something that will not suggest Confederate ties."

"Understood. Timeline?"

"Soon. You'll be returning to Liverpool within a fortnight. In the best of company. We're sending two men to London and Paris to provide us with a more effective diplomatic presence than Yancey, Rost and Mann have been able to provide."

Percy thought that the three had done disservice to their cause rather than advancing it. He only said, however, "A needed move. Who?"

Judah paused to re-light his cigar. He then drew Percy into his assignment, enticing him with its gravity. "Both were U.S. Senators. That will carry weight. You know John Slidell already. The other is a Virginian, James Mason. He's being sent to London and John to Paris. They're knowledgeable on our plans, but we need you bring them up to date on what they will find in Britain and France. No one here is better qualified to do that. And you already know John. I hope you don't mind leaving so soon after your arrival."

Percy nodded. Maybe now the sense of unfinished business in England would go away. Purchasing a ship was a pleasant prospect that he looked forward to. What he had learned in working with Bulloch on steamships he could now put to his own use.

Perhaps just beneath the reach of his conscious mind, without his accepted awareness of an inner drive, Percy's sense of unfinished business in London touched on that glimpse he had had in scene five of *Colleen Bawn* of the young actress playing Kathleen Creagh, Miss Grace Tarkenton, formerly of Godstow, Warwickshire, daughter of a Member of Parliament.

Chapter 35

Destiny in Foreign Lands

Percy stood with Joseph Quintero at the platform of the Richmond & Danville rail depot as the latter awaited his departure south. The Cuban Confederate was now officially the confidential agent to Governor Vidaurri, to reside in Monterrey

"What are your instructions, if you can share them?" asked Percy. He wondered if he and Quintero might overlap in their missions abroad. The Tehuantepec Railroad project might be an occasion for cooperation.

The two men had sought out a quieter room adjacent to the crowded station. It was the principal intersection of soldiers and civilians to and from the Confederate capital from the south. There was hardly an hour of the day without the bee-loud buzz of a busy hive. Quintero outlined his mission. "Along lines that you must have suggested to Mr. Benjamin. I'm to advise Governor Vidaurri that President Davis reciprocates Vidaurri's expression of friendship and goodwill. Commercial and social ties are to be expanded. However, I am to respectfully suggest in the interest of both parties that it would be impolitic to annex Mexican states to the Confederacy."

"That's good." Percy was encouraged that maybe reason would prevail. "Anything on relations with the North?"

"Yes. I am to persuade Governor Vidaurri to block Union troops across northern Mexico while we pursue purchasing war supplies. At the same time, I am to find the best route to send supplies from Mexico to the Confederacy. Of course, I am to keep my status a secret."

"Well, secrecy should be easier for you than for your predecessor Pickett. With his height and rude manners, he stood out as a sore thumb in every Mexican's eye. You will be indistinguishable from any other Mexican of Spanish heritage. No one will suspect you of being a Harvard man or a Confederate agent." Winking, Percy added, "You might even pass as a Latin poet."

As they stood and shook hands in farewell, Percy said:

Destino amargo y severo
a tierra extrema nos lanza.

"Yes, my friend." replied Quintero with a broad smile. It was the opening to the poem that he had given Percy: *Destiny, bitter and harsh, sends us to foreign lands.* "You are one of the few Confederates I've met who can appreciate poetry."

It was a heartfelt selection; Percy knew the quote was fitting, for both men.

Quintero was one of those remarkable men whom Percy considered a friend, even after the war ended. Years later, when Percy returned to New Orleans, they did have a reunion and reflected on their experiences and regrets. That is a tale yet to be told. He was a man of principle and ability. And a poet to boot! I ask you, what if the Confederacy had had more men like Joseph Quintero and Percy Moorhead and fewer Thomas Picketts?

Chapter 36

Richmond's Social Salon

Returning to Judah Benjamin's office that afternoon, near dusk, Percy found the Secretary of War leaving his office. Jovial, Benjamin greeted Percy, "You're just in time Percy. You can join me for a light buffet. At a good friend's home."

This was a surprise. Judah had not included him in a social function in the ten years since Percy and Philomena had entertained guests for Judah's political activities. Percy asked, "Am I dressed appropriately for the occasion? I'm afraid I don't know Richmond's wartime social etiquette."

Judah put Percy at ease. "Your uniform is perfectly good. It's an informal gathering. My friend has regular guests in for a Friday buffet. People come and go throughout the evening. It's a good way to maintain a regular social life and camaraderie in these difficult days. You need to meet some of Richmond's society."

Although Percy's late wife had grown up in Richmond society, Percy had not spent any time with her in the city. He welcomed the opportunity to meet others outside a military setting. "A very good idea. Whose your friend?"

"You'll meet her very soon. A lovely widow. Her place is only a few blocks from here."

Benjamin and Percy walked up 9th Street to St. Paul's church and turned left on Grace. In two blocks Percy found himself in front of an elegant town home that he recognized immediately. He had been here twice before.

"Is this it?" he asked Benjamin. "The Stanard home?"

It was Judah's turn to be surprised. "Yes. You know it?"

Percy, intently querulous. "You said your friend is a widow?"

They arrived at the open door to the house. "Yes. Mrs. Robert Stanard. Here she is now to greet us."

Martha Stanard exclaimed, "Judah! Where on earth did you find Percy Moorhead?" The hostess was as vivacious as Percy remembered, though she was a decade older. But a widow? When Martha Pearce Stanard opened her home for the wedding reception after Percy and Philomena married in 1851, her husband was away on legal business in Washington.

Speaking to Martha, Judah asked, "You know each other?"

Percy graciously answered for her, in case she may have forgotten. "Mrs. Stanard lent her beautiful home for our reception when Philomena and I were married. I'm amazed she remembers me."

Martha Stanard was sensitive to subtle expressions on the faces of her guests. She sensed the sadness to Percy's words. Without asking Percy to speak about Philomena if he were reluctant, she said tentatively, "Philomena's family were Randolphs. I'm afraid I've lost touch with her mother." She did not let on that she knew of the death of Percy's wife. She had attended Philomena's funeral in Richmond but had remained in the rear of the church. She was uncertain whether Percy had seen her.

Percy quickly spoke; to avoid awkwardness, he was vague, even though he recalled seeing Martha at Phil's funeral. "My wife passed a few years ago. Her mother has kept to herself since then. She is well."

With delicacy, Martha said, "I was saddened at your loss. Do you still have your home in Louisiana? You're in the uniform of a Confederate officer and not of the Washington Artillery from your state. Since Manassas, they have camped nearby."

Benjamin returned to the conversation. "I took Percy from his professorship at William and Mary to represent the Confederacy in legal matters abroad. He's just returned from England on the *Bermuda*. I'm afraid his stay in Richmond will be brief."

A young black maid presented herself at Martha Stanard's side and quietly said she was needed by two other guests. Martha excused herself, expressing the hope she would see more of Percy before he left.

Percy asked Judah, "What happened to her husband?"

Moving slowly to a table on which an assortment of well-prepared dishes were ready for guests, Judah explained, "Illness. He was somewhat older than Martha. She has taken it upon herself to knit the Confederacy together in a way that President Davis and our legislature can never do. She brings together our leading figures – political, military and business – and gives them the chance to become familiar with one another in a casual setting. Sectional interests are set aside in favor of pleasant society. What controversy could continue among us in the presence of her charm and optimism?"

Percy readily agreed. "She's an amazing woman. She has a gift of intimacy. Not unlike Phil before our losses."

"I can only imagine," said Benjamin quietly. After a respectful pause, he called Percy's attention to a man in the doorway to the living room. "Over there you may recognize Thomas Jenkins Semmes. Perhaps you encountered him in New Orleans when he was practicing law. You were in Virginia when he was elected Louisiana Attorney General. Now he's one of our state's senators. As chairman of the joint committee on the flag and seal of the Confederate States, he wrote our motto, *Deo Vindice*."

Percy remembered seeing the lawyer in New Orleans. "So it

was Senator Semmes who invoked God as our vindicator. As I recall, the Senator spent as much time in the Boston Club as he did in the courtroom."

"As did I," chuckled Benjamin. "Fortunately, I had a capable young attorney to carry my load. And you still are indispensable."

"Who was responsible for the preamble? As I recall, it differed from the U. S. Constitution."

Judah was not surprised at the fact that Percy had examined the new constitution of the Confederacy. He had an eye for telling detail. "Yes. The people are citizens of their own states, not citizens of a United States. Words matter, whatever their source on the foundation document. Even if few people read it closely."

"I'll look at it more closely," Percy promised. Words mattered, he thought, even when lofty sentiments conceal less savory ends.

Returning to his jaunty air, Benjamin noticed another regular guest. "Our hostess has also long been a patroness of Southern literature. She and Robert feted their friend, William Makepeace Thackeray, when the novelist was in Richmond to lecture on English Humorists of the Eighteenth Century. See the sallow figure over by the buffet table? That's John R. Thompson."

"Of course," answered Percy. "I should have recognized him. He's another friend of Edgar Poe. Thompson was editor of the *Southern Literary Messenger* when I was a student of Beverly Tucker. I heard Poe speak here not long before I joined your practice. It was Thompson who introduced Poe. The Stanards hosted a reception for the poet afterwards. That was my first visit to this home. But he doesn't look well. Too thin for his height."

Benjamin led Percy over to Thompson, whispering, "Consumption, but he's in remission now. He's returned from Georgia where he moved after leaving the *Messenger*." He introduced Percy as a special envoy to England to assist in trade matters. When Percy told Thompson he was familiar with his writing and his poetry, he responded, "I'm flattered. Are you a fellow scribbler?"

"My aspirations unfortunately outrun my talents. I studied law with one of your contributors. Judge Tucker."

"Really! I confess I studied law as well. In Charlottesville, where I heard lectures by Judge Tucker's brother. But I found the muse of poetry more seductive than Lady Justice. Mrs. Stanard has always been a generous supporter to the *Messenger*. Come, if I may borrow you from Judah. You've got to meet another alumnus of the magazine. One of my predecessors as editor. He's seated over there, by the window."

"Marvelous!" exclaimed Percy. "I've just recently met your successor, Dr. Bagby. It's a wonder that he can continue to publish in conditions of war."

Thompson smiled good-naturedly at the mention of the current editor of the *Messenger*. "Old Mozis himself. It is with a great deal of grumbling, I would imagine if I know the good physician." He took Percy by the elbow and led him to the seated gentleman, a well-dressed man in his mid-fifties, of stout physique and balding forehead. The man stood and greeted Thompson cordially, who then said, "Let me introduce Lt. Percy Moorhead. This is Commander Matthew Fontaine Maury. Confederate Navy but an editor of the *Messenger* after Poe."

The name and reputation of Maury were well-known to Percy. An accident, a fall from a coach, had disrupted Maury's career at sea. He had turned his restless energies to charting the winds and currents of the seas all over the world. Few ships on the ocean did not draw upon his monumental collection of data that he had assimilated into charts that cut days or weeks off sea voyages. That Maury had also edited the *Messenger* was, however, new to him.

"Moorhead, you say?" said Maury, warmly surprised. "I know who you are. You've been working with Bulloch and Huse in England. I wasn't aware you had returned."

Matthew Fontaine Maury

Percy's reply was intentionally nonchalant, as if to downplay the importance of his work compared to Maury's achievements. "I come and go as the Confederacy requires my services. Just now, I'm between assignments. They also stand and wait who only serve."

Grinning at Percy's allusion, Maury insisted, "Sit. Sit, Percy. You must tell me everything you can about the ships that are under construction in Liverpool. Nothing could capture my attention more."

For more than an hour Percy poured out to the naval officer everything he could remember about the designs of the *Oreto* and the *290*. The land-locked mariner took it all in eagerly, peppering Percy with ship-building questions that only Bulloch could have answered to his satisfaction. Percy was more comfortable describing the challenges of complying with the English statutes that promoted her neutrality. "At the construction phase, it's like trying to make a bear look as harmless as a cow."

Maury laughed, adding his own animal imagery. "Or a sea-wolf covered in a sheep's skin. Are you returning to England?"

Percy's quick answer showed his readiness. "Almost immediately." Judah had briefed him adequately on his assignment.

"Excellent," said the naval legend warmly. "I hope our paths may cross again. Our President and Secretary Mallory think I may do good service there."

Three days later, Percy began his return to England. His work would overlap Maury's own mission to Britain and Europe.

But first he had to get there. The challenges were to be much greater than his first trans-Atlantic journey of the war.

Chapter 37

Stormy Start

The moonless night's weather was ominous for the beginning of a voyage into the dark Atlantic Ocean. Still dripping from his wet walk from the South Carolina Railroad depot on Meeting Street down Hazel Street, Percy stood under the relative shelter of the eaves of Winslow & Co.'s warehouse. Midnight approached, the time for boarding. The mid-October storm drenched Patton's Wharf with cold, wind-driven rain; the *Theodora* was tied at Patton's not seventy yards from Percy. Amid lightning flashes, he could make out some of the figures who stood under an overhanging roof, his fellow passengers waiting to plunge into the black night.

Percy recognized Benjamin's fellow former Senator from Louisiana, John Slidell. With him were his family – his wife and their four children. Huddled nearby was James Murray Mason, the Virginian Judah Benjamin had mentioned. Other passengers could be glimpsed, awaiting departure. Among them, he was to learn, were Slidell's secretary, George Eustis, with his bride, and James McFarland, Mason's assistant. When the group began to board the steamship, Percy fell in with them. The vessel would carry the Confederacy's best hope for British and French recognition of the

South's independence.

Silence prevailed. All knew how critical the journey was, and perilous. The uncommonly foul weather added to the apprehension the travelers felt. For the captain and crew, the conditions were a godsend, making less likely their detection by the Union squadron lurking just beyond cannon range. Better to chance thunder bolt than cannon ball.

Once aboard the steamer, an ex-privateer, the passengers and crew continued in hushed tones, as if whispers might carry across the sheets of rain to the blockading Yankee ships. The only lit lantern was shrouded, allowing the helmsman to read the compass. They had to slip past the Union gunboats that kept vigil, like a pack of curs with heavy ordnance for teeth and claws.

The five-hundred-ton sidewheeler gave a quiet shudder, and the passengers briefly swayed as the pilot engaged the engine. The paddles began to lap slowly the water of the harbor. A light at Fort Sumter and another on shore allowed the *Theodora* to steer, despite the dark and rain. Passing within a mile of the nearest ship of the Union squadron, the passengers could see its lights, but they escaped observation.

After the *Theodora* was beyond the blockaders by three or four miles, Percy heard Captain Lockwood instruct the helmsman to abandon the coast and put directly out to sea, making direct for Nassau. She was a small, fast ship, capable of running at sixteen knots. Though no match for a Union war ship, she was armed with one large pivot gun, a 32-pounder. Those passengers who had remained in the salon now went below to attempt some sleep.

⚬ - ⚬

Coming on deck as the sun rose, Percy encountered another early riser, a man in his mid-forties. Thick-set and a gentleman in manner, the man had a florid complexion and round face set off by mustache and goatee. Though the man was traveling under a false name, Percy learned he was Louis Coxetter, a mariner who had operated as a privateer for the first few months of the war. Coxetter was a taciturn man who had settled in Florida in his youth. Now he was traveling to England to assume responsibility for a Fraser, Trenholm ship the firm would use in running the blockade. Neither man divulged much about himself as they conversed about what lay ahead. Intermittent rainstorms kept most of the passengers in their cabins for the day.

That evening, when Percy had drinks with Mason and Slidell after dinner, the two envoys told him they were glad he had arrived in time to accompany them. Benjamin had informed them of Percy's work in England.

"I was glad," said Slidell, "that Judah was able to persuade you to serve with him. He always spoke highly of your work in New Orleans and how you helped with our Mexican railroad project. I'll have to tell my wife to visit with you about your association with General Beauregard. He's now married to her sister."

"Really? I didn't know." Percy was pleased that Slidell remembered their associations. "I saw him in Charleston in May as I was leaving for Liverpool. Our acquaintance is not such that he would mention it."

Not to be left out of the conversation of two from Louisiana, Mason interposed. "Judah tells me you were teaching at William and Mary." Mason was a somber man of sixty-plus years, square jawed, with wide lips and flowing hair that emphasized the baldness of the top of his head.

"Yes. I had studied law there with Judge Tucker. Later I was employed by President Ewell to teach Rhetoric."

"Good man, Tucker. I knew him and his father. William and Mary is where I studied the law as well."

James M. Mason   John Slidell

Despite Mason's clumsy effort to make conversation, Percy perceived a certain hauteur in the Virginian, a patrician distance that sprang from an uncongenial aloofness. Though America had always rejected hereditary titles, Mason's lineage was such that he was certain he possessed a natural nobility that set him apart from common folk. The family motto was *Pro Republica Semper*: For the Republic always. Mason saw no contradiction that the Republic to which he was forever faithful shifted as time suited, now Virginia, now the United States, now the Confederate States of America. The Republic of his fidelity was an ideal Republic, a Platonic Republic or even the Roman Republic, in which he was confident he would also have been a Senator. His Republic was an intellectual construct of a state committed to Principle and Freedom and Duty, the content of which qualities varied with occasion. His Republic was a Republic with more Liberty for people such as the Masons – propertied, responsible, refined, but less Liberty for poorer whites, and none at all for those of African descent.

Mason was unaware apparently that his manner was felt as patronizing by Percy. "I served with Secretary Hunter in the Senate. He's a good pick by Davis. He's been Secretary of State for a few months. Very few reports have come back from our commissioners. You are in a position to tell us what we need to expect."

Percy tried to cut through Mason's reserve with candor. "I can't speak about Paris because I've had little to do with activities there. Most think that Louis Napoleon will follow the British lead. Your focus will be on Prime Minister Palmerston and Foreign Minister Russell. You will make your own assessment whether they are open to charm and persuasion. They will do what is best for Britain."

"Hmmmrmp," grunted Mason. "And the British masses?"

"You will find the better sort are with us. We have friends in Parliament but also opponents, especially Mr. Bright. I must warn you, you will be watched everywhere you go. From the first day when he arrived in London, Mr. Adams has employed hundreds of agents to pursue every man and woman who might be working for the Confederacy."

"Hundreds? Surely you exaggerate," Mason interjected, scoffing at the notion the Yankees would pay the costs of such extensive surveillance.

"No, sir." Percy was emphatic. "You will underestimate their determination at your peril. If they can prevent a shipment of 10,000 Enfield rifles, they will have disarmed a Confederate regiment without the loss of a single Yankee soldier. If they can prevent the launch of just one Confederate cruiser they will save two dozen or more Yankee merchant ships." He was beginning to doubt whether Mason would prove better at representing the Confederacy than Commissioner Yancey.

Slidell had paid close attention to Percy's words. He asked, "How do we counter their efforts?" He had not fully realized the vital importance of the work of the Confederate agents already in England, such as Percy, Bulloch and Huse. Lincoln and Seward labored under no such misperception. The Union government invested heavily to counter the handful of Confederate agents, who were working effectively to arm and supply the Confederate soldiers.

Percy was more comfortable engaging with Slidell than with Mason. He answered Slidell's question: "Two words: discretion and deception."

"All right. Explain, Lieutenant." Mason was not a man who easily took direction from a man half his age, even if they shared an alma mater. He insisted that he be persuaded.

Percy turned again to Mason. "Discretion – avoid connections that can be used by the Yankees against us. Don't provide them with evidence that can be used to show violations of their Foreign Enlistment Act."

"I can't imagine us giving them evidence," Mason said, dismissive of the possibility.

Percy persisted, trying to sound patient, "If you are seen in Liverpool, where ships for the Confederacy are being built, it will be presented to the English authorities as a confirmation that they are our ships, that they are not being constructed for the Italians or Egyptians or Mexicans. The Union detectives are watching the shipyards day and night to see who is inspecting the vessels under construction, who is meeting with the shipyard owners and engineers. They have placed their agents on the work crews."

"Like carpenters?" asked Slidell, more receptive to Percy's admonitions than Mason.

"Indeed. And mechanics and painters. The words of the English statute are 'equip, furnish, fit out, or arm' a vessel in violation of British neutrality. Adams and his agents want to have workers who will give evidence that a ship is being readied for war purposes, not commerce. If they can show that and link it to you, the Foreign Office or a court will stop the vessel's construction or prevent its sailing. They have men in a dozen Liverpool pubs each night to try to overhear if anyone is bragging about building or crewing a ship for the South."

"My God," exclaimed Mason, "our fate rests on the sobriety of workmen and sailors."

Percy could not imagine Mason mingling with workmen or common sailors. He cautioned, "Our fate depends on discretion."

"You had mentioned also deception." Slidell was more interested in Percy's experiences than was Mason. If Benjamin trusted Moorhead, he would too.

"Yes. We might send a false message knowing that Adams's detective will intercept it – for example, saying that our man will meet with an arms dealer at a certain time and place. Then the minister's men will show up and waste their time on nothing, for no one is there."

Mason insisted, "Gentlemen need not resort to trickery."

Percy shook his head in reluctant disagreement. "I wish it were so, Mr. Mason. But to give an example of when it has been effective, to ferret out one of the workmen bribed by Minister Adams in Liverpool we had one of our men install rail fittings for a cannon so that the Union spy would report it. By the time an inspector from the Foreign Office arrived, our man had removed all trace of the fittings, thereby undermining the minister and identifying his spy, who was immediately fired by the shipyard."

Slidell said with a grim smile, "This would be amusing, if so much were not at stake."

Percy said, "There are many who believe the ends justify the means – any means. We've been told by someone who was present that a bitter argument took place between Adams and Henry Sanford."

"Sanford? The Union minister to Belgium?" asked Slidell, who knew of Henry Sanford as a diplomat to Paris when Slidell was a U. S. Senator.

"Yes. He's spent most of his time in England organizing their agents. He was overheard arguing to Adams that they would be justified in using sabotage to stop us from getting arms and ships."

Mason was surprised. "Sabotage?"

"Yes. Burning the hulls of ships being built. Destruction of crates of arms in warehouses."

Indignant, Mason asserted, "But that's not lawful. Or fair."

Percy said wryly, "War is brutal – when not conducted by gentlemen." Almost under his breath, he added, "I'm not sure if the consequences of secession have been fully appreciated by those who initiated it."

"What's done is done," Mason said. He paused as he loosed tobacco juice into the spittoon next to the table then wiped his lips with a napkin. He looked harshly at Percy, measuring his words before he spoke. "You sound of recrimination, sir."

"No sir. Not recrimination," Percy quickly retreated. Mason had a closed mind. "Anticipation. Preparation. Too many of our people dismiss Lincoln as a country bumpkin and Seward as a wild-eyed radical. They fail to see both their determination and their competence. If we continue to underestimate them, we will be unprepared to meet their challenge."

"Hmrruph," responded Mason. "We'll see about that, won't we? Soon enough the English will be persuaded that we are their true descendants in America. My ancestor George Mason of Staffordshire was a member of the House of Commons during the reign of King Charles the First. He commanded a regiment of cavalry in the Royal Army and came to Virginia rather than live under Cromwell. The English will appreciate our close connections to them, and they will recognize our cause as representing their values and traditions. Lincoln and Seward should not be overestimated. In Jefferson Davis they have more than met their match."

Slidell's raised eyebrows showed he likely did not share Mason's sentiments. To end the exchange, Mason turned and went below.

"Well now," said Percy to Slidell with irony and a wink. "That was interesting. Do you suppose Mr. Mason will tell the Queen that he has come round to conclude that the American Revolution was a mistake? That George Third was unduly maligned by the colonists?"

Slidell smiled but said nothing that would undercut his fellow emissary. His eyebrows had been enough.

Chapter 38

A Cuban Detour

Percy emerged on deck from a nap after lunch, awakening to the awareness that the *Theodora* was no longer moving in the water. He saw Louis Coxetter walking away from Captain Lockwood. Two other men were descending to a pilot boat at the side of the ship. "What just happened?"

Coexetter did not look happy. "Those were the pilots who were to take us into Nassau. They've just informed Captain Lockwood that British ships from Nassau to England all stop in New York. We can't risk it. Our envoys would be immediately recognized. And there is no steamer from here to St. Thomas, which is the only island that would be the port of departure of a British steamer line. This ship can't take us to England."

Percy took the news in stride. He was growing accustomed to erratic travels. Schedules were aspirations at best, guesses the rest of the time. "Okay. Where does that leave us? We are two days out of Charleston. This is a blockade runner, not a ship for crossing the ocean. In another day or so we'll run low on coal, and we're three days from St. Thomas. Do we put into Nassau for more?"

"The pilots recommended that we not. Union ships patrol these islands. If we put in, we probably won't get out. The captain says we'll head to Cuba if Slidell and Mason concur."

Percy made light of their predicament. "At least Cuban coffee is likely to be better than what the cook on board here puts out for us."

Coxetter chuckled. "And the cigars."

A day and a half later, off the harbor of Cardenas, Cuba, they met with a small Spanish war steamer. When the captain of the *Theodora* raised the Confederate flag and asked to speak with the Spanish captain, their salutation was returned, and the Spaniard lay to. Slidell went on board the Spanish ship and was received with kindness and civility. The coal remaining on the *Theodora* was running low. It was doubtful she could make it to Havana. The Spanish ship escorted her into the port of Cardenas, much to the anger of several Union ships that were also anchored there but would not risk an international incident. While refueling, a Cuban who was married to a Virginia woman rode into town to invite Mason and Slidell and all their party to spend a few days at their sugar and coffee plantation. Upon being informed there would be no steamer to St. Thomas for another three weeks, the two envoys and their immediate entourage accepted the hospitality of the Cuban grandee.

Percy and Louis Coxetter remained aboard the *Theodora*. It departed the next day for Havana. On arrival, they took a room with two beds at a hotel. The *Theodora* began loading goods to carry back into Charleston, while Percy and Coxetter sought information on ways to get to England that might be earlier than Mason and Slidell anticipated. That evening, a knock on their door was from a man who introduced himself as Charles Helm. The three went downstairs to the bar of the hotel. Helm told them he had just arrived from England to assume the post of Confederate special agent to the Spanish, English, and Danish Islands of the West Indies.

Percy shook his head ruefully. "We had not expected to come to Cuba on our way to Liverpool."

Helm sounded equally regretful. "No, I suppose not. If you had, perhaps the Confederacy would have sent me funds by you. Secretary Toombs promised me that I would be furnished with ample funds in credits on London banks to pay the port charges of vessels sent to me, to pay the storage and commission in the discharge and reshipment of cargo, and in the charter or purchase of vessels to transfer cargo. This wasn't done, and I've not heard yet from the new Secretary, Mr. Hunter."

"The delay is not from neglect. The Yankees are tightening the blockade," volunteered Coxetter. "That's why we set out on the *Theodora* instead of the *Nashville*. She's faster than any of the Union ships off Charleston. I'm being sent to Liverpool to take charge of a blockade runner. We expect to run it from several ports of the West Indies. It's certain your role and agents at Nassau and Bermuda will be of greatest importance. My best guess is that communications just didn't reach you in London."

Percy added, "We're both trying to reach Liverpool."

"Yes," replied Helm. "Your friends there await you. I've spent time with Huse, Bulloch and Anderson. They've explained your work to me."

Percy joked, "Not much secrecy in being a secret agent."

Helm was reassuring. "No, I think your cover story is pretty effective. In England Percy Moorhead is thought to be a resident of Vera Cruz and a representative of an English firm, the Anglo-Mexican Tehuantepec Company."

Percy understood the challenges Helm would face. "My associates in Liverpool and London have had their own difficulties with the transmission of funds through Fraser, Trenholm."

"So they told me," said Helm, sounding frustrated. "But I don't want to be on the hind tit of the hog. If my coordination is to be effective, there should be no delay in placing funds at my disposal. A failure could result in serious inconvenience to the government. My personal credit at Havana will enable me to negotiate on the best terms any bills of exchange or drafts that may be forwarded to me via London or Liverpool. I hope you can convey this back to Richmond."

Unable to help Helm, Percy hoped Helm could help him. "We first must get to England. Any suggestions? Our companions on the *Theodora* said it would be three weeks before they can move on."

Setting aside his own difficulties, Helm brightened. "In fact, I may be able to get you on your way. Did you notice the Spanish ships in the port and the soldiers who've just arrived?"

"Yes." Percy was uncertain of the relevance. "Are they anticipating another revolt or a filibuster expedition by Confederate sympathizers?"

"Not at all," laughed Helm. "Though who knows? Revolutions can happen any day. But no, not today. As to concerns about Confederate designs south of her borders, among my instructions is to convey our earnest desire to Governor-General Serrano that we have no designs on Cuba and wish only to expand trade and commerce with a near neighbor. The Spanish are the vanguard of a planned expedition of Spain, Britain and France into Mexico to demand repayment of debts. The ships you've seen are an early arrival of supplies and soldiers."

Skeptical of a plan to bring Mexico into submission, Percy asked, "And that helps us how?"

"As the representative of a Mexican railroad project, I think you and Louis could find passage on the return of one of two vessels leaving in the next day or two. You could easily make the transition to England from a Spanish port."

"You could arrange that? But you've only just arrived."

Helm laughed again. He had an easy laugh, a sign of his readiness to setting up shop as a Confederate shipping and commercial agent. "Actually, I'm returning. President Buchanan made me consul general here three years ago. Seward offered to keep me here, but I resigned. I'm well-known to the Spanish and the Cubans. I've built up a fund of trust. We have seen eye-to-eye in the past, and we can be of use to one other in the future."

This was good news to Percy and Coxetter. Percy was enthusiastic. "Give us an hour's notice, and we'll be on board. Can we forward communications for you once we get to England?"

Helm shook his head. "No. My letters to our government will go with Captain Lockwood. Right now he's loading the *Theodora* with swords, pistols, lead, coffee and 200,000 cigars of Cuba's finest tobacco. She can't carry much cargo but her shallow draft and speed allow her to hug the coast and use the protected waterways that the Yankee ships are too deep to enter. Hot coffee and cigars will give our soldiers some comfort in the cold, wet days of winter soon to begin in the camps in Virginia and Tennessee."

Percy would have liked to have spent a day or two exploring Havana. When he was a boy, Odessa had told him stories of her living in the city where she learned needlecraft from an old Jewish tailor. He was especially interested in seeing Castle Morro, a prison with a long history. It had once held captive Percy's new friend, José Quintero, who was on his way to Mexico even as Percy sought return to England. But there was no time. He was on assignment, not a turista.

Fourteen hours later Percy and Coxetter were aboard a Spanish ship steaming out of Havana. In fifteen days they were in London. After Percy made a morning visit alone to Mr. Russell Sturgis of Baring Brothers, they boarded a train in early afternoon for the final five hours of their journey to Liverpool.

Chapter 39

The *Herald*

Percy and Coxetter were eating breakfast in Percy's Liverpool hotel. It was the morning after their arrival. "Listen, Louis, we shouldn't be seen together going from here to 10 Rumford Place. The Fraser, Trenholm offices are known as the beating heart of the Confederacy. A Union spy keeps watch on everyone coming and going. They know me. If we're seen together, it'll confirm that you are a Confederate agent."

"You got it, stranger," Coxetter grinned. "Will they have good coffee there? I miss it." He gestured at his teacup. "This English tea is brown water."

Percy, equally cheerful. "Awful it is. And their bread. But it sure as hell beats field rations, hardtack and weevils. I'll see that coffee's waiting for you."

"I'll count on it. What I'll do is delay my arrival at Rumford Place by at least fifteen minutes."

"All right. That may do it. Henry Wilding is acting consul at the United States commercial consulate pending the arrival of Bev Tucker's replacement from America. He supervises a network of detectives and spies for Ministers Adams and Sanford. Someone is supposed to be the new consul, but that's all I know."

Pleased to see Percy, Charles Prioleau inquired of conditions in his native city. Percy told him of the good spirits prevailing at home with the blockade's limited effectiveness at sealing the city from seaward commerce. He explained that he and Coxetter had to leave the envoys Mason and Slidell behind in Cuba. Their arrival might be delayed several more weeks. From his leather case, Percy presented Prioleau a stack of dispatches, letters and financial instruments from Richmond and from the Charleston office of Fraser, Trenholm.

When Louis Coxetter arrived a half-hour later, Prioleau told them that the ship that was the reason for Coxetter's journey was almost ready to take up her mission.

"The vessel I am to command. Does she have a name?" Coxetter sipped his hot coffee approvingly.

"The *Hay'ld*," said Prioleau, which was understood as the *Herald* by Percy and her future captain. "Y'all need to go to Dublin to inspect her and finish the paperwork for her purchase."

"Dublin?" This surprised Coxetter.

"Yup. She's a fast ferryboat. Ran the Dublin to Glasgow route until coupla months ago. We had the firm of Cunard, Wilson negotiate her purchase through an agent, Mr. Chaals Taylah. I think y'all will like what y'all find. Large capacity, low freeboard and loaded draft of 10.5 feet. Oughta be just what y'all need for running the blockade. I wouldn't want to cross the Atlantic in her too many times."

"When?" asked Percy.

"The sooner y'all go to Dublin, the sooner y'all can bring her back here for modifying."

Percy was eager to learn more., "And the *Oreto*? Bulloch's back in the South, and we haven't had any updates."

"She's shaping up. And the *290*, across in Birkenhead, in the Lay'd yards. Best materials. Best workmanship. Union agents doing all they can to interfere."

To throw off any of the agents who might be watching them, Percy and Coxetter traveled to Dublin by separate routes. A night's long ferry ride on the *Iron Duke* took Coxetter across the Irish Sea to Kingstown Harbour, Dublin. Percy took the train from Liverpool to Holyhead, where he caught the ferry of the Dublin Steam Packet Company at 1:30 in the morning, sailing to the same port. Percy arrived at the offices of A & C Taylor, agents for the Dublin and Glasgow Steam Packet Co. at 9 Eden Quay, an hour before Coxetter. The Confederate captain was already busy inspecting the *Herald*.

The managing agent for A & C Taylor was a slender Irishman of forty, dapper in dress and cheerful in outlook. He introduced himself as Finn Dooley. In his accent, Percy thought he heard traces of his own father's long diminished Irish tongue. It carried a bit of charm for him. But the recollection of Grady Boyle's more pronounced brogue chased away the pleasant memory.

Finn Dooley handed Percy the paperwork for the transfer of ownership of the Herald. As Percy reviewed the documents, he noticed the agent eyeing him in an odd manner. Percy stopped reading and pleasantly asked, "Yes? You wanted to say something?"

"Oh," was the sly reply. "I was just thinking it is a pity that Mr. Prioleau was unable to purchase the *Herald*'s sister steamer. Pay no attention. Just an idle thought."

Of course, Percy's attention was immediately aroused, as the Irishman intended. But he pretended indifference, grunting and burrowing down in the papers before him. Finally, Percy looked up and said indifferently, "Mr. Prioleau's had a lot of offers, I gather."

"Oh well," said the agent. "The people we represent purchased three ships in anticipation of receiving government mail contracts. The contracts were awarded to a rival."

"Sister ship, you say?"

Finn perked up. "Yes. Built by John Reid & Co., Port Glasgow.

Two hundred twenty feet length, iron hull, side wheeler."

Percy, sounding indifferent. "Still for sale?"

"For Mr. Prioleau?" said the agent, alertly sensing Percy's interest.

Percy, casually. "No. On this I would represent another principal." Shrugging, he added, "If he's interested." The undisclosed principal was the Anglo-Mexican Tehuantepec Company, which is to say, Percy himself.

"I'm sure we can work something out." The shrewd, dark-eyed Mr. Dooley added, "You would, of course receive the same agent's commission as Mr. Prioleau."

"Agent's commission?"

Dooley responded, "Yes. In Britain, it is the custom that a portion of the purchase price be remitted to the agent of the purchaser."

The British custom was not the American, as Dooley seemed to understand. A *commission* for the purchaser's agent had the unsavory appearance of a bribe. Recalling Major Anderson's concerns about commissions, Percy countered, "Could that amount not be deducted from the purchase price? It's not our way of doing business."

"Hmmm," was Dooley's only response, saying nothing about Prioleau's acceptance of a commission on the purchase of the *Herald*. "I'm afraid that is out of the question. It would be contrary to our regular business practice and could set an unfortunate precedent. And the sellers we represent would think we had lowered the price of the vessel without their consent. We cannot require you to keep it, so you may simply pass it on to your principals as a savings to them."

"Yes. I suppose I could." No doubt Anderson had told his superiors in Richmond of British commissions in his reports. From Prioleau's extravagant style of living in Liverpool, Percy surmised that Prioleau was not returning his commissions to the

Confederacy or to Fraser, Trenholm. Of course, Prioleau was the representative of a private firm, not an employee of the Confederacy. For the other purchasing agents of the Confederacy, he had his doubts as to their practices. There was no way to inquire of them how they accounted for commissions. There is no delicate way of asking about kickbacks. New Orleans political realities had taught Percy that lesson long ago.

Louis Coxetter arrived and joined with Percy in taking charge of the *Herald*. Percy paid close attention as Coxetter and Finn Dooley worked out crew arrangements to move the *Herald* from Dublin to Liverpool for final fitting out. He would need to make similar provision for obtaining a crew and taking charge of the steamship he would buy through A & C Taylor. He admired the discretion of Dooley for making no mention of the sister ship of the *Herald* in the presence of Coxetter. As they left the broker's office, Percy said he would return the next day for additional discussions.

"You're not going with me on the *Herald* to Liverpool?" inquired Coxetter.

Percy demurred, without raising suspicion. "No. I have other business. And it's best we continue to travel separately. The Yankee spies will be watching new ship arrivals in Liverpool."

The "other business" of Percy was not only a ship for Judah Benjamin but something far more personal . . . . Percy's father and the Boyle family. He had waited for this opportunity. Now it was here.

Chapter 40

The Boyles Priest

IN the reception salon of Macken's Hotel on Dawson Street, near Trinity College and St. Stephen's Green, Percy opened the small notebook he carried to record important information. He was warmed by the fireplace opposite his chair. Two years earlier, in the court proceedings in St. Francisville, when Grady Boyle established his competing claim to be the rightful heir of Howard Moorhead, *alias* Redmond Boyle, he had jotted down the christening record for Grady Boyle, which named the church and the full names of Grady's parents. The Church of Ireland baptism had taken place at St. Luke's on Coombe. Seeking out the church's location from a city map, he arrived there in early afternoon. A servant took him to the parish rector, Rev. Thomas Fitzpatrick, a weary, thin man in his early sixties. His face was lined by the cares of his parishioners.

Percy asked the priest if he was familiar with the Boyle family.

"Now which would that be?" the priest replied with a wizened half-smile. "We have three families of Boyles, two O'Boyles and a few Boylans."

"The one I'm looking for is Maureen Boyle, Mrs. Redmond Boyle. She would be about your age I would imagine."

The priest was not hesitant in responding. "Ah yes, I knew her. A sad woman."

"She is deceased?" Grady Boyle had represented her as still living to the court in St. Francisville that took Percy's father's estate and awarded most of it to Grady Boyle as agent for his mother, the wife that Percy's father had abandoned in Dublin many years earlier. Or so Grady Boyle had claimed.

"Yes. Nearly two years now. A long time widow. Are you related to her?"

Percy did not stray far from the truth. "Friends of the family, in a manner of speaking."

"I wasn't aware of family in America." The priest had lost quite a few of his congregation to the Irish migration across the Atlantic.

Percy gave no account of the American connection of the Boyle family, merely saying, "Yes. What happened to her husband?"

"A sad story, it was, as she told it. He had been at sea. He was in Dublin after a voyage when he was accused of participating in piracy off the coast of France."

Percy was immediately disheartened. "Yes, a terrible thing." The minister was substantiating the story laid out in court when Grady Boyle asserted his primacy in inheriting from Howard Moorhead. "What happened to him?"

Father Thomas gestured with a sad shake of his head. "She always said it was a mistake. He had been taken hostage by pirates and escaped them and returned to Ireland."

"Was he found innocent?"

"I don't believe he was ever tried. The treasure was recovered a year after the piracy, and the shipping company that had made the claims dropped the case."

"Is that when he fled to America?" Percy based his question on Grady Boyle's account.

The priest was plainly confused. "America? I don't understand."

Percy related the facts as he understood them. "Redmond

Boyle set up a new life in America. I suppose that's why she may have regarded herself as a widow, not knowing if he were still living. She was as good as a widow."

"Oh dear," said the priest, shaking his head. "Now you may be mistaking him for another Boyle family. Redmond Boyle drank himself to death many years ago. I buried his wife next to his grave. You can see his headstone next to hers. He died in 1819, I believe. Or 1820. More than forty Easters ago, before I was assigned to this parish. I can't be certain without looking at the parish records." He started to rise from his chair to look for the records. Percy motioned him to remain seated.

Not permitting himself to hope that the priest would rehabilitate his father's reputation, Percy drew the priest on. "Yes, perhaps there is a mistake. The Boyles of whom I speak had a son named Grady."

Sinking wearily into his seat again, the priest was relieved that he was not mistaken. He said, "Ah, then it must be the very same. Grady is their son."

"Was he a parishioner?" Percy was still puzzled. Was this the same Grady Boyle who had dispossessed him?

"Grady Boyle was registered to this parish. But he was a poor church member. And a poor son to his mother," the priest said disapprovingly. "I met him a few times – nine or ten years ago. Handsome man, attractive to the women, though not of the best sort. His mother always said Grady was his grandfather's child. The grandfather was a famous Dublin actor or singer. Grady fancied himself a businessman, but he was a schemer. When we tried to find him for his mother's funeral, no one knew his whereabouts."

It wasn't adding up. He wanted to know more about the Dublin actor, but that connection clearly was long before Fr. Fitzpatrick's tenure. Sensing he had received as much information as he could from the priest, Percy donned his hat, stood and asked,

"I'd like to pay my respects. Where might the cemetery be?"

"Just behind the church here." The priest opened the door for his curious visitor from America, pointing him the way.

Percy found the headstones of Redmond Boyle and Maureen Boyle. His showed the stains and wear of forty-two winters of Dublin weather. Hers was identical, the two monuments purchased together years earlier when she still had a little money, the date of her death not yet carved into the stone. Was Grady Boyle aware of his mother's death? Did he care?

The neighborhood was poor. A woman in a worn coat and shawl who must have been nearly as old as Maureen Boyle, widow, was selling flowers at the entrance to the cemetery. Percy thought too of his own mother. He gave the flower lady a shilling for a small bunch and placed it between the markers of the two deceased Boyles. They had some relation to himself and to his father, but he could not imagine what it was. But Redmond Boyle, father of Grady Boyle, was not Percy's father. Redmond Boyle had never moved to Louisiana, or if he had, he had returned here to die.

The story of the Boyle family related by the Irish priest seemed very close to the story told by the old sailor in the St. Francisville courtroom three years ago – the story of Redmond Boyle aboard the sailing ship *Hybla* that was taken by pirates off the coast of France. However, the Redmond Boyle buried here had died in 1819, as the tombstone verified. Grady Boyle had not invented the story out of whole cloth. There had to be some reasonable explanation, but for now Percy could only speculate.

A light drizzle, mist more than rain, was lingering in the cold air as Percy walked Kevin Street and Cuffe to St. Stephen's Green. A gate had been left open, by which he entered. He sat on a bench and absorbed the information he had gathered. He was hardly aware that his face and hands were wet.

What was clear to Percy was that Grady Boyle had defrauded Percy out of his inheritance. Grady Boyle could not be Percy's long-lost brother. The papers used in court in St. Francisville to prove that Grady was the son of Redmond Boyle were the same papers that established Grady was not the son of Percy's father, Howard Moorhead – whatever his real name may have been. How was it that Grady Boyle had come to New Orleans and made it his business to take over the plantation built by Howard Moorhead and the townhouse deeded to Percy by his father? It was an audacious undertaking and had taken time and effort for Grady Boyle to bring about. He was clever, but how did he embark on this grand scheme?

More to the point, what could Percy do now to undo the injustice done to him? Could he go back to Fr. Fitzpatrick and get him to sign an affidavit that Redmond Boyle and Maureen Boyle were the parents of Grady Boyle and that both were deceased, with the dates on which each had died? Would these be sufficient to set aside the judgment obtained by Grady Boyle in district court in St. Francisville in January 1859, well more than two years ago?

If he had his hands on Grady Boyle right now, he would pistol whip him into an inch of his life; he would strangle him to almost his last breath. He would not kill him. He needed him alive to tell Percy the truth, the truth about Grady's scheme, the truth about Percy's father – for Grady Boyle must have known more about Howard Moorhead than Percy himself knew. He could never have pulled off the great fraud without certain knowledge of Percy's father. Grady Boyle was so sure of himself, so brash in carrying it out. He needed Grady Boyle to tell Lucy Moorhead that her husband of thirty years was neither bigamist nor pirate.

Yet, there were unfortunate possibilities that Percy had to consider. It seemed from the priest's story and the testimony of the sailor in the probate proceeding that there had been a piracy at sea and that Redmond Boyle, Grady's father, had been complicit in it. Was Howard Moorhead a co-conspirator in the piracy with Redmond Boyle? Perhaps Howard Moorhead had absconded with Grady's father's share of the piracy and started life anew in New

Orleans under a new name. Perhaps Grady had decided to track him down and threaten to expose him unless he was paid to keep silent. When Grady discovered that Howard Moorhead was incapacitated, he had revised his plans from confrontation to displacement, to shift from extortion to outright fraud. This was a plausible explanation but one that did nothing to restore the estate to Percy nor the good name of his father. He would get the truth out of Grady Boyle one way or another. He had to learn the truth about his father.

If nothing else, Percy wanted vengeance from Grady Boyle. There was nothing else to pursue in Dublin to solve the mystery. Dublin was far, far from New Orleans; there was no way to confront Grady. He had other things he had to do, a part to play in a war for the Confederacy's survival as an independent country. His personal vendetta would have to wait. He exited the park by a gate close to Dawson Street and found his way to his hotel.

He had a ship to purchase for Judah Benjamin.

Chapter 41

The *Scylla*

T he next morning, Percy returned to the office of Finn Dooley to further the purchase of the companion of the *Herald*. He was told that the vessel was still in Glasgow where the two engines were being retrofitted to boost their horsepower, increasing her speed by two knots.

"Splendid," said Percy. "How soon can she be ready?"

"No later than three weeks, I'm sure." If Finn said it, it was so.

"Let's work this out like this," proposed Percy. "I'll sign the papers here, today. From London, I'll have Mr. Sturgis of Baring Brothers send you a letter of credit for the purchase. Once you notify me at the Adelphi Hotel in Liverpool of the readiness of the ship, I'll send a captain and crew to Glasgow to take delivery."

"That will be most satisfactory, Mr. Moorhead," replied the dapper Irish broker in his understated cheerful manner. "When I have received the remittance from Barings, shall I send your commission to your hotel?"

Percy, reluctantly, "If you must. I'll see to it that it is credited to my principals."

"Shall the registration of the vessel be in your name? Or in the name of Cunard, Wilson – as with the *Herald*?"

"No. I am acting as agent of the Anglo-Mexican Tehuantepec

Company. Use its name. This transaction will raise no questions about British neutrality."

"Very good, sir. And sir, do you wish to retain the name of the vessel?"

"Ah, yes. I had forgotten that detail."

"Yes. The purchaser traditionally may re-name her. Her name now is the *Eugenia*."

Percy rejected the name immediately. "That won't do. Let's call her the *Scylla*. S – c – y -l – l – a."

Writing as he spoke, Mr. Dooley spelled out the new name. "Very well, sir. S – c – y - l – l - a."

A ferry returned Percy to Liverpool. At the bow of the ship, while looking over the rail at the moon's glint on the wake of the hull gliding over the dark water, Percy felt the throb of the steam engines. He grinned at the thought of the sensation he might feel when it was his own ship, the *Scylla*, steaming him over the seas. Then he thought again of Fr. Fitzpatrick and the revised story of Redmond and Maureen Boyle and of the two headstones and of an Irish actor, Grady Boyle's grandfather. What were they to him and to his father? He thought of the pathetic woman selling flowers at the cemetery. Was she someone's mother? Who was his father's mother? or father? His father had never spoken of them. Of his own mother he knew nothing now of her present life. He had written to her several times while he was in Virginia but had heard nothing since he had left St. Francisville, several years ago.

The cold air whipping across the Irish channel slapped Percy's cheeks. He had turned sad, not for himself as much as for the unhappiness that so many people inflicted upon others – and on themselves. The war back home was very far away; it seemed unreal. But the war was real, and somehow it had brought him here, to a foreign country, to a past he had never known, to Boyles and Moorheads he had never imagined. He felt it somehow, in his blood, in his bones, in a new way. Their blood was his blood. He felt it in a way different from his mother's side of the family. Although he resembled his mother, her memory was almost as a stranger.

The ferry bore into the darkening night, still hours from Liverpool. The next day Percy would learn of the surprise turn the war in America had taken. It was an incident at sea that Percy had narrowly avoided himself.

Chapter 42

The *Trent*

When the desk clerk called out to him, Percy was half-way up the staircase at his Liverpool hotel after his night voyage. He was tired from his travel and ready for a few hours of sleep.

"Mr. Moorhead? You have a message."

Percy set his bag on the landing and retrieved a folded slip of paper signed by Louis Coxetter. "Come to my room. Important." It was a sign of his fatigue that Percy decided Coxetter could wait while he deposited his bag in his room. He washed his face in the basin in his room and put on a fresh shirt and jacket.

On opening his door at Percy's knock, Coxetter handed his caller a Liverpool paper. "Have you seen the papers?"

"No, I've just arrived. You look uncommonly cheerful. Have the British granted us recognition?"

"Come in," Coxetter grinned. "Almost as good, maybe better. There's talk of their going to war against the Union."

"Go on!" Percy exclaimed. "How can that be?"

Coxetter, with a sly expression. "Recall our companions on the *Theodora?*"

"Of course. Slidell and Mason. We left them in Cuba."

"A Yankee warship seized them from a British mail packet, the *Trent*."

"What? They can't do that. It's a violation of neutral rights." Percy was emphatic. "How could the Union make such a stupid blunder?"

Coxetter now picked up a London paper and handed it to Percy. "Of course you're right. The Yankee captain, Captain Charles Wilkes, claims that Slidell and Mason are contraband of war being carried aboard the *Trent*."

"What? That's novel. People as contraband? Even so, if a neutral ship is carrying contraband, the ship itself is supposed to be seized and taken into port for an adjudication, not individuals aboard the vessel." Percy had already examined the question in connection with the supplies they were sending to the Confederacy on English vessels for transshipment in the Bahamas or Bermuda.

"Wilkes knows that." Coxetter was well-aware of the rules of capture on the high seas. As Percy had learned from him, at the outset of the war he had successfully operated as captain of a privateer under letters of marque for the Confederacy. After his ship sunk, he turned to work for Fraser, Trenholm. "But seizing the ship and all the other passengers would clearly be an act of war. He acted just short of that. And the Union papers are treating him as a national hero."

Percy looked up from the paper. "Do you know anything about him?"

"Only by reputation." Coxetter sat on a chair and threw his leg over its arm. "He's arrogant and ruthless, a publicity seeker. On an exploratory expedition to the South Seas he ordered the killing of natives in Fiji and the burning of villages. He court-martialed any officers who opposed him. On his return he was court-martialed but not relieved of duty."

"Ah, that Wilkes. The explorer who claims Antarctica is a continent. Any reports in the papers about the British government's reaction?"

"Nothing official. Too soon. But there are calls in the press for war against the Union."

Percy forgot his weariness as he examined a couple of other newspapers that Coxetter handed him. He mulled the facts from the excited reporting, then observed, "I suspect that Mason and Slidell are now more valuable to us as pawns than as envoys. The British will surely remind the Union that the seizure of the two and their assistants is like the search and impressment practices that brought on the War of 1812 between them and America. If it were *casus belli* then, it is *casus belli* now. Even if there's no immediate declaration of war, the British are unlikely to hinder us as we contract for ships and arms. We may make common cause with them. Have you visited with Prioleau on this?"

"No, we should."

Standing up, Percy donned his cap and declared, "Then let's go pay our respects."

❧ . ❧

Percy and Coxetter found Prioleau as he was when they last visited – convivial. When the Fraser, Trenholm partner offered refreshments, Percy realized he had forgotten breakfast after his overnight journey. Prioleau had a clerk bring in rolls, coffee, and tea.

"Captain Wilkes could not have made a bigger blunder than if we had written the plan ourselves, don't y'all reckon?"

"Amazing," agreed Percy. "Have you heard anything from London?"

Prioleau shrugged noncommittally. "Y'all know the English by now. They don't say much. Not given to hollow threats or bluster. I'm told they've sent word to the top military to make preparations to send troops to Canada. If Lincoln and Seward back Captain Wilkes, other hotheads may demand they take over Canada. In for a penny, so to speak. Now that the Yankees have assembled a big army they could suspend their invasion of the South and pivot to their north. Might be more popular than fighting us in the South."

"We can only hope things still break our way. In the meantime," continued Percy as he put his plate and coffee to the side and placed a sheaf of papers on the table, "here are the *Herald's* registration and purchase papers. We're well on the way to putting Captain Coxetter at her helm."

"Mahvelous," replied Prioleau. "But there's a new reason for us to be cautious. The new Union consul to Livahpool has finally arrived. His name is Thomas Haines Dudley."

"Oh? Never heard of him," Percy admitted. "What do we know about him? Not another writer like Hawthorne, is he?"

"Hawthowne was here when I first got here. We got along just fine. He even brought his friend by to say hello, author of that silly whale book. Needed us to negotiate a letter of credit for his further travels."

"Melville? Wasn't that his name?"

"Yep. Same writer wrote a novel about Livahpool. *Redbun,* I think it's called. Can't say I recommend it. Now this Dudley is a genuine abolitionist. A Quaker lawyer from New Jersey. Abe Lincoln owed his nomination at the Republican convention to Dudley. Livahpool is his reward. They say his chief purpose is to keep us from getting any ships or supplies out of our port."

"Maybe we should have someone follow him like the Union agents follow us here and in London."

Prioleau was open to the suggestion, "They have more money at their disposal than we do. Let's talk with Huse and Bulloch and see what we can do. Bulloch's supposed to be back soon. In the meantime, there's a new man Richmond has sent to London y'all need to get with. His name's Hotze. Henry Hotze."

"Name's new to me," commented Coxetter, who usually remained silent.

"Swiss, but he has been living in Alabama. He came through

here a few months ago. He's convinced Richmond that the South needs a public voice in London to overcome the news the Yankees put out about us. He wants to publish a newspaper that'll give the British news from our point of view."

"Newspaper man?" The name was also new to Percy.

"Yep. *Mobile Register*, as I recall."

"Another of Forsyth's disciples."

"You know Fo'syth?"

Percy shrugged in a way that showed his unpleasant memory of Forsyth. "We had dealings when he was ambassador in Mexico. We won't hold that against our Mr. Hotze. What are his marching orders from Richmond?"

Prioleau attempted to smooth his ungovernable hair and said, "He showed me his instructions from Secretary Hunter. He's to make every effort to impress upon the public mind abroad the ability of the Confederate States to maintain our independence. He's to publish whatever information he possesses, calculated to convey a just idea of the South's ample resources and vast military strength. Whatever it takes to raise our character and the Confederate government in general estimation."

Percy quipped, "He will wage a war of words while we supply the boats and bullets." He knew nothing about Hotze, but surely he could do no worse than the Confederacy's ineffectual trio of Commissioners, Yancey, Rost and Mann. They had expected to be welcomed like visiting potentates by the crowned heads of Europe and had no inclinations to stoop to persuade the masses; outreach to the public throng would have been vulgar. "Maybe Hotze can stir the British government and people to anger over the insult to British sovereignty by the Union aggression against the *Trent*."

"Why, I do believe you and Mr. Hotze will get along just fine. You both have a way with words," said Prioleau with a broad grin.

Percy and Coxetter finished their coffee and left the Fraser,

Trenholm offices, with Prioleau looking in a mirror to judge his success in taming his hair. Or to admire its eccentricity.

On the way back to their hotel, Percy reflected on what he could do to limit the interference of the new Union consul to their plans to set upon the seven seas the Confederacy's ships. It was especially pressing because among those steam-driven vessels was one in which Percy felt a paternal pride, as though it were his own, the *Scylla*.

Chapter 43

Spaulding – Investigations

If Prioleau could not hire an agent to learn what he could about Consul Dudley, Percy would. The expense could be paid by the commission he received on the *Scylla* purchase or by Anglo-Mexican Tehuantepec Company, which Percy would reimburse from Confederate funds when they became available. An hour after leaving Prioleau, on Harrington Street, he had noticed a discreet sign that said simply *Spaulding – Investigations*. After a late lunch, he called upon the office. A young man of about twenty showed him in to see Michael Spaulding, a greying, gruff, paunchy man of mid-forties.

Percy explained his needs: surveillance of the new American consul to Liverpool, Thomas Dudley.

Spaulding's comment was low-key and droll. "The consul, is it? I take it this is not an insurance claim or a domestic dispute." Percy thought, if a Basset hound could speak, it would sound like Michael Spaulding.

Percy's tone nearly matched Spaulding's. "To be equally blunt, Mr. Spaulding, I know he has hired spies to investigate the activities of Confederates in Liverpool. Mr. Wilding, his assistant, has been doing the same. And Mr. Adams, the Union ambassador in London. If you're unwilling to help me, I will look elsewhere."

"No, I can help you," replied the detective, putting down the paper he had been reading. "I can't help the Yankees. They wanted to hire me to report on activities at the Miller & Sons shipyards. Couldn't do it. Me wife's brother is chief of carpenters. They wanted me to get him to tell them everything going on there. Your war won't last forever, but he'd be out of a job if the Millers found out I was working against them. And I'd come near to losing me wife. That's one of our sons who showed you in. No secrets in this family."

Percy took an immediate liking to Spaulding. "Good. When can you start?" The detective was direct. There was nothing hesitant in his manner, no pandering to a potential client. Percy surmised, correctly, that he would be able to trust any intelligence *Spaulding – Investigations* provided him.

Spaulding splayed his hands on his desk, as though he would use them to stand. "Starting's no problem. The question is what you need. Do you understand what is necessary for your purposes? I can have three, maybe four, men working for me. But you'll probably need more to be thorough."

"Because the Yankees have so many working for them?"

"Yes. From what I hear." Spaulding was in a business where hearing was key to success.

"You know some of them?" Percy knew that could be useful.

"A few."

"Let's start with Dudley and an agent named Maguire and go from there."

Spaulding chuckled. "So, you've become acquainted with Matthew Maguire."

"You know him?"

"We've had a similar background. We have sparred from time to time."

"Let's give him a taste of his own medicine. The watchdog

watched."

"That'll be a pleasure." The detective's face had the look of a dog thrown a bone to chew.

Sparred, indeed, thought Percy, inferring from the detective's expression that there was no affection lost between the two. They agreed on a price, and Percy gave Spaulding an advance on his services, drawn on funds with Baring Brothers.

Four days later, Percy received a note from Spaulding proposing to meet at a coffee house on Lord Nelson Street, opposite the railway station. Percy was seated when Spaulding appeared precisely at three as promised, a roll of paper in hand. He began his report with no small talk, before he received his coffee.

Without consulting his notes, Spaulding said in his terse manner, "The consul is living at No. 3, Wellesley Terrace, Princes Park. He's forty years old or thereabouts, a tall man with a long face, gray eyes, and a dark, trimmed beard. He leaves his residence before eight each morning and returns late, habitually well after seven. There are two entrances to the consulate. A hundred or more callers each day. It's impossible to say who Dudley or Wilding may be meeting in the consulate. Or who of the callers may be taking out messages. Or what messages and mail may be going into the consulate. Unless you can get a man inside their operations, it will be near impossible to know what they are doing."

Percy wasn't disappointed. "All right. I suppose I should have expected this. But I think I saw your eyes glimmer when you said 'near' impossible."

"You did, sir," confirmed Spaulding with a toothy smile. "Very perceptive of you. An old friend heard I was making inquiries. Sent me a note, he did. Said to meet him at an ale-house. So I did. When he asked if I was working with the South, I didn't say yea or nay. He then told me if I was, pass on that he'd meet my contact at the same pub tomorrow night."

The coffee arrived, along with a small plate of cookies the

English called *biscuits*. These had an almond flavor.

The coffee Percy sipped was not as strong as he would have preferred. "Meaning me. Are you to come with me?"

"No sir. Alone, he said."

"Do you trust him? Is he setting me up."

"I couldn't say, sir. I've used him meself. He's good when he's sober. But he's a mean drunk. Welshman. Rhys Morgan. He can hold a grudge. I wouldn't want to be on his bad side."

"Should I meet him?" asked Percy, with raised eyebrows.

"How important is it that you get good information?"

"Enough that I will take risks. How will I know him?"

"He gave me a scarf for you to wear. It's hanging in the corner next to your coat. I put it there as I came in the door."

"And what about Maguire?" inquired Percy.

"Oh, I've got two men on him. One for him to see and lose. One to keep following him. Once Maguire thinks he's escaped his stalker, he moves more freely. Then he's pretty open about meeting with the agents he directs. I'll give you a list of them."

Percy thanked Spaulding and shook his hand. "By all means, continue to follow Dudley and Maguire until further notice."

On returning to his hotel that evening Percy was surprised to discover Bev Tucker in the lobby of his own hotel. Tucker had arrived in Liverpool late that afternoon and was now checking in. They agreed to meet for dinner in the dining room in an hour.

On reuniting, Tucker told Percy of his journey to Virginia through Canada into Kentucky. Once at home, he had volunteered to serve in the Confederate army, but the government thought his commercial associations overseas would better aid his country. And he was eager to get his young sons out of Europe.

Tucker explained how he had come to return to England. "In late August, President Davis endorsed a commercial mission proposed by me and my business partner to procure medical and military supplies in Europe."

"Do I know him?"

"Doubt it. His name's A. T. D. Gifford. We go back a while. Did you know we just missed each other? In Richmond."

"How's that?"

"You were on the way to Richmond from the *Bermuda* as I was leaving the capital. Gifford had sailed from Savannah in the *Bermuda* only a short time after you had arrived with the first cargo to the South. She had been reloaded with cotton. After successfully eluding the blockading squadron, she refueled in Havana made it to London."

"That's good news. But how is it that I got here before you?"

"My own efforts to leave by way of Savannah a few weeks after Gifford were blocked. I went to New Orleans where I was stuck for six miserable weeks because none of the officials trusted the Southern Steamship Company to work for the Confederacy. The owner was in New York and his son-in-law was in charge. Officials wouldn't okay the use of his ships, so nothing got done."

Percy wasn't surprised. "That's New Orleans for you. I'm guessing the food was good though."

Tucker sighed. "Eventually I was able to board a steamer called the *Calhoun* and reached Havana. By the way, our key man there is a fellow named Charles Helm. He says he helped you get out of Cuba. He found me a berth on a steamer to Southampton. Traveled the rest of the way here by rail finally."

"Where's Gifford now?"

Bev's expression changed from genial to grave, even anxious. "I'm concerned at not hearing from him. I got word that he left six weeks ago in a steamer fitted out with a valuable cargo for the Confederacy. She's owned by the house of William S. Lindsay & Co. Gifford placed the orders and sailed with her."

"Lindsay is very reliable for us." Percy tried to reassure Bev Tucker. "Perhaps he's successfully delivered his cargo. Communications are slow. We encounter delays in Bermuda and the Bahamas." Percy's words did not have the desired effect. Tucker's outgoing nature, often ebullient, could not hide his worry. What little capital he still had was in the venture, which could yield substantial profits – or bankrupt him if lost.

To draw him from a slump, Percy told Bev Tucker of his meeting with Spaulding and enlisted his help. "The setup with this Welshman named Morgan seems suspicious to me. The mystery man could be part of a trap by Consul Dudley or Minister Adams."

"So, what would you want me to do?" Tucker was ready to contribute and let go of his worries.

"Go to the pub a half hour early. Keep your eye out for anything strange. You know this city almost as well as any Liverpudlian. Maybe better. You've had to rescue American merchant sailors and visitors from troubles of all sorts. If you see something that makes you uneasy, step in before it gets out of hand."

"Cloak and dagger," grinned Tucker. "In case there's a frog in the ointment."

"Who would have thought?" laughed Percy.

Chapter 44

Rhys Morgan

The next evening, Percy had nearly finished a pint of lager when a man in an overcoat slipped into the chair next to him in the Saxton Arms pub. The man was as non-descript as the scarf he had sent for Percy to wear. Neither the man nor his clothing would stand out in a crowd, as you would expect of a sleuth who doesn't want to be identified. One moment Percy thought he was thirty-five, the next, fifty. The beard and long hair concealed wrinkles that come with age, if there were any such signs.

"When did your state secede?" the man asked, barely above a whisper.

"What?" Percy was briefly off-balance at the unexpected opening to the conversation.

The man's voice was a rasp abrading an oak board. "If you're from the Confederate states, you'll know when your own state seceded." Spaulding had said the man was Welsh. Percy guessed that accounted for the unfamiliar accent.

Percy, without hesitation, "I'm from two states. Louisiana seceded on January 26 and Virginia on April 17."

"Good," growled the odd visitor. "A Yankee posing as a rebel wouldn't know. Now what is it you be looking for?" The sly sleuth was anything but shy now.

Percy was brusque. "That depends on who you are and why you might have something of use to the cause of Confederate independence." He had no time to waste on a man who would react poorly under pressure. "The less you know about me, the better. And the more about you I know, better still."

The man's response was not what Percy expected. But Percy was new to the spying game. Nothing, it seems, is ever as it seems. Percy thought his blunt manner would give him the upper hand. It only made clear that he was out of his element.

A mischievous grin flashed on Rhys Morgan's face. "Oh, I know a lot about you already, Percy Moorhead. I asked you about secession to see if you would lie to me. You're Judah Benjamin's man. You arrived last May and left again on the *Bermuda* in August. You were staying at the Adelphi and are now at Queens Hotel, where Major Anderson had stayed. You had your friend Beverley Tucker come before you tonight so he could watch for me."

Percy could not conceal his chagrin. His natural response was to laugh at himself. The man opposite him was clearly more experienced in intrigue. He motioned his head for Bev to come over. The Virginian's bulk made the Welshman appear even less noticeable.

With self-effacing amusement Percy said to Bev, "Mr. Morgan here has been following us for months. He's doing nothing to conceal his employment by our foes." Turning to the Welshman, Percy continued, in a more relaxed tone than a few minutes earlier, "So why have you gotten us here, Mr. Morgan? If that's really your name. Did the Union minister send you to run me off?"

"Aye, Rhys Morgan's me name. But I'm no longer working for the man I was working for. You weren't the man I was directly following." Morgan was visibly pleased with himself at the discomfort he caused Percy. "That was Major Bulloch. But since you and he and Huse hang together at Rumford Place, I come to know about you. You were another detective's subject."

Looking closely at Morgan, Percy said, "I had my own hound?"

"Yeah. Hazelwood and then Dickinson as I remember. But no more. Not since you left in August. They may put a new man on you, now that you've turned up again."

"Interesting. I suppose I should feel honored. So, who were you working for? Maguire?"

"Ignaz Pollaky," sniffed the Welshman.

It was a new name to Percy. "Pollaky? What sort of name is that?"

"Pollaky's a Hungarian Jew. He worked under the chief Inspector of the Metropolitan Police, Inspector Field. Pollaky speaks five languages and passes for a native in any of them."

"I thought Minister Adams was using Maguire for his spying."

Rhys Morgan leaned forward. "That he is, he is indeed. Maguire probably followed you, too. But there's the rub. Another American, name of Sanford, he was the bloke who hired Pollaky. He had eight men working in London and six of us in Liverpool."

Bev Tucker joined the conversation. "Sanford's the Union envoy to Belgium. He's an experienced diplomat, unlike Dudley. I knew him while I was consul here, and he was *chargé d'affaires* in Paris. He's also been posted to Russia and Germany. He thinks he knows more about Britain and the Continent than Lincoln's political appointees like Adams, Dudley, and Morse."

Morgan agreed readily. "That may be true. Sanford was in London and hired Pollaky last June. Then we was all fired six weeks ago."

"Go on. Why was that?" All this was news to Percy. He had thought Maguire was the Union's man coordinating the spying.

Morgan hesitated. "I might be able to speak a little better if I weren't thirsty."

"Bev, can you get our friend here a pint? His speaking ability is hampered by a lack of a lubricant." Percy thought to himself, perhaps the abrasive sound of Morgan's voice would be smoothed with liquid but not his grating manner. Bev came back with a full mug. And one for himself.

Sipping his brew, Morgan said, "That's more like it." He raised his brew and toasted:

Your wines and brandies I detest,
Here's richer juice from barley press't.

"Another Welsh poet," said Percy with a hint of a smile as he resumed his interrogatories. Morgan was nothing if not a talker. "You were about to explain your departure from Pollaky's service."

With a wily wink, Rhys Morgan told Percy, "If I tell you all I know, then what worth would I have?"

"So you're ready to turn on the people who hired you?" Percy's distrust of Morgan was little concealed, even if the man had an amusing quality.

The Welshman looked up sharply and shook his head, indignant at the charge of disloyalty. "No sir! The North didn't hire me. It was Pollaky. I don't owe the North nothing. I don't owe Mr. Adams or Mr. Lincoln or Mr. Seward nothing. They fired Pollaky, and now I lost my work. I'm going to have a hard time finding other work, especially if anyone knows I'm talking to the Confederates."

"What do you want from us?" interjected Tucker.

"Five hundred pounds is my price," he demanded, looking to Percy. "Not a shilling less."

"And what do we get for our five hundred?" asked Percy.

"Everything I know. And for twenty-five a month, I'll find more. Here and in London."

It was Percy's turn to be crafty with Morgan. "And what is it that you know that is worth a princely price?"

"The names of the men working for Wilding and now Dudley. The men in Liverpool working for Maguire. The men they pay in the shipyards. Why Pollaky was terminated. Maybe more."

"That's still steep." Percy was skeptical.

"But worth it." Morgan's confidence showed he knew the value of his intelligence even without reading Percy's expression. "You'd have to pay five men for three months to get the same information. And then you still wouldn't have it all." Morgan was displaying his cards. They definitely had value.

Practicing law in New Orleans for the better part of a decade had taught Percy how to read a man in a negotiation, how to keep a man engaged without conceding too much of your own position. He said with a shrug, "If we give it all to you, nothing's to keep you from selling what you know of us to others. Here's what I'll do." Percy reached into a breast pocket and withdrew some British notes and laid them in front of Morgan. "Fifty pounds now to know what happened to Sanford and Pollaky. The rest in increments as you tell us what you know, and we check it out. You'll get what you ask for."

"Fair enough," said Morgan after reflecting on his alternatives. The five £10 notes Percy had placed on the table had the desired effect. "Pollaky was tracking Major Bulloch in London and found out about your ship, the *Bermuda*. Sanford wanted to sabotage her while it was in port and still being loaded. Failing that, he wanted a Northern ship to intercept her at sea and sink her."

This revelation surprised Bev Tucker. "But those would be acts of war in England or on the high seas. The *Bermuda* was registered as English and had an English captain." Percy had already heard of the arguments between Sanford and Adams – and conveyed the rumors to Slidell and Mason - but nothing specific as this involving Pollaky. This confirmed that Morgan had insider knowledge.

Morgan continued, "That's why Mr. Adams wouldn't allow it. Then you had another ship. The *Gladiator*. It was loaded in London. Sanford had bribed the pilot of the *Gladiator* to run her aground while she was still on the Thames. Before that happened, Adams had had enough of Sanford and Pollaky. He was afraid Sanford was about to get the North and England into a war. The British cabinet might still consider war over the seizure of your envoys on the *Trent*."

Bev Tucker interjected, "Sanford's a reckless man."

Percy found that Morgan's story had the ring of truth. The man could be of value. "Morgan, I'm going to trust you." He pushed the bank notes across the table. "You've earned the first fifty." The Welshman folded the bills and put them in his shirt pocket. Percy proposed, "Let's meet again tomorrow. But tell me, why would Pollaky share all of this with you?"

Morgan had no reason to conceal the truth. "Pollaky's first wife died. Then he married my niece. They met through me. I gave her away at their wedding."

The personal connection helped explain why Morgan would be so offended by the dismissal of Pollaky and why he would be ready to turn against Pollaky's former employer. Percy commented, "Well, I can understand that. My companion here performed the same service when my wife and I were married. Do you think we might engage Pollaky in London?"

"Maybe." Rhys Morgan sounded cagey. Percy decided not to pursue the matter. There was too much chance of a *volte-face* with Pollaky.

After Rhys Morgan left the pub, Percy spoke to Bev Tucker, who was on his second mug of ale.

"What's your reaction, Bev?"

Wiping a fleck of foam from his upper lip, Bev responded with a grin, "I'd take anything the Welshman says with the proverbial grain of mustard seed. The Welsh are a byword for mistrustworthiness."

"We'll see," replied Percy, smiling again at Bev's locutions. "I'm told prospectors in California have to sift a ton of sand for the occasional ounce of gold."

Over the next few weeks, Rhys Morgan provided the names and information he had promised Percy. Its value lay in making the Confederate agents more cautious in all their dealings. They were surprised at the extent – and expense – of their surveillance by Sanford and by Charles Francis Adams and the Union's London consul, Freeman Morse. Morgan told them that Dudley was being given a greater role and budget to expand the spying in Liverpool.

Morgan's contacts were able to alert the Liverpool Confederates about the Union's informants among shipyard and dock workers and when British inspections were about to take place. Percy had made a sound investment. The dividends would more than repay his outlay when the trial of the *Alexandra* took place in the Court of the Exchequer months later.

In the meantime. Percy needed to meet the newcomer to the Confederate in England, the magnetic Mr. Hotze.

Chapter 45

The Index

When he next came to London from Liverpool, in late February, Percy had difficulty locating Henry Hotze. The resourceful Confederate agent was in the middle of moving from his first quarters in Bury Street, St. James, to Savile Row, Mayfair. The new location was a step up in prestige for London real estate. Arriving, Percy found a youthful man, slender and of moderate height, sharply dressed, directing laborers unloading furniture from a horse drawn wagon. The new offices were in a four-story, stucco-fronted building capped by an isosceles trapezoid attic.

Percy, congenially, "Moving day, Mr. Hotze?"

The man turned to Percy. A good-humored smile played upon Hotze's sensitive mouth, beneath a bushy mustache ornamenting an oval face. His dark eyes were intense in their focus and showed an uncommon intelligence as he assessed the man who spoke his name.

Hotze extended his right hand for a warm greeting. "Indeed. And you sir, can only be Lieutenant Moorhead. Charles Prioleau said I should expect you any day now."

Instantly charmed, as were many, by Hotze's boyish affability, Percy introduced himself. "Percy Moorhead, at your service, sir."

Hotze was animated and playful. "Please come inside where it's warmer. You'll be the first official visitor to the Confederate States Commercial Agency and future home of the *Index* – Henry Hotze, resident agent, editor, publisher, proprietor and general factotum." From the reports given to him in Richmond and in Liverpool, he had every reason to expect to find in Percy Moorhead an able ally.

Percy followed his host upstairs while workers continued unloading and arranging chairs, desks and sofas on the ground floor. "Please be seated," Hotze said, stirring the coals of a fire in a welcoming hearth against a side wall. "I'm eager to have your thoughts about our approach to shaping British opinion."

Taking a seat opposite the fire, Percy replied, "I'm not sure I'm qualified to speak so broadly. As a lawyer, my persuasive efforts were all directed to a few judges or the occasional jury, not a whole nation as diverse as the British."

"Oh, come now, Percy. May I call you Percy? As we will be working together, we should not stand on formality." Hotze's courtly manner and confidence immediately put others at ease. Percy Moorhead was no exception to the younger man's appeal.

"Of course, Henry."

"You are far too modest, Percy. Your friend Judah Benjamin spoke highly of you when I made my proposals in Richmond. And Prioleau and Yancey say you are competent for any task you undertake. I am told you are a man of letters, a professor at the College of William and Mary."

"Would that I were yet. This war sought me, not I it." Percy meant this in all candor.

Hotze grinned in approval. "See there! Exactly as I meant. A fine turn of phrase and a modest, well-placed sentiment. It is just as we must have the British see things. The South did not seek this conflict. It was thrust upon us. We never wanted war. We are victims of Northern aggression. Is it too early for brandy for you?"

"A brandy would be well-received." What Percy had heard of Hotze's appeal had not been exaggerated.

Hotze stood and walked to a wooden crate next to a stack of English and French newspapers. Prying off the lid with a large knife, he took a bottle from among a dozen of its companions in sawdust packing.

Holding the brown bottle to the light, Hotze said, "The best I could purchase from Spain. More expensive to import in bottles than casks, but it impresses the English when they receive the gift of a Spanish bottle. And after finishing it, they prize the Spanish cork. Brandy will have to serve until we can get a shipment of Kentucky bourbon through the blockade." He poured a generous amount into two glasses and handed one to Percy.

"Thank you," Percy said. "It's good that Major Anderson is not still in London."

"Ah, I've heard stories of the good major, if he's not made colonel already. A stickler for military regulations and a close eye to the bottom line. I take it that is your reference."

Nodding as he sipped, Percy said, "Yes. Anderson was skeptical about expenditures of Confederate resources and disapproved of personal extravagance."

"Not a fan of the major?"

Shrugging, Percy was laconic. "We can choose our friends and our enemies but not our associates in times like these."

"Of course, of course. You are subtle in your expression. I'm sure he would be the ideal sort of officer in charge of a commissary or a naval engagement in which powder and shot must be husbanded. But the spirits and the two casks of Havana cigars are not for me and thee. Politicians and newspapermen have in common a love of alcohol, tobacco and gossip. The two former lubricate the latter. We must distribute them freely if we are to win friends in our campaign for recognition. Libations, sir. Libations are indispensable to persuasion – ceremonial offerings even to the ancient Greeks, essential as a token of hospitality and good will. And tobacco is the gift of the new world to the old. What man does not enjoy a good cigar? To share the aromatic fumes of a Havana *parejo* in the male enclave of a paneled library of a home or a city club is to bond with other men."

"Granted," said Percy, "that prominent Englishmen and journalists like to smoke and drink as much as we do. But there must be a case made to them. And to a wider public. What is the substance that will advance your mission? Gifts and charm alone do not carry over to newsprint."

Hotze showed no surprise that Lieutenant Moorhead would immediately turn to the business at hand. He had a reputation as efficient but never ruthless. Gesturing with his brandy glass, Hotze began, "Heroes. Villains. Glory and infamy. We have a story, and we have our people who are participants and contributors to the story. We must make the British see us as they prefer to see themselves. They want heroes and villains. They want to hear of acts of glory and deeds of infamy."

"Yes," an intrigued Percy encouraged his new colleague, "Tell me more."

"Recall this, as I am sure you will, dear Percy, when Caesar Augustus wanted to gain the support of his people, he got a story teller to tell the tale of a people who fought against odds to found a new civilization. And those Romans were an unruly lot, weren't they? Augustus hired a writer to provide that story: Vergil. The Latin poet gave them heroes. He gave them villains. He gave them battles at sea and on land against great odds. That's what we will give the British."

With no hint of skepticism, Percy asked, "Do you have candidates to be exalted in this pantheon?" Percy recalled the essay in the *Southern Literary Messenger* comparing the Battle of Manassas with the victory of Caesar over Pompey at Pharsalia. Did Hotze intend to be equally explicit with the British?

Waving his arm as though unveiling a tableau, Hotze said, "We will start with General Jackson, the Stone Wall. The British are already most favorably disposed to Stonewall Jackson, their Napoleon of the Confederacy. It would be useful to have portraits of the general to distribute to leading Englishmen."

Nodding agreeably, Percy responded, "An excellent suggestion. We can see that some are sent out by blockade runner. We can engage a copyist here." Percy would not mention to Hotze that he recalled serving in the same artillery company with the humorless, plodding Stonewall Jackson when the fresh young West Point graduate was firing cannons at Belen Gate, Mexico City.

Percy accepted a cigar that Hotze handed him. He bit off the end and spit it towards the fireplace. Hotze pulled a thin strip of pine from a spill vase next to the fireplace and, igniting it, used it to light Percy's cigar. Percy inhaled and savored the Havana. It reminded him of Judah Benjamin's pleasure at a good cigar. Hotze resumed his enthusiastic discussion.

"Now Percy, I ask you what book has done more than any other to shape English views of the South?"

"Mrs. Stowe's," replied Percy without hesitation.

"Indeed so. *Uncle Tom's Cabin*. It has sold in the millions here. We must give the British alternative stories, alternative facts they can associate with the South. The English-reading public will want stories they are familiar with. We can look to Charles Dickens, Walter Scott, Mr. Makepeace Thackeray, Miss Jane Austen."

Percy showed his surprise. "What? Will you publish books and stories of Southern authors?"

Shaking his head, Hotze said quickly, "No sir. Not at all. You misapprehend me. We will use the same sorts of stories as Dickens and Scott, but they'll come from our correspondents in the South. We will publish the tearful but brave letters of the wives of soldiers and their valiant efforts to nurse and sew for the Confederacy. Our correspondents will tell of the sufferings of widows and children whose husbands have perished in the struggle for their freedom."

"Where will you obtain these?" Percy was intrigued that Hotze had given such thought to a method of swaying public opinion in favor of the Confederacy.

"Friends, Percy. Friends. Here is a letter from a Mobile mother that passed through the enemy blockade to her sister in England." Hotze picked up a letter that rested on a shelf. He read aloud:

Dearest Ruthie:

John, too, is gone to the army; Dr. Hamilton kept him out a long time on account of his delicate health; but no one with a drop of blood in his veins can keep quiet in these times. If I had a dozen sons, I should say, "go" to each of them, and could not love them if they were sluggards in such a cause. The women are working, too, in their way — nursing at the hospitals, and doing all they can to aid the soldiers. I was one of a party of ladies who cut out 3500 sandbags in half a day; 50,000 were ordered, and done almost as soon. We stand ready to do and to die if necessary. General Knowles is confident that we can hold Mobile. If the city is shelled, we are beggars. But I would rather live in Europe as a lady's maid or housekeeper, than remain here, if the Yankees are to overrun us. I do not believe that any man or woman of gentle birth or rearing, will want to live here with that vulgar barbarian to rule over them. Apart from these considerations, I do admire the Queen. She is a noble and a good woman, and was a devoted wife. I do really sympathize with her in her afflictions . . .

Looking up from the letter, Hotze said, "Only a heart of stone could not be moved with such an outpouring." Percy had no reason to think it was not genuine, even if it appeared tailor-made for Hotze's purposes.

Percy, with a hint of drollery in his voice, "A nice touch to invoke the Queen of England."

"But of course. Our paper will recall to the British that the South, for generations back, has been proud of its closer affinity of blood to the British parent stock, than the North, with its mongrel compound of the surplus population of all the world, could boast of. The South has always claimed a more aristocratic, or at least, a more honorable descent, looking upon itself as the lawful offspring of the common mother. We will remind the British that we share a past. We should share, as well, a future. We will have them reflect on the bonds and reciprocal duties of parents and offspring."

Percy nodded in agreement, putting aside that the sentiments were voiced by a recent Swiss émigré. He told Hotze, "I'm sure you've found James Mason singing the same tune since he arrived here after the *Trent* debacle. He hopes to persuade the British that the South is England's true and legitimate heir."

Hotze's invocation of bonds and duties existing between parent and child had triggered an emotional response from Percy that gave a sharpness to Percy's own words: "true and legitimate heir." Unaware of Percy's past, Hotze could not know the reason for the ironic tone in Percy's voice. Was Percy not the true heir of Howard Moorhead? He could never come to grips with the idea that he was the bastard child of a bigamist whose real name was Boyle. After what he had learned in Dublin, he was growing in the conviction that he was a victim of fraud, and his father was not the perpetrator.

Overcoming Percy's brief distraction, Hotze brought the *Trent* affair into the conversation as he stressed the enduring relationship between the South and English traditions. "The Union made a grave error in seizing our envoys. Britain has been disposed to treat the North, if not as a bastard, at least as a relative of doubtful legitimacy. The political institutions of Great Britain always have had their warmest and most sincere admirers among our people of the South. The North is arrogant and self-conceited. It's too fond of change. With a population largely composed of the proletarian elements of Europe, the North can see in the governmental fabrics of the Old World only rotten monarchies, and petrified corpses. It fancies itself as the chosen reformer and apostle of a new social and political system. The South is conservative by instinct. We feel humbled instead of elated by the 'glories' and 'grandeur' of the vaunted Union. So, we cling to our English heritage and her traditions, rather than to the industrial future and its false promises."

Peering up from his brandy, Percy asked, "And the war itself? The battles won, the engagements lost?"

With sweep of his hand, as though brandishing a sword, Hotze said, "We will celebrate Southern victories and diminish Northern ones. But we must never print falsehoods nor ignore Yankee military success. To the contrary, when the Yankees win a battle, we will emphasize the enormity of the slaughter and the huge odds against which the brave Confederate soldiers struggled valiantly. We will give our readers stories of the life and trials aboard a Confederate naval vessel. Commander Raphael Semmes has forwarded accounts of his adventures aboard the CSS *Sumter* and its taking of Northern prizes on the high seas."

"And our peculiar institution? What will you say of our African slavery?" Here Percy was doubtful that a good or convincing account could be given, even by one so persuasive as the Swiss-born Confederate.

Again, Hotze showed the careful consideration he had given to the subject and the task before him: "We shall speak with more delicacy, I trust, than Commissioner Yancey. The British found him belligerent on the subject, a proselytizer. His pronouncements all ran to property rights and Southern superiority. Our appeal should be more sensitive to English sensibilities. There is the matter of religion. Perhaps not so much on the Bible commending slavery as much as how we are spreading Christian salvation to the African heathen. We do the work of the Lord in bringing the good news of salvation to the black man and woman and child. They will embrace Jesus Christ as their Savior and reject Paganism. Piety, Percy, we will stress piety."

Without diminishing Hotze's point, Percy said, "I've long held an opinion that abolitionists are less interested in the salvation of the slaves than they are in punishing the sin of the slave masters."

Percy could have added his own father had come to regret owning slaves. When Howard Moorhead had wished to free them, the law of Louisiana would not allow it. Even now, Percy felt that the taint of slavery had passed to him through his father, that the privileges of his youth were the unearned yield of forced labor. Yet, here he was, working with Hotze to gloss over the evils of the institution. Percy felt there was no contradiction. A Northern victory would unalterably disrupt the lives of all black and white Southerners. The North would destroy the old order but would be unable to replace it. Percy must continue to work to forestall that disaster.

"That's very good, my friend. Puritans punishing sinners, not saving the enslaved." Hotze walked over to his desk and made a few notes of what Percy had said. Turning again to his guest, Hotze continued, "We'll use that. And we can use to good effect the fact that the British empire encompasses a great many darker races over whom the white Britons maintain superiority. We may with justice stress the natural racial superiority of the white peoples over the black and the brown the whole world over. Do not the British fear revolt of their dark masses throughout their empire, just as we must fear the revolt of our Africans against their masters? The living conditions of our African laborers are as good if not better than their non-slave counterparts on British plantations in India or the West Indies and East Indies or the Cape. If you've not seen my translation of *L'Inegalite des Races* by Count Gobineau, I'll supply you with a copy."

"I confess my ignorance of the Count."

"When I finish unpacking from my move, I'll send it on. We will also report on the harsh conditions in Lancashire resulting from the inability of Southern cotton to reach the mills on which so many depend for their livelihoods. Thousands of English families are as much victims of the Union aggression as our own citizens of the Confederacy. We will call attention to and seek wider circulation of books and pamphlets favorable to our cause. Do you know, for example, of Lord Beresford-Hope?"

Smiling, Percy recalled his attendance at Arklow House. "Yes. He gave a celebration of our victory at Manassas when the news arrived."

Hotze paced as he talked. "Good. He has spoken often of our country and our right to be free. We will assist in publishing and advertising his lectures. And James Spence. Do you know him?"

"I have met Mr. Spence. A Liverpool tin and iron merchant. As I remember, he's published a little book called *The American Union* which supports our right of secession. An able fellow, I believe."

Hotze shared his other plans with Percy. "Perhaps he will be useful to us. There is the difficulty that he opposes our slavery. He may be open to persuasion as he may not fully understand our conditions. I have visited editors at the *Morning Herald* and the *Standard*. They have assured me of access to their columns for such facts and opinions as we may provide. I plan to engage columnists who will report favorably on our behalf. We must do so to counter the North's own journalists in England. You may have seen a little paper called the *London American*. Each Wednesday it publishes a feature most partisan of the Union, the *Progress of the Great Rebellion*."

"I'm afraid I've not seen it."

"No matter. And do you enjoy the theater, Percy?"

"I do. When I have the time."

"Good. I frequently have tickets. It is good for us to be seen and to be able to converse with our English supporters, to show that Southerners have cultivated tastes and share interests with them. And have you seen that the great Dickens will soon be giving another series of public readings here in London? I will obtain tickets for choice seats if you are interested."

Indeed, Percy was most interested. But he could not have imagined the turn the invitation would take, and how it would profoundly affect the course of his life.

"Yes, please. I think I would enjoy that very much. He was in Liverpool at the end of January for readings. I was unable to attend."

"As good as done, my friend."

Percy left, reassured by his meeting with Hotze that he was a superb choice by the Confederate government to put a more positive face on its cause for independence. He would avoid the mistakes of commissioners Yancey, Mann and Rost. Percy looked forward to seeing the first issue of Hotze's paper.

A WEEKLY JOURNAL OF POLITICS, LITERATURE, AND NEWS.

Vol. 1.—No. 1.]　　　LONDON—THURSDAY EVENING, MAY 1, 1862.　　　[Price 6d.

Chapter 46

Bulloch's Return

L ooking as though he had just emerged, fully clothed, from the Mersey River, James Bulloch dripped his way into the library of 10 Rumford Place. Still wearing hat and cloak against the foul weather outside, he was soaked and tired but smiling. In gruff good humor, he said, "I hope you boys have plenty more of that coffee, 'cause there's nothing I need more right now." Percy and Charles Prioleau were seated at the conference table reviewing what steps were yet to be taken to ensure a timely launch of the *Oreto*. Bulloch removed his damp outerwear and hung hat, scarf, and coat in the corner stand before collapsing into a chair opposite the other two.

A grinning Prioleau welcomed him. "Damn, Percy, it looks like ol' Neptune swallowed ol' Bulloch whole and coughed him back. We reckoned you were lost at sea when we didn't see you back in January or February." It was now early March 1862.

Bulloch chuckled. "I proved indigestible. It's been a helluva roundabout journey. Haven't slept, getting back here by way of Queenstown, Dublin and Holyhead. I was gonna have a full load of cotton on the *Fingal* out of Savannah. The cotton was slow to arrive. There's just not enough the South's trains can do to carry men and supplies everywhere they're needed. When we were finally ready to weigh anchor, we found we were bottled up. The

Yankees had taken Tybee Island and the lighthouse and set up a battery. If we could have left, we could have used the back channel through Warsaw Sound. By the time we tried it, the blockaders had closed off that route, too. Next, I took the train up to Charleston. No luck there either. Finally, I was able to get out through Wilmington on the *Annie Childs*. She was never intended for trans-Atlantic crossings. In a few days she'll arrive, after they refuel her and repair some damage we sustained."

Bulloch explained the difficulties of his most recent voyage. He'd left on the fifth of February, a terrible time of year in the North Atlantic, with rain and Arctic gales churning the ocean. The *Annie Childs* couldn't carry enough coal for such a rough voyage. "Damn me if it didn't feet like we traveled as far up and down, rolling on the great waves, as we had going east. We had to refuel in the Azores and were delayed by the Union consul. Even then, we ran out of coal as we approached Queenstown. The engineer steamed us in by burning the sweepings of the bunkers mixed with rosin and spare spars that the crew cut up. Altogether, we were thirty-six days when it should have been twelve."

Savoring slowly a second cup of coffee, Bulloch turned more somber, his furrowed brow showing his worry. "Tell me that the British haven't seized the *Oreto*."

Percy grinned reassuringly. "Happily, no. We were just going over what we need to do to see her off. After all your work, it would have been a shame for her to launch without you."

Prioleau instructed a clerk to bring fresh coffee. Bulloch visibly relaxed as the good news sank in, saying, "That's a relief. Richmond was insistent that I return and send her and the *290* to sea as quickly as possible. They are our best hope of diverting the Union blockaders from our ports."

"Here, this'll warm you." Percy handed Bulloch a cigar from his coat pocket. "Since you left, a new American consul is in charge here in Liverpool. His name is Dudley. He leaves the regular consular business to Wilding. Dudley has a singular obsession with defeating our efforts to get ships. That is his preoccupation from when he arises, which is early, until he retires at night, which is late."

"You have a man watching him?" Bulloch asked, drawing on the cigar, then rolling it appreciatively between his thumb and two fingers of his right hand.

"Yes. And a maid where he is boarding. She says he leaves all of his papers at the consulate. Dudley's agents are working in shifts. During the day he's got men pretending to be laborers scouring the Merseyside docks and shipyards, learning all they can about construction of every ship being built. He's got a dozen or more crawling the pubs and dram-shops of Paradise Street for rumors about the men being hired as crews for new ships. Who is buying ships? Where are they expected to go? He seeks every bit of intelligence he can gather."

Bulloch looked concerned. "Is he getting anywhere with his efforts?"

The American consul in Liverpool was proving to be a formidable opponent, a real challenge to Percy, as was his close relation to the embassy in London: "Consul Dudley is hand-in-glove with Minister Adams. The Union's minister is a regular visitor to Lord Russell, demanding that the Foreign Office investigate everything about the *Oreto*. Russell has sent men to inspect the ship twice. Others from his office are keeping close watch on her. Miller and Sons is sticking with the story that the vessel is built for the Italians, and her destination is Palermo."

"Anybody buying the cover story?"

"Yeah. For now," answered Prioleau, "Most are. It's credible. The man the Millers have supervising her construction is John Henry Thomas. You know him. He's also the local agent of the Thomas Brothers of Palermo. With the political turmoil in Italy now, it's plausible that the ship is bound for Italy. We're listing him as owner on the *Oreto*'s registration papers. Thomas has spread the

Italian story among all the men working on the ship. He puts on a good show."

Bulloch was grateful for the report. "That should buy us some time. What are y'all doing to counter Dudley's spying?"

"I'll claim responsibility for that." Percy's counter-intelligence work had largely displaced his role in providing legal guidance. He found it surprisingly stimulating. "Charles here has too many other activities to oversee agents. We can count on Price Edwards, the Customs official, to let us know about complaints lodged by Dudley and if an inspection is ordered by London. But Price Edwards is not privy to the spying efforts of the Union. He's our friend but not our agent. He's not the sort who can be bought. We must respect his integrity and maintain his trust. Some of the workers on the ships are sympathetic to us, and they want to keep their jobs. So, we've let it be known we'll pay for tips about the men working for Dudley and Adams. In fact, we're paying a few to give false information to Dudley." With a sly smile, Percy added, "When the Foreign Office sends out an inspector to check out a lead and it proves wrong, it undercuts other reports by Dudley and Adams."

The Georgian asked, "Is Dudley aware of the *290*?"

Bulloch looked older. Percy wondered if maybe it was just the weariness of travel. Or maybe it was a year of intense activity with the weight of the future of the Confederate navy on his shoulders. Or maybe he had experienced frustrations dealing with officials in Richmond. Likely, it was all of these, concluded Percy. While back in America Bulloch was much closer to the war than he had been since it began. As Percy had experienced himself, the hardships were made vivid firsthand instead of what he read in print in the Liverpool and London papers. He saw the maimed, the wounded, the fevered. He had visited the hospital tents. He had heard the bickering of the military men and listened to the pettiness of the politicians who demanded answers to questions that had no answers. Now he had no doubt but that the war would be longer than any of the secessionists had claimed. It worked a toll on a man like Bulloch whose family, like so many others, was divided by the war. Bulloch had told Percy that his favorite sister was living in New York, and her husband, a Roosevelt, was prominent in support of the Union.

Percy wished he could allay Bulloch's worry, but he had to be candid. "He's not discovered the *290* as far as we can tell. His men are snooping around. They're starting to look at ships under construction across at Birkenhead. It's just a matter of time before they recognize that the sister ship of the *Oreto* is being built by Lairds."

Bulloch frowned. "We need to get the *Oreto* out of here as soon as we can. The Yankee blockade is proving effective. We have to have our cruisers to draw the Union warships away from our coasts."

Percy nodded in agreement. He stood, walked to the window, pulled the curtain aside, and looked out. The rain had increased again, pelting the panes, demanding entrance to the cozy interior.

Turning back to Bulloch, Percy spoke quietly. "There's another development that may prove important. After I left on the *Bermuda* in September, you met a few times with our man Henry Hotze. He's back in London now and is proving himself very useful in more ways than one. He's been cultivating a source in the Foreign Office. He won't give us the man's name. Calls him Albion. Hotze says Albion will tell him of messages going to and from Lord Russell that relate to the Confederacy."

Bulloch grunted in approval. Percy saw Prioleau raise his eyebrows; he had not informed Prioleau of Albion's existence. It was not in his interest to know details.

Bulloch leaned forward. "Richmond said they had plans for Hotze. He's smooth, I'll give him that. If he's got a Foreign Office source, that could be most valuable. Are we sure it's not a trick? I wouldn't put it past Adams to spread stories to throw us off-guard – just like we're doing."

Percy had considered the possibility. "We'll have to take that chance. To show his worth to Hotze, his secret source made him a copy of a report Dudley sent to Adams a short time ago, and Adams then shared it with Russell, urging the Foreign Office to act." Percy reached again into his pocket and unfolded a sheet of paper to show to Bulloch and Prioleau.

"Here's the copy. It's about the *Oreto*":

The builders say she is intended for the Italian Government. Fawcett Preston & Co. are fitting her out, supplying all the machinery etc. From this fact and some other suspicious circumstances I am afraid she is intended for the South. She has one funnel, three masts, bark rigged, eight port holes on each side and is to carry sixteen guns. Her coal is now being put on board and she will go to sea most likely the latter part of the week. Her armament is not as yet on board and the appearances indicate that she is to leave Liverpool and receive armaments at some other place.

Bulloch looked up at Percy with some alarm. "Are we sure no one is betraying us? It sounds like Dudley has got everything just about right."

Percy, reassuringly. "I trust our people. Most of Liverpool is sympathetic to us. They're beginning to feel the cotton famine, as they call it. Unfortunately, Adams and Dudley have agents everywhere. We can't hide the construction of a large ship that is designed for a belligerent's needs. As long as we comply with the English law to the letter, I don't think the government will stop us." Percy sounded more sure of himself than he felt. Expressing doubts would not alter the only course of action available to them.

Bulloch, rising to leave, "Good. I'm counting on that. If there's nothing pressing right now, I'm going to a hotel for a few hours of sleep. Then it's back to work after too long a break."

Chapter 47

The *Oreto*

Bulloch and Percy spent most of the rest of the week shuttling back and forth from 10 Rumford to the Toxteth Dock where the *Oreto* was berthed and to the offices of Fawcett Preston and W. C. Miller & Sons. Bulloch was frustrated that he was to have no hand in hiring crew members. Working late one evening at Rumford Place, Percy expressed his sympathy. "We have no choice. British law forbids raising recruits within England for a foreign war. Both of us are known to be Confederate agents. Enlisting sailors for the *Oreto* would lead to our arrest and the interdiction of the ship."

Bulloch complained, "I still don't like it. We spend all this time and money on building our ideal cruiser, and we have to put her in the hands of a crew we can't even meet. What if Dudley or Adams gets one of their agents aboard?"

"A chance we have to take. Captain Duguid is master of the ship. The fact that his wife is the daughter of the ship's builder, W. C. Miller, ensures we have a credible cover for the English authorities and raises no suspicion among the crew. Lawyer Hull tells us that once the *Oreto* is clear of British waters, the sailors can be given the opportunity to stay aboard for the Confederacy or accept return to Liverpool."

"If we must, then we must." English law made Bulloch

disgruntled, not Percy or Captain Duguid. "Has Duguid been told he is to follow the instructions given him by Low?" Although nominally a civilian in port, John Low was an officer in the Confederate Navy. Originally from Liverpool, Low had settled in Savannah after an illness at sea some time before the war. Recruited for the navy by Bulloch, Low had proved himself with Bulloch when they took the *Fingal* to Savannah six months earlier.

"Yes. Duguid understands that the less he knows, the better for him. If he encounters problems in port, he can truthfully say he received his instructions from Messrs. Fawcett, Preston, and Co. for a voyage from Liverpool to Palermo, and those instructions were to be governed by John Low for Fawcett, Preston, and Co. Low will have custody of the ship. He will see to it that the *Oreto* is fitted with the armaments you bought in Hamburg." Bulloch had gone to Hamburg to purchase four seven-inch rifled guns and all the necessary equipment and fittings, shot and shell. He had engaged a Fraser, Trenholm ship, the *Bahama*, to transport the weapons. "You do have Captain Tessier to transport the guns from Hamburg, along with other supplies the *Oreto* needs, don't you?"

Bulloch confirmed. "Yes. Tessier was stalwart getting you and the *Bermuda* to Savannah. But we haven't set where the *Oreto* and the *Bahama* should meet to transfer the weapons. Your thoughts?"

"That's a tricky question. The Azores is relatively close, and we would have her cruising much earlier. But you say the American consul there nearly kept you from leaving with the *Annie Childs*. And once the ship gets guns, the crew will know for certain she's a Confederate ship. A number might bail on us when they learn of her true colors. We couldn't get a fresh crew in the Azores even if she could leave. That leaves us with Bermuda or Nassau. Either is close enough to the South to get a crew from the blockade runners. Both have ports big enough to have anything the *Oreto* might need to put the ship and arms in working order. I say Nassau is best, if for no other reason than the presence of our agent there."

"Who's that?"

Before answering, Percy walked over to the iron urn on the office cupboard to refill his coffee mug. "Lewis Heyliger. I got word through Henry Hotze that he's been appointed by the Treasury of the Confederacy as the depository of Confederate funds in Nassau. Among his chief duties will be to coordinate shipments of cotton and tobacco to England. He's our man to organize the purchase of incoming cargoes, and he would help with hiring a crew. Good man. I knew him in New Orleans. He's the treasurer for the Tehuantepec Railroad Company. Or was."

Indecision was as alien to Bulloch as fear. "Nassau it is. I'll let Captain Tessier know where he's to go. Now let's get the *Oreto* out of here."

"Once her papers are transferred to the Confederacy, what will you name her?"

The ship was Bulloch's project, but not his to name. "Not my call." His shrug suggested something other than indifference. "Though I wish I had naming rights, the Secretary of the Navy is from Florida. He's the man paying for her, so he's named her the *Florida*."

"A loyal son of Georgia gets her built, only for Florida to appropriate her name." Percy sensed no hostility of Bulloch towards Mallory.

"She's still my offspring, and if she does her work well, that'll be enough for me."

Bulloch still expected to get command of his favored ship, the No. 290 taking shape across the way at Birkenhead. Years at sea, waiting on time and tide, had taught him patience. Those years had also taught him that some hopes must forever remain unfulfilled.

Chapter 48

A Dickens Reading

As much as he enjoyed working with James Bulloch, Percy could not help feeling concern that Bulloch might sense that Percy was occasionally deceptive. They spent weeks together working closely in preparation for the departure of the *Oreto/Florida*. At the same time, Percy spent a significant amount of time getting the *Scylla* ready to sail at roughly the same time. Both Bulloch and Prioleau were completely unaware of Percy's purchase of the vessel in the name of Anglo-Mexican Tehuantepec Company. Judah Benjamin had wanted Percy to keep the *Scylla* off the records of the Confederacy, so he had to keep them in the dark. Percy let his Liverpool associates think his unexplained absences were attributable to his secret work against consul Dudley's spying; this was in part true. So much surreptitious activity took a toll on Percy's nerves.

A welcome relief came unexpectedly. Percy was at his desk at the Fraser, Trenholm offices when a clerk handed him a telegram from Henry Hotze. It was an invitation to public readings by Charles Dickens this Thursday. Percy quickly scribbled a reply, accepting the offer. A few days in London could be used to gather supplies for the voyage and a couple of books for his bag; it could clear his head of deceit, if not salve his conscience.

On the appointed day, after walking from the rooms he had

taken at Hatchett's Hotel, Percy arrived at St. James Hall, London. The Dickens performance was to be in the huge auditorium that could hold an audience of more than two thousand. Two smaller halls were at street level, as was a restaurant where Hotze was waiting for Percy. Hotze walked to the door to greet him, then led him to a table, at which were already seated two young women.

Hotze smiled and gestured to the well-dressed guests, both in their early twenties. "Percy, allow me to introduce Miss Dorothea Rainsford. I believe you have made the acquaintance of this other young lady, Miss Grace Tarkenton. They will accompany us for the evening's performance."

Percy was at a loss for words. Grace appeared to be amused by his discomfort. It was as she intended. Her auburn hair was thick and finely curled – loosely caught back and topped by a fashionable hat. She filled the silence. "I'm sure Lieutenant Moorhead has entirely forgotten the thirteen-year-old girl who annoyed him across the Atlantic. On a visit to our home soon after, he was kind enough to pretend to enjoy my juvenilia upon the piano."

Recovering, Percy bowed. "Forgive me, ladies. Our host gave me no reason to expect that a Dickens performance would be augmented by such charm. And, no, Miss Tarkenton, I had not forgotten you. Not many months ago I saw you in *Colleen Bawn*. How are your father and mother?" In the Adelphi Theater where Grace was briefly on stage, Percy had been unable to see what an attractive woman the child had become.

"They are well, thank you," she said slyly. "And they remain tolerant of their daughter's peccadilloes." The dress she wore was fashioned of an exuberant mauve fabric.

Concealing his sense of being flustered, Percy recovered his confident manner. "As I recall, they expected your enthusiasm for the theater would diminish." Why was she here? Hotze would have to explain himself.

"A misapprehension on their part," she said as she raised her wine glass to him. "Neither their first nor their last."

Small talk disclosed that Dorothea "Dotty" Rainsford had recently moved to London from York, where her father was an import merchant. She had come to care for her aunt, a widow living comfortably on the three percent per annum paid on Bank of England consols. Grace met her when, on a whim, Dotty auditioned for a part in a play in which Grace would appear.

Hotze engaged in witty repartee with the two women, while Percy shifted awkwardly in his seat, rarely making comment, and only occasionally glancing at Grace. He was uncertain what it was about her that disturbed him. Wasn't their age difference prohibitive of attraction? As she was a child when he met her, shouldn't he so regard her now?

When the two women excused themselves, Percy demanded of Hotze, "Henry, if you have set the meeting with Grace Tarkenton as a means of getting access to her father, it calls into question your judgment. I have no acquaintance with her, and no desire for her company. She was irritating as a child and seems not to have advanced much since."

Hotze patiently responded, "Why, Percy, I'm afraid you are quite mistaken. I would never presume to use you in so coarse a manner."

"Then why are they here with you?"

"Not my idea at all. It was unavoidable. I met with Sir James at his office. A routine call. He's a former consul in New York and an MP now. His opinion is likely to be held in esteem by the Foreign Minister. While there, his daughter appeared. Your name came up when her father identified me as an associate of yours from the Confederacy. He seemed as annoyed with her as you. I mentioned I was taking you to hear Dickens. She took me aside and insisted that I bring her and a friend. I could hardly say no when her father is influential with Lord Russell, now could I? Had I refused her, it could have been taken amiss. Luckily, I was able to obtain two more tickets."

Percy pressed, still not satisfied. "Does Sir James know of this outing?"

"Not from me. Whether she has told him I can't say. This other woman I just met."

No longer suspicious of Hotze, Percy reassured him, "Then, sir, I owe you an apology. I can only assume the attraction for Miss Tarkenton is an opportunity to see the great Charles Dickens and not to share our company. She is herself an actress."

"Ah, Percy," Hotze said with a sly wink, "perhaps you underestimate your charm and the impression you made on a young girl. She's as pretty as she is voluble. You may take a liking to her and her keen wit."

Scoffing, Percy grunted, "Voluble? She just talks too much. I fail to find the charm. Where you perceive wit, I see a peevish brat." Percy was as annoyed by Hotze's amusement as he was uncomfortable with the unexpected appearance of Miss Tarkenton.

When Dotty and Grace returned, the four mounted the stairs to the balcony. Lighting the interior were gas stars of seven jets each suspended from the ceiling. They found their seats, near the platform from where Dickens would perform. Seated next to the rail, they could peer into the dress circle below.

Grace chattered on about the design of the St. James Hall while they awaited the celebrated speaker. As the lights began to dim, Grace whispered to Percy, "Note the two women in the third row at the end who were just seated."

"All right." Percy was just able to make them out. "They are?"

"Mother and daughter. Fanny and Nelly."

The names meant nothing to him. "Should I recognize them?" Percy was again annoyed. Could others hear her?

"Actresses. I'll explain later," she whispered, *sotto voce* as to a fellow conspirator.

Lighting much closer to the stage now brightened as gas was increased to the lamps, framing the area around a desk on the center of the platform, bathing it in light. The desk was covered with a greyish-green material. A little shelf to the side of the desk held a flask of water for the performer. A few feet behind the desk was a maroon backscreen, designed to project the sound of the speaker's voice forward into the great auditorium.

Now a door opened, and a bearded man with a large, unruly mustache walked briskly across the stage. His hair was long and casually arranged on either side of his head. Deep furrows creased his face, though he was not more than fifty years in age. In dark evening dress, with a bright buttonhole, a purple waistcoat, and a glittering watch-chain, he paused at the desk, placing there the book he carried.

Dickens was conscious of the effect of his great sense of presence upon the spectators and made the most of it. They all were here to see him and him alone on this vast stage. Slowly he removed his gloves and laid them on the same shelf as his water flask. Self-possessed, he received the round of applause bestowed by the admiring audience. They were in the presence of the greatest living author. Only Shakespeare was more famous than Charles John Huffam Dickens. Though he was of medium height, the screen and his erect posture made him appear taller. The lighting system minimized shadows thrown onto the backscreen.

Holding his book in his left hand, propped on a small box atop the desk, and gesturing with his right, Dickens began his reading; first, passages from *David Copperfield*. The performance continued for two hours without break, with only brief pauses when the author drank from his glass. The audience was enthralled, noting every gesture, every change in voice and inflection. The roar of applause could be heard a block away.

As the four emerged from St. James Hall after the performance, Hotze suggested they walk to Marlborough Tavern, a favorite of theatre-goers. Despite the crowd, Hotze found them a table at which to stand while he fetched them drinks. The two women requested claret.

Percy told Hotze, "See if they have Armagnac or Calvados."

"What did you think of the performance?" asked Grace with an impish expression.

Dotty responded first. "It's not quite like a play, now is it? It was just bits and pieces of a story and not a whole story. I mean, I read the *Copperfield* book a long time ago, and I can hardly remember it at all. Still, I was glad to see so famous a man. I did not imagine him so old."

Grace smiled at her companion's critique. "Why, Dotty. I think you could play a Dickens character yourself. A Minnie Meagles. Or even Tattycoram. Why yes, Tattycoram herself." Percy looked at Grace and suppressed a laugh, which would have been at the expense of Miss Rainsford, whose blush and thanks showed she was unfamiliar with these Dickens characters. With no indication of her insincerity towards Dotty, Grace turned to Percy,

"And you Mr. Percy Moorhead? Have you read *David Copperfield*? What did you think of our Dickens?"

Without pause, Percy asserted, "It was the most extraordinary experience I've ever had from the stage."

Hotze reappeared with four glasses. "Claret for the ladies. I'm afraid they were out of Armagnac and Calvados. Cognac for us, Percy."

"Close enough." Percy raised a glass to the other three.

Grace said to Hotze, "Our Virginian visitor was beginning his review of tonight's performance." She turned to Percy, challenging him. "Elaborate, if you will, please."

Percy decided that Grace needed a come-uppance for her needling manners. For some inexplicable reason, she had taken to provoking him, even at the expense of her companion, Dottie. He began, "As I say, extraordinary. It was not so much a Reading as it was a Re-creation. The man is a spell-binder — a storyteller who suddenly fractures into different individuals on the stage. Dickens has a way of engaging his audience, as if he is talking with each person in the hall. He reaches into his listeners like an invasive force. One has the same sense reading his work, an intimacy with the reader. I would say it is a voice. But now, upon the stage, it is as though he is talking to each of us about Dickens the writer."

Grace, skeptical, "Aren't you just saying that he's a good actor?" She was surprised at the depth of Percy's response to the performance. She had assumed he would be bored.

Percy countered, "No. Not that, not that at all. He's a writer who has created something entirely new from his writing. I had the sense he was not reading *to* us but reading *with* us, that he was himself aware of his performing and winking, like a magician who knows his audience is perfectly aware that he creates an illusion, and he is pleased with the success of his illusion."

"An illusion?" Was Grace perhaps attempting to mock Percy?

Uncowed by Grace's interruption, Percy held forth, "Call it that or by any other name. My point is this: He re-created his characters with a subtlety that can't be achieved through the printed word. It is a new way of coming to know them. He lets us see them new. Now we hear Micawber's voice, and a minute later we see the expression on Micawber's face, the gesture of his hand. Dickens does not perform or impersonate Micawber. Rather, he adds detail, much as a painter adds a feature to a portrait, a new shading. Or as polish on a fine cabinet enhances the grain of the wood. The form and substance were already there, but they have a new luster. He has a power beyond acting."

Not wishing to be eclipsed by Percy in front of the two women, Hotze said, "I was impressed too. His ability to project his voice to be heard throughout such an auditorium is a finely developed skill. Think what the man could do if he turned his fame and ability to political oratory! Why, he could be Prime Minister. If only we could enlist him for our cause."

Grace laughed, not generously, but at Hotze's expense. Having herself been upstaged by Percy, she now turned on Henry Hotze. "Mr. Hotze, I fear you have not come to understand the people whom you seek to persuade. The English ruling classes distrust actors even when they do not despise them. And you know too little of Mr. Dickens himself. I suspect his notion of freedom does not correspond to yours." She showed no diffidence to the host who had provided the tickets to the performance.

Hotze stiffened at Grace's dismissal, replying. "Speaking strictly, Mr. Dickens is known as a writer rather than an actor. And I understood that the rumors of an intimacy with his wife's sister were dispelled." Hotze now shared Percy's opinion of the irritating Miss Tarkenton.

Notwithstanding Hotze's attempt to patronize her, Grace shot back, "Writers, yes. Actors, no. Our Disraeli is a successful writer and politician. But those of us who perform upon the stage are regarded as immoral. I will speak no further as to Mr. Dickens's reputation. His estrangement from Mrs. Dickens is too well known."

Percy felt no need to endure the sharp exchanges. He excused himself to return to his hotel, leaving Hotze and the two women to their own devices. It was not his responsibility to see them home. He could not fathom why Grace Tarkenton had taken upon herself a purpose of embarrassing him and Hotze.

He accepted Hotze's word that he had not been responsible for drawing him into company with the unpleasant and inaptly named Grace. If her presence was the cost of enjoying the great Dickens, it was worth it. At least, he was now rid of her. Or so he thought.

Chapter 49

Visit to the Sojourner

Percy returned to his room at Hatchetts Hotel, made himself comfortable on a sofa, and resumed his reading of Disraeli's revised *Alroy*. Twenty minutes later, his tranquility was disturbed by a knock at the door. Opening it, he discovered Grace Tarkenton with a sly smile on her face. Her head was covered with a scarf and her long coat was slightly damp from a fine mist deposited by the chilly London night air. In her hand was a bottle. Calvados. She thrust it forward and entered the room, removing her scarf and putting her coat on a tree just inside the door.

"What am I to do with this, Miss Tarkenton?" Percy accepted the French brandy from her. "A peace offering?"

"Why, drink it of course. Or are you as naïve as your silly friend, Mr. Hotze? You asked for Calvados? You have Calvados."

Taking the bottle, Percy chided Grace, rather than thanking her. "You were rather curt with Henry, weren't you? Graceless, I might put it. He was trying to show his enthusiasm for Mr. Dickens. He thought you shared that interest."

Scoffing, Grace rejected his criticism. "Interest? The man is single-minded. Mr. Henry Hotze is trying to spread Confederate propaganda in London in any way he can. He's been buying pro-Southern opinions to appear in our newspapers. It would be a feather in his cap if he could get a piece favorable to the South published in *All the Year Round.* Everyone reads it every Saturday. Charles Dickens manages very closely every item that appears in his weekly. He's instructed his staff to avoid entirely your civil war."

Percy was not to be intimidated. "You seem to know what Henry has been up to. And Dickens."

"My father warned me. He says your friend Hotze is very persistent in looking for support in the press and in government offices. He is charming and cunning like an Indian cobra. Stay away from him, my father insisted. Beware, he said."

"Yet you sought tickets from him for the performance this evening? You didn't heed your father's admonition."

"I rarely do."

Percy, dryly, "That's the first thing you've said that doesn't surprise me. Was Dickens so great an attraction that you finagled tickets?"

"No," she shrugged, "I can see Dickens at any time."

"Then what? Were you trying to embarrass Hotze? Do you so hate the South?"

She replied curtly, "I don't hate the South," then added, to Percy's surprise, "How else was I to meet you again?"

Percy was immediately confounded. All he could reply was, "Me? But you don't know me."

She brushed past him and examined his hotel suite, ignoring his comment. She complained, "Must we stand? You have a comfortable sofa and chairs. Shall we try the Calvados?"

Grace made herself comfortable. Percy shrugged and poured brandy. Handing her one glass, he sipped from his and sat on the chair opposite the sofa where she had settled.

"Why are you here, Miss Tarkenton?"

"Grace. You must call me Grace. Do I not interest you,

Lieutenant Percy Moorhead?"

Percy leaned back in the chair. He tried to assess her intentions. "Interest? Perhaps. Annoyance is what I most remember about you. You were an insufferable child. I've seen nothing to alter my opinion."

"Then I was successful. I intended to provoke you. You reminded me of Pierce Butler. You know of him, I'm sure."

"Who could forget? He was the Southerner who married the actress, Fanny Kemble. You were very taken with her, as I recall."

"I still am. She's an admirable woman, much abused by her husband — like many independent-minded wives. And like him, you are a slaveholder. Or were. We did not often meet slave owners when I was in New York. Those we did had beards glistening with tobacco juice and spoke coarsely."

With a half-grin, Percy replied, "Faint praise to be sure. I'm a Southerner who doesn't slobber and swear. Where is your friend Miss Rainsford?"

"Dotty? I hardly know her. Someone had to come along with me to the performance. I sent her to her aunt's directly."

"You were more than a trifle unkind to her, weren't you? Tattycoram? Really!"

"The girl is a trifle. As light as the wind. She'll be a pretty ornament in some gentleman's household. If Dickens knew her, he'd savage her like he has others. He's not known for patience."

Percy pretended to wince. "Ouch! You can be brutal, Miss Tarkenton. I would not like you as an enemy. You were equally hard on Hotze. Henry's a decent fellow. Tenacious, yes. Determined to advance the cause of the Confederacy. Patronizing on occasion, tedious sometimes, but never obnoxious. You seemed to think him ignorant of Dickens in some respect."

"Do you recall that when the lights went down, I pointed out two women below us?"

"Yes. Mother. Daughter. What has that to do with Hotze?"

"The younger woman was Nelly Ternan. The other was her mother, Fanny."

Showing his indifference with a shrug, "Yes? Should I recognize the names? Should Henry?"

"Actresses. Nelly has left the stage. Dickens has provided her a home. She is his paramour. That's why he can't enter politics. Other men may have their mistresses, but Nelly is an actress. Or was. He fears a scandal if their relation is publicly known."

Percy now understood her point, nodding, "I see. And because Hotze was unaware of this, he was foolish to think Dickens might be brought to say favorable things about the Southern cause?"

Grace, scornful, "Southern cause? What cause? The South's cause is slavery. Dickens would never associate with slavery. He has hopes of making a return trip to America. He could give his Readings in New York and Boston and Philadelphia. But not if he were thought to be a friend of Southern secession."

Percy, sarcastic now, "So you came to Hatchett's Hotel to be sure I suffered from no similar misapprehension about Mr. Dickens. You were concerned that I might embarrass myself if we should by chance encounter. How thoughtful of you!"

"No. The hour is late. Your hotel was near the theater. I was curious to know if you are the man I think you are."

Percy, showing some amusement, "Oh? And who do you imagine me to be? Pierce Butler? Heathcliff? Simon Legree? Jeff Davis?"

"None of those," she asserted confidently. "You're one of those ancient figures who descends into the underworld. You're an adventurer, but one who is haunted by what you have lost."

Percy instantly was on guard. Her penetrating statement braced him. This was no longer frivolous banter.

"How could you possibly know what I have lost?" His sense

of mild amusement at an impertinent young woman vanished, his privacy invaded.

Grace saw that he had been stung. She softened her manner and explained quietly. "When I first met you, you were a Louisiana lawyer and plantation owner. You were married and said you had a child on the way. But when you next came to England you had become a college professor in Virginia and a widower before joining the Confederate government. You had lost everything except your connection to Judah Benjamin."

Percy's eyes darted from side to side as he leaned toward her and demanded, "You learned all this how? And why?"

Soothing now, Grace said gently, "I mean no offense. You are well known among certain people in London and Liverpool. My father has sources. He told me your story. It touched me." She did not elaborate.

How had his personal information come to be known in London, Percy wondered. He tried to puzzle it out. The Union spies must have gathered it. He had arrived in England in May. If he had been identified as a Southern agent in June associated with Bulloch, Huse and Prioleau, the Union agents could have sent queries back to New York and Washington for further information about him. The Union had spies and secret supporters in Richmond, New Orleans and other cities who could have supplied details on Percy Moorhead. Or perhaps Richmond had sent letters to the South's commissioners about him and the letters were intercepted. Maybe the Union's hired men Ignaz Pollaky or Maguire were known to Sir James Tarkenton and they had passed on what they knew of Percy Moorhead directly. Surveillance, he had come to expect, was a game. But this information touched a nerve. It was deeply personal and beyond the reach of surveillance. Who had betrayed him? Someone he knew must have.

Percy stepped back from Grace, as though she were bent on harm. "So, your father has told you. Has he encouraged you to meet with me to learn more of what I am doing? For Lord Russell or Palmerston?"

Grace was surprised at his speculation. "No, he warned me to stay away from you. For the same reasons as Hotze. England must remain neutral. He will be a friend to you, but do not expect help from him. He knows nothing of my plans for the evening."

"Then why are you here?" he snapped.

Opening herself with candor, she said, "Your sneaky sad eyes. They see everything outside and conceal everything within. And I plan to win your affection."

Shaking his head vigorously, Percy protested, "Miss Tarkenton, you do have the ability to startle and to provoke. But you mistake me. I am no Don Juan."

"Nor I a trollop. You will not have me tonight. My favor is not lightly given."

Intrigued by her boldness and frankness, Percy was beginning to find her more interesting than threatening or irritating. Before she was derisive or mocking; now she was softer and sincere. Why not respond in kind?

Bantering, he challenged her. "How am I to prove myself? Will you drop your glove into the lions' pit?"

Grace was amused. "You have just shown you have wit, Percy Moorhead, by recalling Leigh Hunt's poem. Hunt was once our house guest, as were you. I am sure you have imagination equal to your wit."

Percy again jested, alluding now to *Macbeth*'s gatekeeper. "I'm at a loss for words. I am at once provoked and unprovoked."

"Ever the equivocator, Mr. Moorhead," she laughed, returning the reference. "As I called you on the *Baltic*. Then would you turn me aside?" she asked, taunting him, mischief in her voice. "Is it my features you find unattractive? Or my manner? Am I too forward? What part must I play to awaken in you desire? Come, come, I'm waiting for an answer. Show me more wit. Show me you are clever.

Challenge me." She was enjoying herself.

Percy had never met so mercurial a woman. He thought for a moment. "Ten years ago I looked out the window of your father's house. You were in the garden, dressed as Ganymede."

Grace stood and moved Percy to a chair next to the sofa and had him sit.

"Ah, yes. Like so?" Moving away from the chair, Grace pulled her hair to one side and turned her back to Percy. She stepped over to the coat rack and pretended it was a tree from which she plucked a note. With a dramatic turn of her head towards Percy, she read from the imagined note, affecting the voice of a young man.

All the pictures fairest lined
Are but black to Rosalind.
Let no face be kept in mind
But the fair of Rosalind.

She continued, "But that reading must be done in the guise of Ganymede. I suppose you would rather I play Rosalind to your Orlando. Do you find danger in love?"

Altering her voice to a more feminine pitch and subtly shifting her posture, she came closer to Percy, looking down on him in a mocking manner.

The poor world is almost six thousand years old,
And in all this time there was not any man died in his own person, videlicet, in a love cause.
Troilus and Cressida? Leander and Hero? Are these the patterns of love?
These are but lies. Men have died from time to time, and worms have eaten them,
But not for love.

From Rosalind, she reverted to Grace, shaking her head and saying more seriously, "No, Rosalind won't work for Percy Moorhead, soldier of fortune, a sojourner. She is too strong a figure. Not admiring her man enough. Might I do better as a fawning Miranda who has never seen so grand a creature as the newly arrived Ferdinand to the island where she has been confined by her father?"

Grace approached Percy, placed her hands on either side of his head and with false effusion said, in yet another voice,

There's nothing ill can dwell in such a temple.
If the ill spirit have so fair a house,
Oh, brave new world
That has such men as Percy Moorhead in't!

Percy allowed himself to feel amused. Her performance was extraordinary.

Laughing at herself and seeing his reaction, Miranda again was Grace, talking and walking around the chair where Percy watched in fascination.

"Perhaps you would have me be a Cordelia. Would you defer to my father and take half my love to have a rich dowry? Do you fancy yourself Burgundy or France?"

Grace stepped back two steps and knelt on one knee before Percy. In a meek, even piteous, voice she said,

Haply, when I shall wed,
That lord whose hand must take my plight shall carry
Half my love with him, half my care and duty.

She swooned and lay still a moment. Then Grace rose again and resumed her march around the chair, now lecturing to Percy.

"No, the Percy Moorhead I see, Lieutenant Moorhead, sees himself as the Confederate Hamlet. He has before him a petulant Ophelia who will not leave him so he may suffer the slings and arrows of fortune alone. No, Percy Hamlet would send me to a nunnery. I can only lament.

O, what a noble mind is here o'erthrown!
The courtier's, scholar's, soldier's, eye, tongue, sword   ,
Th' expectancy and rose of the fair state,
The glass of fashion and the mould of form,
O, woe is me
T' have seen what I have seen, see what I see!

Grace bowed as if on stage. Percy clapped his hands. He wondered at her command of the Shakespeare plays. With new appreciation, he said, "Bravo. Okay, Grace Tarkenton, I surrender. You know your Shakespeare far better than I. But why would you have the slightest interest in me? You are young and lovely. And your talent is unquestionable. Surely you should have your choice among many of the squires of your class."

As though the question was puzzling, she said, "Really? You are an attractive man, handsome in the crude American fashion. Not sweetly scented like our gentlemen whose hands have known no toil. When I first met you, you were Pierce Butler. The slaveowner who was stealing Fanny Kemble's children from her. But you had charm. And you treated me as an adult. You encouraged me to play the piano for you. And to become an actress. My father's friends had never done that. Children here are neither to be seen nor heard. England has freed her slaves but not her women. You were different. And now the wicked, charming man from ten years ago has become a sad and lonely man." She was no longer playful. Percy even sensed sympathy in her.

Percy, laughing lightly, "Sad and lonely? I rather thought I cut a dashing figure. At once, both wicked and debonair, calluses and all. Now I think you offer your favor as an act of charity to a lost soul. Which is it? Am I challenge or charity?"

"Don't make mockery of my judgment," she insisted seriously. "It's in your eyes. You trust no one. You are wary of everyone and afraid to let down your guard. You need to make a human connection that can bring you no harm. We can come together for a brief time and take leave of one another with no regrets. We have no future together. You are a slaveholder. Or were. Now you have only a pocket full of Confederate dollars. You have no property. You have no standing in England. My father respects you but does not embrace your cause. He warns me away from you. If you live through this war, you will return to a ruined land. Your loyalties are misplaced. But you are safe for me."

"Safe? As in *Lucrece*?"

"Safe in that you are in England only a short time, my sojourner. Unlike Dickens, you're not married. I have no intention of letting a man interfere with my acting. Nelly Ternan has had to stop acting so she won't be in the public eye, embarrassing Dickens and calling attention to their affair. Proper Englishmen, the squires whom you deride, are reluctant to associate with a lady of the stage. There is no such delicacy in you. You can provide me with intelligent companionship for a brief period, and we can share desire and affection."

"You are nothing if not bold. But nothing tonight? You said I will not have you tonight."

"No, not tonight. And don't sound patronizing. I will sleep with you, but I will not sleep with you."

"What makes you think I would want to see you again? If you would withhold yourself tonight, and if I am lonely and fear betrayal, why would I subject myself to future disappointment?"

"Because I provoke you. As I performed, I saw your desire. I could be your Rosalind, your Miranda, and it would excite you." She paused, adding with a sly smile, "Perhaps I can entice you with something more than my engaging wit in performance."

Percy, now curious, "Oh? Persuade me what that might be."

"You need not encounter Dickens by chance. He fascinates you. You made that clear. I will introduce you to the great Dickens himself. You will not have to share him with two thousand Londoners."

"Yes. I admire him very much. Not for the same reasons as Henry Hotze. Since Judah Benjamin and I first discussed Dickens, I've read most of his books. I wish I had his talent."

"You want to be a writer?"

Percy, with an amused chuckle, "I do write – as a lawyer. Briefs. Appeals. Letters for clients. In legal writing, I am a past master. And I've written my class lectures. Someday I'd like to collect them and publish them, like my Rhetoric professor at Princeton. Very few writers make the money of a lawyer with an equal amount of words."

"No? Dickens is wealthy."

"Yes, but atypical. Take Edgar Poe. Famous everywhere when I heard him lecture in Richmond a dozen years ago. A month later he was dead at forty. Penniless and alone. I was deeply moved by his lecture, his theory of the beauty of a poem. After the lecture I attended a reception at a wealthy lawyer's home, a childhood friend of the poet, and there I met Poe. A strange man. Incandescent eyes, as though fevered, haunted. I returned to Louisiana determined I would be a writer. The newspaper reports of his death shocked and frightened me. Instead of emulating Poe, I followed the path of his host that night, his lawyer friend. Mr. Dickens is the rare exception of a man who can earn his living as a novelist or poet."

"Hmmmm," Grace mused aloud. "Wealthy lawyer or impoverished Poe. Why do you seem to admire still the latter more?"

"My words made me well-to-do. Poe's lines have purchased immortality. What was Dr. Faust's bargain? Make me immortal with a kiss. And just that line alone has placed Marlowe among the immortals."

"And Dickens has wealth and literary fame. Yet, the devil has not taken his due. So, would you like to meet the man himself?"

"Yes, of course I would. Don't tell me he's a friend of your father's."

"No. My father and I travel in different company. But I can arrange for you to see him."

Percy was intrigued. "You have my attention, young lady."

"Come to my rehearsal tomorrow afternoon. I'm in a new play, *The Maid of Melrose*. I play the part of Emily, the sister of the lead character, Henrietta. And Maria Ternan plays Sarah, Henrietta's rival for the affections of Rodney Rolandson."

"How does that involve Dickens?"

"Maria is Nelly Ternan's sister. Nelly, Charles Dickens's secret lover. Unlike Nelly, Maria still is an actress, and Dickens is helping advance her career. So he comes to our rehearsals and gives suggestions to the writer and director. If you come to our theater, I'll have Maria introduce you to him."

"All right. It is late. Do you really intend to spend the night here?"

"Yes. But you shall not have my favor tonight. And not until you answer a question to show you have imagination as well as learning."

"And what riddle might you have for me?"

"Do you recall the women whose lines I performed?"

"That's not difficult. There were four. Rosalind, Ophelia, Miranda and Cordelia. I'm sure I can identify their plays, when the hour is not so late and my mind not affected by Calvados."

"Yes. Of course you can. But what have they in common?"

Percy struggled to find an answer. "I can't recall enough detail. You're a better Shakespeare reader than I am. All I can say is that two live and two die upon the stage. That's not in common."

Grace laughed. "Not bad for a lawyer. But no actor can expect to be taken seriously unless you can play not just a few but many roles. Since I was six, I have prepared to perform Shakespeare. Every serious actress must. Some parts have greater meaning than others for each of us. I'm sure lines involving lawyers and the law have more meaning to you."

"True. But soldiers, too. When I was in Mexico, I thought of Henry the Fifth in France."

"You were in Mexico?"

"That fact must not have made it into the spy's dossier on me.

The one that your father must have seen or been told about."

"Say no more of him," said Grace." It's late. Get into bed. I will join you."

"I will respect your conditions. Reluctantly."

"It will only increase your appetite. A night is but small breath and little pause for matters of consequence."

Percy fell asleep, feeling the warmth of Grace's gentle breathing upon his neck, her firm breasts upon his back. When he awakened at seven, he was alone.

Chapter 50

Maid of Melrose

G race had left directions for Percy to the Raven Theatre, near
Clerkenwell. He entered from a side door. Rehearsals for
The Maid of Melrose began a little after ten. The venue was
scruffy and seldom used, relegated now to foreign players or to
rehearsals. Had he attended the Raven in its glory days, he might
have seen Boots Blackthorne immortalize the role of the laughing
captain of the HMS *Wivern*. Here, Harold O'Shea had filled the hall
with his booming soliloquies, and Anna Templeton had drawn
rivers of tears from countless audiences at her anguished cries
when she realized the small figure on the floor was her own
beloved Lily Belinda. Now, several acting companies stored their
costumes and unused sets in the hallways and rooms behind the
stage. The Raven's feathers were no longer glossy; though shabby,
the theatre was serviceable.

Percy spotted Dickens seated on the third row, commenting
intermittently to another man, perhaps the playwright or a
producer of the play. Seating himself five rows behind them, he
maintained a respectful distance so he would not appear to be
eavesdropping or presumptive. The actors were reading their lines
from their playbooks and pacing from place to place on the set as
instructed by the young director. Grace was upstage, saying her
lines with animation, unaided by a prompt book, to another young

woman. Her powers of memory were extraordinary. She glanced in Percy's direction briefly but made no sign to acknowledge his presence, remaining in the character of Emily as she continued to rehearse.

Dickens now looked older to Percy than he had appeared on stage. The furrows on his face were more pronounced, his hair more unruly. When the director announced a recess of twenty minutes, Dickens approached the stage. An actress of about thirty descended at the side and greeted him with affection. Percy guessed this was the Maid of Melrose's best friend, Maria Ternan, sister of Nelly.

"The play is just the thing for you, my dear," Dickens said warmly. "You bring Sarah Weaver to life. So many possibilities. I'll share some ideas when we meet with our director."

"Your support is generous," Maria responded. "I won't disappoint you or Nelly." Seeing Grace approach, Maria reminded Dickens, "You remember Grace, don't you? She's brought someone to meet you."

Dickens turned, "Grace, of course. Emily, the Maid's sister. The MP's daughter."

Percy could see something pass across Grace's face, a moment of hesitation as her mouth briefly pursed before broadening into a smile at Dickens's greeting. If something disturbed her, she was a good enough actress to conceal it well.

Grace caught Percy's eye. She motioned for him to come forward.

Dickens continued, "Well, Miss Tarkenton, it would be clumsy wordplay of me to say you bring grace to your role. Emily – what an opportunity for an actress. How is our Sir James?"

Grace, terse, but cordial, "My parents are well, thank you."

Dickens, giving a wry smile, "Your father would have no reason to remember, but I nearly became a barrister because of him.

I was a fifteen year old at the firm of Ellis and Blackmore, Gray's Inn. For a short while I was a courier of messages and documents. I watched his appearances in court and hoped to do the same."

Grace, more courteously, "From your novels, Mr. Dickens, the reader would think you are a lawyer. My only court experience has been from your Jarndyce case."

Nodding in the direction of Percy, Dickens said to Grace, "And this gentleman. Is this who Maria said you wished me to meet?"

Turning towards Percy, Grace introduced him to Dickens. "He is. We attended your appearance last evening and loved your performance. Allow me to present Lieutenant Percy Moorhead of Virginia."

Dickens examined Percy from head to boot, assessing every feature of the man in modest civilian attire who stood before him. He took Percy's extended hand and shook it casually. With no suggestion of criticism, Dickens commented, "A rebel, are you? Your secession, your domestic discord, has stirred no small misery here. The looms and mills of Manchester and Liverpool have fallen silent. When will your war be over?"

Percy, showing a subtle smile, was amiable. "Your Prime Minister could end it with a single sheet of foolscap tomorrow by recognizing our independence."

Dickens frowned slightly. "Would that it were so simple. Many of our English think your war is like the burning out of a very dirty chimney, at which the neighbors may look on with composure and self-congratulation. Some desire the utter ruin of the North to render Canada safe. Others would be glad to witness the annihilation of the South to remove, as they think, the most formidable competitor of India. None wish to see the expansion of slavery into the Caribbean nor the revival of the traffic in humans from Africa."

Affable despite the criticism, Percy replied, "Our firebrands in the Confederacy are an outspoken minority. Were it not for the invasion of the South by the Union, our peculiar institution would have been gradually but surely superseded by wage labor. Human servitude is highly inefficient. It ties up too much capital. A phasing out of forced servitude would be possible if it were not for the extreme abolitionists in the North. They have no love for the African. They are what you might call telescopic philanthropists."

Dickens registered the phrase as one of his own making and smiled. He looked Percy over with a new appraisal. "Well, Moorhead, I see why the South has sent you to represent them."

Shaking his head, Percy insisted, "No, that role lies with Henry Hotze. He's the man who obtained our tickets last evening. My job is not to defend the institution of slavery. A solution cannot be forced upon us at gunpoint. I'm only a lawyer trying to keep his client within the boundaries of British law."

Dickens remained vaguely aloof. "Oh? I have labored under a rather different impression of those who appear before the bar. In my experience, they try to redraw the boundaries when they don't ignore them entirely. Indeed, you may prove to be the exception. Did you practice in Virginia before the conflict?"

"A long time ago, I had a commercial practice in New Orleans. A wag could have been speaking of me when he said, others had cases to plead, while I had to plead for a case. When the Union demanded the submission of the South, I had already given up my practice to become a teacher of rhetoric at the College of William and Mary, in Virginia."

Showing more interest in the Confederate lawyer who was also a man of letters, Dickens said, "Really. And did you prepare your scholars for the rigors of war?"

Percy, earnestly, "Could any man? Each generation must learn for themselves the great lie of war's glory."

Impressed by the lawyer's turn of phrase, Dickens replied, "Jack Falstaff could not have said it better. And you Mr. Moorhead, if you are indeed skeptical of war's glory and the Confederate program, why do you fight in this war?" Dickens's eyes were the penetrating eyes of an inveterate skeptic, an agnostic of sentiment and a skewer of piety, pretense and sanctimony.

Percy, without hesitation. "Loyalty. Debt."

"Loyalty. To Virginia? To a new country?"

"No. To family. To friends. To the people I've known and worked with since I was a child. To my colleagues and students at my college. How could I turn from them when they are challenged by people whom I don't know, who have no use or care of me? I don't like slavery and would not fight to defend it. I preferred maintenance of the Union. But my choices were limited. I had no voice on secession. President Lincoln himself has said the Union government has no goal of abolishing slavery. My college closed its doors. If I had stayed out of the Confederate service, it would have been only a matter of time before I was subject to conscription by the Confederacy and carrying a rifle. If I abandoned the South and moved North, it would only have been a matter of time before I was subject to conscription and carrying a rifle against my own family and friends."

Dickens's forehead furrowed deeper as he looked intently at Percy. "You, sir, sound like a reluctant rebel."

Percy did not contradict him. "Let me put it another way to you, Mr. Dickens. Troy is falling. You are a Trojan. Would you remain with the Greeks, who have no use or regard for you, or would you sail away with Aeneas to an uncertain fate? When reason is overthrown, whirl is king. A man must find his way in a world of confusion, chaos, and challenge."

Dickens ruminated at the thought-provoking response and nodded. "You expect a long war. You mentioned debt. Are you a candidate for debtor's prison?"

Percy thought he heard something poignant in Dickens's voice. He immediately remembered Micawber in *David Copperfield*, whose imprisonment in the Marshalsea was based on Dickens's own father. But Percy made no reference to it. "My debt is not of the monetary kind. It is to Judah Benjamin."

"A Confederate official as I recall. Vice-president to Jefferson Davis?"

"Close. He was Attorney General. When I asked to join his law firm years ago, as I began my career, he took me in. When he asked me to work for him in his new office, I could not refuse him."

"Ah, yes, Mr. Moorhead. Friends, family. An employer. Well and good. But will they reciprocate when your time of trial comes? Or will they abandon you upon some sign of disagreement?" Dickens was speaking now to Percy with the world-weary distrust of human nature that Percy had found permeating Dickens's novels. "Do not harness your talents to causes in which you have no faith. When they fail, you will find yourself alone."

Percy showed no disagreement with Dickens's perspective, even if it seemed cynical. He said nothing of the irony that Dickens was himself the husband of a wife who was now alone as Dickens had abandoned her. This, in itself, reinforced Dickens's opinion.

Hearing the director call the players to the stage, Dickens nodded politely to Percy and returned to his seat. Grace told Percy she would meet him outside the main entrance to the Raven in two hours.

Chapter 51

The British Museum

L eaning against a lamppost, Percy watched the smoke of his cigar curl towards an ash-gray sky, when Grace finally exited the Raven, a half-hour late. She was wearing a dark blue coat and had changed from the outfit she had worn for the rehearsal. Her face was slightly flushed, and she seemed preoccupied until she saw Percy across the street, as though she had forgotten she was to meet him. By the time he reached her, she had nearly regained her composure.

"Are you all right?" he inquired. "For a moment, you appeared distraught."

Managing a nervous half smile, she waved her hand to dismiss concern. "Nothing. A misunderstanding. Some changes perhaps."

"If this is no longer a good occasion . . . ."

Shaking her head, she insisted, "No, please. It will pass. Let us proceed as we planned."

"And we had planned?"

"The British Museum. Didn't you say you wanted to see it?"

"I suppose I must have."

"We have time. It's fifteen minutes by coach. And then two hours til closing."

Percy did not recall having mentioned the Museum, but it was something that he had intended to visit. Grace said little in the cab as it made its way to High Holborn and then Great Russell Street. Her eyes were directed out the windows, but she saw nothing. When they were inside the museum, she asked, "Now, what is it you wanted to see?"

"Let me start with the catalog," he said, quickly examining a synopsis of exhibits on a counter. "Why not begin with the most ancient? Would that be Egyptian or Greek? Let's visit Egypt first."

"Yes, let's," she agreed, indifferently.

Walking slowly through the hall, Percy examined the exhibits and consulted the printed guide. Here were statues of pharaohs and ancient Egyptian deities. At the north end of the gallery were stone sarcophagi – bases and lids and a giant scarab beetle. Grace matched his steps but paid little attention to the ancient objects, her thoughts elsewhere.

Percy paused before a four-foot-tall slab of dark gray granite, its width half its height. The sign below identified it as the Rosetta Stone.

Coming beside him, Grace asked "What do you think? The most famous writing in the world."

Peering intently at the obscure characters chiseled into the stone, Percy paused and said with mock sincerity, "It's all Greek to me."

Grace laughed, in spite of herself. "Well, we do have Shakespeare to share, don't we? You have a quote for every occasion."

"Had it not been for France's Capitulation of Alexandria, this stone would no doubt be on display in Paris. The divine cult of a ruler for whom the decree was made is long dead, but the words – lapidary scrawl in three languages no less – live on."

"Lapidary. I like that." Her mood seemed to brighten at the

wordplay. "Well, we've exhausted most of an hour on the Egyptians. Can we do the Greeks and Romans in less time? Closing will soon be upon us."

Encouraged by the improvement in Grace's mood, Percy remained playful, saying, "Small Latin and less Greek. We will fleet the time, my dear. If you are up to it."

"You are capable of charm, Lieutenant Moorhead. When you put your mind to it."

Smiling and taking her arm, Percy said, "If I can draw you from an ineffable sadness, then I will have done something worthwhile. Yes, we can walk quickly through the Greeks and Romans; I recognize most of the things here. Throughout the Confederate states you will find that the public buildings, the capitols, the mansions – all are built along the lines we see here. We model our society on Greek and Roman ideals, or what we claim them to be. It even extends now to Southern names. When I saw Judah Benjamin in October, he introduced me to one of his friends from Mississippi – whose name, as I recall, is Lucius Quintus Cincinnatus Lamar."

"Was that the name of a Roman consul?"

"Maybe we can find the answer here, among the statuary. I wouldn't be surprised to return to Virginia and find our Solons clad in togas and declaiming in Latin."

"And her capital renamed Richmondium?" She was smiling.

"Exactly so! And I will tell them all I have just returned from Londinium. See, you can be chipper after all."

"And I'm famished. Let's find somewhere to eat."

"When was your last meal?"

"You were still asleep when I left this morning. I had a roll and tea while rehearsing my lines at a shop near the old theatre. So much for that."

"That?"

"Let's not dwell on it. The Blue Posts is a quiet place to eat. Cork Street is a short ride."

Twenty minutes later they were seated in a pleasant dining room.

Percy, after ordering, "When is the premier of *Maid of Melrose*?"

"Three weeks from now."

"I'm afraid I'll have to miss it."

"You're returning to America?"

"To the Confederate States of America." He had no meaning to correct her, only to clarify his destination.

Grace, again curt. "Same thing."

Was it something he had said? Perhaps it was mention of the *Maid of Melrose*.

He tried to revive the moment. "I won't quibble. What can I do to amuse you now?"

Grace was staring at flowers in a vase at the side of their table. She turned her eyes toward him. "Don't ask about the play. Or Mr. Dickens."

"Oh? Has something turned you on him? I was very glad to meet him."

"There. You asked about him."

"So I did. You're quite right." Percy doubted that he could say anything that would be well-received.

Their food arrived. They ate in near silence, Percy briefly giving his impressions of the Museum without a response from her. She ate little despite professing hunger earlier. Upon leaving, Grace gave the coachman her address, near fashionable Belgravia. Percy got out of the coach and assisted Grace in stepping to the curb. He started to get in the coach, but Grace held his arm.

Grace, anxious, "No. I don't want to be alone. Stay a while. You should stay."

⋘ - ⋙

"It was March 14, 1862, Tom." Percy was somber, reflective when he said this, maybe even wistful. It was a few days after the funeral. He was collecting things to put them away. He had asked me to come by. We sat in his backyard, with its gentle slope down to the river Stour. On the other side, sheep were grazing; the spring grass in their field was in full green growth. A tenant's border collie was darting back and forth among them, herding them back to a safe enclosure as the day was drawing to a close.

"You remember the exact date?" I was surprised. That was well more than a quarter-century ago.

"Yes. And the day. A Friday."

He had a sadness about him. Was it solace he sought, the company of a friend to share with him profound grief mixed with a sort of release? It was almost exactly a year after that date that I first met Percy in the Tarkenton backyard in Godstow. I first met Grace on that same occasion. We had been friends ever since.

"The What-Ifs, Tom. It's the What-Ifs. I don't mean regrets. Regrets are useless, more like self-pity than anything else. What I mean, can we imagine how different a life might be based on a single, simple What-If. We know the past, don't we? We know what happened for the want of a nail."

"Isn't that Shakespeare?" I asked.

"Close. You'd be thinking of Bosworth Field. Same proverb. Same point. What-If the horse's shoe had not lost a nail? Would English history have been different? Life, history, is often on an exquisitely balanced beam. You've heard me on Kairos before, how it differs from Chronos. An ever so small a weight can tip the beam, and everything is different."

"Yes," I said. "I see." Of course, I didn't see at all. But I knew he would get to his point. I would learn what it was he wanted me to hear.

And then he explained.

"That evening with Grace, coming to her flat from the museum, was such a moment on the balance beam. I intended to walk away from her at that moment. She had teased me the night before, and it left me with an odd taste, almost unpleasant but lingering. After her rehearsal, she was obviously disturbed. Something about Dickens had upset her. At the museum I had difficulty trying to break through her distraction. She was troubled. She was brittle. She was anxious. Should I have turned and walked away? I was inclined to. What if I had? What small thing tipped the balance and affected the course of my life? The lock of loose hair over her eye? The depth and passion of her earnest glance when she urged me to stay? What-If?"

Chapter 52

What If?

Pulled by her hand, Percy turned and followed Grace to the door. Her rooms were on the ground floor. He placed his hat on a table and seated himself on her sofa. Without asking his preference, Grace poured two brandies and handed him one. She sat in a chair opposite him and sipped from her glass, saying nothing, downcast.

Percy, breaking the awkward silence, "So, tell me what we can chat about?"

"You begin." She was not eager to explain why she was upset. "Tell me what it was like to live on a cotton plantation."

"Fairy tale? Or bad dream? Which version would you prefer? I'm sure you've already read the book."

Grace, abruptly, "You can't mean Fanny Kemble's. I've read some of it. She hasn't published it yet, but people know it's coming."

"The same Fanny Kemble we talked about earlier? When you took me to be a Pierce Butler."

"Yes. She's encouraged me in acting. Now she wants to show everyone how wrong the South is. Everyone who knows her knows about her book She's let me read some of it."

Percy was hopeful that she was turning from whatever was

upsetting her. He encouraged her to go on. "What sort of book is it?"

"It's a diary from her two years living in Georgia on her husband's cotton and rice plantations."

"That should be timely. I'd love to see it. No, the book I was thinking of was Mrs. Stowe's."

"Of course. *Uncle Tom's Cabin*. Everyone in London has read it. The nightmare. Or was she wrong?"

Percy acknowledged the power of Harriet Beecher Stowe's work. "There's a lot of truth in her book. She put much of her plot in Louisiana, but she had never visited a Louisiana plantation. Or any other. Now, your Fanny Kemple lived on one. That would be more authentic. My father's plantation, he named it Bolingbroke. His views were not unlike those of Stowe's character, Augustine St. Clare. Little Eva's father, the man who bought Uncle Tom. My father ran the plantation through a black overseer with the same efficiency as Alfred St. Clare ran the St. Clare plantation."

"Alfred St. Clare?" Grace didn't recall the name.

"Augustine St. Clare's brother in the novel. He ran the family plantation that the brothers inherited."

"I don't remember him. But who could forget Simon Legree?"

Percy shared with her some of the dismal events at Bolingbroke. "I don't deny that Mrs. Stowe got that right. My sister's husband would have been just as bad, if slavery hadn't killed him first."

"How did slavery kill him?"

"It made him who he was. His name was Calvin. He was a pathetic little man who hid his own deficiencies behind his brutality to slaves. You can inflict only so much violence on another human. Even a slave will revolt. One did. The worst evil of slavery is its denial of redress to gross injustice. Human nature is no worse at the South than at the North. But in the South the law protects the worst abuses to which human nature is capable."

"But your father was different?" Grace sounded skeptical but open. Although testy, she had no wish to quarrel with Percy.

"Yes. He was a generous man, a kind man who disliked the idea of owning other people. He was determined that no black person was made worse off by coming under his authority. No black person – man, woman or child – would have found a better life if he had sold or freed them. The slaves at Bolingbroke worked hard, but so did all of the free people. To me, it seemed as natural an order as I later found in the army. My home was as much a part of who I am as were my parents."

"But your father treated the slaves like farm animals, didn't he? Horses are well fed and often treated kindly."

"No. He treated them as laborers. And he treated them better than many of the workers in the mills of Manchester or factories in Birmingham. One of the last things we talked about was his plan to free his slaves. I approved. But Louisiana law would not allow it. If you're not convinced, I'll tell you something I've never told anyone else – he loved a black woman."

Grace, less agreeably, "Mrs. Stowe talks about slaves used as mistresses."

Percy, earnestly, "No! You misunderstand. She was a free woman of color. She has her own shop in New Orleans. I only learned of their devotion to one another after his death. After I had lost everything to an Irishman who claims he's my older brother."

Grace, surprised now, and with more sympathy, "How? I knew you no longer had a plantation. I just assumed your family went bankrupt like many others. What happened?"

"That's a long and complicated story. For another occasion." Sensing a change in her mood, Percy plunged ahead, "Now I've told you one of my secrets. You must tell me yours. What upset you so today?"

Grace took a deep breath. She spoke slowly, resentful. "They're changing the play."

"They? Who are they?"

"The author. The director. Dickens."

"Is your part written out?"

Grace, glumly, "It might as well be."

"Emily is still in the play?"

"Yes, indeed. With an enhanced role, a bigger part."

"Isn't that good?"

"For Maria Ternan. Not for me. She's to play the part of the Maid's sister. I've been changed to the part of Sarah. The Maid's rival."

"I don't understand."

"When I was Emily, I was Henrietta's younger sister and her confidante. It was an important part and allowed me to play the ingenue. Sarah, however, is a supercilious character, ill-natured and unpleasant, at whose expense laughter is expected from the audience. Dickens suggested enhancing the Emily part for Maria. Now Emily is an older sister of Henrietta, and she's worldly wise. It is Emily who teaches Henrietta how to prevail against her rival, Sarah. Now me. The revised Emily will be the moving spirit behind the bringing together of the Maid of Melrose and Rodney. Don't you see what they are doing?

"Somewhat. Perhaps. Tell me. I want to understand."

"All right. I'll spell it out for you. Maria Ternan is Ellen Ternan's older sister. In the play, Emily is changed from Henrietta's younger sister to her older sister. Dickens promised that he'll write a new scene and revise two others. The role of Sarah is being cutback. The role they've stuck me in."

It didn't make much sense to Percy. He had no reason to know any of the play's plot or characters. "Would Dickens draw on people he actually knows? Wouldn't that prove embarrassing?"

"He does it in many of his books. You haven't heard about Dickens and Leigh Hunt?"

"I know a few of Hunt's poems. Nothing more."

"Leigh Hunt was always a good friend to Dickens. But Dickens caricatured poor Hunt mercilessly. He made him Skimpole in *Bleak House*, a weak man-child who sponges off all his friends. Everyone knew what Dickens had done, but he denied it. Hunt took it as a very personal betrayal. It was public amusement at Hunt's expense. So, what Dickens and the director are doing now is making Emily like the real-life Maria, and Henrietta will be made more like Nelly. I wouldn't be surprised if Dickens doesn't make Sarah an MP's daughter."

"Why are they doing this?"

"To make Maria Ternan almost the leading lady. And I think they were concerned that I might up-stage her. I'm sure that Nelly is behind this. Even if she can't perform because it would draw attention to being Dickens' mistress, at least her sister will get important roles. And it will be a little joke at the expense of everyone in London who disapproves of his relationship with Nelly Ternan. Being a great writer doesn't make him a nice man."

Percy tried to soothe Grace. "There, there. Would it do any good to tell the playwright you think the play was better, as he had written it or as the director has staged it?"

Grace was angry at Percy's inability to understand. "No! Do you think any director in London would refuse the advice of the most famous writer in the world, one whose own weekly publication would bring all England's attention to the play? And the author of the play – he was a writer for Dickens's magazine until three years ago. *Household Words*. He's a Dickens acolyte."

Percy, determined to show his support of Grace, "Then quit. Take a part in another play."

Grace shook her head fretfully, rejecting the suggestion out of hand. "That's impossible. As soon as it became known that I walked out so soon before opening, I'd never audition for another role again."

Percy, taking a different tack, "Hmmmm. Let's look at it another way. When people know that Dickens has written part of the play, won't that bring out audiences like we saw last night? It'll mean more people will see you and your talent as an actress. A successful play will lead to more roles in the future. A rising tide lifts all boats in the harbor."

"Maybe." She did not sound encouraged. "That won't change the fact that they have taken something from me that was mine. I earned that role. Every word Maria Ternan speaks will remind me they should have been my words. Every crossing of the stage was my moment to cross the stage. They've embarrassed me. My father will think this confirms all of his warning not to mix with theatre people. They'll use me, then ignore me."

"Then embrace the role. Make it your own, a showcase for your talents."

"That's not what I want to hear."

Out of ideas, Percy confessed his frustration. "So, what do you want to hear from me?"

"I want sympathy. I want you to tell me I've been wronged. Tell me I've been treated unfairly. Share my anger. Take my side. Say how awful Charles Dickens is to have done this to me."

"Dickens is doing what men always have done. He's looking out for his own. You've told me that this is what Nelly Ternan would want for her sister. And how could Dickens resist the wishes of the woman he loves?"

Grace would not be consoled. "Forget it then. Forget I said anything." She turned her hostility to Percy himself. "I should never have talked about it. But you insisted. That's what I get for telling you my feelings. They're just ignored. I shouldn't have let you stay."

Percy was quiet for a minute. He sighed and said, "Words fail me. I will leave you to your anger and self-pity. You prefer them to my company." He picked up his hat from the table.

Turning petulant, Grace demanded, "No! You were to stay the night. And so you shall. I thought you wanted to have me. When I'm going through all this, will you reject me, too? I thought you were more gallant. Or was that just pretense?"

"You are not the same woman now. Sure, I wanted you. The Grace I saw before was charming, provocative, self-assured. Lively. A woman of mystery and riddle. A beguiler. But she's not here."

"I don't want to be alone," she implored, now frightened.

Percy shook his head, "Percy Moorhead can be of no comfort, I'm afraid. Self-sorrow is a bottomless pit. Give in to it and you give up the possibility of future happiness. I know, I was nearly seduced by it. And when I saw what it might do to me, I despised that person."

"So now you despise me? Is that it?" Her voice and expressions vacillated between testiness and fear.

"I said no such thing. You behave like the peevish child I met on the *Baltic*. The truth is, you're angry with Dickens because you are angry at your father. I saw your expression when Dickens remembered you as the MP's daughter. You recoiled but held yourself in check from showing it. And you returned to it only a moment ago. Dickens saw you as Sir James's daughter, not Grace Tarkenton, the actress and rightful heir to Fanny Kemble."

"How dare you!" she blurted out, stepping in front of him, slapping his face hard.

Percy ignored the blow that left his cheek red. He said calmly, "Your anger at your father provides the answer to the puzzle you gave me. Your Shakespeare heroines have troubled relations with their fathers. Rosalind, Ophelia, Miranda, Cordelia. Each is controlled by her father. Each suffers from the father's overbearing nature. That's why their roles are so meaningful to you. You expected Dickens to be a different father to you. Now he, too, has disappointed you."

Grace lunged at Percy again with her open right hand. He grabbed it with his left.

Percy, sharply, "No!"

"Damn you." She was defiant, pummeling his chest with her fists. He held both her wrists tightly and drew her to him. As their faces met, he looked her in the eye. And she returned his look. The warmth she saw, the calm manner, dissipated her anger and fury. Her arms relaxed, and she turned her head slightly to receive his kiss. Their lips touched tentatively, each uncertain now of the other. Of resistance, there was none. Relief of the tension of angry confrontation turned to eagerness and passion. They unbuttoned each other's clothing with fumbling awkwardness that embarrassed both of them, about which they would later laugh. A half hour later, they lay in each other's arms, exhausted.

The morning after their love-making, conversation was awkward as Percy and Grace shared a breakfast of cold buns and tea. Nothing was said of Dickens or the *Maid of Melrose*. Percy said, "I must leave for Liverpool. And Richmond soon after. Will I see you again?"

Her expression was inscrutable. "Will you?"

With no more, he departed for Liverpool. Should he have made a welcome of indifference? He wondered now if she would play the role of Sarah, as re-imagined by mighty Dickens.

Two weeks later, the many months of preparation for the *Oreto* and the *Scylla* were complete.

Chapter 53

Ships Set Sail

Saturday, March 22, was a cool but sunny day, drawing many residents of Liverpool to the promenade along the docks. Following Percy's suggestions, James Bulloch and Charles Prioleau had arranged for some of their friends and families to enjoy an outing aboard the *Oreto* for a brief run on the Mersey, notice of which was well-circulated in Liverpool society. A block from the dock Percy Moorhead, with quiet satisfaction, looked on with binoculars as guests walked on the ship's deck and peered over the rails. Shifting his view, he observed a man he recognized as one of Consul Dudley's spies amble over from the dock to the United States consulate. No doubt he would inform the consul of the activity on the *Oreto*. As Percy and his associates had planned, the spy surmised it was just another trial run, the third in a week. No cause for alarm.

Then Percy saw the angular shape of Consul Dudley emerge from the consular building. Dudley was familiar with the distinctive two funnels and sleek outline of the *Oreto*. Any day now, he had made it known, the English government would nail an order to one of her masts forbidding the removal of the ship from the dock.

Dudley's posture suddenly stiffened. Percy knew what must be going through his mind. Why were there two small boats beside the *Oreto*? Why were the visitors getting into the boats rather than returning to the dock with the ship?

Percy smiled; he could see the look of consternation on Dudley's face as it dawned on the consul that the Southerners were pulling off a surprise departure on a weekend, when most of the harbor officials and the foreign ministry in London were off-duty. The first Confederate cruiser built in England would have a two-day head start on any effort to prevent this sailing. Percy could read the anger on Dudley's face; he could almost feel the deep chagrin. He could see Dudley's gestures of distress at the success of their ruse. The rebel mouse was escaping the Yankee cat.

Percy imagined Dudley's state of mind, fuming impotently and vowing that it would not happen again. He had failed his first big challenge as Union consul. How many Northern merchant ships would be lost from his ineffectiveness?

CSS Florida (1862-1864)
Clary Ray, December 1984. NH 57835
Navy Art Collection, Washington, DC

Even now, a second Confederate raider was rising in the shipyard at Birkenhead, just across the Mersey River, known to

Dudley only by its number: 290. Ostensibly, it was destined for the Spanish government, just as the *Oreto* was supposed to be en route for owners in Palermo. If he wrote immediately, it would take weeks to get a response from Spain. From what Percy had learned of his opponent, Dudley must be swearing that the *290* would not leave England, even if he had to sink her himself.

Percy could not, however, wait and share the moment with Bulloch when he returned to the dock. He must hurry to get back to Richmond. Now that the *Oreto* was launched, his work in England was, for now, finished. Were it not for the fact that the *Oreto* was going to Nassau under sail for most of the voyage, he could have gone with Captain Duguid and John Low. They would be at sea for as much as forty days or more, in no great hurry, for they needed to meet up in Nassau with the *Bahama* under Captain Tessier. Instead, Percy had his own ship ready to sail, the *Scylla*, near twin of the *Herald* which had already departed under Captain Tate, with her future captain aboard, Louis Coxetter. The *Herald* was to be an ideal blockade runner for the Confederacy. The *Scylla* was her equal, if not superior.

Percy's coach was ready with his bags to take him up Regent Road to Sandon Dock, where the *Scylla* waited in the basin. No Matthew Maguire followed him this time. Percy was now a master of evasion.

A quarter hour later Percy stepped from the coach. He paused to admire his new craft. She was one of the finest specimens of a Clyde steamer, with her rakish profile – long iron hull, narrow beam, a draft of only ten feet and powered by two engines of over 300 horsepower. For her purpose as a blockade runner, her staterooms had been removed, her stowage areas increased, her smokestacks replaced with retractable funnels. Her masts were now mounted on hinges so that they could be lowered to reduce her silhouette. Percy had ordered that the *Scylla* be painted a light gray to further reduce her visibility. As she was not of a design suited to be armed, the *Scylla*'s arrival in Liverpool for refitting had attracted little attention from Union spies. A blockade runner was unarmed so that if she were captured, her crew would be treated as civilians by the Union, neither spies nor pirates.

The *Scylla*'s captain was Joe Morrissey, an Irishman whom Percy had hired in Dublin for a year's service. Morrissey had worked on ships of the Collins line on trans-Atlantic crossings before its bankruptcy, and then as a ferry captain in the Irish Sea. The ship was registered to a Liverpool owner, a business associate of Charles Prioleau who was nominally a shareholder of the Anglo-Mexican Tehuantepec Company. Percy left it to Morrissey to assemble a crew – three engineers, twelve firemen, and a total of thirty-six hands all told – who were signed for a voyage only to Bermuda, Nassau or Vera Cruz, with guaranteed return to Liverpool. Having discussed the arrangements at length with Bulloch, Percy understood that a crew from England and Ireland might refuse service to the South. He intended to obtain a new crew once he got the vessel closer to the ports of Wilmington, Charleston, and Savannah or perhaps Mobile or New Orleans. Bulloch urged him to consider Wilmington; it was the port from which he had sailed on the *Annie Childs*.

Captain Morrissey had filled the bunkers two-thirds with the cheaper coal that produced a dark smoke. The remaining space in the starboard bunker held a more costly coal, anthracite from Wales, which made no smoke, for the approach to ports that might be blockaded or monitored by Yankee ships. Caleb Huse had been responsible for arranging the purchases of the military components of the *Scylla*'s cargo, though Percy kept Huse ignorant of the ship and her destination.

Percy had consulted Henry Hotze on what luxury goods might be in greatest demand. He then turned to Archibald Hamilton, one of the founders of Sinclair, Hamilton & Company, as his commission merchant to acquire the long list of items suggested by Hotze. As before with the *Bermuda*, the cargo was concealed under false labels. Percy's gifts to Customs officer Price Edwards, including an Edward Lear painting of a colorful parrot that he had purchased in London, made it unlikely he had to worry.

Leaving Liverpool, Percy remained below deck to avoid being seen by Union agents. When the Mersey pilot left, Captain Morrisey, his pipe tightly clenched in his teeth, took control of the sleek vessel. Now in late afternoon, sunlight still permitted Percy a close walk around the open deck. From the wheelhouse, he walked aft and climbed the steps of the portside paddlewheel box. Through his feet and legs he felt the churning of the water by the paddles, in syncopation with the steam engines. Captain Morrissey had her moving at a steady thirteen knots to get a feel for her under full steam, sails furled. The sea was gentle, with low rolling swells, which the *Scylla* rode like a seasoned rider posting on a graceful thoroughbred. Eight of the crew of thirty-seven men were in their quarters, four at cards and four sleeping in their hammocks. At 7:30 they and all others who were not in the wheelhouse or boiler room would gather in the galley for the evening meal.

Going below deck, into the after-cargo hold, Percy found a hundred and twenty crates and barrels all neatly stowed, their weight evenly distributed on either side. Looking up, where light was streaming from the open hatch, he could see the hoists that would raise the cargo when they arrived in port. He climbed the ladder again and gazed contentedly at the wake of the *Scylla* on the open ocean.

Only now could he feel at ease. For weeks he had prepared for this moment, worrying at every step. So many things could have gone wrong. The Foreign Ministry could have stopped the *Scylla* at any moment prior to her sailing. They could have seized her. The deliveries to the dock of rifles, pistols, cartridges, lead for bullets, molds, and powder could have gone astray. But it was all on board, enough to arm and outfit two regiments of Confederate soldiers.

Descending into the forward hold, Percy examined four bronze Austrian 24-pounder howitzers that would make up a formidable battery. Looking at them, aft of the ladder, Percy thought back to the 12-pounder mountain howitzer that he helped haul up the hill at the battle of Cerro Gordo, before the Mexican soldier shattered his arm, breaking it in two places. He still had the scar where the femur had protruded through his forearm. The 12-pounder was a lighter, more mobile cannon but far less destructive than these four he was carrying aboard. They would be used by the Army of Northern Virginia.

Opposite them were saddles and sabers, four hundred Enfields in crates of ten, boots, belts and buckles, medical provisions, instrument kits for surgeons, cloth for uniforms, buttons, thread, stockings, boiler-iron, ingots of copper and zinc, barrels of saltpeter and more. Bev Tucker had worked with Percy in buying all these military items.

"With these arms and supplies we're buying," enthused Bev one evening at dinner, "the army of Virginia ought to be ready to take on the forty horsemen of the Apocalypse."

Percy laughed, "Now there would be a cavalry company from Hell, for sure. But as necessary as arms are, they are not sufficient. They must be the right arms and supplies and rightly put to use. A man will starve if he is armed for soup with a fork as will another who has only a spoon for beef."

Looking quizzical, Bev asked, "Don't the Russians eat their peas with a knife?"

"From experience I couldn't say. Perhaps my simile isn't sufficiently apt. Let me put it another way. What was Caesar's greatest weapon?"

Bev's brow wrinkled. "The sword?"

"No. The Gauls and the Picts had swords aplenty and outnumbered the Roman legions four or five times over."

Bev tried a second time. "All right. The stabbing spear."

"Same answer."

"It's a trick question." Bev frowned. He had never been a good pupil, and though an experienced journalist he read little besides newspapers. He was especially fond of the London dailies and immediately turned to the police reports. At breakfast when he and Percy were staying at the same hotel, he would read aloud to Percy the accounts of a crime, quoting the police in different voices as he imagined the officer as he may have spoken.

Percy supplied the correct answer. "Nope. Caesar's great weapon was the shovel or pickaxe. *Dolabra*, I think was the Roman word, if I remember my Latin readings. Caesar's army used the *dolabra* to construct fortifications that no sword or spear or arrow could penetrate. This is how Caesar won at Alesia, how he captured Vercingetorix."

Not wanting to be outdone, Bev Tucker said, "Interesting. And where did that get him in the end? A shovel was no good against the knives of the assassins."

"No, Bev, you're absolutely right. You can't bring a shovel to a knife-fight and expect to prevail against a mob of Senators." Percy's affection for his cousin-by-marriage made him indulge Bev without further discussion.

❧ · ❧

Percy crossed under the ladder to look over the less bulky goods that were stowed forward of the military arms and supplies; these carried greater monetary value. A thousand or more of goods that were luxuries in the middle of war conditions: perfume, umbrellas, jewelry, scented soaps, teas and coffee, fine English textiles for ladies' garments, corsets, Spanish sherry and brandy, formal leather gloves, fifty sets of Wedgwood bone china for tables of eight, eighty-five porcelain vases, and still more. These goods were necessary if the voyage was to pay for itself.

Percy had had no difficulty in selecting the luxury items from the best shops and commercial suppliers. They were familiar household items in the plantation home in which he was raised,

Bolingbroke. Only in recent years had he come to realize how few of the goods in his own home had been produced in America. The fact that industries in the North were finally beginning to produce quality household goods only served to highlight how poorly equipped was the South to provide for the well-being of its citizens. Now that purchases from the Northern states were cut off, only imports from abroad could elevate a Southern home from rustic coarseness.

Percy and his fellow agents could not count on the Confederate government to provide the funds to pay for the war materiel they were expected to acquire or for crews for transporting it or for coaling. The inflated prices that could be charged for the importation of luxuries were a form of tax upon the wealthy of the South, voluntarily remitted by citizens who were philosophically opposed to excise taxes by a central government they distrusted. And who in the South could afford the prices of these blockade-running luxuries? Why, some of the same people who were profiting from charging the Confederate government outrageous prices for beef, for pork, for lumber, for cavalry horses, for mules, and for hundreds of other items necessary to keep the armies in the field and the navy, such as it was, afloat. The money flowed in a circular fashion. How many Confederate agents, however, were as scrupulous as Percy Moorhead in accounting for the money circulating through their hands?

Percy climbed the ladder to the bow of the *Scylla*. He had spent enough time reflecting on his efforts and weighing options for insuring that his cargo would reach the Confederacy.

A favorable breeze had arisen while Percy was below deck. Captain Morrissey ordered the crew to raise sail and let the winds carry the ship, saving coal for future need. Percy made his way to the galley for coffee and a slice of cake the cook had left out, then retreated to his cabin for slumber. The day had been long, eventful, and a success. If the South were not to secure her independence, it would not be from a failure on his part.

He looked forward to returning to Virginia. Lying in his bunk, a glass of brandy in his hand, his only regret on leaving England was that he had not had the chance to see Grace Tarkenton before leaving London.

Would he ever see her again? He wasn't sure he wanted to.

Chapter 54

Comes a Squall

Once his ship arrived at the port of St. Georges, Bermuda, Percy spent three days taking on additional coal and recruiting a pilot who could guide the *Scylla* into Wilmington, lying sixteen miles up the Cape Fear River. The pilot, called Skeet Daniels, was known as a boozer and brawler in port but, on all accounts, sober and competent when the need for sobriety and competence came due.

"Pay me half-now, half on arrival. That's the deal," Skeet demanded. He and Percy were seated at a table in a tavern just up from the docks. His unshaven face had the gritty appearance of brown sandpaper. The figure he had named was equal to a year's pre-war earnings for coastal pilots.

"No," Percy insisted with finality, smiling blandly. "One-third, two-thirds. Final payment only when all goods are unloaded at the wharf."

From the master an English merchantman, Percy had learned that at least five pilots familiar with the coasts of the Carolinas were milling about in St. Georges waiting for a ship assignment. Long familiar with the role of pilots going up the Mississippi River, Percy knew that no ship captain could chance sailing to an inland port without the guidance of an experienced pilot who knew the shifting subsurface river channels that had to navigated. Without one, the risks were great that a ship could run aground or become stranded on a sandbar. The value of any cargo on a ship successfully running the blockade made the expense of a pilot seem small, so a pilot could demand a large premium. But the uncertainty of ships ready with a cargo to attempt to run through the Union navy lessened the bargaining power of a pilot, as Percy had calculated in approaching Skeet Daniels. Percy held the advantage: his *Scylla* was the only blockade runner ready to leave port.

Scowling, the pilot grunted his assent. He held out his palm to receive an advance. Percy handed him five dollars and instructed him to be ready to sail at noon the following day. Skeet again grunted, stood, and walked to the bar.

Nine crew members who were unwilling to continue the voyage on the *Scylla* now that they knew that she was a Confederate vessel were discharged by Captain Morrisey with pay and passage for return to Liverpool on an English ship. They were replaced with sailors from the Confederacy.

The *Scylla* departed the port on April 5 for the 690-mile voyage to Wilmington. After two days averaging twelve knots, they were not many miles out from North Carolina when Percy asked Captain Morrissey, "How close are we?" It was an hour past midnight.

"Thirty, thirty-five miles."

"When do we begin burning our anthracite?"

"Now. Gave the order below twenty minutes ago." Morrisey's briar pipe, held fast between his teeth, did not inhibit the clarity of his response. His thin hair was covered by a navy-blue captain's hat that he had worn on the Collins line.

Percy stepped outside the wheelhouse and focused on the forward funnel. Only wisps emerged from the smokestack. He saw, moving in the dark, members of the crew preparing to lower the main mast, removing the pins of the hinge on which the mast was fastened upright. They would then turn to the aft mast and perform the same procedure. It went smoothly. Percy had insisted on practicing the function a good fifteen times on the way en route to Bermuda and twice since refueling.

Word was passed through the ship to extinguish all lights and to maintain absolute silence. Skeet Daniels took a position next to Captain Morrisey at the ship's helm. They steered the *Scylla* a hundred yards closer to the coastline, hugging the shore. When the early morning fog briefly thinned, off their port side Percy could dimly make out a distant silhouette of a large, clumsy warship, the USS *Albany*. Though bristling with firepower, she was no match for the *Scylla* for speed and maneuverability.

The fog thickened again as the *Scylla* glided quietly past her brawny foe. Twenty minutes later, the still air was broken by the sound of a shrill whistle that pierced the dark silence. The lookout on the mainmast of the *Albany* had spotted the *Scylla* through the gloom and raised the alarm. A drummer below beat a tattoo calling all hands to quarters. The *Albany's* first mate, standing next to the helmsman, shouted to the gun crews to ready their cannons.

Silence aboard the *Scylla* was abandoned. Captain Morrisey called down to the engine room, "Full steam ahead."

"How far?" shouted Percy to the pilot who was now at the wheel.

"Three miles to New Inlet," yelled back Skeet Daniels, "if you want to try it. Fifteen–twenty minutes. An hour to Old Inlet."

"Which one, Mr. Daniels?" asked Percy impatiently.

The pilot called back, his voice urgent, "Old Inlet is the main channel for the Cape Fear. Deeper. New Inlet's shallow, treacherous. Old Inlet is safer."

Two of the forward guns of the *Albany* boomed simultaneously. The shells whistled through the air and fell short of the *Scylla* by a hundred and fifty yards. The Yankee ship weighed anchor and unfurled more sail to get closer to the Confederate blockade runner. Percy had moved to the top of the port paddlewheel box to get a better view. If that was the best the

Yankees could do, the *Scylla* could easily outrun their pursuer. Perhaps there was time to make Old Inlet.

Again, the cannons boomed. This time they straddled their target fore and aft. The closer shell arced over the *Scylla* and splatted the water fifty yards away from Percy, then skipped towards the sandy shore. The *Albany's* gunners had only been getting their range. The next shells would be still more accurate.

"More steam," shouted the pilot to the engineer below. "Dammit, more steam." Were Vulcan himself stoking the ship's boilers, the engine room could not have produced more power to the churning paddles of the *Scylla*. Swift as she was, she could not outrun a cannon shell.

From his post, Percy peered at the *Albany* through binoculars. Behind her outline he could see a wall of black. As if in answer to a plea, the heavens suddenly intervened. A squall rolled rapidly across the waters behind the *Albany*, swallowing the gunship in ripping rain and black clouds. Unable to see more than fifty feet in front of them, the cannon crews ceased firing.

Using the ladder rails, Percy vaulted down from the paddlewheel housing to the deck and rushed over to the pilot and captain.

"New Inlet," Percy commanded. That's it just ahead, isn't it?"

"Yes," the pilot replied, still protesting, "but it's too dangerous. I've come out it, but never up. With the current, never against."

"It's a luxury we don't have time for," Percy was growing angry at the pilot. "This squall won't last. When it lifts, we're easy prey."

Cursing under his breath, the pilot shook his head but did as he was told, turning the ship to starboard, into the channel. The wind was from their back now. Rain pelted them, stinging their faces. Percy noted the shift in the color of the water where the fresh water of the river current mixed with the salt sea of the Atlantic. Burdened by silt, the river water was darker.

H.M. Ship Scylla. In a Perilous Thunder Squall
Public Domain

Though the sun had begun its rise, the sky was dark with the squall. The banks of the passage upriver were obscure, occasionally thrown into sharp relief by flashes of lightning. The pilot made constant adjustments to the course for the next quarter hour until suddenly Percy and the crew were jolted. The *Scylla* struggled and then resumed its forward progress.

"Sand bar," snarled the pilot. "We're over this one." He was nervous and agitated. "I told you this route would be treacherous." He gripped the handles of the wet wheel tightly.

"Continuing to the Old Inlet as we were was certain disaster. The Yanks would have gotten us for certain." Percy was determined. "This way, we have a chance. We have a cargo to deliver — deliver it we will." Wind-driven rain stung his face, but he hardly noticed. He paced the deck behind the pilot, his eyes shifting back and forth between the river ahead and the *Albany* to their rear.

A few minutes later the ship again struck something. This time she halted completely.

"Engines stop!" ordered the pilot to the engine room. He turned to Percy and Captain Morrisey. "We're stuck fast. Another bar."

"All right." Percy demanded, "What do we do?" He stood only three feet from Skeet.

"We reverse engines. Try to back her off."

"What are we waiting for?" Percy was growing exasperated with the pilot. His mood matched the sudden storm, dark and furious.

For his part, the pilot sounded desperate. "If it doesn't work, we've got to lighten the load. Throw the cargo overboard."

"We must give it a try. With the cargo." Percy would not give up without a fight. "We've come too far and gotten too close to give up."

Upset, the pilot heeded orders and hollered down to the engineer to reverse the engines. The hull was wedged hard in the sand, but the paddle wheels were still free to turn. The ship shuddered as the paddles operated in reverse, now struggling to rotate clockwise. Their efforts were futile.

After a minute of churning uselessly, the pilot was becoming frantic. "Can't do it with all this weight. We gotta throw it all overboard. That Yankee ship can't follow us, but we're still in their range. When this storm lifts, they'll destroy us and the cargo."

Percy was adamant. "No, we're not going to give these arms and supplies to the Cape Fear River. Our soldiers must have them. There's got to be another way." Percy was no mariner, but he knew there must be some means of moving a large ship. Something nagged his memory. But what?

"My job is to get this ship into port safely." The pilot was frustrated and fearful. He fretted, "No way 'cept by dumping our weight."

Percy was now angry that he was having to fight his pilot and the blockading ship about to fire on them again. "And my job is to get this cargo to our soldiers. We've worked too hard and long to collect these arms and supplies to toss them overboard." Again, he struggled to recall. Something about a naval battle that stuck in his head long ago.

Vehemently, Skeet Daniels spit out, "Ain't gonna be no good to no one when that Yankee gunboat gets its guns on us again. Believe me, it's certain death, Lieutenant. When I signed on, I told you there were no guarantees of safe passage. And it was you who put us in this channel. That was your mistake."

Talking to the pilot was futile. Turning to the Irish shipmaster who had stood near in silence, Percy asked, "Any ideas, Captain Morrisey?"

"This is outside of my experience, Mr. Moorhead," Morrisey admitted as he and Percy walked forward. Standing at the bow, they looked down at the water where the ship was held fast by the sand just eight feet below the surface. The river current divided at the bow, carrying leaves and fallen limbs against each side of the hull as it flowed past. The rain began to lighten. Percy was about to speak when they heard a voice yell out.

"Man overboard!"

Five crew members, as well as Percy and Morrisey, rushed to the starboard side. One of the crew was pointing in the water. Despite the rain, a figure could be seen swimming, heedless of the current.

The man overboard was the pilot, Skeet Daniels, swimming to shore, abandoning ship and crew. He was unwilling to risk his life further for the sake of a cargo of arms and luxuries. Even if he forfeited the rest of the pay, he already had received more than enough money to last a while.

A crew member, Larkins, a beefy, bearded Georgian who had previously served on whalers, stepped into the deck cabin and grabbed a loaded rifle. The swimming pilot was now seventy yards from the *Scylla*, easily within range of the Enfield. Larkins raised the rifle to his shoulder and was about to fire, without seeking the approval of Percy or Captain Morrisey. Percy shoved the barrel down just as Larkins fired; the minié ball hit the water behind the starboard paddlewheel.

"He's a deserter," protested the crewman, upset that Percy had stopped him. "In a time of war." The pilot was deserting not only the ship but an entire crew that depended on him.

Though disgusted by the pilot's cowardice, Percy said, "Yes, Larkins, we are in a war. But the man you would execute is not a member of the Confederate army or navy. He's a coward, and he has breached his contract to pilot our ship to Wilmington. Still, he's a private citizen. War is savage, but we are not."

Obviously disgruntled, Larkins nevertheless gave no challenge to Percy and replaced the rifle inside the entrance to the cabin.

Percy added, "And there's no need to shoot the poor man."

"Sir?" Larkins was puzzled. The deserter a poor man?

"Watch." Percy nodded in the direction of the swimming pilot and gestured upriver.

An uprooted tree bobbed in the water as it moved rapidly downstream. When it struck Skeet Daniels, the man gave out a hopeless scream. He clawed on the trunk of the floating tree, but it was too thick to hold. His cry for help was unfinished when he went under.

"I see." Larkins seemed to have a new understanding of the ship's owner. Rain streaming from his face did not hide his grim smile of satisfaction. "Do you have a way to get us off of here, Lieutenant?"

"Perhaps." Percy turned to Captain Morrissey. "Any experience with kedging, Mr. Morrisey?"

Morrisey shook his head. "Not except by way of stories from old-timers. Not much use to steamships."

"No. But it proved the difference between victory and defeat in our war with the British in 1812. I remember as a boy reading stories of how the captain of the *Constitution* – Old Ironsides – escaped the English ships chasing them. Before steamships. There was no wind that fateful as British squadron of seven ships sought the *Constitution*. Hunters and hunted were dead in the water while calm prevailed. The captain of the *Constitution* sent out row boats with anchors and long lines. Dropping those anchors would pull the ship towards the anchors. I think they called it kedging. Or warping. She slowly glided away It's worth a try. Worked then."

Speaking now to the former whale boat sailor, Percy said, "Larkins, I want you to take five men. Get an anchor from forward and put it on the ship's boat. Attach a stout long rope to our stern and then row out a hundred feet to the rear. When I give the signal, we'll have the engine room engage the paddle wheels hard in reverse while you drop the anchor. And you might as well try rowing hard to add to the pull of the anchor on the boat. Got that?"

Larkins saw the logic of Percy's plan. "You're trying to yank the ship off the bar."

"Exactly right."

Morrisey nodded approvingly. "It's worth a try. And if it works?"

"If it works, you'll have the helm again, Captain. You'll have to give it your best shot using the old charts to get us into Wilmington."

While the crew members worked with the anchor and lowered one of the two boats of the *Scylla* into the water, the rain continued to diminish. Percy eyed the sky anxiously. Soon, the storm will have passed, exposing the *Scylla* again to fatal fury of the *Albany's* guns. He saw no reason to tell Larkins to speed his efforts as the man was carrying out his instructions without hesitation.

Morrisey went below to talk with the engineer about getting the maximum thrust from the engines in a burst of power that could shake the ship free from the sand without damaging boilers or drive train.

Ten minutes later all was ready. Before Percy could give the signal to drop the anchor and engage the wheels, another boom of the *Albany's* cannons could be heard. A shell burst overhead but thirty yards too far to port to cause damage. Shrapnel from the projectile slammed into the water creating dozens of splashes. Time was urgent. A few more shots and the *Albany's* gunners would have their range and a target that was dead in the water. Percy swooped his arm downward as the signal to Larkins in the rowboat while Captain Morrisey commanded the engine room to engage. The *Scylla* shook. Another shot from the *Albany* arrived, but its fuse was timed wrong, so the shell landed nearby with no harm.

Abruptly, the *Scylla* popped free from the sand bar like a bottle being uncorked. Morrisey stopped the engines to allow Larkins and the small boat to cut the kedge anchor's line.

Suddenly the sounds of a half dozen cannon firing all at once startled Percy and the crew. They came from a different direction, off to the starboard of the *Scylla*, not her rear.

"Oh God," said the ordinarily imperturbable Captain Morrisey. "Is it a second blockader?"

"If so," replied Percy, "they're shooting the wrong way. Here, look through the binoculars. The shells are hitting near the *Albany*."

"By damn, you're right," declared the Irish captain happily. "What the hell is happening?"

Percy had surmised the answer. "Someone in Bermuda told me our army was planning to fortify Federal Point. Skeet Daniels hadn't heard about it. But it was a reason I was willing to take a chance on New Inlet."

The small Confederate force at Federal Point had heard the rounds of fire from the Yankee ship and sent a scout the mile distance from the fortified position to see if there was a Southern vessel leaving or entering New Inlet. He rushed back to the position and informed Colonel Fremont that a ship bearing a Confederate ensign was stranded on a bar. When the squall lifted and the *Albany* could be seen by a lookout perched in a tall pine, the Confederates had opened fire. The *Albany* hurriedly hoisted all sail and retreated to safety, out of their range to reach the *Scylla* with their guns.

The crew of the *Scylla* raised a cheer. A contingent of fifteen Confederates from the fortified position were marching to the shore near the *Scylla;* one of them hollered out to see if they needed help. While Morrisey held the ship against the current, Percy sent Larkins and the ship's boat to confer with the Confederate soldiers. Two of the soldiers had enough experience on the inlet and river up to Wilmington that they could pilot the ship upriver safely. The *Scylla* took them aboard and steamed the eighteen miles up the Cape Fear in bright morning sunlight. The new men informed Percy that the fortifications were now called Fort Fisher and were being expanded with new batteries. They had recently received more powerful artillery up from Charleston and were happy to see it so effective in chasing off a Northern blockader. The commander of Fort Fisher telegraphed to Wilmington that a blockade runner was on its way.

A crowd of nearly fifty greeted the *Scylla* at the Wilmington wharf. Some waved flags. Others stood in front of the row of buildings and warehouses adjacent to the wharf waiting to see who and what came off the successful blockade runner.

Percy stepped off the ship in his lieutenant's uniform to loud cheers. He grinned at the good fortune that had brought him and his ship safely to port. *His ship.* Yes, it was his ship. And she had performed beautifully under heavy fire. Elation overcame his weariness. His voyage was, however, not complete. He still had to dispose of his cargo and to get to Richmond.

⤳ · ⤳

Percy left the *Scylla* in the control of Captain Morrissey with instructions to off-load and store the cargo until a Confederate official could take possession of the military supplies. A commercial agent recommended by Charles Prioleau was employed to sell the luxury items and to remit the funds to Captain Morrissey. Whenever possible, the agent was to barter the luxury goods for cotton and tobacco that might already be on hand in Wilmington. Morrissey and the agent were told by Percy to use the cash they had received to furnish a full load of cotton and tobacco for export. The *Scylla* would pay for herself coming and going and then some on this, her maiden voyage as a blockade runner.

"What then?" queried Morrisey. He had signed on for a year with the *Scylla*, but the terms of his employment after this maiden voyage were unspecified.

Percy himself would have to confer with Judah Benjamin for the longer term use of the *Scylla*. He instructed the captain, "Take the *Scylla* to Nassau and place the cargo in the care of Louis Heyliger. He's our agent. After unloading, you should sail to nearby George Town and await word from me." With all arrangements made and placed in the hands of trusted associates, Percy boarded a train for Richmond.

A new assignment awaited him that would entail disastrous consequences for New Orleans and the Confederacy.

Chapter 55

Private Bensonsuh

The train returning Percy to the Confederate capital pulled into the Richmond & Petersburg depot at a little after four in the afternoon. As it was creaking to a halt, Percy dashed off a note to Judah Benjamin announcing his arrival in Richmond: He would be at the Exchange Hotel, if he could get a room. Not in uniform, he identified himself as Lieutenant Moorhead, Headquarters Staff, to a private at the depot entrance and told him to take his message to Secretary of War Judah Benjamin immediately.

"Suh, I can't," the young man drawled. He was a green recruit up from Alabama. His uniform was ill-fitting, the trousers too long and with awkward cuffs, the tunic small in the chest and large at the waist – as if sewn by an inept seamstress for her tubby husband. The pants and jacket were of contrasting shades of butternut.

"You can't?" Percy repeated.

"No, suh. Mr. Benjamin's not Secretary of War." The lad was red-haired and freckle-faced and not a day over eighteen. His youth was matched by his earnestness.

"Then who has replaced him?" The last time Percy had returned to the Confederacy from England, only six months earlier, he was greeted at the Savannah wharf with news that Benjamin wasn't Attorney General but had been appointed Secretary of War by President Davis.

"Secretary Randolph, suh," said the callow private.

The young soldier was obviously perplexed by the lieutenant's evident confusion over the chain of command. A lieutenant should know who was Secretary of War.

"Which Randolph?" Having married a Randolph, Percy was familiar with the identities of Philomena's extended range of relatives. "Thomas Randolph, the rector of the University of Virginia? Or his brother, George, the Richmond lawyer."

Eager to affirm the officer, the lad quickly replied, "Yessuh. That's Secretary Randolph, the Randolph whose grandfather was President Jefferson."

Percy sighed. The Randolph brothers, who had both been appointed Confederate officers when Virginia seceded, were indeed related to Percy's wife, Philomena. George Randolph had attended their wedding in 1851.

Percy was beginning to enjoy his conversation with the gangly young recruit, so eager to help. He brought to Percy's mind his students from William and Mary; they would be about the same age as this youth. All of them were surely in the army but Percy knew nothing of their whereabouts. Were any of them casualties of this conflict?

"What has happened to Secretary Benjamin?"

The lad replied, not understanding the lieutenant's continuing confusion, "Nothing suh. He's still Secretary Benjamin."

"I thought you said Secretary Randolph is Secretary of War."

"Yessuh. He is."

"So do we have two Secretaries?"

"Yessuh."

"Is your name Dogberry by chance?"

"Nosuh. Benson, suh. Private Benson, suh."

"Bensonsuh. That's an interesting name." Percy's smile was playful, not unkind or mean.

"Suh?"

"A little joke, private. Now please explain yourself. I've been out of the country for a while. Speak slowly, if need be. I am sometimes obtuse."

"Obtuse?" The private was puzzled but undeterred. Perhaps the lieutenant meant he was hard of hearing. He raised his voice. "Yessuh. Well, suh, Secretary Benjamin was Secretary of War. Now Secretary Randolph is Secretary of War. You know, the one who's the grandson of President Jefferson. Secretary Benjamin is now Secretary of State. President Davis made the appointment just a few weeks ago."

Putting his hand on the young man's shoulder, Percy looked him in the eye. "You may lower your voice, soldier. I am a tad thick-headed but not hard of hearing. Now, Private Bensonsuh, would you kindly deliver the message you hold in your hand to Secretary Benjamin at the Secretary of State's office."

"I'm afraid I can't do that, suh." The youth was earnestly apologetic.

"Pray tell," sighed Percy again. "Why now, private?"

"Secretary Benjamin hasn't yet moved to the Secretary of State's office. He's still in the office for the Secretary of War."

"Then please take the message wherever you can find Secretary Benjamin."

"Yessuh," beamed Private Benson. "Right away, suh." He was proud to be in the Confederate army, proud to be stationed in the capital. If he were still in Possum Hollow, Alabama, he'd be slopping hogs with his father and two brothers at their pig farm.

Percy watched soldier Bensonsuh proudly salute before

marching rapidly away with the message entrusted to him. It was a pleasant and amusing start to his latest sojourn in Richmond, even if it was to prove unexpectedly brief.

ᠻᡡ - ᡣᠵ

Percy had never seen Richmond so filled with people and so busy or so noisy. After a coach ride to the Exchange Hotel, he found it was fully occupied. He walked from one hotel to another, dodging wagons, coaches, and riders on horseback as he crisscrossed the streets, bag in hand. All of the hotels were full. As he was a traveler and not in uniform, he was asked for papers by patrols a dozen times; none were as personable as Private Bensonsuh. The citizens were hurried but did not appear worried as they went about their business. Finally, he decided to call upon his mother-in-law, Emily Randolph, and ask if she could put him up, pending other arrangements.

On the way to the Randolph house, Percy passed a florist's shop on Fifteenth Street, next to a confectioner's. Inside, he marveled that in the midst of a war a business of flowers and plants thrived. The women of Richmond wanted to keep up appearances of normality. They continued to entertain their old friends and to welcome into their homes the new associates of their husbands who were part of the government of the Confederacy. Here, among the floral arrangements and bouquets, were some of the high-value English and French goods that had run the blockade – Piesse and Lubin perfume, scented soaps, Belgian lace and other items that would mark their possessors as ladies of taste, the same sort of goods that were brought in by the *Scylla* and even at this moment were being sold to speculators in Wilmington who swarmed like locusts on wheat. They would distribute them to other places throughout the South, with prices doubling at each transaction.

Percy found that Emily Randolph was delighted by the unexpected appearance of her son-in-law and pleased by the spray of flowers he presented to her. They visited for several hours that evening. She was glad that Percy might work with her cousin

George, but she wondered if George would find the post congenial. He loved his books and home more than commanding others. She feared he would be treated as a mere place-filler by President Davis and the generals. Her home already had boarders but if Percy didn't mind, he could sleep on the sitting room sofa.

He didn't mind at all. Mrs. Randolph's house was the closest thing Percy had to a home now. When he asked, she regretted to tell him that there were no letters from his mother or sister, though he had sent them letters directing return correspondence to Mrs. Randolph's address. As he struggled to sleep on the sofa, his lingering loneliness began to reassert itself. He hoped he could hold the dogs of depression at bay for a few more months. He tried to focus his thoughts on Philomena, but the voice that he heard in his head belonged to Grace Tarkenton. He continued to hear a single word that she had called him, meant in sympathy, not scorn. *Sojourner*. Percy was a sojourner. She may as well have called him a vagabond. No matter where he found himself now, he was only a visitor, a man with no fixed home.

Chapter 56

A New Assignment

An orderly escorted Percy to Judah Benjamin's office promptly at 9:00 the next morning. The Secretary did not arrive for another half-hour. As Percy knew from their practice in New Orleans, he preferred to prepare for the day's work at home, even if it meant he was not punctual for morning appointments. When he finally arrived, Judah greeted Percy warmly. "I received your dispatch of December in which you reported your purchase of a blockade runner. If you didn't receive my reply, I heartily approve. The *Scylla*, wasn't it?"

Percy settled into the stuffed chair near Judah's desk. "Yes. I'm happy to say she's an excellent ship. And the *Oreto*, now the *Florida*, was successfully launched from Liverpool despite the Union efforts to interdict her. The *Scylla* and I left the same day, but we proceeded under steam. She'll go from Wilmington back to Nassau with cotton and await further service. The *Florida* has to be refitted for her mission."

Benjamin talked with Percy about the developments in England, with interruptions by aides bringing telegrams and reports to Benjamin. After an hour, Benjamin apologized that he had to leave; he had to meet in another room with the President and other Cabinet officers. As he rose, his manner changed, and he spoke in a lower voice. "You've learned by now, Percy, that I've taken on the State Department post. George Randolph isn't ready to assume his responsibilities just yet. I doubt he'll ever be more than a clerk for the War Department."

Percy stood to follow Benjamin. "That's just what Emily Randolph suggested to me." He had the sense that Judah was withholding something from him. Reluctant to press him, he only remarked, "You'll probably enjoy State more than War in any event.

"Enjoy is not the word I would choose." A wry expression briefly lingered on Benjamin lips. Then his eyes narrowed. He became grave, almost ominous. "You should know, however, the President has asked that I continue to control our operations in Louisiana. George Randolph knows nothing of our state. I need to talk with you about that before the day is out. Meet me in front of the capitol in forty-five minutes. We will walk, so we won't be overheard. It's urgent."

Benjamin was inscrutable when he indicated urgency. Percy could only conclude that it must be serious, very serious.

༄ - ༄

Arriving ten minutes late and but seeming unhurried, Benjamin, in silence, walked Percy down 10th Street to the Great Basin where the barges and passenger boats of the city's intersecting canals could turn. Benjamin was as somber as Percy had ever seen him. With his back now to the basin, he spoke to Percy with uncharacteristic emotion, the mask of imperturbability displaced by worry.

"New Orleans is threatened. You've just returned, but I need you to go there right away. Let me explain the difficulties. Whether it would be me or George Randolph with the title of Secretary of War, it's President Davis who exercises the authority of the position. And he is attempting to be the superintending general of all the military. It's his sense of responsibility. It weighs on him."

Percy agreed. "I suppose he knows his record as first president will be examined as closely as George Washington's. The first president of the United States will be his measure."

"Precisely so. Below him, at the operational level, he is keeping authority divided. In charge in New Orleans is General Mansfield Lovell. Do you know him?"

"Not to speak of." Percy stiffened slightly at an unpleasant memory of Lovell as a brevet captain in Mexico. "We were both at the assault on Belen Gate when we were in Mexico City. We had a brief encounter at the Aztec Club."

Percy recalled vividly, but did not mention, the mortification he had felt that Christmas Eve day, 1847, when he had stumbled as he carried a crate of wine bottles for the officers' festivities at the Aztec Club. He had knocked over a stool. Captain Lovell had embarrassed Percy in front of the other men in the room and showed his contempt for a private performing a menial task.

A cold wind came up from the turn basin, carrying the sounds of clamorous activities of a city at war. The Tredegar Iron Works were a short distance southwest of the basin, at work night and day, turning out cannons, rails and spikes for the South's railroads, steam engine shafts, and a thousand other items without which the Confederacy would already have failed. Benjamin was wearing a winter coat with fur collar. Leather gloves kept his hands warm. Percy's hands were in the pockets of his wool jacket. The felt hat on his head did not prevent his ears from feeling chill.

Benjamin shrugged. He had no personal connection with Lovell. "I have found him to be competent and efficient. But there are many who distrust him. He's from the North. When Lincoln declared war, Lovell was in command of the City Guard in New York City. He didn't join the Confederacy until August when he moved to Richmond, eight months ago. General Twiggs was too old to command in Louisiana. He was ineffective in New Orleans, so Davis assigned Lovell to command Military Department No. 1. Braxton Bragg thought the appointment over New Orleans should have gone to him. He's spread distrust against Lovell. Davis tried to appoint Bragg to take command of the Trans-Mississippi Department a month later, but Bragg was still brooding about New Orleans."

"All right, Judah. But I'm puzzled. Why didn't that command go to Beauregard? It would have been a natural fit."

Benjamin paused to put a cigar in his mouth. He chewed on it but did not light it. "Seemingly. But New Orleans is not an active theater. Yes, Beauregard and even Bragg would have been better in New Orleans for political reasons. Both know the city. Lovell had never even seen New Orleans. Beauregard and Bragg, however, are needed where there is combat."

"Where's Bragg now?" Percy wondered why Judah was relating these army details to him.

Benjamin, briskly, "Bragg commanded a corps under Albert Sidney Johnston at Shiloh a week ago. When Johnston was killed, Beauregard appointed Bragg his second in command. They're on their way to Corinth, Mississippi. The president has just made Bragg a full general for his attack on Grant. Now, you've been away from the country and the news for some time. How familiar are you with the Anaconda Plan, Lincoln's plan to put a watery snake's coils around most of the South?"

Percy knew the plan was conceived by General Winfield Scott. "Circle the South with the blockade on the coasts and control the interior by the Mississippi and its tributaries."

"Yes. And they're coming at New Orleans from both directions, above and below. President Davis is army and does not have a high regard for the navy – whether ours or the Union's. As the Union has thrown its troops at us at Fort Henry and Fort Donelson, the President demanded Lovell send the soldiers, cannons and riverboats defending New Orleans up the Mississippi. This has stripped Lovell of much of his men and resources. Now the Yankees have amassed a fleet of gunboats and mortar boats on Ship Island and the entrance to the Mississippi. Our latest reports are the Union fleet is moving up the river, planning to attack New Orleans from below."

Percy, remembering a conversation in Charleston a year earlier, "As I recall, we are counting on two forts south of the city to prevent the Union from using that approach."

Benjamin, lighting his cheroot, "Right. Forts Jackson and St. Philip. Lovell's done the best he can with getting them ready. The President has paid more attention to Beauregard than to Lovell on the defense of New Orleans. Beauregard's ten years as the Army's chief engineer on the Mississippi gives him authority with Davis. But Beauregard's needs in the Western theater cloud his judgment. Like most generals, he wants more men and artillery for his operations and expects others to make do with less. Beauregard claims that the two forts, coupled with a river barrier of chain and hulks are adequate to stop the Union fleet."

"What's the strength of the Union fleet?" The defense of New Orleans had nothing to do with Percy, and he could give no advice concerning it. He assumed Judah simply wanted the sympathetic ear of a fellow New Orleanian whom he trusted. Percy had played the role of sounding board often when they practiced law together.

Benjamin shook his head. "We can't be sure. Our intelligence is faulty. We can't get eyes on them off the coast. Some reports count a few gunboats. Others, many more. Their ships of the blockade are spread out across the three entrances to the Mississippi, not massed. We can't know what they will throw at us from the Gulf of Mexico. Or when."

Percy frowned. "And what's the fallback if they get past the forts?"

The worry showing on Benjamin's face, usually all enigmatic smile, held Percy's attention despite the unpleasant weather. He knew Benjamin had family and properties in and around New Orleans. They would be threatened by Union capture of the city. Worse, the Yankees might destroy the city and seize Benjamin's properties.

Benjamin's expression was grim. "We've been counting on two ironclads to defend the city and to clear the Union navy from the entire Gulf coast. They're a project of the Navy Secretary. Competent man, Mallory, but jealous of protecting his authority. He's named them the *Louisiana* and the *Mississippi*. There's a third that's already been launched, a smaller ironclad with a single gun but also useful as a ram, called the *Manassas*."

"The other two are not ready?"

Benjamin spit a bit of tobacco at the ground. "No, damn it. When construction began in October, the builders promised the *Mississippi* would be delivered by mid-December. Mind you, the *Mississippi* project was the product of two brothers named Tift who had long been friends with Mallory. He knew them from Florida. They had no experience in shipbuilding but figured they could use the same techniques of house building to construct a better ship than the navy has. And they could use house carpenters and the same lumber as in building houses. On paper it is brilliant, so our naval review board approved it. The brothers moved to Louisiana and set up a shipyard north of New Orleans."

Percy's skepticism couldn't be suppressed. He was now very familiar with what work must be done for sound ship construction. "House builders for navy ships? Unseasoned planks?"

"Necessity. Pure function. They are the exact opposite of the two ships you and Bulloch have built in Liverpool. We don't need speed, nimbleness or the ability to travel great distances without coal. We just need mass: iron plate and heavy cannons – an elephant matched against horses. If they hold together just for a year, that will give us time to have first-class ironclads delivered from England and France."

Percy saw the attraction of the plan. But he remained doubtful. The *Oreto* was built by a well-experienced Liverpool shipyard with access to materials and machinery and skilled labor. The keel had been laid in June, and it had taken until mid-March to launch her. "You said there's another, the *Louisiana*. Same builders?"

"No. The *Louisiana* was proposed by a Kentuckian – E.C. Murray. He's more experienced in shipbuilding than the brothers. His boat's to be about the same size as the *Mississippi*. Its size, too, was so large that the only logical place to build it was on the Mississippi River. Jefferson, couple of miles north of New Orleans. The land is owned by Laurent Millaudon."

Percy recognized the name. "He was a friend of my father, as I recall. His banker."

"And my client at one time. You won't be surprised that E.C. Murray found a location next to the Tift brothers and the *Mississippi*. One boat carries 16 guns, the other 20. Both will be heavily armored with iron plate or rails. Murray's contract called for completion of the *Louisiana* by January 25."

"This is April. Have they been fitted out and launched?"

Shaking his head sadly, Judah said, "I'm afraid there have been delays."

In a voice tinged with scorn, Benjamin briefly elaborated. The construction problems were tragic when not farcical. Because the ships were being built by private contractors, the laborers building the ships were not exempt from the Louisiana militia. They were treated no differently than a baker or shopkeeper in New Orleans. So, they were frequently called out to drill by the state's militia officers who cared not a bit whether the ships were completed timely. The militia officers had their own responsibilities and would see to it that they were properly performed. And the workers were required to take part in parades, even if they interfered with construction.

"Let me see," summarized Percy laconically. "The defense of New Orleans depends on two house builders from Florida and a Kentuckian. They are newly arrived in the city and have no existing connections in the city. Command of the city is under a man who moved there from New York City who must have found himself immersed in an alien culture. It would be a huge challenge for someone with lifelong experience with bankers, contractors, and local officials. I know what I had to go through to get a casino developed and licensed. I'm not surprised there would be delays. New Orleans has always been reluctant to welcome newcomers. Her reputation for inefficiency is well-earned."

"You've always had a gift for succinct analysis of a party's situation that exposes the tenuous position they occupy, Percy. Our city, I'm afraid, has lacked a sense of reality and urgency. It is about to catch up with them. We need you to go post-haste to New Orleans with orders for General Lovell."

"Of course I will." Percy now saw why Benjamin was confiding in him. It was all a briefing for Judah's new assignment for him. "Without hesitation. But why? You still have telegraph communication. You have many officers available. With higher rank, they would carry more authority than a lieutenant. General Lovell wouldn't know of me. I was only a private at Belen Gate."

Benjamin turned to face Percy. With his right hand he grasped Percy's shoulder. "The orders you will carry are oral. From President Davis's lips, and mine, to your ears only. And from you, only to General Lovell. The city of New Orleans and its people must not know in advance what will be done in their crisis. And no one must ever know that Richmond has planned the fate of New Orleans. Any message sent by telegraph is little different from publishing it in a newspaper."

"So, Judah, you must have concluded that it is more than likely that the Federal fleet will make it upriver. And what follows?"

"I'm afraid that is the case. When the event becomes inevitable, we must immediately abandon New Orleans, salvage what we can, and make the city indefensible for the Union. The French would say, *sauve qui peut*. An outcry will be heard throughout the country, 'You have abandoned New Orleans to the Yankees. You have betrayed the city's people and Louisiana without a fight.' Every major city of the Confederacy will wonder whether it will be the next to be abandoned."

Percy saw immediately that Benjamin's analysis was exactly what would happen. Left to his own instincts, a general like Lovell would stand and fight. But that stand would only compound the disaster.

Was Percy to bear the onus for the loss of New Orleans? "And this is to come from me. Glamis hath murdered sleep, and Cawdor shall sleep no more. I am to murder sleep, as it were."

Judah was sensitive to Percy's concern. "No. Not Percy Moorhead. You will be relaying the orders which will then be issued by General Lovell. He, not you, will be abandoning New Orleans. The fact that Lovell wouldn't remember you is of no matter. The principal point is that you are known to the people who are relevant in New Orleans."

Percy was dubious. "I've not been back in three years. I have nothing left there."

"True. But you're well known to key people. Pierre Soulé is one of the men in charge of martial law in the city. He has not forgotten your solitary meeting with President Comonfort and his minister of *fomento*, Siliceo, in Mexico City five years ago. You turned Comonfort around completely on the Tehuantepec Railroad. Don't worry, he won't hold that against you. He knows you carry authority and will understand that you speak for me and our President should Lovell resist you. Yancey, our commissioner in Europe with whom you have worked closely, is now in New Orleans and advising the city's leaders. The mayor and others around him remember you as well and they know of our long association – if it comes to that."

Percy reluctantly saw that Benjamin was right. He acknowledged, "No one will know what I will have told to the general. To all the world, it will appear that General Lovell is removing his troops from defending New Orleans against the invading Yankees. And Lovell will have no reason to doubt my bona fides."

Benjamin consulted his pocket watch. He was already late for his next meeting. "A good soldier does what he must. General Lovell will be given opportunities to rehabilitate his reputation in other engagements. He may yet win the bubble reputation. New Orleans need not be his Battle of Poitiers."

A reason Benjamin was always comfortable with Percy was their ability to communicate elliptically by allusion and yet be fully understood by one another. They worked well together to achieve a common objective.

Percy, nodding his assent, "If we are to make this happen, I need to be tutored on the military conditions in south Louisiana before I go. I can't convey orders I don't understand. I must be knowledgeable to be convincing."

"Of course. No one prepares as diligently as you. Let's go back to the War office. Major Thurston is expecting you. He's an assistant adjutant-general of the army. He has maps and reports to share with you. You should plan to leave tomorrow afternoon, after we meet with President Davis."

⚮ - ⚭

Judah left Percy at the War Department Building; it fronted on 9th street, opposite Bank Street. Percy remembered the imposing structure, surmounted by a large observatory, as the location where the Virginia secession convention met in the shadow of the Capitol building. Before being taken over for the War and Navy Departments, it was a school for apprentices, the Virginia Mechanics' Institute.

Inside, Percy was directed to the second floor where he found Major Louis Thurston seated at a table in a large room waiting for him. Filing cabinets occupied three walls. A half-dozen men and two women were seated at other tables copying or organizing war reports and dispatches. No record would be made of Lieutenant Percy Moorhead's orders or mission on this occasion.

Thurston was a lean man several years younger than Percy. His long, wavy hair and full beard gave him a leonine appearance that belied his spare frame. From small talk Percy learned that Thurston was a West Point graduate who began his service at Fort Brady, Michigan, before his posting as assistant Adjutant-General, in the Department of Texas. When secession began, he was serving in the Adjutant-General's office in Washington, at which time he resigned and was appointed a Major in the Adjutant-General's Department of the Confederate Army in Montgomery. His neat appearance the careful arrangement of maps and three file folders prepared for Percy hinted at his talent for organization.

Thurston began the conversation. "All I could gather from Secretary Benjamin is that he wants me to fully acquaint you with the resources and readiness of the army under General Lovell in Military Department No. 1. I hope these maps and his most recent reports will answer your needs. Shall I leave you with them?"

Percy was open to guidance. "It looks like you must have reviewed them to prepare me. Perhaps you could point me in the right direction."

"This war is about to enter its second year but so far the major campaigns have been along the northern boundaries of the Confederacy. There's been little fighting in our southern parts. So General Lovell has not experienced battle casualties. Instead, his losses are of an entirely different sort. Not a week goes by without at least two or three complaints from Lovell that all the men he trains are being taken away from him. He's got a point."

"Yeah? I know New Orleans, but I've been out of the country for most of the last year. What's his grievance?"

Thurston cleared his throat before summarizing Lovell's dispatches. "After he took over control of the Department from General Twiggs in October, he had close to ten thousand men. He had drilled them and armed them. Half of them were ordered by the army to Kentucky in February to try to hold back Union advances under General Grant. After the fall of Forts Henry and Donelson, another three thousand of Lovell's New Orleans defenders were sent north to reinforce General Beauregard at Shiloh and Corinth. As it stands today, Lovell has only a few thousand men to defend a city of a quarter of a million people. "

"Other than the two forts, what's to protect New Orleans? Why take all the troops away?"

"As I understand the back and forth of the generals, sending troops north was part of the defense of New Orleans. New Orleans is vulnerable from the south, to be sure, but the city is just as vulnerable from the Union coming down the Mississippi."

"I see," Percy agreed. "It looks like the Union is getting closer to control of the upper Mississippi. Once we surrendered Island No. 10 a few days ago, it means the Yankees are going to hit Fort Pillow and Memphis next. If we can't hold them there, only Vicksburg will be the last stronghold keeping the Union from New Orleans coming downriver." Percy was aware that the Confederacy had some fortifications at Port Hudson downriver from Bayou Sara and his home, but it lacked manpower and ordnance to successfully serve to protect the river.

"If your visit can lend support to his constant requests for more troops, then he'll be glad to see you. His other complaints relate to his difficulties with the local government in New Orleans. They have complained about him to their legislators here in Richmond, and he has tried to answer their charges against him in his reports to President Davis and the Secretaries of War. With your own background from New Orleans, you'll surely be able to make the assessments that Secretary Benjamin must be looking for."

༺ - ༻

After three hours of briefings with Major Thurston and a review of the defenses of New Orleans, Percy fully understood the necessity of his mission and why it was imperative to abandon New Orleans in order to save it from devastation. That evening he began planning how he should deal with Lovell.

The next afternoon, Percy was again in a railroad car on an assignment for Judah Benjamin, sealed by a still, silent handshake of President Davis. Emily Randolph had prepared a small package of cookies and fruit to carry with him. He felt she was the only family left to him. Three years had elapsed since he had seen his mother and sister. Would he have a chance to visit St. Francisville while he was in Louisiana? Would the Yankee ships make it as far north as Bayou Sara and St. Francisville? Where might he encounter Grady Boyle and confront him with what he had learned about the real Redmond Boyle in Dublin? In the midst of war, private scores were secondary but not forgotten. He would fulfill his mission for the Confederacy. And then he could come face to smirking face with Grady Boyle and finally learn the truth of his father.

Or would he again be disappointed in his quest?

Chapter 57

Grady Boyle Reappears

After their first night together, Marnie Dennett did not see Grady Boyle for another two weeks. She walked by his townhouse several times and saw his upper windows open to the street, curtains stirred by an afternoon breeze. She wondered if he had left the city.

Grady, and the absence of Enoch Dennett, had awakened something in Marnie. And it was the war, too. War upends sense-numbing routine. War brings excitement, soldiers marching, huzzahs as they parade. War brings commerce, carts and wagons in constant motion carrying goods to and from the ships on the wharfs and at anchor in the river and to and from the New Orleans, Jackson and Great Northern Railroad depot twenty blocks from the river. Marnie felt more alive than she had in years.

Twenty years of marriage had dulled her ability to enjoy simple pleasures that held her interest as a young girl in New Jersey – trips to the shore, church socials at the Methodist Hall, games of shuttlecock and maypole dancing. Enoch had bought the New Orleans pharmacy when he learned of the owner's death seven years ago. New Orleans held much more opportunity, he said, than continuing to work for another druggist in New Jersey, where they had lived for twelve years. From their arrival, Marnie found New Orleans an alien place, intimidating in its diversity and stifling in heat and frequent rainstorms. She withdrew into herself, to lessen feelings and desires that could not be indulged. Enoch was preoccupied with his proprietorship, now responsible for an independent business.

Marnie was curious about this new man in her life. Mr. Boyle had been vague. He made allusions to a plantation he owned. He was a part owner of the casino, Toulouse Gardens. He dressed well, as though he were wealthy, far grander than the clothing her husband wore daily. Did he also have money in Ireland?

Grady Boyle had owned slaves, Marnie knew, for she had seen the papers on the sale of two, a woman and a boy, to a woman named Maisie. The address of the owner on the sale papers was on Old Levee Street. Perhaps she could learn something about Grady Boyle if she looked there.

On a slow Wednesday, she closed the pharmacy for a few hours. When she arrived at the address for Maisie Dastugues, she was surprised to discover that it was Lalande & Co., a small shop that sold notions and such-like, which she had visited a few times. A little past one in the afternoon she entered the door, which was held open on this warm spring day by a cast-iron yellow cat door stop. A pleasant woman-of-color of about sixty greeted her politely.

"May I help you, Mrs. Dennett?"

Marnie was surprised. "You know me?"

With polite deference, the woman answered, "Yes. You have been here several times. Your husband we know better, when we have been to his pharmacy."

The mixed-race woman was slender but not thin, and more self-possessed than other women-of-color that Marnie had encountered in New Orleans. The complexities of race distinctions, manners and customs were too much for Marnie to contend with, so she avoided encounters that might prove embarrassing to her. Having been raised in a northeastern state, Marnie did not treat Maisie in the superior way that a white native of Louisiana would.

But she was also more distant than any long-time resident of New Orleans.

Marnie told the woman, "You must forgive me. I've been minding the drug store while Mr. Dennett is away. I don't recall seeing you."

"Perhaps you have seen my employee or her grandson." The shopkeeper was unassuming. "They help me with errands."

Marnie was discomfited by the fact that Maisie knew who she was. She was reluctant to reveal more about herself. She guessed that the servant and grandson of whom the colored woman spoke were likely the Odessa and Julius whose names she had seen on the papers in Grady Boyle's townhouse.

"Yes, perhaps."

Maisie, quietly, "And what can I help you with today? I regret that my stock of goods is running low. With the blockade, we get few new items. And the costs from upriver are nearly beyond our means."

"In your display, I saw some exquisite embroidery," Marnie improvised. "May I see what you have?"

From a drawer behind the counter, Maisie pulled a shallow, rectangular tray containing a dozen pairs of cotton and satin gloves, embroidered with flowers or patterns, and placed it on the counter. "Certainly. We have a nice selection of scarves, handkerchiefs, and gloves." Next, she took from a shelf below three needlepoint reticules and placed them beside the gloves.

"These are lovely. Do you do them yourself?" Marnie found herself relaxing with the calm, polite attentiveness of the shopkeeper.

"No, I'm afraid my fingers are becoming clumsy. My assistant, Odessa, is the one with talent."

"She does excellent work." While inspecting the pretty items, Marnie tried to make sense of the information she had. Had this mixed-race shop woman purchased a slave at a significant price merely to do needle work? No matter how talented she was, the cost could not justify the purchase. And she called the woman her assistant, not her servant. Purchasing also the slave's grandson at an equally high price, disproportionate to any revenue his work at a young age could possibly generate, made even less sense. Assuming Maisie Dastugues was a free woman-of-color, surely she could not afford to buy two slaves for her individual service. Could the Percy Moorhead who bought the two from Grady Boyle and sold the pair to Maisie be the owner of Lalande & Company? How might she approach an inquiry?

Marnie, after trying on a pair of gray cotton gloves, "I'll purchase these gloves. They fit me nicely." Trying to sound casual, she added, "By the way, one of our pharmacy customers recommended you. Do you recall a Mr. Boyle?"

Maisie stiffened visibly and looked up warily at Marnie. "I know of a Grady Boyle." The curt reply displaced her former polite deference to a paying customer. Handing the tissue-wrapped gloves to Marnie, Maisie added frostily, "Why he would recommend our shop, I couldn't say. He's not a customer."

Marnie, quickly, as if apologetic, "Perhaps I am mistaken." The mention of Boyle was obviously unpleasant to Maisie. She thought better of mentioning the name Moorhead. Whatever the relationship Maisie may have had with Grady Boyle, it was no cause for jealousy.

⋘ · ⋙

Two days passed, and in late afternoon Grady again entered the pharmacy. From Marnie's expression, he knew his reappearance, after another lapse of several months, pleased her.

Marnie smiled coyly, "Well, stranger, you've made yourself scarce. Have you run out of pills?"

Boyle, with a wink and a grin, "Ah, milady, are you not an Irish colleen? You have the sauciness of a lass from County Limerick."

"And you, sir, have the honeyed words that are the gift of your nation."

"It would be ungallant of me to intrude myself upon you if it were not reciprocated. I was concerned you may have had misgivings." Raising his eyebrows, he added, "Or that Mr. Dennett may have returned."

"The last I heard he was sent to Tennessee with General Bragg." She added, "Far from home."

"I see. Soldiers do what soldiers must do. You are keeping the store open?" He put an elbow on the counter and leaned toward her.

"Yes. In spite of being nearly out of supplies of all kinds. What else is a lady to do all day? I can't sew uniforms. I've already cut up most of my sheets and rolled them into bandages and dressings for the soldiers."

Sure of her response, the confident Irish gentleman said, "Martial law and a curfew are in effect, but there are some restaurants still open. May I escort you to dinner?"

"Oh, you are a wicked man, Mr. Boyle. You disappear for weeks then return with sweet words and smiles. What's a lady to do?" Her effort to sound coquettish fell flat. But charm was unnecessary. They both knew where their flirtatious dance would take them.

After dinner, the curfew furnished a reason for Marnie to remain again in Grady's townhouse for the night. Their ritual – his appearing at her shop at closing time, dinner, and a shared bed for the night in his townhouse – was repeated three more days. And then he disappeared for yet another week.

This time, Marnie was concerned that something may have happened to her smooth-talking Irish gentleman. Tensions had been rising in the city. She feared that perhaps he had been conscripted into military service. The latest militia law brought under its authority all able-bodied men, with no regard to nationality. Louisiana's Governor Moore issued a statement that nothing extra would be required of foreign nationals, no more than the duty that they owed to the state whose law protected them and which is exacted of them by the laws of nations – meaning that foreigners and Louisianians were equally to bear arms against the Union. His earlier promise that companies made up of foreigners would be limited to service in New Orleans no longer applied, now that there was imminent danger of invasion. The defense of New Orleans would not be kept within its city limits but required military service anywhere the military was needed, so far as Marnie could understand the effect of the governor's statements.

So, Grady may have been drafted into service and sent away without an opportunity to tell her he was forced to leave. Perhaps he was among the 5,000 troops sent to reinforce General Beauregard and counter the advance of the enemy at Nashville. Everyone in the city was aware of the order and the hurried massing of the men. The trains going north were loaded a thousand men at a time, together with car after car of provisions, powder, cannons. Who would now defend the city, and with what? The five thousand were the trained soldiers. Who was left? Only the Home Guard – consisting of hundreds of older men, poorly drilled, armed with old muskets and shotguns.

Hope for Grady sprang up when Marnie saw in a newspaper a public invitation from the British Neutrality Association to a meeting of British citizens who desired to maintain the neutrality that Britain had adopted as its official policy. Although they didn't talk about politics when they were together, she knew Grady had nothing but contempt for the military and had no intention of serving. He had not volunteered for any of the foreign companies organized for local defense. Nor had he reported to register for service as required by the new militia law. The acting British consul in New Orleans was doing all he could to protect the interests of British subjects and to prevent them from having to fight against the North. He urged repeatedly the British ambassador in

Washington to charter a ship to take British subjects out of harm's way.

The outcry that followed against the formation of the British Neutrality Association was a surprise to Marnie. Two newspapers issued editorials condemning the Association and calling for the arrest of everyone connected with it. To refuse service while depending on Louisiana to protect them and their property from an invading army was tantamount to treason. Only cowards would refuse their natural duties to defend the helpless women and children of the city from a murderous foe.

Chapter 58

Mobbed

When Marnie next saw Grady Boyle, it was a chance encounter in early afternoon in mid-April. She had closed the drug store for an hour while she went to the produce market near the levee to see if any vegetables were available. Fear of invasion had driven prices beyond the reach of most citizens. Only a few boats could be seen floating high on the river, which was swollen by melting snow and heavy spring rains. The air was cool and clear, conditions being such that the constant volleying of mortar and cannon seventy miles to the south seemed distant, unbroken thunder, Thor's hammer blows on the two massive forts upon which the city depended.

The cannon had begun two days earlier and were unrelenting. A deep feeling of insecurity and uneasiness pervaded some in the community, yet others were walking as if it were an ordinary day. Many said that they heard nothing, that others only imagined they heard the roar of ordnance. Most saw nothing threatening in the rising of the river, the swiftness of the current, the churning of the brown, sediment-laden water. The levees held the turbulent river from them.

Grady Boyle was among the insouciant strollers, nonchalant as he chatted with a woman he escorted into a shop opposite the statue honoring Andrew Jackson. Marnie saw them as she crossed the square, just in front of the cathedral, and looked into the shop. Boyle turned and saw Marnie was looking at them. His indifferent glance made clear he did not care that he had been discovered with another woman, a blonde who seemed to be the current recipient of his fickle affections.

Marnie fought her inclination to enter the store and slap Grady Boyle across his lying face. She held back. Maybe there was something she didn't understand. Was she better off without him? She didn't miss Enoch, but she missed Grady. He was capable of charm, when he charmed. She could give him another chance. She had been wrong to suspect a relationship existed between Grady and the woman named Maisie. Maybe she was wrong about this woman. He would have an explanation.

The distant cannon and mortar fire continued to roll upriver and across marsh, a low ominous rumble for those who listened. There was no change that would indicate it was growing closer. People in the streets who were concerned tried to reassure one another by saying it was a sign the forts were succeeding in holding Yankee ships away. The soldiers in the forts were giving more than they were taking. Reports said that the Union ships were all wooden and old – no ironclads among them. Soon, the guns of the forts slamming against their wooden sides would take their effects, splintering them, knocking out their boilers and their masts. They'd soon be dead in the water. Just be calm and go about your business, the citizens were instructed. Soon, Jeff Davis would send General Beauregard back down the river with 10,000 soldiers, and Billy Yank would turn tail and run like the coward he was. Marnie Dennett believed all that, just as she wanted to believe Grady Boyle would return to her shop before closing this afternoon. She would at least give him the chance.

By 5:00 Grady had made no appearance at Dennett's Pharmacy. Nor by 6:00. At 6:30 Marnie's patience had worn out. Her charitable inclinations towards her Irish suitor were exhausted, supplanted by jealousy and anger. She went out into the evening and found her way to Canal Street, where the Committee of Public Safety staffed a station that volunteer patrolmen could use as a base for making their rounds in the city, looking for spies, invaders, abolitionists, undocumented slaves and other suspicious and unpatriotic persons. The volunteer guardians, who by age or disability were disqualified for conscription, all wore red sash around their left arms as their badge of office, their sole license to serve and protect – or harass and humiliate, as was the more frequent case. Each man was outfitted with a shrill whistle, the only other item of defense or uniform that they had in common. A few carried ancient muzzle-loading pistols, capable of a single shot, or wore swords in ill-fitting scabbards that had to be steadied to prevent their banging against walls on their patrols.

Marnie found one of the stalwart patrolmen and reported to him her belief that a member of the British Neutrality Association was an Irishman named Grady Boyle. She gave the man, who identified himself as Cyrus, a description of Mr. Boyle, the address of his townhouse, and the names of two restaurants where he might be eating. She expressed a citizen's concern for her fellow New Orleanians that he might be spreading discontent among the foreign. The armed citizen thanked his informer and said he would see to it immediately.

Cyrus hurried to another station of the Committee of Public Safety, this one near the Cabildo in the French Quarter. He marshaled the support of three of his fellow patrollers. Together, they set forth in search of the suspicious Irishman. It was their intent to make a citizens' arrest under the authority of martial law in the name of the Committee of Public Safety and to detain him until a committee of the Committee could decide whether or no Mr. Boyle was a threat to the city.

As the four, wearing their red insignia, made their inquiries at three restaurants, other men and women began to follow them, to ferret out a man who might be an agent of hostile powers lurking among them. It was their civic duty. The four patrolmen did nothing to discourage their supporters – who might be useful in an emergency. This Boyle fellow may be one of many Britishers ready to welcome the Northern invaders aboard enemy ships a short distance down from New Orleans.

It was now dark when the small mob arrived at the townhouse where Grady Boyle was reported to live. Two men and one woman at the front of the group carried torches that spread flickering light on the door and the street. Across the street, half a block away, Marnie Dennett watched. Cyrus, the leader, called out Boyle's name. On the third call, a curtain was pulled back from an upstairs window. The light of a table lamp next to the window revealed to Marnie that Grady Boyle had just finished putting on a shirt. Behind him was the same woman she had seen him with that afternoon. Her resentment grew. Now, she thought, his duplicity would be obvious to everyone. It did not occur to her that no one knew of his relationship with Marnie; if they did, they would know only that it was she who was betraying her own husband.

"I'm Boyle. What the Hell do you want?" His hands gripped the sill of the window as he leaned out. He was surly, unintimidated by the crowd below him. They may as well have been revelers at Mardi Gras; Boyle was unaware that celebration of Mardi Gras had been canceled because of the war.

"Come down from there," called out Cyrus. "We know you're disloyal. You're one of them, British neutrals."

When he opened the front door, Grady Boyle had buttoned his shirt, but the shirt tail was not tucked. His hair was uncombed and on his feet were fleece-lined doe-skin slippers. An angry scowl was his response to the crowd demanding his attention. His right hand held a gutta-percha walking stick that he had found in a closet. It had a brass knob head that reflected the light of the torch Cyrus held.

"I've got nothing to do with your war, one way or another," said Boyle in a loud, indignant voice, slightly slurred by drink.

"You've got no reason to accuse me of being disloyal. I'm a subject of the Crown, not the Confederate government."

"Then do you deny you didn't report for duty under the militia law?" demanded Cyrus.

Grady was defiant. "I've got no duty to your Confederacy."

"Then you admit you're a damned neutral." Cyrus took a step toward Boyle. "You're coming with us to the station." He reached his left hand to Boyle's right arm.

Marnie suddenly became alarmed as her desire to see Grady merely embarrassed turned into a violent confrontation. She watched as Boyle struck the patrolman's arm with his cane. Cyrus let out a cry and stumbled backwards from the top step of the townhouse porch, falling against one of the women of the group gathered behind him. She screamed, more in surprise than pain.

For a moment no one moved. Grady Boyle raised the walking stick in menace. Of a sudden, four of the men jumped as one and dragged him from the open door. Boyle's cane clattered against the bricks of the street. He curled himself, all knees and elbows, as the mob began beating him with the broom handles and fireplace pokers they carried as weapons. Boyle's angry yelling turned into cries of pain until he could barely be heard even to moan. Two of the men grabbed his bloody body by each arm and began dragging him. They had dragged him a short distance when a Confederate soldier approached, carrying a double-barrel shotgun. Knowing nothing of what had precipitated a savage attack in the middle of town, he cocked the gun and demanded that the crowd stop. Immediately the mob dispersed, cowards one and all.

While the soldier went after the ribbon-wearing vigilantes, a now frantic Marnie stepped from the shadows and, struggling, dragged the body of Grady Boyle into an alley. She discovered he was still breathing. Blood covered his face. Skull was exposed above the socket of his right eye. One arm was twisted and broken.

"Oh no," Marnie sobbed. "What have I done? I only wanted

them to arrest you. I never thought they would hurt you. They weren't supposed to hurt you."

Grady Boyle was much too heavy for her to try to get him back into his townhouse. Not knowing where else to turn, she would have to seek out the only other person she knew who might know something about Grady Boyle. That was Maisie, eight blocks away on Old Levee Street. Marnie covered Grady's torso with the light jacket she wore and ran through the night until she came to the shop. After banging on the shop's door repeatedly, it was finally opened by a mulatto woman a few years younger than Maisie. Marnie recognized the woman who held a candle as the colored woman who had on occasion picked up medicine ordered by someone.

Marnie, hurriedly, "You must be Odessa. Please, you must come and help me. You and Maisie. I'm afraid he will die. And it's all my fault."

Odessa demanded curtly, "Who's gonna die?" She knew the woman before her was Mrs. Dennett, whose husband was the pharmacist. But her husband was away. Why would she be here looking for her or Maisie?

"It's the man who used to own you, Mr. Boyle."

Odessa turned and began to close the door. "I don't want nothing to do with that man. He's evil."

Marnie implored, crying, "Please, please for me. A mob has beat him half to death. I can't have his death on my hands. We've got to try and save him."

"Who is it, Odessa? Who is at our door?" called Maisie from the stairs.

The door still in her hand, Odessa called back to Maisie, "It's the druggist's wife. She's saying Grady Boyle has been beat to death and she wants help."

Marnie pleaded to the woman in the back, "He's still alive.

Please come. Please."

"Where is he?"

"In the alley across from his place."

Maisie sighed and said "Awright. Odessa, we got to see what we can do. He's still Mr. Percy's brother no matter how bad he treated him. We got to try. What if Mr. Percy comes back and we let his brother die? Leave the boy here to sleep."

Chapter 59

Ozymandias

The last segment of Percy's hurried journey from Richmond to New Orleans was the two hundred miles due south from Jackson, Mississippi, with a brief interval at Camp Moore. Only parts of the rail line had been in operation when Percy was last in New Orleans early in 1859.

He was surprised to find the bustling activity of Camp Moore just a few miles south of the state line, near Greensburg. This was where Louisiana's soldiers were trained before being sent to fight in Kentucky, Virginia, Tennessee, and Arkansas. His train stopped at Camp Moore for just over two hours to unload provisions for the soldiers stationed there – and more. Its population was about to increase substantially, which would come as a surprise to the camp's commander. He was not privy to Percy's secret orders from President Davis and Judah Benjamin. No one was, not even the new Secretary of War, George Randolph. They were never transmitted to the clerks within the Confederacy's Bureau of Orders and Correspondence whose duties were to copy and record all orders and official communications. It was an order that was never ordered – as Davis and Benjamin could claim, if the truth ever made an appearance.

Percy was in uniform as he arrived in New Orleans a little after two. A few minutes after the train halted, he stood before a mirror in the depot, combing his hair and adjusting the fit of his jacket after hours of cramped sitting on the train seat. He knew the crucial importance of a commanding appearance when he was to engage a general who outranked him. Outside the station, he was just able to discern the distant volleys of roaring guns as their muffled sounds rumbled up from the two forts below the city. He could only imagine how deafening was the effect on the men who fired the cannons and mortars and what the conditions must be like in the two forts under siege – the constant pounding, the shaking of the timbers above the men in the casemates where the Confederate cannons fired intermittently and uselessly through the forts' embrasures, the smoke and grit from the discharges covering and choking the unfortunate souls manning them without relief.

~ · ~

Walking up Canal Street, Percy made inquiries of soldiers where he might find General Lovell. His crisp officer's uniform ensured that he was given quick response.

"In the Custom House, Lieutenant, sir."

Percy identified himself to a sentry at headquarters. When he said he had orders from Richmond, he was immediately taken to the general, who was seated at a table putting entries on a map from reports open next to him.

At forty, Lovell was not many years older than Percy but seemed as weary as a man of sixty. The general's grey eyes were bloodshot from fatigue. His uniform looked as though it had been slept in, which it had, on a cot on one side of the room where he had resided for near a week. Bushy whiskers ran across his upper lip but did not extend to his square, dimpled chin. His hair, thinning at the forehead, was as neglected as his uniform.

Lovell looked up at Percy suspiciously. "You're the man sent by Richmond?" He was as wary as he was weary.

"Yes. Percy Moorhead, General."

General Mansfield Lovell

Lovell was testy. "They wouldn't send a name. He wired a shibboleth to identify you."

"That's right. Ozymandias. Long O."

Lovell winced. He immediately understood the allusion. "Was that Benjamin's choice or was it the new Secretary, Randolph?"

"It was Benjamin's choice. He's still the Cabinet secretary that the president trusts on New Orleans. As far as Richmond is concerned, Benjamin remains in charge of operations here." Percy was truthful if not entirely candid. It was Percy who suggested the code word to Benjamin. Smiling wryly when Percy said Ozymandias, Judah himself quoted the key lines from Shelley's poem: "My name is Ozymandias, Look on my works, ye mighty, and despair!"

Putting down a pencil, Lovell snapped, "Benjamin is not subtle."

"Take it as you wish. New Orleans cannot be made a boundless and bare wasteland."

Lovell scowled. "So, he sends a lieutenant with my orders? That says something in itself."

"Rank has nothing to do with this meeting, General. I am here to convey orders, not to give them." Percy had decided he needed to be tactful in his treatment of Lovell, not assertive.

"I know nothing about you. Morehead, is it? Do you understand what I face here?"

"Moorhead. Two o's. Moor. Like a marsh or like Othello." After a pause, he continued, "My answer is, I understand it better than most. I grew up just north of here and practiced law in New Orleans for ten years before the war. I know these people and how difficult they can be. Now, your situation. Six months ago, you were assigned authority over a city and region of two hundred thousand people you knew nothing about. They did not know you and they haven't cottoned to you. At best, they can be coldly cordial to an outsider. I was told in Richmond that New Orleanians think you're a Yankee who left New York because a politician bought you an appointment as a general in the South."

Percy saw that he was coming across as sympathetic to Lovell. It was what he had planned.

"That's a slander. Don't they I was brevetted captain for my leadership and wounds at Chapultepec? But that was before your time. You had to have been a boy."

"Believe me, General, when I say I know firsthand of your record of service in Mexico. I was wounded at Cerro Gordo. I was among the soldiers with Battery K who assaulted the convent at Churubusco. Our unit took the greatest losses that day. Our battery supported you and Quitman with your assault at Chapultepec. I, too, was at Belen Gate."

Percy's calm statement took Lovell back. The general had spoken too hastily. He was embarrassed by his own presumption. Percy saw that he could expect greater respect from Lovell now that he was aware they shared combat experiences. Percy further softened his approach as he prepared a proud man for a bitter pill.

"General, you were put in a position that would have been a

nearly insurmountable challenge to any soldier. Richmond knows that full well."

"Do they? Do they know what I have accomplished here in such a short time? Under Twiggs the Department was a shambles. He was a relic of the War of 1812. I started from scratch. Within six weeks I had constructed fortified sites all around the city. I increased the armament of Fort Pike by four 42-pounders, Fort Macomb with five 42s and an 8-inch gun, Fort Livingston with an 8-inch columbiad. I garrisoned and armed and provisioned the two forts down river, Jackson and St. Philip. Now they are nearing a total of two hundred guns. I took eight thousand men and made them into soldiers in a cohesive, trained unit. I armed them and scrounged uniforms for them. Richmond should see the massive raft of cypress logs and iron cable I constructed to make the river impassable for warships coming up from the Gulf. I've worked day and night fortifying this city. And still the city complains, at the St. Charles or at Antoine's or while drinking and gambling at the Boston Club."

"What you say, General, is absolutely true. Richmond is thoroughly impressed with your energy and effectiveness. Major Thurston at headquarters briefed me on your achievements."

"Major Thurston? Yes. The overseer of Logistics. Of course. They know what I have accomplished."

Lovell's estrangement from 'Richmond' took a new turn. "They knew the resources I had gathered. That's how they took most of it from me. I expected to lead my own men that I trained for battle. What has Richmond left me? Just one company and less than three thousand militia. They're armed with shotguns harmless at twenty yards. I've never seen people quite like what I've found here. The rich care only for their property. And the rest? A miserable mixed breed. How do you train men who can't speak our language?"

Percy didn't disagree. "I'd feel just as you do. But Richmond made a judgment that the greatest threat to New Orleans is from upriver. The soldiers were needed to protect New Orleans by denying the Union the upper Mississippi, the Tennessee and the Cumberland."

Lovell wasn't placated. "That's why they took the ships from here as well. Hell, they never even gave me command of those. I had no say in what they did with them." Lovell stood, his back stiff from sitting too long period. He walked to a window and pointed at a closed curtain.

"Listen outside, Moorhead. You can almost hear those mortars. There's been no let-up for five days. I was down there yesterday. I hear them always. Day and night barrages. I would have thought they'd run out of powder by now. The Union has planned this well. They've positioned their mortar boats where we can't even fire on them. If we had the boats the Secretary of the Navy called upriver, I could have sent them down to the forts to engage the enemy. Hollins and Whittle and I wanted to attack Farragut on the river well before he could mass a squadron below the forts. But the Navy Department ignored us."

From Thurston's briefing, Percy had anticipated Lovell's railing against the Navy, and reasonably so. "General, I'm not here to defend Richmond. But there are political realities that we must all live with. The division of authority between army and navy is unfortunate. Secretary Mallory is very insistent in maintaining absolute control of the Navy Department. So that his resources are not dissipated as yours have been. President Davis favors the army, and he leaves it to Mallory to do what he wants. Neither of them has thought the Union ships could withstand the fire from our two forts."

Sitting again, Lovell returned to his treatment by the leaders of New Orleans. "You know what the worst of it is? I'm doing everything I can for the people of this city to defend them. But they say that I'm the one sending the soldiers away. They say I'm selling ships and the cannon to other states. They say I'm really working for a northern victory and a fortune for myself."

Percy could not deny the New Orleans was an insular city. "They're frightened, general. They grasp at anything. Rumor stuffs the ears of men with false reports – surmises, jealousies, conjectures. The city needs someone to blame."

"Yes. And Richmond, too. Richmond's politicians need someone to blame. General Lovell is their scapegoat. Was I was sent here to take the blame from the outset? Braxton Bragg had wanted this posting. I thought President Davis was favoring me. But look at us now. Bragg commands a corps in battle. I'm struggling in an ungovernable city of speculators, creoles, half-breeds and immigrants. Did Benjamin and Thurston tell you what is happening in the city?"

Allowing Lovell latitude to vent his frustration would add to his trust in Percy. "Only in the most general way." He encouraged Lovell to continue.

"You know I declared martial law last month, don't you? I set up four districts and put good men in charge to keep order. I instituted a curfew. How did the good citizens of New Orleans respond? They created a Committee of Public Safety to help defend the city. Help? They took martial law out of my hands."

Percy commiserated. "Yes, General. I know New Orleans."

"Did Richmond tell you about the petition the Committee submitted to the Confederate Congress two weeks ago? They complained bitterly of what they called the languor of Government in the conduct of the war. Languor! They spoke of all I've done as a deathlike lethargy. Those were their very words. They were acting, they claimed, as citizens of this place, not as a stranger sent here to work by the year or by the job for pay. That's how they see me, a stranger working for hire. They put themselves in charge of the city. Have you been accosted by men wearing red ribbons on their arms? If I try to do anything that the Committee of Public Safety disagrees with, then I'll have to do battle with them."

Percy, empathetic, "Outrageous, I agree." Nothing about New Orleans's dysfunction could surprise Percy. Had Percy guided Lovell, he might have co-opted his opponents, stroking their egos with meaningless responsibilities and assignments. But it was too late for conciliatory gestures.

Lovell continued his bitter complaints. "You can tell Richmond that the Committee are the source of many of the city's problems. Those businessmen are the speculators who have driven up the prices on food and the goods people need to live their ordinary lives. With martial law I was going to requisition their hoardings and distribute food and supplies. But they checked that. I'm fighting against the people I'm trying to protect."

Pausing and looking thoughtfully for a moment at Percy, Lovell asked, "Do you read, Lieutenant?"

"A little."

"Then you wouldn't know your Byron. 'I'd learn'd to love despair'."

Percy recognized the line but knew that displaying his knowledge would only embarrass Lovell. "Despair is not appropriate for an officer of your rank. I know you will do your duty. Now we must turn to your orders from Richmond and how you will carry them out."

Even Percy's mild statement caused Lovell's resentment to surface again. "And you are to supervise me?"

Sensing Lovell's stiffening, Percy sought to placate him. "No, General. My assignment is only to convey the orders and report on conditions upon my return to Richmond. If I can give you the benefit of my knowledge of New Orleans, I will do all within my power." Pausing, Percy added respectfully, "As you command."

Lovell picked up a pen. "I shall take notes. Do you mind if I memorialize my orders?"

"If you wish. They should reflect that they are *your* orders."

Lovell, putting the pen back on his desk, "I think it is becoming clearer to me as you speak. The orders must seem to be my orders and not Richmond's."

Percy, understated, "Would you prefer to be thought of as having been removed from command by a lieutenant sent by Richmond?" His quiet delivery was not soothing.

Deflated, Lovell paused, "Moorhead, I see why Benjamin has chosen you as his agent. You perfectly convey his Roman subtlety in compelling a man to suffer at his own hands."

"Or Biblical. Isaac was made to carry his own faggots. But the Lord saved him." Percy gave a small smile intended to encourage Lovell. "You may yet be saved. Let us begin. Is there any reason for believing that the Union fleet will not pass the forts in the immediate future?"

Lovell reflected on his preparations and challenges. "The melting snow, the spring rains, have made the river rise to the levees' heights. The current is strong and has brought down masses of fallen trees and debris. It's already destroyed one obstruction. The new one is stronger, but the chain barrier cannot hold against such force."

"Other measures?"

Lovell became more focused. "As many as resources have allowed. I have ordered Commander Mitchell to position fire rafts. Let me correct myself. I requested that Captain Whittle see to it that Commander Mitchell use fire rafts against the Union fleet. My requests have no authority on the Confederate Navy. If they choose to ignore them, they may do so. When our naval operations are not coordinated with the cannons firing from the forts, they are bound to fail. If the barrier is breached, if the fire rafts fail to slow the Union steamships long enough for the forts' cannons to smash them, then yes, the fleet will make it to the next line of defense. We've set up fortified batteries at Chalmette and across the river at the McGehee line. But there's too few cannon there to stop the full fleet. We can't long detain the heavy ships of the enemy armed with

9 and 11 inch guns."

Percy took Lovell's response as a disclaimer. He pushed back. "In a word then, yes. The forts will be passed. And soon. Correct?"

Lovell, reluctantly, "Probably."

Looking the fatigued Lovell in the eye, Percy now conveyed the orders he had been charged to deliver. "Then you must immediately begin to abandon the city. You are not to put up any resistance. If you wait until Farragut's lead ship drops anchor off Canal Street, it will be too late. Both your army, what's left of it, and the city will be destroyed."

Lovell seemed stunned by the cold clarity of the commands. "I see. You are telling me I must dismantle everything I have done since my arrival."

"That and more, General. President Davis and Secretary Benjamin will want to re-capture New Orleans later. And they will do so by land. It is imperative that you leave nothing that the Federals can use to defend their hold on the city. In Richmond they told me about two ironclad vessels under construction here. The *Louisiana* and the *Mississippi*. What is their status?"

"The *Louisiana* was launched unfinished two days ago and was towed into position off Fort St. Philip, above the raft obstructing the Yankee fleet. A work crew is aboard, trying to finish her engines. I've tried to get the navy to move her below the obstruction. She's not in a position to enfilade the enemy fleet."

Percy cocked his head, quizzical. "The navy won't comply?"

Lovell, agitated, "They say they are considering the option. Damn it, this is the problem of the divided command. The navy is so protective of their jurisdiction and their ships they won't cooperate."

"And how about the *Mississippi*?"

Lovell, gesturing helplessly at papers on his desk, "Yet another sort of problem. It's still under the control of its private contractors, the Tifts. Even the Committee on Public Safety tried to move them to launch. It's in the water but immobile. The builders say they'll try to get her ready for attacking the Yankees, but they don't seem to think the event is imminent."

Percy returned to the orders for Lovell. "All right, let's assume Farragut will make it up to the city. You must quietly collect all rail cars and locomotives at the depot and begin loading them with all military supplies – powder, bullets, guns, cannon."

Lovell looked up from his desk. "Just in the city?"

Percy, emphatically, "No. Everything that's not immediately trained on the Union fleet's route up the Mississippi must be moved. Fort Pike on Lake Pontchartrain and Fort Macomb on Lake Borgne must be evacuated, as must be Forts Berwick and Chène, on Berwick Bay. Spike any cannon that cannot be carried away."

Lovell resisted. "They face no immediate threat from the Yankee fleet. Why not leave them?"

Percy shook his head. "I'm a messenger, not a negotiator. Richmond wants to consolidate elsewhere in the state. Everything should be taken to Camp Moore. You will commandeer all of the horses and mules of the city streetcars. Every bale of cotton in storage must be put on the levees and burned. Not one bale or one hogshead of tobacco must go to the enemy. If we can't sell them abroad, then the Union shouldn't be able to profit from them. All of the food and provisions that are stockpiled must be destroyed. Every barrel of sugar and molasses. All commodities awaiting export. You must enter the banks and seize all the gold and silver they hold."

Lovell was suddenly surprised. This was a non-military turn he had not anticipated. He protested, "That's private property. The people of New Orleans will want their money. It's their money."

"Yes, you are absolutely right. But that won't matter at all to the Union soldiers. They will say it is rebel property that can be confiscated in a time of war. That specie would be used by the Union against us. You must seize it so we can use it against the enemy."

Lovell, bitterly, "And all New Orleans will blame me for stealing their money," "They will say it is for my own use."

"That can't be helped. It's little different from the necessity of tearing down a line of houses when a city is on fire, to save the rest of the city beyond the buffer line. Some property must be sacrificed to prevent greater loss. It is harsh for the few, and they won't accept it. But those who have care of the community must bear the bitter resentment. As soon as you telegraph Richmond that Ozymandias is arrived, Richmond will order more food, provisions, and tents be sent by rail from Jackson to Camp Moore for you and your men."

Lovell, with resignation, "That's it? Not even a display of seven or eight hundred armed men and a battery of cannon near the wharves to show we're defending the city? The Committee of Public Safety has proposed raising another thousand volunteers who will attempt to board the Yankee ships. We will be seen as cowards if we just turn tail and run."

Percy knew he had to convince Lovell of the urgency of full compliance. "General, you must leave the city to save the city. You've never seen New Orleans in a hurricane or a flood. I have. Let me tell you what will occur if you make a stand. Commodore Farragut's ships will steam a couple of miles above the city while the remaining vessels anchor with their guns trained down on every block and building in the city. The ships upriver can either plant explosives on the levee or cannon can begin firing shells into the levee until it is breached. Then all the fury of the swollen Mississippi will rush through the great chasm, just like it did in 1849 through Sauve's Crevasse when a weak spot flooded us. Two hundred city squares were under water. Twelve thousand people were forced out of their homes. If the Yankees blow the levee, soldiers and civilians alike will be flooded. Any efforts to fire guns at the Yankees from upper floors of city buildings will lead to bombardment that will level the great mass of buildings down to the rising floodwaters. Tens of thousands of civilians will die from flood, from starvation and from disease. They will be unable to flee. Conditions will be ripe for a return of the yellow fever a month later. The horsemen of the apocalypse could not wreak more havoc."

Lovell, grimly, "From what you've said, New Orleans was indefensible no matter how many men and guns we had."

"Almost. If the Union had not sent a powerful naval squadron, nothing would have happened by land either. The swamps and the river protect the city like a moat. If you had ironclads to reinforce the two forts downriver, they probably would have done the trick. A great amount of work has to be carried out very quickly." To palliate the bitter tasks imposed upon Lovell, Percy added, "Davis and Benjamin are confident that you have the character and skill to carry it out effectively. They have left it in your hands. They could have sent a replacement, not a messenger. They have confidence in you."

General Lovell was quiet as he weighed Percy's words. The lieutenant was not his enemy. Moorhead had not judged him as negligent in the conduct of his command. He conveyed no message of criticism from Richmond. He was a man trapped in conditions not entirely of his making. Ambition had brought Lovell to the Confederacy and to New Orleans, and it was here that he must accept the deserts of that ambition. His character would be defined by the grace and courage with which he accepted his fate.

Buttoning the top button of his uniform, Lovell stood slowly and said, "Well, Lieutenant, we must do what we must. Is this not the nature of duty?" Lovell composed himself. Percy saw that the general was aware of the impression he must make on the officers and soldiers in the next room and everyone after them, all whom he had to lead in this awful assignment Percy Moorhead and Richmond had burdened him with.

Chapter 60

Chez Maisie

Two hours had elapsed when General Lovell opened his office door to the growing number of soldiers demanding his urgent attention. Percy stepped in the outer room where they had congregated. Majors and captains who had met regularly with the general over the past five months eyed suspiciously this newcomer in a fresh uniform. None had ever seen him. How could this lieutenant have occupied their commanding officer for so long?

Percy lingered before leaving. He gave an orderly a note with instructions to locate Judah Benjamin's sisters, Harriet and Penny, and let them know messages from Judah would be waiting for them at the St. Charles. This gave him an opportunity to observe the general's exchanges. After the intense discussions with Percy, Lovell would hear no argument from his subordinates contrary to the course he must take. He demanded that each man speak his piece. He barked his responses, always making sure that every order he gave corresponded to the directions from Richmond.

An aide to Lovell had already been sent to the St. Charles Hotel with Percy's bag and instructions that a room be secured there for Lieutenant Moorhead for the duration of his stay.

Emerging from the Custom House as dusk descended, Percy realized how tired and hungry he was. He had not eaten since breakfast twelve hours earlier. The restaurant he preferred was on

Royal Street, a few blocks past the townhouse that Grady Boyle had taken from him. With reluctance, he would pass by the townhouse. If it were still occupied by Boyle, he could not let his personal animosity and desire to confront him interfere with the assignment that had returned him to New Orleans. Nothing could be accomplished by challenging the Irishman just yet.

As he approached the townhouse, he saw a small woman emerge from its entrance and walk north. Even in early evening's shadows her distinctive gait looked familiar. Suddenly, he realized she was Odessa. He called her name, gently, so as not to frighten her.

Turning, the black woman exclaimed, "Percy, is that you? The lord knows we need your help." She was surprised but not distressed at his sudden appearance after three years.

He embraced the small, fierce woman who had nursed him as an infant. "Odessa, I can't believe I have found you. But why are you coming from the townhouse? Did Boyle try to claim he never sold you to me?"

"Mr. Boyle, he's dead," Odessa blurted. "Maisie is with him now, on the sofa in the parlor. And Miz Dennett."

Percy was puzzled. "Mrs. Dennett? Who is she?"

"I got no time to 'splain. I got to go see about Little Jay. He's by himself at Maisie's place. Everything's crazy in the streets an' I can't leave him by himself."

Percy opened the door to the townhouse without knocking. He had entered it a thousand times before. But he had not been here in more than three years, when he had cleared out, shortly after Judge Albritton had rendered judgment against him in St. Francisville in the case of *In re: Estate of Moorhead, alias Boyle*. He would be damned before he would knock for Grady Boyle – living or dead. Under the judgment of the court, he still had a part-interest in the townhouse, subject to the usufruct of Maureen O'Neal Boyle and the power of attorney Grady held as to her interest. Only Percy knew that

Maureen was now deceased. Only a new judicial proceeding could get his present interest recognized.

The living room was just as he had left it. He entered the parlor-cum-library without a word, startling the two women in the room. One he knew immediately, Maisie Dastugues, once his father's mulatto mistress, who was sitting. The woman standing near the mauve satin sofa was a white woman whom he did not recognize. It must be the Mrs. Dennett Odessa had mentioned. His eyes took in the corpse of Grady Boyle stretched out on the sofa, a ragged cut on his right forehead, his left cheek severely bruised. Someone had dressed the dead body in clothing that showed no signs of the beating he had suffered. Percy could feel no sadness at his passing, but he was deeply frustrated that Boyle's death deprived him of the confrontation he had long wanted.

The other woman — about forty, twenty years younger than Maisie — was obviously frightened. She stepped away from the dead body, distancing herself. She had mistaken Percy to be a Confederate soldier who had come to arrest her.

Maisie Dastugues stood up and greeted Percy, relieved at recognition of the unexpected visitor. "Percy Moorhead! We heard you were in the army. But all the regular soldiers were sent to Mississippi and Tennessee."

Percy hugged Maisie, then stepped back while still holding her hands. "Judah Benjamin sent me here to meet with General Lovell. I just saw Odessa. She told me Boyle was here, dead. What happened?"

"Mrs. Dennett can explain better than I could. She saw it. Do you know her? She's the wife of Mr. Dennett, the druggist on Carondelet Street."

Percy looked at Marnie with a reassuring expression. He was well-practiced at putting people at ease. His ability to establish rapport had made him popular with his law clients. "Mrs. Dennett, I met your husband a few times after he purchased the pharmacy."

Marnie Dennett extended her hand to Percy, who accepted it with a gentle gesture of his right hand. She had had most of a day to come up with a plausible explanation why Grady Boyle, now dead, was in her care in his townhouse. She tried to sound convincing, as she had rehearsed to herself. Though this Confederate soldier appeared friendly, he was still a Confederate soldier. "I met Mr. Boyle as a customer of our drug store. I gave him the courtesy of delivering pills to this place, as I do for some of Mr. Dennett's regular customers. He was a casual acquaintance. By chance I was near here when I heard a commotion in the streets last evening." Marnie was nervous. She hesitated, trying to adhere as close to the truth as possible.

When she paused, Percy invited her to continue, with his skeptical, "Yes?"

Stammering, she continued. "A crowd was gathered around Mr. Boyle. He lay in the street where he had been beaten by a mob. With the Yankees at our doorstep, law and order has broken down completely. It is a danger to be outside. He was still breathing when we brought him in here."

As he absorbed the woman's tale, Percy still had questions. "When did he die?"

Nervously looking at the dead man, she lowered her voice, as though someone might overhear outside. "About noon today. We tried to find a doctor last night. And again this morning. We know we must report his death to someone. But who, in this turmoil?" She pleaded to Percy, "Tell us what to do."

There was much for Percy to absorb and to sort. He declared gravely, "We're about to go through a lot more turmoil." Checking himself, Percy knew these women could help him, but he needed not to sound ominous. They needed a calm hand to reassure and guide them. He smiled. "Let's think this through. I can't do that on an empty stomach. Any food about?"

Marnie was ready to do something other than answer

questions. She stood and told Percy, "I went out at noon and found some bread and cheese and a jar of jam and some apples." She went to a pantry and prepared a plate and brought it back into the living room where Maisie and Percy were sitting.

Percy turned to Maisie, "How did you end up here in the townhouse caring for Grady Boyle?" Applying his pocketknife to a golden apple, he ate eagerly as she answered.

The mulatto shopkeeper explained, "Mrs. Dennett came and brought me and Odessa here. We helped her get him in the house."

"Yes, I understand that," he persisted. "But how did Mrs. Dennett happen to seek you out?" Percy was a lawyer now, seeking answers to questions that were relevant to his circumstances, not theirs.

Marnie, not Maisie, could explain. "I found some papers in a drawer upstairs. They showed a Percy Moorhead – I guess that's you – purchased a slave named Odessa and a boy and then sold them a few days later to Maisie Dastugues. There seemed to be some connection between Mr. Boyle and Maisie. That's why I sought their help."

Percy always recognized misleading testimony and was immediately skeptical of Marnie Dennett's account. If Mrs. Dennett was only a casual acquaintance to whom she delivered medicine, she wouldn't have been rummaging in his papers. If Maisie and Odessa had helped her carry Boyle into the townhouse, it would mean she had left him in the street, gone upstairs, searched his papers and hit upon the idea of locating a woman she didn't know, then bringing her and a slave woman to carry a badly beaten man into his home. No, there was more to the relationship between Marnie and Boyle. Even though there was little reason for Percy to pursue it, he had just learned that there was a paper trail that might tell him things about Grady Boyle's fraud in stealing Percy's heritage.

"Are there other papers?" Percy was careful not to alert her to his doubts.

Marnie, nervous. "Yes. Would you like me to get them for you?"

Percy, flat. "Please."

When she returned Marnie carried a sheaf of papers. Inside a folder were documents and papers of different sizes, the papers most important to Grady Boyle. Percy wondered how Boyle had gotten the papers by which he had conveyed Odessa and Little Jay to Maisie. Then he remembered. He had left them in a cabinet drawer upstairs when he moved out. He'd had no further use of them. Maisie had her own copies.

Percy found a British passport issued in Dublin for Grady Boyle in 1857, as well as copies of the documents his attorney had submitted into evidence in the court proceedings over the estate of Percy's father. One paper was especially curious. It was handwritten verse:

There was an old hermit of Halford
Whose tongue stumbled on every word
All day he stuttered and stammered
All night he muttered and yammered
That wealthy old hoarder of Halford.

Percy showed it to Marnie. "Any idea what this is?"

Marnie, recalling Grady, "He thought it was funny. It was about somebody's uncle. He said it came from a lawyer, I think."

"Odd." Percy meant both the verse and Marnie. Obviously, Marnie knew Boyle much better than she had admitted. No matter for now. Focusing on the paper, he wondered where Halford might be. And why would the limerick come from a lawyer? A random fact? Or part of a puzzle with pieces that would fit together? Other documents revealed that Boyle had made a sale of Bolingbroke but evidently had not secured payment from the buyer who now held title: Newton Sutter, of Memphis, Tennessee.

Just then the front door opened. Odessa returned with the boy,

Little Jay, whose complexion of mixed African and French heritage was a close match to his grandmother's. How old was he now? Nine or close to it. A little older than Rand would have been, had he not been attacked by a swarm of yellow jackets, a toxic effusion from the depths of the soil near the deceptive placidity of Bolingbroke's pond. Rand and Little Jay had played together, just as Percy had grown up with and played with Little Jay's father, Julius. Percy had not seen Little Jay or Odessa since he had signed papers transferring their ownership to Maisie Dastugues; Louisiana law had made freeing the boy or his grandmother impossible. This was as close to giving them freedom as he could do under the law.

"Jay," Odessa told her grandson, "this is Mr. Percy Moorhead. You be carrying his name. You 'member his boy Randolph."

The boy was shy – polite and quiet but not frightened. When Percy held out his hand, the boy slowly put forth his own and shook it.

Odessa, with pride. "Jay is reading now, Mr. Percy. Real good. He likes to read. His Aunt Maisie is teaching him his numbers too, so he can help in the shop."

Percy, to the boy. "That's real good, Little Jay. I'm very glad to hear that. Your father and I learned to read together. He was my friend Julius, and I know that's your name. What am I to call you? I can't call you Julius because that was his name. And you're too big for Little Jay. How about Jay-Bird? Will you be my friend, Jay-Bird?"

"Yes, sir. Jay-Bird is okay." Little Julius remembered Mr. Percy and Miss Philomena as parents of his playmate Rand. All the other white people on the two plantations ignored Jay. Not Rand's parents, who were warm and friendly - until their son died. And they, too, then ignored him. It was only when Little Jay's mother and father both were killed that Jay again came to Mr. Percy's attention. He was surprised when Mr. Percy told him and his gran'mere that he had found them a new home in New Orleans with a woman who would take good care of them. And that was the last he had seen of Mr. Percy until now.

Marnie was growing anxious. "I can't stay here any longer. My drugstore has been closed all day and I've got to go back there. Tell us what we should do."

"All right. First, tell me who did this. What sort of mob was it?"

Marnie, hesitant. "To tell the truth, it was mostly some of the patrol from the Committee of Public Safety. A man called Cyrus was the leader." Her eyes avoided Percy's.

Percy, pressing. "Interesting. And where might I find this Cyrus?"

The presence of a dead man stretched out on the sofa on the far side of Percy Moorhead added to Marnie's obvious discomfort. "There's a station for the men on patrol, on Canal, near Chartres."

"All right. Any idea who is the provost marshal for this district under General Lovell's edict of martial law?"

Maisie spoke up. She knew New Orleans political figures from long observation and protecting her little shop from interference. "I think it's Mr. Dufour. Or Senator Soulé. One of them."

Percy, turning to Maisie, "That must be Cyprien Dufour. He was district attorney when I began my practice. Very good. And for better or worse I have made the acquaintance of Senator Soulé."

Refreshed by food, Percy laid out a course of action. "Now here's what we will do. We will carry the *corpus delicti* back to the alley where you found it and deposit it without ceremony. Then you will come back here while I pay a call on the civic guardian who fancies himself a Persian king. Maisie, I want you and Odessa and Jay-Bird to gather your things from your shop and move into this townhouse. Chaos is about to break out in New Orleans. The Yankees will occupy the city soon, very soon, and you will be safer here than near the wharves."

Maisie seemed unsure about leaving her rooms and shop. "How do we explain that we are living here?"

"Make up a story. Tell them you're the housekeeper for Mr. Boyle and that he's a British citizen who has gone to St. Thomas on business. You can keep these papers that say it's his townhouse. You can show them to the soldiers who will come. If no one is living in it, the Yankees are liable to take it over. But they won't oust a Briton or the people who are taking care of it for him.

Marnie, still fearful of arrest, still full of guilt that she had brought about her lover's death, and growing more nervous, asked, "But won't they find out that Mr. Boyle is dead?"

Percy grunted, "No. Cyrus will make it so no one will ever find the body."

Marnie seemed even more anxious. "How are you going to do that?"

Looking up from the townhouse papers, Percy replied bluntly, "Human nature. I'm going to approach him in my uniform and tell him I've come from General Lovell's headquarters. Which is, of course, true. I will then tell him that the provost marshal for this district has received a report that a group of men wearing red armbands have beaten a British citizen, and the man was seen crawling into an alley on Royal Street. I will appoint Cyrus to find the man and to investigate the crime. I will tell him that the general would be very disturbed to learn that harm had been done to a British citizen when relations with Great Britain are of great importance to the Confederacy. The men who did this must be brought to justice and punished so as to keep Britain from siding with the Union. Trust me, Cyrus will immediately go to the body and dispose of it so that it can never be recovered by man, beast or bird."

"How can you be sure?" Marnie was doubtful but eager to be convinced.

Standing, Percy dismissed Marnie's concerns with a grim grin.

"Experience, madame, experience. The actions of men of little character are uniformly predictable. Self-preservation is their sole instinct. Now I'll need your help returning the late Mr. Boyle to the site where he fell. First, we'll have to change him back into clothing that shows he was beaten and gives no hint that the body was removed from the place to which he had crawled."

Within three hours, everything had occurred just as laid out by Percy. War brings out the best in some men, but the worst in men of low character. Cyrus was at his station and snapped to attention when a Confederate officer approached. He accepted the assignment with alacrity. When Percy left, Citizen Cyrus found two of his fellows and they recovered the mortal remains of Grady Boyle. They placed him in a large canvas sack and used a pushcart to take a route through alleys to a wharf. Ten bricks from a pile set aside for street repair were added to the sack, its top tied tight, and brick, body and sack were rolled off the pier. And the deed was done – no more evidence that harm had come to a British subject who had the misfortune to reside in Louisiana in the midst of a civil conflict.

While Cyrus and his men accomplished their disappearance magic, a weary Percy was experiencing the comfort of his room on the third floor of the St. Charles. A major who was required to vacate the room had left, with no intention of gift, a half-full bottle of bourbon. Percy removed the tunic of his uniform and sat down to enjoy a drink. He was glad to be back in New Orleans but felt no elation to discover that Grady Boyle was now dead. He was instead frustrated. He had planned to confront the Irish deceiver with the information he had collected in Dublin. The force of that revelation might have made Boyle tell the truth about Percy's father.

From the papers in the townhouse, it was clear that title to Bolingbroke had passed to a buyer from Tennessee but was now clouded by the failure of the buyer to pay Grady Boyle. Transfer of title to an innocent buyer meant Bolingbroke was now unrecoverable, even if he could prove fraud by Boyle. Perhaps Grady Boyle would have known something about Percy's mother and sister at Jericho Hill. He would have to ask Odessa if she knew anything of his remaining family. Through the open window, a breeze blowing the curtains, he could just barely imagine the distant, relentless shelling of the two forts by Porter's mortars.

Soon, he would see and hear for himself.

Chapter 61

Before the Fall

Percy arrived at General Lovell's headquarters early the next morning, Wednesday, the twenty-third day of April. An orderly ushered him into the general's office. He found Lovell leaning over a map on his desk, pointing out to a colonel where he should take a detachment.

"Good morning, General," Percy called out cheerily, ignoring the colonel.

Lovell stood upright and dismissed the other officer with a gesture of his head. "And to you Lieutenant Moor-head." He exaggerated the pronunciation to show he acknowledged Percy's correction from the day before. "Did you find your accommodations at the St. Charles satisfactory?" Lovell was less hostile now. His uniform was fresh. His attitude had improved, which relieved Percy. The orders Lovell must follow were not his own, but Percy saw that he would carry them out as a good soldier.

"Indeed, I did, General."

"Good. You should know that the mayor's office sensed some new direction in the increased activities emanating from these headquarters after you left. They sent an anxious delegation to meet with me. I informed them that nothing has changed. The citizens of New Orleans are in no greater danger today than they were the day before. Telegraph communication with Fort Jackson has continued without interruption, and the two forts hold strong against the Union ships and bombardment. I have promised them I will again personally visit the fortifications to survey them. When that happens, I'll inform you."

"I would be glad to join you, if you have no objection. Until then, if you have no need of me, I'll attend to a few other duties."

"I know where to find you, Lieutenant."

As Percy left, soldiers were bumping into one another coming and going from the headquarters; some were officers receiving the orders that Percy had relayed to Lovell, others were messengers. Percy was satisfied that the directives from Richmond were being fully implemented. Lovell was resolute in carrying out a duty that would leave his military reputation in tatters.

Percy decided he would see if Westbrook Haydel was still in the city at his old office in the bank building. Westie was the friend he had appointed as his business agent to liquidate his interest in Toulouse Gardens, the casino he had helped establish a decade earlier. He had used the proceeds to purchase Odessa and Little Jay from Grady Boyle.

Westie was sitting at his desk, just as Percy had last seen him. His round face was rounder and his bald forehead was balder, but he was the same old Westie. Sure of himself, even as everything disintegrated around him.

Westie, with a toothy grin, "Percy Moorhead, as I live and breathe. And a Confederate soldier. Look at the uniform. Sharp. Are you assigned to the general's staff?"

Percy, smiling as he warmly embraced his banker friend, "Hello, Westie. Polly still putting up with you?"

"How could she find anyone more charming? Good to see you." Standing back to take Percy's hand, he chuckled, "Or should I salute?"

"As in my earlier incarnation, I'm still on assignments for

Judah Benjamin. Not much more than a junior attorney. The uniform is window dressing. You could put a uniform on a monkey, and he would still be a monkey and no soldier. Or a lawyer. A lawyer in a uniform is still a lawyer. More seriously, I'm surprised you're still here."

Now sitting, Westie sighed, "Can't leave. Polly's father, Herb as you remember, and I are both on the Committee on Public Safety. We're trying to save the city. We're not sure what is worse, Farragut's ships or Richmond's incompetence. Everyone says Lovell has sold us out and is returning to the North if the city should fall."

Percy was surprised that Westie was on the Public Safety Committee. Should he have been surprised? Westie was always eager to make his place among the businessmen of the city. Many of them had made their money by sharp practices. Maybe Westie had adopted their ways. He would have hoped better of him.

"Are you prepared for that?"

Westie, with a sly look, "The change might not be such a bad thing. Lot of us in New Orleans didn't want secession in the first place. This was Governor Moore's secession, not ours. But, no point now in wasting a crisis. Herb and I have been doing pretty well so far, buying things up that people will pay good money for when the time is right. It's all in the timing. Now it's about time for us to pick up and go back to Mobile where my family is from. Polly's already packed."

Percy was disappointed that his friend was one of the profiteers making life difficult for General Lovell and ordinary citizens. He only remarked, "I've heard the prices for everyday goods have risen quite a lot in the last few months." Percy looked closely to see if Westie felt the implied criticism of his speculation at the expense of the people the Committee on Public Safety claimed to protect. Seeing no reaction, he continued. "You may need to leave sooner than she's anticipating."

The banker, narrowing his eyes, "Sounds like you may have some inside information. Maybe you could help us get away when the time comes. I can make it worth your while. When the invasion approaches, there's more than a few others you know who'll be leaving with a tidy amount of gold and silver."

Percy sharply, no longer disguising his disapproval, "That's not something I could justify, Westie. Even for friends like you and Polly were to Philomena."

"Don't be self-righteous, Percy," Westie spit out, leaning forward in his desk. "I didn't ask for secession, and I don't owe any loyalty to the people who brought it about. If you choose to fight and die for the honor of Confederate manhood, that's your business. And don't invoke your late wife to make me feel guilt or pity. You may have forgotten that I know about your cheating on her with Diana whatever-her-name was and how your father made her leave."

"I expected better from you, Westie. Decency at least." Percy was sad that true character is revealed in crisis. Friendship that cannot survive crisis was never friendship.

Dropping his pen on his desktop, Westie was scornful. "You've come to the wrong place for sympathy or patriotism, Percy Moorhead. And I don't need your help in any event. I've got a major and a colonel ready to make good our escape to Mobile. I thought you might need the money. Last I saw you, you were broke and broken and turning tail to Virginia."

Percy shook his head sadly and turned, without asking Westie if he had heard anything about his mother and sister. Coming here was a mistake, but it dispelled illusions about the past that he had entertained.

⤝ · ⤞

The military preparations for evacuation following Lovell's orders made the city's civilian population aware that something was underway, even if the general had rebuffed the queries by the city fathers. The streets were filling with people trying to learn news, looking to take their own precautions. Something was about to happen, their senses keen, like birds and animals before a hurricane. Why else would soldiers be directing crews to empty warehouses and ships of bales of cotton to place on the levees? Why else would railroad cars and locomotives be gathering at the railroad depot? What could explain the absence of street cars as members of the militia collected the horses and mules that pulled them?

As Percy walked back to his town house (for it was now again *de facto* his) he saw that panic had not set in. No one was smashing windows or looting stores, as happens when a terrible storm engulfs the city with tree-toppling winds, when rushing waters flood the streets. Residents were not retreating indoors or covering their faces as they would when the dreaded words *yellow fever* are on every pair of lips. Citizens were hurrying to the markets to lay in stores of any available food they could find. But they weren't fighting one another for loaves of bread or jars of jelly. Not yet. They were apprehensive but not alarmed, fearful but not frightened. Not yet. Percy knew that alarm and fright would follow. Panic would come when peril became patent.

On his way to his townhouse, Percy ignored the men and women who tried to stop him, who pleaded with him to tell them what was going on. He was in uniform. He looked official. They wanted answers that he would not give them. Arriving, he found Maisie, Odessa and Jay-Bird downstairs, seated in the living room. The boy was drawing with pencils on paper spread neatly on the table in front of the sofa. His grandmother was seated, reading a book in French. Her native language was French. Here she had access to many books in French and welcomed the opportunity to read. She was already teaching Little Jay French as well as to read English, and the townhouse library made it easier.

Percy was glad to see that Maisie had already brought in two baskets of food in response to Percy's words the night before.

Marnie Dennett, they said, would return, bringing supplies from her pharmacy. The three women and the boy would ensconce themselves in the townhouse as though under siege. They would bar the door and nail boards over the windows.

Sitting with a fresh cup of coffee at the living room table, Percy spoke to the two women. "Tell Marnie that she need not worry what happened to Grady Boyle. The vigilant Cyrus performed as expected and removed all traces of Boyle's death. Now let's see what Boyle may have left behind."

Searching all drawers, shelves, and cabinets in the townhouse, the three found a few more papers of no value and near $500 in silver coin and U. S. paper currency. Less than $50 was in Confederate money.

Percy, pleased with the discovery, "Excellent. The Yankees won't use the Confederate paper. Spend it as quickly as you can before they get here. The minute they arrive it will be worthless. I'll show you a place to hide the rest."

Climbing a ladder in the second-floor hall, Percy pushed aside a hatch into the attic. Odessa followed him up, and he showed her a place between the attic joists where she and Maisie could hide the hard money. He had hidden his own treasures here when he was a seven-year-old.

In the upstairs bedroom where he and Philomena had slept, they found Boyle's clothing. When Grady Boyle thought he was wealthy, he had outfitted himself fashionably, using New Orleans's best tailor. Percy felt himself violated by Boyle's remaining presence in the room.

Percy again gave instructions to Maisie and Odessa. "Do not remove any of Boyle's clothes. In fact, leave a few items on display downstairs."

Odessa, puzzled, "Why, Mr. Percy?"

Percy explained to her and to Maisie, "As far as the world is concerned, and especially any occupation officials, their owner

Grady Boyle is a British subject, away on business at an island in the Caribbean. He could return any day. In fact, I will send to you at this address some letters in the coming weeks. They will appear to come from him with instructions to you, Maisie, as his housekeeper."

Maisie trusted Percy. But he would not be around if the Yankees occupied the city. "I don't know. What if someone catches on?"

Percy, reassuringly, "Don't worry, Maisie. In chaos, there is opportunity. The court judgment out of St. Francisville giving Boyle possession of this townhouse and recognizing as owner his mother in Dublin give us all the leverage you need. Neither the state of Louisiana nor the Union government will try to confiscate the property held here by a British subject. Eventually, I will see to it that papers are sent to this address establishing the death of his mother, which in fact has already occurred, and later of the death of Grady Boyle. After things settle down, we will obtain papers in Nassau that will show that Grady Boyle was lost at sea or that he died on the stormy Bermudas. The townhouse will again be in my name in full ownership. And I promise you this: that the three of you will be taken care of as my own family. So long as I live, you shall never want."

Odessa, though relieved, still showed concern. "What of Miss Lucy and Eliza?"

The subject was painful to Percy. He had been to reluctant to inquire before now about his mother and sister. "Yes, what has become of them? I was hoping you could tell me."

Odessa told him what she knew, speaking softly and carefully, apologetic that the news was all second-hand and discouraging. "Mr. Boyle sold off all the slaves he could what hadn't run away. I heard some were still living at Jericho with Miss Lucy and Miss Eliza, but everything was runnin' down with nobody to keep it goin'. They were fixin' to move to a hotel in town but that was last year and whether they did or did'n I don't know."

Percy wished that he had more information. It occurred to him that Odessa might fear that his mother could claim the townhouse. Or that Lucy might even try to assert authority over Odessa as when she had been her mistress. It was Eliza's husband who was responsible for the death of Odessa's own son, Julius. Odessa surely felt about Lucy and Eliza as he felt about Grady Boyle.

Percy again assured Odessa and Maisie about their own futures. "Don't worry that they'll show up here. They both dislike New Orleans. They have no claims to the townhouse. Maisie has papers that will protect you. You can settle in for a long time even if Maisie's shop won't have any business in the turmoil of occupation. When you run low on money, I'll see to it that more comes to you. Do you have questions?"

Maisie, grateful, "You've always been a man of your word. Just like your father." Odessa nodded her agreement, though she was not so sure that Lucy Moorhead would not pose a problem for her in the future. Jay-Bird continued to read quietly in a corner, lost in a book and unaware of the storms breaking just outside these sturdy walls. He had lost father and mother but was secure with his gran'mere.

Confident that he had prepared them for the coming upheaval, Percy looked a last time upon the small community under his care. Stepping outside, he put on his lieutenant cap and returned to his hotel.

The Confederacy was crumbling on this entrance to the most important river in America, the principal gateway to the great interior, the heartland of the country.

Chapter 62

A River of Fire

At this early evening hour, the dining room of the St. Charles Hotel was the city's hub of activity, as busy as General Lovell's headquarters and the railroad station. Sitting alone in the only quiet corner Percy was well positioned to observe the ongoing commotion. Three tables over from him he spotted the Louisiana governor, Thomas Overton Moore, conferring animatedly with Mayor John Monroe. Both were interrupted frequently by aides and officials. Just then another man joined Moore and Monroe at the empty seat at their table, a handsome man of sixty. With a square jaw and a full mane of greying hair, he carried a commanding presence. The seat must have been saved for him. Percy remembered him immediately. It was Pierre Soulé.

Judah Benjamin had alerted Percy that Soulé was in the city, participating in its governance. He had last seen Soulé five years earlier in Mexico when they had been on competing sides for obtaining a grant for a railroad concession across the Isthmus of Tehuantepec. Percy's side had been successful, largely because of Percy's ploy with the Mexican president. Although Judah had assured him that Soulé would hold no ill will, Percy wished to avoid the man; he had no desire to explain his reason for being in New Orleans. He hoped that Soulé would not recognize him in uniform. He quickly finished his meal and slipped away to his room.

After dark had descended, near eight, a messenger from General Lovell requested that he come see the general as soon as he could. Percy put on his tunic, cap, and boots and followed the messenger.

General Lovell was about to leave as Percy arrived. "Moorhead, the telegraphs from Fort Jackson indicate conditions are becoming critical. I have a steamer ready that will take us downriver to see for ourselves. You should come."

Percy agreed. "Certainly." He was eager to see first-hand the imminent threat to New Orleans. He knew it was a critical juncture in the war.

As they walked up Canal Street by lantern-light, Lovell added, "When a court of inquiry reviews my conduct in defending the city, you will have been a witness to my carrying out of my duties. You seem to be a man of honor, Moorhead. I will hide nothing from you, trusting that your account will be full and accurate."

Percy, pleased that he seemed to have Lovell's confidence, "I hope it doesn't come to that, General. If it does, you can count on my testimony." Percy had a grudging respect for a proud and ambitious man who was overwhelmed by events beyond his capacity to manage. All Lovell could hope to do was to mitigate the effects of the disaster.

Accompanied by a dozen soldiers bearing carbines, Lovell and Percy boarded a small steamer, the *Doubloon*, waiting at the end of Canal Street for them. It had just returned from the forts, bringing Major Hudspeth with updated intelligence. Lovell had sent the major down earlier in the day to confer with Colonel Higgins, who was in charge at Fort Jackson, and with General Duncan. The latter, who had stationed himself at Fort St. Philip, had command over both forts.

As they waited to board, Lovell complained, "I asked

Commander Whittle to join with us, but he declined. He said he had important business in the office. I couldn't convince him that there was nothing more important than acting immediately."

"Really? Richmond told me Commander Whittle is in charge of naval operations in this district."

Lovell, sarcastic. "It depends on what you mean by 'naval operations.' Whittle interprets his role as limited to naval activities on land. He says Mitchell is in charge of all naval activities on the water."

"Sir," interjected Major Hudspeth as he brought Lovell and Percy up the gangplank. "I'm afraid that we have more problems. Colonel Higgins reports that Farragut appears to be moving into position to steam past the forts. He's uniting with Porter's mortar schooners."

"Damn!" Lovell exclaimed.

The *Doubloon* entered the middle of the Mississippi River. A swift current carried her rapidly down the river. Percy could see occasional campfires on the banks and levees. Dim silhouettes of sentries observed the passing boat in silence; these men were unaware of events about to unfold in the next few hours only a short distance down from them, events that would unalterably transfigure the role of Louisiana in the war.

⤶ - ⤷

As the small steamboat approached the forts from above, Lovell resumed his questioning of the major. "Has Mitchell repositioned the *Louisiana*? Are the fireboats ready to intercept them at the raft?"

"No, sir. Colonel Higgins told me he crossed over to Fort St. Philip and found Captain Mitchell and General Duncan in a heated argument about their commands."

Percy heard the irritation in Lovell's voice increase. "What's Mitchell's problem now? I had Duncan give him charge of everything afloat down there so he could coordinate the defense."

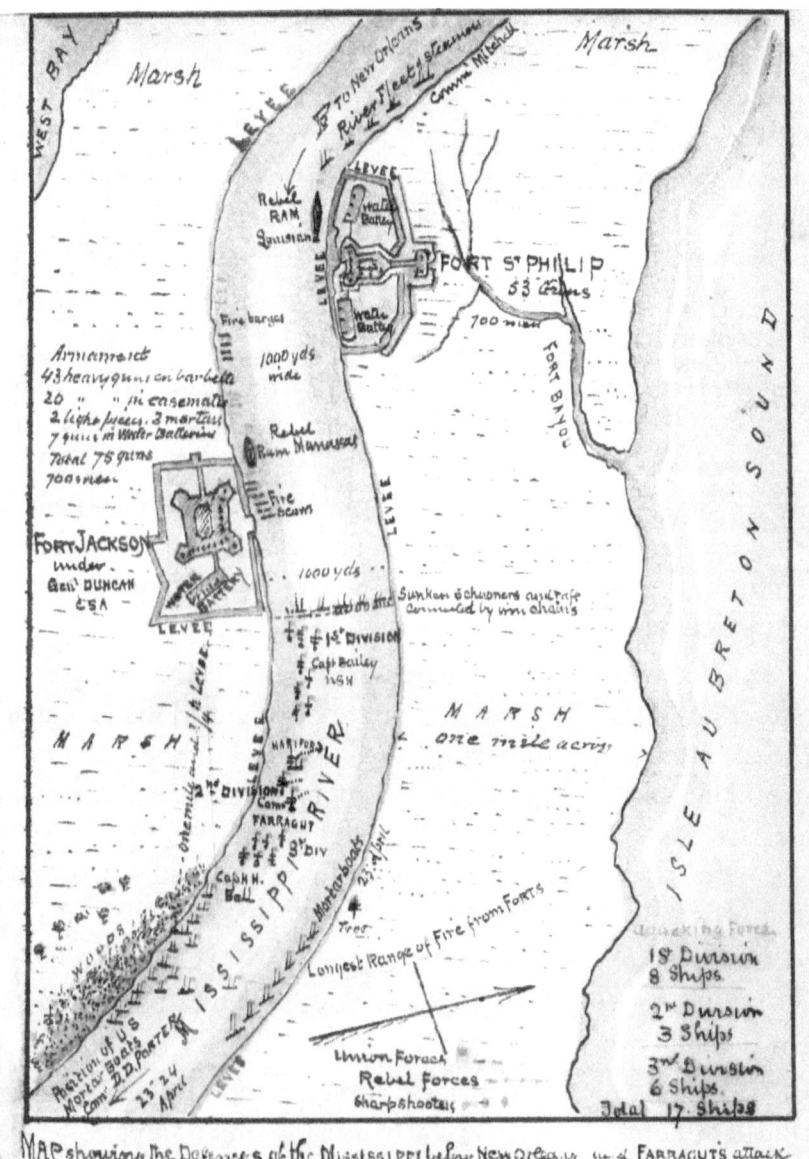

MAP showing the Defences of the Mississippi below New Orleans on of FARRAGUT's attack 24 April 1862.

Major Hudspeth explained, "That's what Captain Mitchell didn't want, he said. So, he turned parts of it back to the general. The captain wouldn't relinquish command of the *Louisiana*. And he declined to move her below Fort St. Philip for at least another 24 hours. The engines still aren't ready, he said, and he doesn't want to risk the loss of his principal ship. Captain Mitchell and General Duncan also argued over how the captain should coordinate the six other boats with cannon that Commander Whittle has him commanding. Captain Mitchell believes the captain of each boat should have the discretion to fight as he deems best. General Duncan said that's a recipe for chaos."

"The son of a bitch." Lovell was angry and frustrated as he told Percy, "If Farragut gets past the raft and the *Louisiana* isn't positioned for enfilading fire, it'll be too late to save the *Louisiana* or New Orleans. We put the largest cannons we could obtain on the *Louisiana*. They're not even going to be used when they must act." Turning again to the major, Lovell asked, "How about the *Manassas* and the fire rafts?"

Hudspeth had more discouraging news. "The *Manassas* is ready, right under Fort Jackson. But her one gun is inadequate to do real damage. She can operate as a ram, but she's slow and difficult to maneuver. She can't take on more than one of the Union ships. Captain Stevenson has had an awful time with the fire rafts. He can't master the current or send the rafts where they can work effectively. At least that was the case last night. Too much current. Too many logs and dead trees banging into everything."

"Anything from Burat?" asked Lovell about a person whose name was unknown to Percy.

"Yes," answered the major. "Burat talked to Colonel Higgins at the fort this morning. He was at four of the Union ships yesterday afternoon. As far as he could tell, it appeared like the Yanks were clearing the decks in readiness to move."

"Did he get a count of the ships?"

"He says maybe fifteen or sixteen are the big gunships. Maybe twenty are smaller boats with the mortars. He wouldn't go near them – they were firing the whole time."

"Not troop transports?"

"They seem to be farther down the river. Some of the other fishermen from his settlement trade with them."

Although he was eager to understand the immediate threat, Percy would not interrupt the exchange between Lovell and his subordinate. When they paused, Percy asked, "Grim news?"

Lovell, teeth gritted, "And growing grimmer. General Duncan refuses to send anything but optimistic reports by telegraph. The line is insecure, so anything he sends leaks. Duncan doesn't want to alarm New Orleans with bad news. And he hasn't got good intelligence of the Union flotilla. Their ships are all behind a bend in the river. Swamps on both sides of the river prevent us from sending scouts to see what the enemy really has. I can only rely on firsthand reports. We've been hoping that the fleet was much smaller and consisted mostly of the troop transports that were at Ship Island. That's where their soldiers have been camped for the last couple of months. The forts can take out transports but not gunships."

Lovell again turned to the major. "What are the conditions inside the forts? Can they keep up their shelling of the Yankees if they try to make a run past them?"

Again, Major Hudspeth's report was not encouraging: "Both forts are holding on, sir. But, after a week of intense mortar barrage, everything is deteriorating. Over 3,000 shells just that first day. The wooden parts of Fort Jackson are all burned away. I could barely make it to the casemates. The destruction goes beyond description. The ground is torn by the shells as if a thousand hogs had rooted it up, holes anywhere from three to eight feet deep. Very close together, only a couple of feet apart in most places. A lot of our guns are dismounted and gun carriages broken. There's filth everywhere inside the fort and gun positions. Water has broken through the levees and flooded the moats around Fort Jackson. It's borne the brunt of the attack. The gunners labor in pools of stagnant water. The odor is awful, as are the mosquitoes."

Lovell fired more questions. "Loss of men? Food? Morale?"

"Only a few casualties, sir. The brickwork is mostly intact. The men are on full rations, and provisions are laid in that will last at least a month even without resupply. The soldiers are holding up but are getting worn out from lack of sleep. Nerves are frayed from the constant pounding of the mortar shells shaking everything around them. They are grimy from all the powder residue and heavy smoke and sweating all the time. Some of the foreigners among the men are complaining."

"Thank you, Major." Lovell turned and gave Percy his assessment of the conditions. "The forts can last. Unfortunately, they are immobile. Once the Yankees are past them, they are of no further use against those ships. But they'll still be essential to keep Union troops from following behind. Those troop boats can't take the fire like the warships, so they're more vulnerable. The Union naval crews can't occupy the city. They'll have to wait for the troop transports to arrive."

Percy was curious about one man Hudspeth had mentioned. "Who's this Burat who can get aboard the enemy vessels with ease?"

Unexpectedly, Lovell smiled. "In war, we meet all kinds, don't we Moorhead? He's a sunburnt old wrinkled Frenchie. He's got one good eye and eight fingers. He lives in a little settlement called Booth's Village down from the forts. Gathers oysters in the marshes and sells them to the Yankees, going ship-to-ship in a little skiff. 'Errstirs, mes amis,' he calls out. His daughter is common-law wife to one of our gunners in Fort Jackson. The Yankees think he's a fool, the way he yammers at them in a patois of English and French. They'd never suspect him of being a Confederate spy. Down there, it makes no difference in their lives if the government calls itself French, Spanish, Louisiana, United States, or Confederacy. It's all one to them. But Burat knows his ships. He's been watching them go up and down the river all his life, with flags from the four corners of the Earth. Two of his sons are river pilots living in the settlement above Head of Passes. He's crude but shrewd – misses nothing around him. Plays the fool when it suits."

Turning grim again, General Lovell paced back and forth on the short deck of the *Doubloon*, fuming in anger and frustration. Percy sympathized but did not envy him. The burdens of a general were far too heavy.

ᥴᕞ - ᥲᕞ

Suddenly, hell broke loose on the water. Two a.m. must have been the designated hour for the furious onslaught of Farragut's fleet now roaring, guns belching fire. There was no delay in the Confederate response, no matter how uncoordinated. The surprise was in the barrier's breach, not the attempt.

Shouting orders was futile, so Percy, standing next to the general responsible for New Orleans, could hear Lovell only curse what he could neither prevent nor control. Amidst the din and the glare, nothing could be communicated, nothing accomplished, here on the deck of an unarmed small steamer.

Percy counted eight or nine ships that must have been the ones the Confederates held above the barrier. Their boilers stoked, they sprang to action and headed down to engage the Yankees in a haphazard defense for which they were caught unprepared. Despite the flashes of cannon fire and the lighting of more fire rafts, it was impossible to see the flags flown by any ship in the water, because of all the smoke from shells and burning rafts. As the Confederate riverboats came closer to the Union ships, it was impossible for the gunners in the forts to distinguish the South's gunboats from the Union's.

Peering through borrowed binoculars, Percy was able to

identify one vessel as uniquely belonging to the Confederacy. Pointing to the oddly shaped ironclad with fuming smokestack and no sails, Percy asked Major Hudspeth,

"Is that the *Manassas*?"

"That's her. Most people call her the Turtle."

"I'd say she's very like a whale."

"As you wish. She's deadly and impervious to the cannons."

A Yankee steamer was headed directly at the whale-like ironclad, trying to ram her before she could maneuver to slam into another Union gunboat.

USS Mississippi running down CSS Manassas
Source – Battles and Leaders

Then, as the shells from the Yankee ships began falling nearer his steamer, General Lovell ordered the *Doubloon* to return with all speed to New Orleans. The ship's log would show that she turned about at precisely three in the morning of April 24, 1862. New Orleans was doomed at that moment. Lovell knew it. Percy Moorhead knew it. Chaos would now follow until the Union could make good its occupation of the largest city of the Confederacy.

Arriving at the wharf, Percy could see that General Lovell's orders were being fully carried out, efficient in destruction. The levees were overtopped with massive piles of cotton bales, thousands of bales, work crews pouring turpentine and other flammables to speed their burning.

As he walked down from the levee to Canal Street, Percy watched as barrels and hogsheads of molasses, sugar, and wine, and crates of meat were upended and either burst open or rolling in the streets. Residents were scooping up foodstuffs and goods in any container they could find, then running home to hide it before it could be seized by Yankees – or their own neighbors.

Near the Custom House, Percy first heard the city's fire bells, as arranged in advance to announce the passing of the Union ships beyond the forts; they were striking twelve times, to be repeated four times each hour. A telegraph operator at Fort Jackson must have sent an urgent message to headquarters in New Orleans that the Union fleet had broken through and would be there in a matter of hours.

Three officers and a platoon of armed soldiers were waiting for Lovell. Leaving Percy behind, the general rushed to headquarters for briefings and to send out new orders.

Percy began a rapid walk around the parts of the city closest to the wharves, absorbing intently all that he observed. Activities of soldiers were orderly and purposeful, if hurried, but among civilians he found only fear and frenzy. Family members were frantically trying to find one another. Laborers revolted against their supervisors, leaving their jobs and casting away their tools. Wheelbarrows left by workers were appropriated by citizens looking for any means to gather up anything of value being destroyed by the soldiers. Shopkeepers bolted their doors and shuttered their windows as they would for a hurricane or a plague. Dogs barked, mules brayed, horses and carriages and wagons all bumped into one another; some overturned, others were made useless by broken wheels.

Percy could see groups converging on Mayor Monroe's office and General Lovell's headquarters demanding to know where they could go for protection. The red arm-band members of the Committee of Public Safety discarded their emblems and sought refuge in anonymity, lest they, too, be blamed by the angry mobs or taken prisoner by the Yankees.

Tied up to a wharf, near the monument to Andrew Jackson, were two steamboats guarded by rifle-bearing soldiers. Smoke chuff-chuffing from their stacks showed that their engines were stoked and ready to depart upon command. They bore the painted names *Magenta* and *Pargoud* on their sides, below their upper decks. Coaches with military escorts were arriving.

As he took a vantage point near the Jackson memorial, Percy recognized Governor Moore from the night before at the St. Charles when he planned his departure. He and other state officials and the families of some of the officers were all boarding the steamers to escape upriver, to Baton Rouge, to Natchez, to other places in-between. Percy also recognized among the boarders a half-dozen or so prominent business leaders of the city with their families making good their escape. Several were members of the Committee of Public Safety, finding their own safety with official help.

An angry crowd gathered, some trying to force their way aboard the two steamers. Mothers wailed and begged that their children be taken on board. The armed guards forced all back with the menace of fixed bayonets – except for the favored few with connections or money.

On the river, behind the two escape steamers, Percy counted six other large riverboats that were burning; they were drifting down river, ostensibly to fend off the Yankees. The order to set them loose and on fire was to prevent them from use by the Union; it was not a defensive tactic to stop the invading fleet. The frantic crowds on the levee thought the boats should have been used to carry citizens upriver. But there were too many people and no crews for the boats. As Confederate soldiers destroyed the shipyards upriver, they launched partially finished hulls, also put to the torch.

Across the river, smoke billowed from the woodyards and workshops of Algiers where other ships were built or repaired. The machinery was all thrown into the river; the floating dock was destroyed by its owners. Nothing was to be left for the invaders, General Lovell's orders.

Percy looked on and marveled at the fiery harvest of the words he had carried from Richmond to the general. "Look on my works and despair." Judah had understood. So had Lovell.

Now the most distressing sight hove into Percy's view and to the shock of the massed spectators awaiting the Yankees – the massive, unfinished hulk of the *Mississippi*, the huge ironclad that was going to save the city and the Confederacy. Her blaze was larger than all the rest that had floated down on fire before her. Her owners had accepted an offer that she be towed up the river, to be completed at a safe location, but the rescue effort had failed. If she did not sink first, perhaps she would make it as far as Fort St. Philip where her sister-ship, the *Louisiana*, was still sitting with non-functioning engines, armed but incapable of inflicting damage upon the enemy, more the result of her incompetent commanders than her state of completion.

The last train would leave the city shortly, carrying most of the remaining Confederate soldiers. Percy left the riverfront and picked up his bag at the St. Charles, assuring himself before leaving that he had put Grady Boyle's identity papers in with his effects. They could prove useful. Passing by General Lovell's headquarters a final time, he saw that only a dozen men remained with him, mostly enlisted guards. From across the room, he waited until the general caught his eye. Percy saluted and gestured that he was leaving. Lovell acknowledged him by a nod and resumed looking at a paper in his hand.

⤳ - ⤳

Percy's rank and uniform secured him a seat on a passenger coach of one of the last trains just before it left the station. It was now dark. He had hardly slept in two days. The final train would leave the city an hour after this one; it would carry the remaining Confederate soldiers, some of whom even now were holding back the crowds of people pleading to get on board Percy's train to flee the tumult and turmoil of the city. Weary as he was, he looked out the window, rain beginning to pelt the window, obscuring what was outside the window. Still, he could make out moving figures, like shadows against a cave-like background when lightning flashed in the distance. He could hear voices crying out in the dark.

"Take me. Take me!" he could hear them yell. "Please, take my child," called out pitifully a woman holding up a six-year-old.

The soldiers had their orders. They would carry them out.

The desperate men, women and children could not understand why they were being abandoned by these trains, by these soldiers who were supposed to defend them. They could not see Percy, who had brought the orders to the city that now would be surrendered because of those orders. They could see the soldiers in the open freight cars, standing in the rain, escaping the Union troops who would occupy the city. They could not see that those rain-drenched militiamen were as miserable as they were. These soldiers, most conscripted, would readily swap places to remain in the city with their own families. The frightened throng barred from the station could not understand, as Percy did, that removing the city defenses saved the city.

Reflecting on the grim necessity of leaving New Orleans to the invading Union ships and Yankee soldiers gave little comfort to Percy. He had taken no pleasure in delivering humiliation to Mansfield Lovell. That was Richmond's doing, not his. Percy had his orders. He had carried them out effectively, with diplomacy and force. Lovell received his orders, distasteful as they were. He was carrying them out.

The city was lost. The city was saved.

Such, too, was the contradiction that Percy felt, behind the rain-struck glass that kept the storm outside from him. Percy regretted that he didn't have time to call on Maisie, Odessa and Jay-Bird before leaving. He had prepared them sufficiently, re-occupying his townhouse in a way that ensured they were unlikely to be displaced by the Yankees assuming control of the city – whether soldiers or civilian administrators who were sure to follow the Union ships under Farragut. Marnie Dennett, a white woman, would add to their protection by her presence, a fortunate coincidence that somehow was linked to the death of Grady Boyle. Percy tried to suppress the conclusion that Maisie, Odessa and Little Julius would be better off under the aegis of the Union government than they were under Louisiana law, but it could not be denied.

Percy felt conflicted also by finding Grady Boyle dead. Surely the Irishman deserved a bitter end after stealing Percy's home and inheritance. But Boyle's death deprived Percy of answers, answers now foregone. He had been more than willing to take Judah Benjamin's assignment to deliver orders to New Orleans because he anticipated an opportunity to confront Boyle in circumstances more favorable to Percy than a hostile courtroom in St. Francisville. A confrontation with a corpse yielded no answers and no satisfaction. The truth, he hoped, was only delayed, not denied.

Too, he had expected to learn the fates of his mother and sister and niece in St. Francisville. There was too little time to travel there or to make further inquiries in New Orleans about conditions in Bayou Sara and St. Francisville. Even telegraph communications were impossible with the impending invasion.

As he thought back on happier times in New Orleans, where he had started his legal career, where he had begun his family with his beloved Philomena, he became disconsolate. All that was now lost. Grace Tarkenton was right. Yes, he was now no more than a sojourner, an Israelite in Egypt.

As the train swayed northward into the depth of gloomy night, sleep came fitfully upon Percy and stole away his cares. Dreaming, he was again at the gypsy's wagon outside Richmond with Philomena, two days before their marriage. Sister Lavinia – Reader of Palms and Tarot. The fortune she told came back to him,

The gods of old have blessed your name
What you lose you will twice regain.

What was its meaning? While this war was on, he would have to wait. No doubt his future lay on foreign ground. This mission fulfilled, what would be his next? What journeys lay ahead?